D0954141

Futuristic Romance

Love in another time, another place.

NIGHT MAGIC

Whatever magic was abroad in the night betrayed him, for instead of continuing down the steps, Dayra came back to stand beside him.

"Coll?" she said hesitantly, looking down at him.

Coll groaned, but he could not refuse to acknowledge her. Her voice alone was enough to compel a response.

Tugged by the night wind, the hem of her shift brushed against his sleeve and as she bent over him a strand of her hair blew across his cheek.

She swayed, as if she, too, were captive to the wind's vagaries. Coll put out his hand to brace her. His palm pressed against the point of her hip as his fingers shaped themselves to the softer curve at her side.

He heard a soft groan, but wasn't sure if it was from his lips or hers.

She moved closer. He had to tilt his head back to look up into her face. What he saw there made him wonder if he were mad or dreaming. He didn't have a chance to decide, for at that moment Dayra placed her hands on his shoulders, leaned down, and kissed him.

FAR STAR

ANNE AVERY

LOVE SPELL NEW YORK CITY

To Beth Anne Steckiel of Beth Anne's Book Corner.
I wish every writer could be lucky enough to have such a
supportive bookseller, and so generous a friend.

LOVE SPELL®

March 1995

Published by

Dorchester Publishing Co., Inc.
276 Fifth Avenue
New York, NY 10001

Cover Art by John Ennis

Printed in the United States of America.

FAR STAR

Chapter One

His foot had started to blister where the sole of his boot was wearing thin. The strap on his bag chafed his shoulder, and the sun on this benighted planet seemed destined to bake away whatever remained of his mind.

Coll Larren sighed, then shifted the heavy bag to his other shoulder. The muscles of his left leg were already beginning to ache where the twisted scar of an old wound sliced across them. Strange he'd never noticed such discomfort when he was in his twenties. Passing his thirty-sixth birthday had evidently sapped the toughness he'd once prided himself on.

Life could do that to a man. He just hadn't expected it would do it to him.

A faint, hot breeze brushed against his skin and stirred the tall grasses lining the side of the dusty road. Nothing else moved in the vast sweep of grasslands and rugged hills that stretched to the pale blue line of mountains on the horizon. He'd been told that Far Star was a young world. There were no birds, no animals, and few insects. Their lack made the land strangely empty and silent.

Coll had expected to find transport before now, but not even a broken-down farm flitter had come by in the past three hours. The preserved meat and coarse bread he'd had for breakfast had become a fond memory. His mouth was dry, but he carried nothing except water in the small canteen in his bag, and water wasn't what he wanted right now.

Not for the first time since the freighter, *Bendrake*, had unceremoniously dumped him at the grubby spaceport two days before, Coll wondered how he could have made the mistake of challenging the first officer. He'd known when he'd signed up back on Artes III that the ship would be a less than desirable berth. No well-run vessel took a crewman like him, a man without proper spacer's documentation. A man without a past, so far as anyone else was concerned.

Coll squinted at the sun. Almost midday. On a world like this, where a day was slightly longer than standard, that meant cooler hours were still a long way off.

And so, it seemed, was any transportation. Not even a hint of dust indicated the movement of vehicles along the roadway. Since this unpretentious strip of ground served as one of the main roads between the spaceport and the world's capital, Trevag, the lack of traffic didn't bode well for his chances of catching a ride any time soon.

Far Star was a colony world, but Coll hadn't thought it would be quite this rough and unsettled. Since he'd failed to find work at the port, which served as the main traffic and supply point for the entire planet, his chances of finding work elsewhere on this backward lump of rock and grass were beginning to look pretty grim.

He could keep going. He could turn back to the port. Or he could take the trail he could see leading off to the left, toward the sea that gleamed blue in the distance. Settlers might have chosen to build their homes near the water rather than the road.

Coll grimaced. None of the alternatives held much appeal.

A drop of sweat ran off his forehead into his right eye, making him blink. With an angry swipe of his forearm across his brow, he brushed away the annoying beads of moisture.

After all these years, he should have learned there weren't many real choices in life. It only looked that way.

Damn shame he hadn't learned that lesson years ago.

With an irritated shrug, Coll shifted the bag higher on his shoulder, where the strap wouldn't chafe quite so badly, then turned to start down the hill toward the trail he'd spotted. As he turned, his toe caught on a rock half buried in the dust of the road and he stumbled, then cursed.

He just wished his canteen held something other than water.

* * *

Dayra Smith swore as the slick, round rocks of the beach shifted under her feet, grating in protest at her weight. Her mother would never have approved of even so mild a word, but her mother had been dead for almost five years. A lot of things had changed in that time, including Dayra's language.

She tossed back the loose strands of her hair that the wind blew into her face, then shifted the heavy bag of fish and the waterlogged net slung over her shoulder, trying to find a better balance as she carefully picked her way over the rocks. The muscles of her arms, shoulders, and back ached from repeatedly throwing the net out and dragging it back filled with fish. She didn't want to think about the effort that would be required to climb back up 70 feet of steeply tilted cliff face on a rope ladder. Unfortunately, there was no other way out of the inlet except by swimming. After an hour of fishing in the icy waters of Far Star's vast, inland sea, Dayra was more than cold and wet enough for that alternative to have no appeal, even if she could have hauled along the fish and her net.

The ladder hung where Dayra had left it, but instead of dangling above dry rock, the end now trailed in the dark, frothy water of an incoming wave, bobbing and dancing maniacally.

Surprised, Dayra glanced around to find the stony beach behind her rapidly disappearing under a rising tide. Either the tide was coming in faster than normal, or she'd spent more time fishing than she'd intended. She hadn't realized how little dry ground remained between the sea and the dark cliffs that ringed the small inlet.

That was what she got for concentrating on her problems and not the work at hand. She'd been so busy worrying about Talman Bardath and his latest demands that she hadn't paid attention to the passage of time.

Irritated with herself, Dayra glanced at the sun, trying to judge the time. A little past noon. She'd be up the cliff before the rising sea could catch her, but she'd have to hurry if she was going to get back to the holding by the time she'd promised. If she was even a little bit late, Jeanella would start worrying and Dayra already had enough problems without adding her younger sister's reproaches to them. At least six-year-old Jason wouldn't heap any complaints on top of Jeanella's. He'd be so engrossed in whatever new devilry he was up to he probably wouldn't even remember Dayra had left.

Heedless of the calf-deep water, Dayra gratefully dumped her heavy load and grabbed the ladder. The rope flapped loosely in her hands. Startled, she stumbled backward, craning her head to look up the length of the ladder.

"Greetings, Dayra Smith," a tall, thin man at the top of the cliff shouted. He waved the loose end of the rope ladder—the end that should have been securely anchored on hooks sunk in the rock—in one hand. "Talman Bardath thought you might like to discuss a little matter of the debt you owe him."

For a minute, Dayra stopped breathing. She knew the man—not by name, but by sight and reputation. He was an outcast on Far Star and a perfect tool for Bardath: vicious, unscrupulous, and not averse to the cruder forms of physical persuasion, if the price was right.

"I stopped by the holding," the man added, continuing to yell so she could hear him over the rush of the incoming waves. "It didn't look like anyone was home, so I followed the trail your flitter left." He paused, waiting for the significance of his words to sink in. "It's very convenient, finding you like this."

Dayra didn't miss the threat behind his words. Her hand tightened around the useless ladder. Thank the stars Jason and Jeanella had obeyed her instructions and kept the gate to the holding locked and themselves out of sight. The muscles of her shoulders and chest tensed at the thought of her younger sister and brother alone in the holding, but she ignored both the tension and the fear behind it, fighting instead to control her breathing and force her stunned mind to work. Too late now to regret having let her hired man, Black Johnny McGregor, accept the offer of a few hours' work on the neighboring holding.

The man at the top of the cliff shook the ladder again, sending tremors through the heavy rope as a not-so-subtle reminder of his power.

"What? Nothing to say, Dayra Smith?"

Even from this distance, Dayra could hear the gloating smirk in his voice. Her throat tight with tension, she shouted, "I can't give Bardath what I don't have."

"According to Bardath, you managed to *take* what you didn't have."

"He *owed* us."

"Yeah? He doesn't see it that way." Bardath's hired thug squatted on his heels, the end of the ladder negligently clasped in his hand.

He looks like an evil dwarf, Dayra thought wildly, staring up the cliff at his foreshortened form.

The man slapped the end of the ladder in his palm. He was clearly enjoying himself. "Bardath wants the boy. Now. That's not negotiable. He suggested you could turn over the girl as partial payment on the debt. She's young, but she'd bring a good price on any of a half-dozen worlds I can think of."

His head tilted to one side speculatively. "Then again, Bardath just might settle for having her himself."

Even from that distance, Dayra could have sworn the man grinned.

He rose to his feet, nodding in satisfaction. "That's a good idea. I'll take the girl *and* the boy. They shouldn't be hard to find. Not around here."

Fear—not for herself, but for Jeanella and Jason—churned inside Dayra, threatening to paralyze her. She shook her fist in impotent fury at the malignant creature above her. "Don't you *dare* touch them! Don't you dare—"

The man laughed. "Doesn't look like you're in

15

any position to argue, Dayra Smith. Come to think of it, if you're dead, Bardath won't be in any position to argue, either."

He laughed again, clearly pleased with himself. "Have a nice swim, Dayra Smith—while you can. I'll come back later to collect your flitter." He casually saluted her and started to turn away, then stopped as if a sudden thought had just struck him. "I guess I don't really have much use for this, after all," he said and tossed the end of the ladder over the edge.

With a rattle of rope against stone, the heavy ladder came slithering down the rock face on top of Dayra. The rope slammed against her face and shoulders with excruciating force. Dayra cried out in pain, staggered, and fell to her knees in the icy waters. The rocks gouged her knees and legs; the sea plucked at her sodden shift with insistent fingers, threatening to drag her under.

Dayra twisted and jerked back, clawing at the entangling coils of heavy ladder. The sea grabbed the trailing lengths of rope and mercilessly twined them even more tightly around her. Spray from a wave drenched her, chilling her through. Dayra gasped and lunged to her feet. She took a deep, shuddering breath, then tugged at the ladder, dragging it over her head and shoulders until she was finally free.

Blinking back tears of pain, she craned her head backward, trying to spot her attacker. Nothing moved along the dark line where cliff met sky.

Her mind spun in dizzying loops, around and around and around, unable to function under the thought-numbing pressures of her fears. Jason and Jeanella. The thin man. The rising tide lapping hungrily at her knees. The ladder that lay in a heap at her feet when it should have been hanging down the rock, waiting for her to climb up.

What to do. What to think. Think. She had to think.

Frustrated and frightened, Dayra pounded her fist against the rock, forcing her brain to work. She had to get out of the inlet, had to get back to the holding, to her brother and sister, who needed her.

A dozen wild plans formed in her mind, only to be instantly discarded. The only sure way out was up the cliff.

Dayra closed her eyes, fighting against the fear that thought brought with it. If there was one thing that frightened her more than any other, it was heights. She had a hard enough time climbing up and down the ladder. Without even the ladder. . . .

Dayra took a deep breath, willing her heart to stop its mad, erratic thudding in her chest, willing the muscles of her arms and legs to stop their trembling. She wouldn't think about the climb, only about the need to get out, to get home to her family.

Moving quickly in spite of her still-trembling limbs, Dayra lashed her net and bag of fish to one end of the ladder, then looped the other end over her shoulders and chest so it hung down her back. There was no place on the beach to leave the ladder where the tide wouldn't take it, and she couldn't afford to replace it; she had no choice but to carry it up with her until she found a secure place to anchor it so she could retrieve it later.

Giving the ladder one last tweak to be sure it wouldn't impede her motion, Dayra anxiously scanned the rock face in front of her, searching for handholds.

Nothing.

She stretched upward, her fingers skittering uselessly across the rock, the muscles of her legs straining to maintain her balance while her toes dug into the shifting stones hidden beneath the foam-flecked waves.

Still nothing.

The rising sea was past her knees before she found a path upward that ought to serve. From experience, Dayra knew the walls of the inlet sloped back away from the sea. Experience, however, wasn't enough to overcome the visual impression that the dark bulk of the cliff loomed over her like some vast and very hungry bird of prey impatiently awaiting its next victim.

Dayra gulped, swallowing the bile that rose in her throat. Then she squeezed her eyes hard shut until the flare of lights behind her lids drove out the threatening visions conjured by her imagination.

Don't think about it, she told herself sternly. Not now.

Eyes still shut, head tilted back, she breathed deep, then rolled her shoulders to ease the tension in her muscles, heedless of the way the rope ladder scraped across her skin.

Don't think. Climb.

She opened her eyes, took a step forward, then another, until her nose was only inches from the cold rock. Then she started climbing.

To her relief, the handholds were more substantial and closer together than they'd looked from below. As she'd known it would be, there was enough of a slope so she didn't have to plaster herself against the rock to keep from falling.

That didn't mean the climb was easy. Even polished by the relentless tides, the rock was punishingly rough against her skin. If the hard work of the past few years hadn't already worn calluses on her palms and fingers, the coarse stone would have quickly shredded her skin. A minor slip left her with a bleeding knee and a scraped arm.

Dayra ignored the pain, just as she ignored the hungry sea beneath her. She couldn't afford to think about anything except the next handhold, the next step up.

She climbed higher. Her breath rasped in her throat as her lungs struggled to cope with the physical demands on her body. Her fingers ached with the strain of clinging to the small knobs and cracks that served as handholds. Her muscles burned, trembling with the effort of lifting her body up the cliff face.

Dayra scrabbled for a firm handhold and foothold, then briefly paused to rest, gasping for the air that eluded her. She shut her eyes and let her forehead rest against the cold stone. Just a minute. That was all she needed. A chance to catch her breath and let her quivering muscles recover before she started climbing again. It seemed as if she'd been on the rock forever . . . or longer.

She forced her eyes open. Her vision filled with minuscule bursts of light as the sun caught at the tiny crystals imbedded in the rock. Seen this close, the hard stone was beautiful, really. Not threatening at all. Her panting breaths reflected off the rock into her face, warm against her chin and cheek.

Though she knew she shouldn't, Dayra couldn't help looking down. The sea churned and roared below her, swallowing the base of the cliff in great gulps. She gasped and squeezed her eyes shut, pressing her cheek against the sun-warmed rock while she fought to control the uncomfortable churning in her own stomach.

The ladder slammed against Dayra's back, startling her, then twisted in the insistent clutches of the wind, threatening to tear her from her fragile perch with its weight. For an instant, Dayra considered releasing it, then just as quickly rejected the thought. She'd hook it over a sharp point of rocks she could see above her. It would be easier to climb once she was free of the ladder's cumbersome weight. Jason and Jeanella would just have to wait for the fresh fish she'd promised them.

At the thought of her younger brother and sister, Dayra stiffened. Already her attacker was on his way to the holding. Jeanella and Jason were alone, with no one anywhere near to help them. Dayra's fingers tightened around the edge of the rock she clung to as if she could dig them into the man himself.

The thought of a threat against her family was enough to dispel both fear and exhaustion. Dayra set her jaw, then started climbing again.

As Coll had expected, the trail led to the sea, following the rugged coastline at a safe distance while providing only an occasional glimpse of the curving cliff walls and the waves that broke against them with such determined force. He'd been walking for a good 20 minutes when he spotted the solitary flitter parked on the flat grassland to one side of an inlet that cut into the coast. Curious, he abandoned the path, angling toward the cliff in an effort to catch sight of whoever owned the flitter.

He almost missed her. He'd been looking for someone walking on the top of the cliff. It was the sight of her light-colored shift against the dark rock cliff that drew his eyes lower.

The woman clung to the face of the cliff like a spider, arms and legs straddled as she stretched for each precarious handhold, fighting her way up the rough stone inch by inch. Something that looked like a rope was strapped over her shoulders and trailed down the cliff face after her.

As Coll watched, she stretched higher, struggling to reach a handhold just beyond her grasp. She stretched farther still. Her fingers wrapped around empty air. Overbalanced, she started to slip and would surely have fallen if she hadn't miraculously found another handhold at the last instant.

As it was, she was awkwardly splayed across

the rock, her body's weight off center, her arms and legs at impossible angles to each other. If she tried to move, there was a good chance she'd lose her grip entirely and start sliding down the steeply angled rock face, headed for the bottom of a cliff that was rapidly disappearing under the eager, foaming sea.

Coll didn't realize he'd been holding his breath until his tortured lungs made him release the pent-up air in an explosive gasp. He tossed aside his spacer's bag and started running.

The girl was more than halfway up the cliff face and climbing steadily again by the time Coll finally reached the inlet. He raced to the flitter and hurriedly rummaged through its contents until he found a length of crudely made rope under the backseat. Unless he doubled it over, it wouldn't be strong enough to hold his weight. Doubled, the rope might not be long enough to reach her. It would have to do. There wasn't anything else.

A quick search revealed the presence of two metal hooks sunk in the ground at the top of the cliff. Coll glanced over the edge to check the girl's position. She'd angled to the side and away from him, following the handholds available to her. If she could get a little higher, he'd be able to reach her. Maybe.

Doubling the rope, he looped it over one of the hooks, then knotted it around the second hook for extra security. With the double length of rope firmly clasped in his hand, Coll knelt at the cliff's edge. Even from this angle he could see the girl's shoulders heaving as she struggled for air. When she stretched to reach for a handhold far above her, he could see blood staining her hand and arm.

He had to get the girl's attention, but an unexpected shout could startle her into losing her precarious hold on the rock. A couple of minutes later she stopped to rest, her hands securely curled over a narrow fissure in the rock. It was the chance he needed.

Cupping his hand around his mouth, Coll shouted down at her. "Hallo!"

The woman's first reaction was to flatten herself against the rock face, her second to glance up. For an instant, her expression twisted with rage. Then it turned to one of hope when she realized help was at hand.

"I'm coming down after you," Coll shouted, displaying the rope he held. "Try to move up toward me."

He didn't need to repeat his command. She understood instantly. Rather than waste her breath on shouting, she nodded once, then started climbing again at an angle that would bring her within his reach.

Tossing the ends of the rope over the cliff, Coll jerked once on the doubled line to test how well it was anchored, then carefully stepped backward, over the edge and down the cliff's face.

His smooth-soled spacer's boots slipped on the rock, but he moved as quickly as he dared. The girl was climbing steadily, her attention focused on the rock in front of her. Only twice did she glance up at him, checking on her next few hand-holds, making sure she was moving in the right direction.

From here he could see the firm set of her mouth. Her eyes were huge, wide with the fear she wouldn't allow to hold her back. Her golden hair had worked free and whipped about her face, tossed by the wind that whistled along the cliff face. Coll couldn't see much else. From this angle, everything was foreshortened until she'd become little more than a face and a pair of hands slowly clawing their way toward him.

Coll's heart jerked as he came to the end of the rope. Not enough. He was still too far away. He wrapped the last couple of feet of rope around his left hand and arm as insurance against it slipping out of his grip. Then he carefully edged to the side, toward her.

She was coming closer, and with each inch gained, it became clearer how near to exhaustion she was. She hesitated before each step up, and once she almost lost her grip on the rock when her hand trembled.

Coll could, of course, abandon the rope and move along the cliff face to help her, but without the rope, there was no way he could take her back up with him. So he clung to the rope that meant safety for them both, and he waited in growing tension and frustration as she slowly moved closer.

A foot. Two feet. Then another, until she was almost within reach.

Coll flattened his body against the rock and

stretched his right hand toward her, straining to bridge the gap that still separated them. The wind tore at him, whipping his hair in his eyes just as it whipped hers. His boots slipped on the rocks, banging his knee hard against the stone.

The woman looked up at him. Her eyes were a clear pale blue, huge with relief at the prospect of help. Above the sound of the wind and the waves, Coll could hear her harsh, gasping struggle for air as she forced her tired body to move closer.

Coll twisted at the end of the rope, fighting to get closer to her as he ignored the sharp pain across his shoulders from the unnatural position.

A foot. Ten inches. Six. She stretched out her hand, straining to reach him. Not close enough. She wrapped her fingers around an almost invisible bulge in the rocks, then pulled herself a few inches higher.

Their fingers touched. The blood from her lacerated palm was warm against his skin. Coll stretched impossibly far, her trembling hand almost within his grasp. Only one inch more. She pushed off from the rock, lunging for him.

A sudden harsh gust of wind grabbed the ladder that was strapped over her shoulders, twisting it around and pulling her loose from the rock.

Coll watched, horrified, as she slid out of his reach and down the slick rock face away from him.

Chapter Two

Dayra would have screamed in fright if she'd had time or the power of thought. Instead, she instinctively flattened her body against the rock as she desperately scrabbled for something—anything—to grab on to.

There was nothing. She was sliding downward, faster and faster, with nothing but the friction of her body against the sloping rock to slow her fall.

Pain lanced through her as the uncaring stone sliced her already bruised and scraped body. Somewhere deep in her mind, Dayra knew it didn't matter. A moment more and the wind and the weight of the ladder would tear her from the rock face and fling her to her death in the icy waters below.

She almost let go and allowed the sea to claim

her. Almost—then her hands once more found a grip on a small ridge of rock she'd climbed along only a few minutes earlier.

Her body came to a halt with a jerk that threatened to tear her arms out of their sockets. Her already battered hands clenched against the agony, but held.

For what seemed eternity, Dayra hung there, her feet dangling in space, her arm and shoulder muscles screaming with the strain of hanging on. A deep masculine voice from somewhere far away commanded her to pull herself up on the ridge, but her overtaxed mind and body refused to respond.

The voice came again, even harsher. She didn't want to respond, but the voice was too insistent to ignore. Slowly, agonizingly, Dayra pulled herself up on the tiny ridge.

It wasn't much. She couldn't sit and she certainly couldn't lie down as she longed to, but she could stand and take the strain off her arms and hands.

Dayra pressed her body against the cold, uncaring rock, heedless of the pain of her scraped face and arms and legs. Her breath came in deep, sobbing gasps. Tears burned behind her closed eyelids.

None of it mattered. She was alive. Against all odds, she was still alive.

"It's all right."

Dayra tensed. There it was again, that irresistible male voice that had ordered her to climb up on this ridge. She opened her eyes to find a giant beside her, his big body pressed tight against the rock, his eyes fixed on her face with a glittering intensity that was strangely reassuring because it was so human.

She remembered then, remembered reaching for his hand, the sense of relief at finding help when she had expected none, the feel of her fingers touching his palm just before the wind had jerked her out of his grasp.

"You have to climb up toward the rope," the giant said. His deep voice was a comforting rumble in her ears, drowning out even the sound of the waves crashing on the rocks below. "I can carry you from there."

His words didn't make much sense. "Climb up?" Dayra asked, dazed. Climb up where? And why? She was safe here.

The thought of moving off the ledge, of risking her life by once more crossing the exposed, pitiless rock, made her shudder. She pressed her body even more tightly against the cliff.

The stranger moved sideways along the ledge, closer to her. "I'm going to take the ladder," he said, gently resting his hand on her shoulder.

Dayra flinched, then relaxed under his touch. His hand was strong, soothingly warm even through the fabric of her shift.

He slid the rope ladder off her shoulder, then looped it over the sharp rock outcropping above him, the same outcropping she'd been aiming for.

Dayra twisted to look up the rock. The sight of that dark, forbidding expanse of cold stone made her stomach heave and her body ache. She couldn't face that climb again

She had to, for the sake of Jason and Jeanella.

"I'll be right behind you." The stranger's voice was gentle, but it admitted no argument and no excuse.

Dayra glanced at him. He was watching her, his expression a mix of determination and understanding.

"Go," he said.

With her hand trembling and her heart pounding in her throat, Dayra stretched to grab the first handhold. The stranger's hand, fingers splayed, was on her back, supporting her and urging her on. Ignoring the agonizing protests of her overtaxed body, Dayra started climbing.

She could hear him coming up behind her, hear his deep, steady breathing and the scrape of his body against the stone. She concentrated on that so she wouldn't have to think about how very, very far away the top of the cliff still was. Once his boot slipped on the rock and he cursed softly. Dayra froze until he started moving again.

She climbed in a mindless daze, one handhold after another, inch by inch up the rugged cliff face. Her world narrowed to the few square feet of rock she occupied, the in-out rasping of each painful breath.

It was the sound of rope slapping against stone that finally roused her. Dayra stopped, disoriented. It took a second before her mind finally dredged up an explanation: she'd reached the rope the stranger had used to climb down.

He moved past her without speaking. Grabbing hold of the rope with one hand, he quickly fastened a loop around his waist and knotted it. He jerked on the rope, then leaned back, away from the cliff face so that his entire weight hung from those two impossibly slender strands. The crude rope grew taut, creaking slightly with the strain, but it held. Satisfied, the stranger kicked off from the rock face and swung around to Dayra's side. His boots scraped on the rock as he danced to a halt.

Dayra watched dully, too tired to figure out what he was planning. When he wrapped his arm around her waist, she could only sag against him, grateful for his warmth and strength.

"Let go," he said, his voice firm. "I won't drop you."

Dayra did as she was bidden. Without releasing his one-handed grip on the rope, he pulled her into the protective cradle of his body, then turned her until she was facing him.

"Wrap your arms around my neck and your legs around my waist. I'll carry you the rest of the way up."

The command seemed perfectly reasonable until Dayra felt her breasts crushed against his chest and the inside of her thighs intimately pressed against the hard muscles of his stomach and sides. She gasped and stiffened at the contact, but he was already shifting her weight so that she was seated more firmly against his body.

"Hold tight."

A moment later he started climbing, hand over

hand, and Dayra had no choice but to cling to
him as tightly as she could. She locked her hands
behind his neck and laid her head on his shoulder,
trying to make herself as small as possible so she
wouldn't interfere with his movements.

His powerful arms encircled her, rubbing
against her shoulders and sides with each movement upward; his muscles bulged with the effort
of lifting their combined weight. He was using his
legs to balance and support their weight, and with
every step his body pressed against her legs. His
broad chest rose and fell with each deep breath he
took, causing his shirt to rub against her scraped
cheek and chin. Once or twice he grunted softly
at the effort of climbing, then breathed deeper,
struggling to get more air for his straining lungs.

When he reached the top of the cliff at last,
he shut his eyes and let his head fall back as he
tried to catch his breath. Dayra clung to him,
uncertain what he expected her to do next, yet
strangely loath to leave the safety of his arms. If
she slipped now. . . . Instinctively, she tightened
her grip around his neck.

The giant let go of the rope with one hand, then
wrapped his free arm around her waist and half
lifted, half shoved her onto firm ground. Dayra
didn't need any urging. Hands, feet, and fanny
firmly in contact with the ground, she scooted
back from the edge to give him enough room to
climb up behind her. She didn't trust her legs to
support her. At least, not just yet.

She was vaguely aware of her rescuer pulling
himself onto flat ground, but all Dayra could really

see was the sharp division between the grass in front of her and the cold blue sea beyond. The cliff's edge was so close, so very close. . . .

Don't think about it, she told herself fiercely. Don't look at it. Don't let yourself imagine what could have happened.

Dayra wrapped her arms around her legs, pulling herself into a tight ball. It didn't stop the involuntary trembling that shook her. She squeezed her eyes shut and dropped her head on her knees, but it wasn't enough to drive out the frightening images that chased each other around in her head.

She had to get back to the holding. Jason needed her. Jeanella needed her. She had to protect them against whatever the thin man intended. She had to move. She *had* to.

The words pounded at her, but they couldn't break through the irrational fear that gripped her. Dayra wasn't even aware of the stranger's approach until he knelt beside her and touched her arm. His voice rumbled soothingly in her ear.

"It's all right. You're safe now."

She raised her head, ashamed that he should see her like this, yet grateful for his presence, nonetheless. Tears stung her eyes but she blinked them back. She forced a shaky laugh and tried to push back the hair that had fallen forward into her face.

"It's crazy, isn't it?" she asked. "Reacting like this, I mean. After all, I'm not really hurt, just scraped a bit, but—" She drew a deep breath.

Her fingers trembled as she tucked the stray lock of hair behind her ear.

"I *hate* heights." The words came out with a ferocity that startled even her. She hadn't meant to say anything—the confession just burst out before she could stop it.

She winced, waiting for her rescuer to laugh at her. When he didn't say anything, Dayra looked directly into his eyes, surprised at his restraint and ready to defend her momentary weakness if he challenged her. Whatever she might have said died unspoken as she suddenly hung suspended, caught in the power of his gaze.

His eyes were a dark green brown rimmed with gold. They were fixed on her with an intensity that was both unsettling and oddly comforting. In their dark depths Dayra read understanding and—was it respect?—but no hint of mockery or amusement.

He didn't smile. Dayra could see enduring strength and the memory of pain carved in the hard lines of his face, but nowhere was there any trace of softness that might have yielded to laughter. Without speaking, he gathered her into his arms, then rose to his feet and carried her toward the flitter. He limped slightly, yet despite his grueling climb up the cliff, he carried her easily. Only the damp sheen on his skin and the dark sweat stains on his shirt beneath the marks left by her own sea-soaked clothes revealed that anything out of the ordinary had occurred.

He was halfway to the flitter before Dayra finally came fully to her senses.

"Put me down," she said, more sharply than she'd intended.

He shook his head. "When we get to the flitter. Not before then."

"I have to get back to my family. You don't understand—"

"You'll get there faster in the flitter. Unless you really want to walk?"

By the time Dayra had thought of a sharp comeback, he was tucking her into the passenger's side of the flitter. A minute later he strapped himself into the driver's seat.

His massive body filled the seat, crowding the narrow compartment. Dayra felt as if someone had compressed the air inside the vehicle, making it difficult for her to breathe. He didn't even glance at her, but kept his attention focused on the controls.

"Where to?" he asked as the flitter rose on its cushion of air.

Dayra pointed to the trail of flattened grass left by her flitter . . . and her attacker. "There. Follow the tracks. They'll lead to my holding."

And to her family, she thought, her hands clenching. She scarcely heeded the pain that simple motion caused her. Her gaze focused on the tracks leading across the grass, straight toward Jeanella and Jason.

Without another word, the stranger turned the flitter and set off along the path taken by the man who had abandoned her to drown.

Urged on by the woman he'd rescued, Coll pushed the decrepit flitter to top speed, following the broad swath of darker green that cut through the tall grass. Flitters were easy to track since the compressed air they rode on invariably left a trail of flattened vegetation behind.

In this case, there were actually three paths: two headed toward the inlet behind them and one headed away, judging by the direction the flattened grass lay in. Already the two older paths were beginning to disappear as the grass sprang back up. The single track leading away from the inlet, the track Coll followed now, was still fresh and clear.

The question was, who was in that flitter, and why had that person tried to kill the woman beside Coll by abandoning her in that inlet?

Coll glanced over at the woman. She was leaning forward, her eyes fixed straight ahead, her body taut with strain. Whatever it was she feared, it was obviously serious enough to have driven all thought of her own condition from her mind.

From this angle he could clearly see the bloody scrapes along her cheek. Since she wore nothing but a short, sleeveless shift, the damage to her hands, arms, and legs was probably worse. He couldn't tell for sure because she was huddled in her seat, her arms wrapped around her and her legs tucked under the seat, as if she were trying to make herself as small as possible.

The thought of her legs roused an unwelcome heat within him. He could remember, all too clearly, the feel of those legs wrapped tight around his waist, the feel of her breasts crushed against his chest as she'd clung to him. He could remember the way loose strands of her hair had blown across his cheeks and lips as he'd carried her, tantalizing him with their casual caress.

When he'd knelt beside her, there at the cliff top, he'd intended to check how badly she was hurt, but then she'd looked up at him and he'd become lost in her ice-blue eyes. He'd seen her fear. More than that, he'd seen the courage with which she'd fought against it, the determination not to give in that had driven her up the cliff and that drove her now.

"Would you mind explaining what's going on?" he asked.

"What?" She frowned and twisted around in her seat to look at him, obviously puzzled. Clearly her thoughts had been on whatever lay ahead, not on the present.

Coll gestured out the windscreen to the green path ahead. "What's at your holding? Why were you on that cliff? Who's in the other flitter and why?"

She blinked, then bit at the edge of her lower lip. A minute earlier she'd been completely oblivious to his presence. Now she was wary, her defenses going up even as he watched. It didn't take a genius to guess she was trying to decide just how much she had to tell him and how much she could keep hidden.

"My brother and sister are alone at the holding," she said at last, picking her words carefully. "There's a man . . . a troublemaker who's been hanging around. I think he may be there now."

"Is it his flitter trail we're following?"

"Yes. I think so."

You know damned well it is, Coll thought, studying her. And whoever it was, he wasn't just some troublemaker.

"What were you doing in that inlet?" he asked, careful to keep his doubts from reflecting in his voice.

"Fishing."

"Fishing?" Whatever answer he'd expected, it wasn't that.

"It's the only place that's even marginally accessible for miles along this coast," she replied, clearly irritated. She looked back out the windscreen. "Can't you make this thing go any faster?"

"No. Can you?" Coll didn't want to call her a liar, but the answer was patently absurd. A woman, fishing alone, on a beach with the tide coming in and the only way out a climb up 70 feet of rugged rock?

His expression of disbelief was wasted, however. Her attention was fixed on the increasingly rough path in front of them, where the grass was giving way to the rocky slope of a low-lying hill.

"It's just over that rise," she said, leaning forward against the safety bar in front of her. "We'll be able to see the holding from there."

A minute later she added, "Watch those rocks ahead! The trail goes through them, not around."

An unnecessary warning, since Coll could now see a dirt path twisting through the massive black rocks scattered across the hillside ahead. The flitter was old and designed for farm work, not speed and maneuverability, but Coll didn't slow down as he guided the heavy vehicle at full speed through the rocks.

The flitter's rightful owner gasped, then wrapped her hands around the safety bar to keep from being thrown against the door. The only protest she made, however, was to throw him an anxious glance before she once more turned her attention ahead.

She ought to be grateful, Coll thought as he roared around one particularly massive boulder. If he weren't so busy watching where he was going, he'd be asking her why the rope ladder had come to be down at the bottom of the inlet with her, instead of looped around the hooks at the top of the cliff, or why she'd left two children alone and vulnerable on a holding so far from any possible help, or why she'd been left to drown in that inlet.

They emerged from the rocky area onto the crest of the hill. From that point, the narrow path ran straight down, then across an open valley directly to the main gate of a walled holding that sprawled across two or three hectares of land. Within the walls, more walls had been built to divide individual fields from each other and from the central compound with its collection of stone buildings. The holding was little more than two miles away, but even at top speed the old flitter they were in would take three or four minutes to reach it.

In that three or four minutes, they had some decisions to make. Or rather, the woman beside him had.

Just beyond the crest of the hill, the trail of the

flitter they'd been following veered abruptly from the path. Instead of continuing on to the holding, the driver had opted to angle across the hill in a sharp descent that would have quickly taken him out of sight of anyone standing on the walls or outside the holding.

It wasn't just anyone the driver had tried to avoid. It was a number of someones, all of them wearing the drab green uniforms of the Combine Protection Forces, the military arm of the government coalition that controlled the lives of the seven known intelligent species inhabiting over a thousand planets within the boundaries of the explored galaxy.

Coll could see three troopers guarding the two armed military skimmers parked near the main gate of the holding, which stood wide open. Another trooper stood near a smaller, faster command skimmer, the kind that was only assigned to officers. The officer or officers in question, along with the remaining troops, were undoubtedly inside the holding itself.

The question was, why? And what were they doing?

Coll glanced at the woman beside him. He only needed a glance to see that she didn't have the answers. She was half out of her seat, pulling against the safety straps that held her as she tried to see what was going on.

"Which do you want," he demanded sharply, "the flitter or the holding?"

"What?" She looked at him, too distracted to focus on his question. A worried frown etched her features, making the scrapes across her chin and cheek stand out sharply.

"Do I follow the flitter or head to your holding?"

She didn't hesitate. "The holding. As fast as you can manage it."

The flitter gained speed on the downhill run, its overtaxed motor whining at the strain, alerting the troops outside the gates before Coll and the woman came close. By the time Coll was slowing to a decorous crawl, another three soldiers had joined the first three. All of them were standing in front of the open gate, eyes glued to the approaching flitter, their weapons within easy reach. The instant Coll brought the flitter to a halt, they had it surrounded.

The woman beside him didn't seem to notice. She was staring down at her stained and dirty shift and her raw red palms.

Coll cursed silently. They'd both forgotten her appearance and the questions it would inevitably generate. Too late now to work out an explanation; he would simply have to follow her lead, however she chose to handle it.

She glanced at him nervously, then set her jaw and clamped her teeth tight in determination. The ragged scrape across her cheek flared an angry red. As though satisfied with some unspoken promise in his gaze, she nodded once, quickly, then balled her hands into fists, shoved her fists into her pockets, and awkwardly climbed out of the flitter.

With every sense alert, and careful to keep his

hands where the troopers could see them, Coll climbed out on his side, then immediately stepped away from the flitter. No sense in making anyone else nervous, especially when they were armed and he carried nothing but a small knife in his boot.

Coll studied the six troopers, who stood silently watching them. The four humans, three men and a woman, carried themselves with the alert, confident grace of individuals trained to deadly perfection. A massive, hairy Graun towered over his companions by a good three feet, his specially tailored uniform oddly bunched over his heavily muscled shoulders, his eyes glittering with excitement over the possibility of a fight. The sixth trooper, a Targ, stood a little apart from the others, its silken fur gleaming in the sun. It might have looked like someone's idea of an exceedingly large house pet if it weren't for the four-inch fangs on either side of its mouth and the even longer claws at the ends of its six-fingered hands.

Every one of the six was armed except the Targ, who already came equipped with weapons that were far more effective for close-in fighting than any regular-issue arms.

Before anyone could speak, a small boy of about six darted through the open gate, headed for the woman Coll had rescued, and excitedly shouting, "Dayra! Dayra!"

"Jason!" Dayra was boxed in by three of the human soldiers before she could move. The fourth, weapon at the ready, whirled to confront the intruder, but immediately relaxed when he spotted the boy. With a grin, he motioned to his companions to release Dayra.

The Graun took a different view of the matter. With a snarl, he grabbed the boy by the collar and swung him off the ground, kicking and screaming.

At that moment, a tall, well-shaped human female dressed in the uniform of a captain of the Combine forces appeared in the open gate. She swiftly scanned the scene before her, then calmly walked over to confront Dayra.

"Good afternoon, Settler Smith," the captain said over the boy's screams. "We've been waiting for you."

Chapter Three

Coll forced himself to remain still, hands relaxed at his side. The last thing he wanted right now was for the soldiers to decide he was a threat. Besides, the boy was in no immediate danger.

"Put him down!" Dayra shouted, fighting against the two soldiers restraining her. "Capt. Truva, tell that . . . that *thing* to put Jason down!"

The captain's eyebrow arched delicately, but she gestured to the Graun to put the boy down.

It wasn't the Graun's fault he dropped the boy. As the Graun started to lower his arm, Jason twisted in his grip and sank his teeth into the Graun's exposed wrist. The creature was undoubtedly more startled than hurt, but he dropped the boy with a roar. Before the Graun could decide what to do next, Jason scrambled to his feet and charged, flailing wildly as he aimed for the Graun's kneecap, which was about as high as he could reach.

Since he'd been ordered to let the boy go, the Graun made no attempt to grab the pint-size pugilist. Instead, in the interests of self-protection, he clamped one enormous paw on the boy's head and held him at arm's length while Jason furiously battered the empty air.

Two of the humans guarding Dayra snickered. The Targ snorted and curled its upper lip back, exposing even more of the vicious fangs. The Graun just looked bewildered.

Dayra slapped at the soldiers restraining her, to no avail. They weren't going to release her without orders, regardless of how amusing they found her brother. "Jason!" she pleaded. "Stop that! Now!"

It was Dayra's fear, more than the boy's predicament, that got Coll moving. He edged around the soldier nearest him, then grabbed Jason around the waist and pulled him away from the Graun before anyone could stop him.

The Graun staggered as his prop unexpectedly disappeared. The soldier, startled by the abrupt tactics of the man he was supposedly guarding, swung around, prepared for a fight.

Coll wasn't about to give him one. He tucked a still-struggling Jason under one arm, partially shielding him with his body, then held up his free hand in sign of surrender. "It's all right. I just wanted the boy."

He didn't have a chance to say more because Jason suddenly squirmed out of his grip. With fierce determination, Jason staggered to his feet and launched himself at Coll.

Coll sidestepped, then pounced on the boy, wrapping his arms around him tight enough so Jason couldn't move. "Stay still, damn it!" Coll snapped.

"Let Dayra go!" Jason shouted, wriggling violently in Coll's grip. "Let her go!"

The captain, clearly annoyed at the uproar, motioned for her people to release Dayra. As soon as they stepped back, Coll released Jason, who immediately raced to his sister, wrapped his arms around her legs, and glared defiantly at the captain.

Dayra threw Coll a grateful glance, then knelt to hug Jason tight against her, murmuring soothing, unintelligible words until he grew calmer. As he relaxed his hold on her, she rose to her feet and, still keeping her hands protectively on Jason's shoulders, turned on the captain.

"What is the meaning of this outrage, Capt. Truva? Where is my sister? By what right—"

The captain cut Dayra's tirade short with cold precision. "Your sister is inside, unharmed. We are here because we had rumors of illicit weapons hidden on this holding, Settler," she said.

Dayra stiffened. "There are no weapons here!"

"None that we could find," Capt. Truva conceded. "Not *yet*, anyway."

Although she was physically smaller than the captain, unarmed, and surrounded by watchful soldiers who *were* armed, Dayra wasn't intimidated by the implied threat. "You would enter my home, frighten my family, and threaten me, all because of a *rumor*? You haven't even shown me a warrant authorizing your search, Captain."

"I don't need a warrant if I suspect rebel activity, Settler. Not here on Far Star."

Coll watched Dayra, caught by the courage that fired her proud defiance. It was love for her family and a fierce sense of justice that made her stand up to the captain, he decided, not any need to conceal illegal activities.

But if she wasn't involved with rebels on Far Star, what had prompted the captain to search a holding as isolated as this one?

The answer walked out of the holding's main gate a moment later, closely escorted by two more armed soldiers and leading a girl of about 11 by the hand.

Coll's eyes widened and his mouth dropped open. He could only be grateful the others were too distracted by the new arrivals to notice.

What, by the red moons of Talkan, was Black Johnny McGregor doing here on Far Star? Coll had thought the old man dead these five years past, so how could he be wearing an expression of repressed indignation and stalking toward them in his familiar, bowlegged gait as if he had every right in the universe to be here?

If the old reprobate really was as alive as he looked, then Coll had no doubt he was the one behind the rumors that had drawn Capt. Truva to the holding. Earthborn and Earth bred, Johnny was 70 if he was a day, and Coll would bet everything he had that not even one of those days had passed without Johnny McGregor meddling in something that was none of his business. The man was addicted to sticking his finger into any nearby pot that might be bubbling, just to give it another stir and see what popped up that might be of interest.

That Johnny had seen him, Coll had no doubt, but the wily codger, steeped in more skulduggery and back-street doings than any ten men his age, was far too experienced to reveal any surprise at Coll's presence.

"There's yere sister, then, lass," he said, giving the girl he was leading a little push toward Dayra. He glanced up at one of the soldiers beside him with a look that dared the young Andorian to object. Then he strode over to confront the captain.

"Well, then, Cap'n," he said, his fists aggressively propped on his hips. "Just as I told ye, yere people have found nothin' for all yere trouble and disruption."

The captain raised that one expressive eyebrow in a silent query. The two soldiers accompanying Johnny merely nodded; the two Mmmrxs that had followed them chirruped an agreement.

Since the tall, slender Mmmrxs possessed an uncanny sense of smell, they were often assigned the task of sniffing out illegal caches of arms or contraband. Coll knew from experience that, if they hadn't found any weapons, there weren't any weapons to be found. Which didn't mean that Johnny wasn't up to something—something that might eventually prove dangerous to Dayra Smith and her family.

Coll glanced at Dayra, but her attention was

divided between the captain and the two children she sheltered protectively against her. She bent to murmur something to the children, then left them clinging to each other in order to confront the captain.

"You have the answer to your question, Captain," Dayra said from between gritted teeth. Her hands were clenched in tight fists and she was leaning forward slightly, balancing on the balls of her feet like a fighter readying for the fight. "There are no weapons hidden on the holding. There never will be. I run a farm, not a rebellion, and I'll thank you not to disturb my family ever again with these illegal and unfounded searches."

Coll couldn't help frowning, torn between admiration for her courage and concern that she might push the captain too far. Truva was rigid with anger, clearly displeased with such blatant defiance, but too much in control of herself to resort to force to silence Dayra.

They'd accomplish nothing with angry tirades, Coll knew, and they might do a great deal of harm through antagonizing the captain. With a silent sigh at the likelihood that his meddling would create problems he'd sooner have avoided, Coll stepped forward.

"Settler," he said, respectfully touching Dayra's elbow, "we've work to finish and the fish. . . ." He let the thought trail off, hoping she'd follow his lead. He still couldn't believe she'd been fishing, not in that inaccessible cove, but as a diversion, the suggestion would serve as well as any.

Dayra started, then gaped at him, disoriented

by his unexpected interruption.

"Who are you?" Capt. Truva demanded, turning her quelling gaze on him.

"A hired hand, Cap'n," Johnny said, quick to pick up Coll's intent.

"I don't recall having seen you around before," Truva snapped, obviously displeased at discovering another suspect she'd have to watch.

"Ah, well, we've kept him hard at work, ye see," Johnny inserted smoothly, saving Coll the necessity of responding. As little as Coll knew of conditions here, the less he said, the better.

"There's a great deal of work on a holding like this, Captain," Dayra added in a milder tone than she'd used thus far. "I'm grateful for the help I'm given."

She turned her head to look directly up at Coll. He blinked, then felt his breath stop halfway out of his chest. Those ice-blue eyes of hers were alive with gratitude and a sharp awareness of what his simple gesture might mean, to him as well as to her. Without even knowing his name, she'd suddenly included him in the orbit of her world along with Black Johnny and the two children. It caught him off guard, left him feeling unsteady and oddly hopeful. There was something in those blue depths that called to him, promising . . . what? He didn't know and now was not the time to find out.

"What's your name?" Capt. Truva's voice clearly indicated she would brook no more foolishness.

With his eyes still locked on the fascinating blue ones of his "boss," he said, "Coll."

The name was out before he could stop it. At the

sound of it, his breath caught in his throat once again, this time from shock. He swayed slightly, startled by the implications of that one simple confession. The world must have suddenly shifted beneath his feet.

"Coll what?"

The captain's sharp question shattered the invisible wall of stunned surprise that enclosed him. If it were possible, he'd refuse to answer. It wasn't possible.

He turned to face the captain, seeking refuge from the dangerous blue eyes that had just led him into betraying himself. "Coll Larren." He had to force the name out. The syllables sounded foreign and strangely harsh on his lips.

How long had it been since he'd last shared his name—his *real* name—with anyone, let alone complete strangers like these people before him? He couldn't remember. Black Johnny knew it, but not many others. Not many that still lived, at any rate, either friend or foe. So why, after so many years, had it suddenly spilled so easily from his mouth?

Coll glanced back at the woman who was responsible for his unwelcome exposure. She was watching him, alert, curious, yet somehow unshaken by his revelation. To her, he was a man who had helped her, twice, and now he had a name. For her, he had no past. It was as simple as that.

The thought was as unsettling as the realization a moment earlier that he'd spoken his name without thinking. The past was so much a part of his present, weighing it down, coloring it in shades of darkness, that he'd never considered the possibility of discarding it, just like that. So simple, really. Just say his name aloud and let all the rest disappear in those two blue orbs as if it had never been.

"Well, Cap'n? The lad's right. We've work to do. Are ye through searchin' for what never existed in the first place?"

Johnny's brash question shattered the spell that held Coll trapped in thoughts of impossible possibilities. Coll turned, grateful for the distraction.

No one appeared to have noted anything odd in his behavior. It had only been a second or so, then, that he'd kept silent. Only a second, and yet. . . .

Coll shifted his weight, easing the strain on his left leg, and found himself pinned on Capt. Truva's sharp gaze. The good captain obviously wasn't pleased with Johnny's facile explanation for Coll's presence, but after failing to find any illicit weapons on the holding, she wasn't prepared to engage in further, possibly futile inquiries. At least, not right now.

She gave a sharp command for departure to her troops, but made no move to follow them. Her steady gaze moved from Coll, to Dayra, to Johnny, then back to Dayra. "A reminder, Settler, should you or anyone else on this holding be tempted to forget: the Combine will not tolerate any subversive activities. I don't think I need to explain myself."

Coll could feel the muscles along his spine

tighten with his sudden flare of anger, but long experience allowed him to keep any hint of the emotion out of his face. The captain was a clever woman indeed. It wasn't Dayra she suspected of rebel involvement, but she was smart enough to realize that a threat against Dayra would prove a far more effective restraint on Johnny's plans—or his, if he'd had any—than if she'd threatened them directly.

Without another word, the captain turned and strode to her skimmer.

The two children, who had remained silent and wide-eyed throughout the tense exchange, immediately reattached themselves to Dayra, tugging at her with their unspoken demands for reassurance.

Coll started to speak, but choked instead when Johnny suddenly slapped his shoulder with such enthusiastic force it drove all the air out of his lungs.

"Well, lad, as ye said, there's still work to be done and the day's a-wastin'," he said, loud enough for the departing soldiers to hear and with just the right mix of unconcern and defiance. He gave Coll a push in the direction of the main gates. "We'll move the flitter once our visitors have gone."

Dayra led the way, with her brother and sister clinging to her on each side. Johnny followed close on her heels. Coll hesitated a moment before turning back to assure himself the soldiers were really leaving.

The soldiers were climbing into the transports,

eager to be gone. Capt. Truva stood, unmoving, beside her skimmer. Her piercing gaze was fixed on Coll with an intensity he could feel even at this distance.

Coll gave no sign he'd sensed her warning, but as he turned to follow the others into the holding, he knew that he would have to be wary, for the good captain would not easily forget him.

Safely inside the holding, with the roar of the departing skimmers fading away, the children once more wrapped themselves tightly around Dayra.

"I was so worried!" the girl wailed. "You were late and Johnny wasn't here and then the soldiers came. I didn't know what to do! If Johnny hadn't come back—"

"*I* wasn't worried," Jason declared proudly. "I kicked the one who grabbed me the first time. And did you see how I bit that tall soldier, the one who grabbed me? Did you see it, huh, Dayra?"

The visit by the soldiers had both excited and frightened the two children, making them cling to their older sister as they bombarded her with their simultaneous reports on events. Engrossed in their own emotions, they didn't even notice Dayra's injuries or her disheveled state.

It was the children and her love for them, Coll thought, that had gotten Dayra Smith up that cliff in spite of everything. He knew her arms and hands were raw and sore from her climb, yet as the children chattered and clung to her, she only held them closer.

Coll suddenly found his own arms aching with

the remembered feel of holding her. With a muttered oath, he crossed his arms over his chest, digging his fingers into the hard muscle of his upper arms as if he could root out the unwanted sensual memories. The memories faded, leaving him with an odd feeling of . . . emptiness.

Though he wanted to turn away, Coll found himself studying the trio before him, trying to trace the characteristics that would mark them as sisters and brother.

The boy, Jason, was towheaded, gap toothed, and scrawny in the way of active little boys. In a herd of other small boys, the only things that would have made him stand out were his engaging grin and sparkling, clear blue eyes, whose color matched that of his sisters'.

The girl had received all the beauty in the family. She was a delicate creature with golden hair, fair skin, and a slender frame that promised an exquisite, feminine grace when she grew to womanhood. She shared the family's blue eyes, but hers were shaded by thick, dark lashes under perfectly shaped brows. In a few years her effect on a man would be devastating.

In contrast, Dayra was thin and angular, not tall, but not so short her thinness could pass for delicacy. Her nose was too long and sharp, her cheeks too hollow, and her chin far too pointed for beauty. Her skin was unbecomingly browned by the sun. Her hair was tied up in a heavy knot that must have started at the top of her head, but had now slipped to one side, making her look slightly off balance. The numerous locks that had worked their way free hung around her face in a disorderly tangle, clinging to the damp skin of her throat and the back of her neck.

Coll blinked, remembering the way those same strands had blown into his face as he'd carried her up the cliff. He shifted his feet, uncomfortable with the memory. He hadn't meant to think of that.

He didn't belong here, he reminded himself sternly. As soon as he could talk someone from the holding into taking him on to Trevag, he'd be gone. If Black Johnny couldn't take him, then perhaps someone else. Dayra hadn't said anything about where the other adults had gone, but one or two of them ought to return soon.

His thoughts were interrupted when Jason, evidently tired of so much affection, squirmed out of his sister's embrace and turned to Coll. "Who are you?" he demanded, tilting his head back to stare up at Coll.

Coll blinked, disconcerted by so direct a question from so small a boy. He uncrossed his arms and let his hands fall by his sides. "I'm Coll Larren." It still felt strange to use his own name, but perhaps a little practice would make it come easier.

"I'm sorry." Dayra released her sister and stood. "I didn't think—that is, I forgot—" With the back of her hand, she brushed aside a lock of hair that had fallen forward into her eyes. The gesture exposed the raw palm that was now darkened by dried blood. "I'm Dayra Smith. This is my sister, Jeanella, and my brother, Jason."

Coll could see her eyes darken as a sudden thought occurred to her. He'd wondered when she'd start to question where he'd come from and why he'd appeared so unexpectedly . . . and so conveniently. Before she could ask, he said, "I was on my way to look for work in Trevag. There wasn't any traffic on the main road, so I thought I might find transport by taking that trail along the cliffs." His explanation covered only the high points, but it appeared to be enough. For the moment, anyway.

The boy, Jason, wasn't interested. "How come Johnny said you work here? Are you gonna stay?" he demanded, obviously delighted at the possibility of having another male around the holding. "I could show you lotsa neat things. We got a—"

"That's enough, Jason," Dayra interrupted. "Why don't you two come with me? I need to clean up and perhaps we can find you a treat. Johnny, I . . . I left the ladder hanging from a rock on the cliff. Would you retrieve it for me? You'll need a long rope to climb down for it. And would you take care of Coll, please?"

She glanced at Coll, then as quickly looked away, clearly too exhausted to deal with any more problems. "We can decide what to do about all this later."

Johnny watched the three with an expression of protective indulgence until they disappeared through the door of the holding's main house. Then he immediately rounded on Coll.

"So it's Coll Larren, now, is it?"

"It's my name," Coll responded sharply, not liking the defensive note in his voice.

"Oh, aye, so it is." The old man's eyes narrowed until they were barely slits. He thrust out his chin and scratched it slowly and very thoughtfully as he continued to stare at Coll. His fingers rasped across the day-old stubble on his jaw.

Coll endured the chin scratching and narrow-eyed stare until he could endure it no longer. "What?"

"What?" Black Johnny shook off his thoughtful pose in feigned surprise. "Oh! I was just wonderin' how long it'd been since I last heard ye use yere rightful name." He shook his head regretfully. "Ah, I'm an old man, lad, an' me memory's not what it used to be, ye understand. Seems I just can't quite remember back that far."

"Tell me another tale I might have a chance of believing," Coll snapped, turning away in irritation.

"Sure, now, and I've plenty. Would ye be wantin' to hear the one about—"

"I'd be wanting to retrieve my bag and Dayra's belongings, Black Johnny McGregor. That and not one thing more."

"Oh, there's a few things left, lad," Johnny said in a tone that would brook no evasions. "I'll thank ye to tell me why ye're here and why ye've come draggin' in with me fine lady boss lookin' like she's gone ten sets with the toughest fighters from Poderis Prime . . . an' lost every one o' the ten."

Coll shrugged. "The first's easy enough. I was dumped here by a ship's master I disagreed with

57

because he thought brutality was the primary requirement for good crew relations. As for the second"—he met the old man's gaze directly—"you'll have to get the story from her. My guess is she'll say the predicament I found her in was a rather unfortunate accident."

"And ye don't think whatever it was was an accident at all?"

"No, I don't. Not any more than I believe you know nothing about those rumors that brought Capt. Truva for a visit. But it's none of my business, after all." And he'd do well to remember that, Coll reminded himself.

"Hummpf." The wrinkles in Johnny's brow deepened in thought for an instant. He glanced toward the house where Dayra had disappeared; then he glanced at Coll, a speculative gleam in his eye. The assessing look was suddenly replaced by a wide grin as he slapped Coll on the back. Hard. "Well, I told the good cap'n ye're employed here, so we might as well make sure she's no chance to doubt me word. There's plenty o' work here to keep ye occupied, and that's a fact."

"I don't—" Coll started to protest, but Johnny ignored him.

"For right now, I'd say the best thing ye could do is help me lady boss tend those scrapes. Nasty things, cuts like that. Ye'll know what's best for 'em."

"Someone else can help her. I'm not—"

"There's no one else, lad. The children would be no use, and if ye can't remember why I won't, then *yere* mind must be the one that's going."

Coll grimaced wryly. "You're right. Where was it? Dorcale? Trinicus? Your treatment hurt worse than that phaser burn the Combine soldiers gave me. But surely—" Coll cut his protest short as the implications of Johnny's words suddenly dawned on him. "Are you telling me there is no one else on this holding except the four of you?"

"Aye, that's what I'm tellin' ye." Johnny said, unconcerned. He glanced up at the sun, now half-way past its zenith. "Well, I'll get some ropes and whatnot so we can retrieve that ladder and yere bag . . . *after* ye've helped me lady boss."

If he couldn't get out of it, Coll thought, glancing toward the house, he could make sure he didn't take any longer than he had to. Clean Dayra's cuts and scrapes, dig out the bits of rock that would be imbedded in her skin. . . .

An uncomfortable heat flared in Coll at the thought of her skin, of the warmth of her flesh beneath his fingers. He opened his mouth to protest that he couldn't help, but Johnny spoke before he could get the words out.

"Dayra Smith could use a little help right now," he said, his gaze locked on Coll's. "There's no one else around to give it to her except one great lump of a man named Coll Larren." With that, he turned and walked away.

All right, Coll decided, watching Johnny go, he'd help Dayra. Then, after he'd retrieved her ladder and his bag, he'd be on his way, even if that meant he walked the rest of the way to Trevag.

He abruptly spun about on his heel, making the muscles in his left leg protest. Coll winced and rubbed his thigh. All right, maybe he'd eat a decent meal and get a good night's rest first. *Then* he'd leave.

In spite of his determination not to get involved, Coll couldn't help studying his surroundings as he slowly crossed the main yard. It didn't take a sharp observer to see the holding had been constructed with grand plans and not much money.

On a world where trees hadn't yet evolved, the builders had relied on raw native rock for their basic materials. Almost everything on the holding was constructed of stone, it seemed—buildings, work sheds, laborers' housing, the protective walls around the property, the main house itself. Even the glass for the buildings' windows had probably been made from local sand.

Whoever had built the place had used architectural principles thousands of years old to shape the rough stone into simple yet eminently practical structures. Only the main house boasted more than one story, and that was limited to a small chamber that probably served both as sleeping quarters and lookout post.

Was it Dayra's room? Coll wondered. Did she climb the stairs each night with the thought that she would be safe, or in the expectation of being able to look out over her small domain and dream of the future?

With the exception of the windows in that second-floor room and one huge window looking out over the compound in one of the ground-floor rooms, most of the buildings' windows were small and set deep in the thick stone walls, as though even locally made glass had been too costly to squander needlessly.

When it came to the holding's doors and main gates, the builders had used some sort of grass, pressed together until it had formed a sturdy substitute for wood or plasteel. The technique was effective, but crude.

Even someone with experience and resources would have had a hard time making a go of this place, Coll thought. What did Dayra Smith have? An old man, one small boy, one medium-size girl, and herself, a woman somewhat the worse for wear. That was it.

Coll frowned, then resolutely shook his head. There was no way he was going to get caught up in Dayra Smith's problems—absolutely no way at all.

She should have asked for help, Dayra decided, wincing at the pain as she tried to extract a piece of gravel that had worked its way into a deep cut in the fleshy base of her right thumb. Perhaps if she hadn't been so tired or felt so battered, it wouldn't have been so hard to ask.

Who was she kidding? She'd never been good at asking for help. She'd taken great pride in never needing to.

Maybe it was time she started learning.

How can I ask a stranger for help? she silently objected, squeezing her eyes shut against the mental image of a tall, tattered man whose shoulders seemed broad enough and strong enough to bear the weight of the world. Excuse me, kind sir, I have this little problem. . . .

Impossible.

No, she couldn't ask for help. She'd managed just fine for the past five years; she could keep on managing just fine, all by herself.

Like you managed Bardath's emissary?

He'd taken her by surprise. That was all. She'd manage better the next time he threatened her and her family.

Really?

Quit thinking about it, Dayra admonished herself. Talking to herself wasn't accomplishing anything.

Not that it ever did, but there wasn't anyone else to talk to except the children and Black Johnny, and she had no intention of burdening them with her problems.

Dayra clumsily picked up the probe with her left hand and once more tried to dig out the tiny rock shard. Her fingers were so sore and stiff it was almost impossible to hold the slim metal tool. Since she was a right-handed person and she was forced to use her left hand for such fine work, the task was almost impossible.

Sweat beaded on her brow. Dayra had to grit her teeth against the pain. Concentrate. *Concentrate.*

In spite of her determination not to complain, Dayra couldn't help but cry out as the probe slipped and dug deeper into the already torn flesh.

"Why don't you let me help with that?"

The deep voice instantly cut through the blur of

Dayra's pain. She jerked her head up and dropped the probe, but didn't bother to watch it as it rolled off the table and onto the floor.

Coll Larren stood in the doorway, his massive form outlined against the sunlight of the open yard behind him. "Let me do that," he added, moving toward her. He bent to pick up the probe, then placed it on the table.

Dayra could tell he was taking care not to meet her eyes, but she couldn't pull her own gaze away from him. Inside her, independence warred with exhaustion and pain and the temptation of letting someone else solve her problems, even if only for a little while. Independence lost the battle.

"Thank you," she said softly, drooping in her chair. "I didn't think it would be so hard."

Coll scarcely heeded her; his attention was fixed on sorting through the contents of the standard medical kit that every holding maintained.

Grateful that he at least hadn't commented on her clumsy attempts at self-doctoring, Dayra watched as he gathered the items he wanted. His hands were big, the fingers blunted and the skin callused from rough work, yet he handled everything he touched with a neat precision she wouldn't have expected in a man his size.

Still without speaking, he drew up a chair for himself and sat down, a damp cloth in one hand. He extended his other hand to her, palm up. Suddenly, his eyes were fixed on her with a steady, questioning intensity that she found unnerving, yet oddly compelling at the same time. Without hesitation, she placed her hand in his.

His fingers curled around her wrist, supporting her as he carefully cleaned first her hand, then worked his way to her wrist and up the inside of her arm where she'd scraped it raw in her slide down the cliff.

Despite the intimacy of his task, there was nothing very personal and certainly nothing deliberately tantalizing in the way he touched her. He kept his head down and his eyes focused on whatever scrape or gouge he was treating, seemingly unaware of her beyond the wounds he tended. Dayra could imagine him working over a piece of machinery with equal care and an equal lack of passion.

As he worked, Dayra studied him from behind her lashes, puzzled by this stranger who had dropped into her life so abruptly. With his rough clothes, unkempt brown hair, and hard, weather-beaten face, he looked like a brigand or a hardened mercenary. A *big* mercenary, she thought—broad shouldered, with legs and arms that were thick with hard muscle. Even seated, like now, Coll Larren gave an impression of raw power that might be used to any dangerous and violent purpose, yet he was fulfilling his self-appointed task of nurse with impressive delicacy.

To her surprise, Dayra realized she'd gradually relaxed under his gentle ministrations, lulled by his comfortable silence and reassuring presence as much as by his soothing touch.

Once he'd cleaned and treated the deep cuts and scrapes on Dayra's arms, Coll turned his attention to the injuries on her legs. This time, he brought his chair around in front of her and lifted both her legs into his lap so he could tend to them more easily.

Dayra stiffened as the back of her legs pressed into the tops of his thighs, but he appeared completely unaffected by the intimate contact.

At sight of her blood-caked knee, he shook his head and said, "This is going to hurt."

"More than it hurt my hands?" Her words were unforgivably rude, but they were out of her mouth before Dayra could stop them. Blame it on him. He was the one addling her senses.

He glanced up, instantly contrite. "I'm sorry. I—"

"It's all right." Dayra grimaced in apology. "I'm just tired. Don't mind me."

Though his touch was extremely light, his ministrations had still hurt. What bothered Dayra was not the pain, but the slow heat his touch had roused in her, a heat that infused her entire body with its disorienting, tempting warmth. She couldn't help but be aware of the warmth of his skin on hers and the pressure of his fingers against her flesh. She could hear the soft rustle of his clothes as he moved and, ever so faintly, the sound of his breathing. She could smell him, a dark, male scent compounded of sweat and something else, something . . . dangerous.

That thought made Dayra flush. She was a fool to indulge in absurd fantasies, no matter how tired and sore and vulnerable she felt.

At thought of the word vulnerable, Dayra swore. Silently. She wasn't about to admit to any vulnerability, not even to herself. If she let just one doubt creep through the chinks in her mental armor, more would come shoving in after. She couldn't afford to let that happen. Not ever.

She almost jerked her legs off Coll's lap, but he chose that moment to place his hand on her thigh, just above her knee. Her interest in running evaporated immediately.

An instant later, she seriously reconsidered the idea of flight when he started bathing her knee, which had taken the worst damage. As he scrubbed away the caked blood to expose the raw flesh beneath, Dayra bit down hard on her lower lip to keep from protesting.

"That hurt?" Coll asked, anxiously glancing up at her.

Dayra expelled the breath she'd been holding from between clenched teeth. "Of course not. I bash my knee on the rocks regularly, just for the fun of it."

He smiled. Just a small smile, but it was enough to light his dark face.

His mouth wasn't hard, Dayra thought. Not like the rest of him. The rest was cut from granite, like the rock that had scraped her raw, but his mouth and his eyes were soft and warm and. . . .

And she was a fool for even thinking such thoughts. Dayra focused on the pain as Coll worked on digging out the bits of rock imbedded in her flesh.

When he finished, she slumped in her chair. That had hurt and no mistake, but it had been a lot safer than indulging her imagination. Dayra swung her legs off his before he could lift them off; then she pushed back her chair and stood up. Unfortunately, he did the same, which left him towering over her. She gulped. Gentle or not, the man was still an intimidating figure.

"Thank you," she said. "That feels much better." She ought to say something more, but her usually glib tongue failed her.

"Your face," he said, his eyes fixed on her.

"My face?" Puzzled, Dayra put her hand to her face. She winced. She'd forgotten the scrapes on her cheek and chin.

"It won't take long."

Before Dayra could think of a good excuse, he'd dampened a clean cloth and delicately started to clean the mistreated skin on her cheek. Since they were still standing, the task was awkward, but Dayra wasn't about to suggest they sit down again. At least on her feet she could run if her self-control shattered completely.

It wasn't the pain; it was his touch that was so . . . unsettling. This close, she could see the pores of his skin, the dark shadow of beard along his jaw. His pupils had widened in the unlighted workroom until little remained but a rim of startling gold around the black. Dayra blinked and tried to look away, but he filled her vision. With one hand firmly holding her chin while he worked, she couldn't move far, anyway.

Was it her imagination, or was he having more difficulty with the scrapes on her face than he'd had with the others? Dayra wondered. She could have sworn his fingers trembled, at least a little, but that was probably due to his trying to make sure he didn't hurt her any more than absolutely necessary. And though it sounded like it, his sigh when Black Johnny appeared in the door to announce that the flitter was ready to go couldn't possibly have been a sigh of relief.

Could it?

Long after the sound of the two men's footsteps died away, Dayra remained standing in the center of the little workroom, staring at the blank wall across from her. Beneath the ache and throb of raw skin, her flesh pricked with the sharp awareness that Coll Larren's touch had so easily roused within her.

It was the whine of the flitter's engine that stirred her to movement. Without stopping to think, without knowing what she would say, she darted from the room, intent on catching them before they left the compound.

Chapter Four

She was too late. The big gate was already swinging silently back into place by the time she was out of the house. By the time she navigated the rough stone steps leading up to the top of the holding walls, the flitter was beginning to climb the rocky hill on the far side of the valley.

Dayra stood, feet braced against the push of the incessant wind, and watched until the flitter disappeared over the crest of the hill. Her thoughts tossed about like the tall grass below her, buffeted by first one emotional gust, then another.

Suspicion. Curiosity. Doubt. Gratitude. Relief. They were all there, along with an undeniable sexual attraction that was probably far more dangerous to her well-being than any other threat the man might present.

No, Dayra thought, hugging her arms to her chest, the sexual attraction wasn't the most dangerous thing about Coll Larren. It was his compassion . . . and his strength. He was a stranger, yet he had risked his life for her. He was a big man clearly accustomed to hard work and, perhaps, an even harder life, yet he had tended her injuries with a gentle skill that had been as soothing as it was tantalizing.

It had been comforting to depend on someone else for a change. She couldn't remember the last time anyone had taken care of her as Coll Larren had taken care of her injuries.

Dayra hunched her shoulders and hugged her arms even closer about her, willing away the dangerous longing to put her burdens in someone else's hands, to give up the struggle that was her daily lot and let someone else fight in her place, at least for a little while.

Tomorrow, when she was rested and her injuries no longer hurt so much and the memory of the thin man had blurred a little, she would laugh at the emotions assailing her. For right now, she could no more ignore the temptation to ask Coll Larren to stay and help her on the holding than she could make the massive stone walls beneath her suddenly disappear.

Dayra glanced down at the stones beneath her feet, then slowly pivoted to survey the sweep of open land and enclosed fields that made up the heart of the holding she'd bought, sight unseen. Most would have called her a fool for investing her money, including the money she'd taken from

Talman Bardath, in so vast a tract of "worthless" land.

She knew she hadn't made a mistake. However hard the struggle to wrest a living from this new world, it was her world now, her land, her living. What she had, she owed to no one, and the success that would one day be hers she would earn for herself.

Until then. . . .

Dayra sighed and eased herself down onto the stones. They were warm to the touch, but not hot. Hard, unyielding, and strong. She wished she could be so hard, so unfeeling. She was tired— tired of fighting, tired of planning, tired of feeling tired. She was especially tired of battling each day's problems without anyone to help her.

She couldn't count Black Johnny's help. Much as she valued the old man's work, he was a hired hand and nothing more. But Coll Larren. . . .

There was something about Coll Larren, something strong and sure that shone deep in his gold-rimmed eyes, something that made her want to trust him even when she knew nothing about him except that he was brave and capable of great gentleness.

Dayra stared sightlessly at the horizon. Maybe her mother had been right. Maybe it was better to find a man to care for you and protect you. Maybe there was something wrong with her that she should be so independent, that she should want so badly to achieve her dreams on her own.

But then, what had her mother known? Beautiful, delicate Triana had spent her life going from one man to the next, always cosseted, always cared for, but never, ever really free. Her life was shaped by chance, dependent on the whim of her latest male protector or the availability of someone new who was willing to assume that role.

If only Jea'nel Shanti, Jeanella's father, hadn't died! He'd loved Triana as none of her other lovers ever had, and he'd treasured his lovely little daughter. He had even welcomed homely little Dayra into his heart. To her, he had been the father and confidant she had never known, and she had loved him even more passionately than had her beautiful mother.

But for all his fine qualities, Jea'nel had shared Triana's complete lack of concern about the future. When he died, Triana discovered too late her lover had made no provision for them. She'd been heart-broken at Jea'nel's death, but it hadn't taken her long to find another protector in Talman Bardath. Had she lived, she would have found someone after Bardath.

But she hadn't lived. She had died, leaving 21-year-old Dayra with full responsibility for two small children, no money, and no skills to earn any. Triana had never seen the need to ensure that Dayra was trained in a profession. After all, Triana herself had never needed any special skills. She'd had her beauty and her charm, and that had always been enough.

Even if she had possessed some of her mother's beauty, Dayra knew it wouldn't have been enough for her. After so many years spent trailing in her mother's wake, Dayra had vowed long ago never to be dependent on a man—for anything. As it was, lacking both beauty and skills, she'd been left with nothing more than determination and her native intelligence to get by on.

Those two qualities had been enough, barely, to provide for the three of them over the past five years, but they hadn't been enough to allow them to escape Bardath.

The thought of the man who threatened everything she'd worked so hard to achieve made Dayra flush in impotent anger. Five years ago, she'd figured she'd run far enough to put her beyond the reach of even so powerful and wealthy a man as Talman Bardath. She'd been wrong, and now he was hounding her and threatening Jason and Jeanella.

For the first time, Dayra wasn't sure she could protect her family or herself. But Coll Larren could. Of that she was certain.

Dayra stared at the hill over which Coll had disappeared with Johnny. Even now he was taking care of what was rightfully her problem. When he came back—

At the half-formed thought, Dayra tensed, then dropped her gaze.

No, she wouldn't think of that. Wouldn't *let* herself think of that. This was her holding, her family, her life. She didn't need anyone to fight her battles and never would. If she hadn't been so tired and battered, she wouldn't have thought of it now.

From somewhere in the house, Dayra caught the sound of Jason's voice, then Jeanella's. Dayra twisted her head to the side, trying to make out the words. At the movement, the clumsy knot of her hair, which she'd tied at the top of her head this morning and which had gradually been slipping to the side all day, suddenly broke free, spilling an untidy hank of hair over her shoulder and down her breast.

Dayra glanced down, ready to shove her hair back, and froze.

She was a tatty, disreputable mess. Her hair was tangled, her shift stained and torn in a dozen places, her legs scraped and raw with a scab forming on each knee. She hadn't realized. . . .

Triana would have been appalled.

Dayra scowled, then awkwardly climbed to her feet. She would bathe and change her clothes and apply more ointment to her injuries. She'd probably have to ask Jeanella to comb out her hair. Not that it would help much.

As she headed down the stone steps on the inside of the holding wall, Dayra decided her appearance had at least one advantage: it was a potent reminder that she was on her own.

If there was anything Triana had taught her, it was that no man was ever talked into anything by a woman who looked the way she did now.

They were just starting to crest the hill dividing the holding from the sea when Johnny said, "I'd heard ye left the Rebel Alliance, my friend."

Coll didn't blink. He'd been expecting the question. "That's right."

"Would ye mind tellin' me why?"

Coll's hands tightened involuntarily around the steering bar. "Yes, I'd mind."

"I see." Johnny sat silent for a moment, studying him, then said, "Given the official visit to the holding, ye'll already have guessed there's a rebel movement startin' on Far Star."

He paused, obviously waiting for Coll to say something. When Coll remained silent, Johnny continued, "We could use yere help, lad. We could use the Sandman on our side."

At the sound of the name by which he'd become known throughout the Rebel Alliance, the name behind which he'd buried his own for so long, Coll sat up abruptly. Anger and the pain of unwanted memories surged through him. "I have no intention of getting involved in the game ever again."

Johnny snorted, his worn face suddenly stiff with fierce determination. "It's not a game, Coll. It never was. Ye know that as well as I."

"It's not a rebellion, either, my friend," Coll responded grimly. "It's nothing but a deadly farce that people like you and me play, people who think they can remake the world in the name of fancy, empty words like freedom and justice and right."

The muscles in his jaw tightened until they ached as he fought to suppress the soul-deep agony that had gouged his heart out on Cyrus IV and that continued to devour him, bit by painful bit. "We were fools, old man, fools and dreamers and madmen, but I came to my senses. Never again—*never again!*"

Coll drew a shuddering breath, shaken by the sudden fury that had risen within him. With an oath, he pulled the flitter to a bone-rattling halt, then forced his fingers to release their death grip on the steering bar.

"Nobody ever said it was goin' to be easy," Johnny growled. "Nobody promised that things would work out perfectly the first time around."

"Nobody said that the same people we fought to free from the Combine would turn on each other like they did on Cyrus IV, either. Or have you forgotten that part?"

Johnny didn't answer. Outside the flitter, the wind swept across the oceans of grass, bending them in tossing waves that broke against the bold black rocks thrusting up from the green like so many islands in the storm. Inside the flitter, anger made the air crackle with tension.

"So," Johnny said at last, "who appointed ye god and judge and jury? Do ye find the job to your liking, Coll Larren?"

He waited. When no reply came, he added more vehemently, "Don't ye ever stop to think of all the people who had enough hope to keep fightin' because the Sandman was on their side? Don't ye remember any of the successes? There have been far more of them than there have been failures!"

Johnny's voice dropped lower, quivering with his vehemence. "Have ye asked yerself how many people died in the last two years because ye *didn't* help them?"

"I helped the people on Cyrus IV. Where did it get them?"

The words hung like ice in the confines of the flitter.

"Where did it get them, my friend?" Coll persisted, shifting angrily in his seat, unconsciously straining against the protective straps that held him. "Dead, that's where. Over six million of them. It took the survivors more than three weeks to say the necessary prayers, and they were praying from one sunrise to the next."

He stared out at the horizon, his gut churning with all the anger and grief and disillusionment that had ridden him ever since he'd stood among the heaped bodies of the dead on Cyrus IV and known, really known, that his dreams of transforming the world were nothing but deadly illusions.

When he was sure he could continue more calmly, Coll said, very low, enunciating each word with care, "Never again will I be responsible for the deaths of innocent people whose only crime is to believe in fancy words and dangerous daydreams. *Never.*"

"Ye take a lot of credit for yereself, Coll Larren," Johnny snapped. "Ye may have trained them, may have given them the skills they needed to break free of the Combine, but ye couldn't eliminate the grudges they'd been harborin' among themselves for generations. Nobody could. If it hadn't been for yere intervention, they might still be at each other's throats.

"Yere problem," Johnny added, his voice coldly implacable, "is ye think that the world is simple, that just believin' in somethin' makes it so, that people who fight for a cause really believe in it, that everythin' can be classed as black or white,

77

good or evil. It isna that easy, Coll. It never was. When are ye going to admit that life is messy and complicated and *human*, damn it?"

Johnny slumped in his seat, worn out by his impassioned tirade.

"Nobody likes the death and the sufferin', Coll," he said at last. "Nobody likes the crooks and the cheats and the people who get so caught up in their role of world saver that they become the same kind of tyrants they fought against. But we keep on fightin', keep on helpin' those who need our help, because we understand that the world is painted in shades of gray, not black and white. We understand that nothin's perfect. Nothing, not even us."

When Coll refused to respond, Johnny sighed, then turned to gaze out the windscreen at the sea of wind-tossed grass. Coll had to strain to catch his last words.

"Until Cyrus IV," he said, very softly, "I thought ye were beginning to learn that lesson, too, lad. I really thought ye were beginning to learn."

Coll's hands once more tightened around the steering bar. The muscles in his arms and shoulders quivered with the strain, matching the tension in his neck and jaw as he fought against the pain and anger and despair—especially the despair.

If only he could once more believe in everything the Sandman had stood for. If only he could reclaim that confidence, that sense of the rightness in what he did that Johnny McGregor still possessed! He couldn't. It had died in the slaughter on Cyrus IV, when the rebels he'd help train had turned their weapons on each other after their victory over the Combine.

Added to all the doubts and uncertainties and failures accumulated over 16 years of fighting against the vast central government that controlled most of the inhabited planets in the galaxy, the tragic waste of Cyrus IV had been too much. Coll had abandoned the cause for which he'd fought since he was scarcely more than a boy and had taken to wandering.

These days he felt like a ship adrift in space, its navigational system destroyed, its motion the product of inertia rather than impulse. A useless hulk whose heart was gone.

And yet he could not—*would* not—take up the cause he'd once fought for with such zeal. He couldn't bear to go through the motions when he no longer believed in the rightness of what he was doing. He couldn't bear to act out a farce.

Slowly Coll forced his muscles to relax and his hands to unclench. When the silence stretched until he could no longer bear it, he asked the question that had been nagging at him ever since he'd seen Black Johnny walking through those gates with two armed soldiers as his escort.

"Is she involved?" he asked, staring down at the steering bar he'd been mistreating.

"What? Who?"

"Dayra Smith. Is she involved with the rebels here on Far Star?" The metal of the bar was worn smooth where numerous hands had rested over the years, Coll noted vaguely. It probably wouldn't be too many more years before the old flitter gave up working completely. And what would Dayra Smith do then? he wondered.

Johnny glanced over at him, then shook his head emphatically. "No. It's all she can do just to keep the holdin' goin'."

"Then why are you there? Aren't you worried your presence might endanger her?"

"How? The military garrison is understaffed and the people assigned there are soldiers, not secret police. They know there're rumblin's of rebellion, but there's not much they can do about it—yet." Johnny shrugged. "Far Star's not important as a military outpost, but the Combine won't give up the mines here, not without a fight. The soldiers will put down any attempt at an uprisin'. They'll kill if they have to. But they won't waste time tryin' to track the movements of every settler on the planet."

"So the captain's visit today was just a friendly business call?"

Another dismissive shrug. "I dinna say that. Cap'n Truva's no fool. An isolated holdin' like this one could serve as an excellent hiding place for illegal weapons . . . and for unwanted visitors. She keeps her eye on the place, just like she keeps her eye on a dozen other holdings."

"Which means she'll be keeping her eye on me now that she's seen me here." Coll grimaced in disgust.

"She would have in any case. Men like ye stand out in a crowd, me friend. Ye ought to know that by now."

Coll knew it. It had made his work as a representative of the Rebel Alliance more difficult, and it still complicated his life even when all he wanted was to be left alone. He frowned. "So why are you here at all, let alone on an isolated holding like Dayra Smith's? I'd heard you were dead."

Johnny studied Coll as though searching for some sign, some reassurance, that his plea wasn't going to be ignored. Whatever he was looking for, he didn't find it.

Instead, he sighed, then said quietly, "Don't ye think we'd best get on with what we came out here to do? Time's wastin' and there's plenty of work waitin' for when we get back."

Coll considered demanding that Johnny answer his question, then immediately discarded the idea. Johnny wouldn't answer any question unless he wanted to. It didn't matter, anyway. Johnny had his life to lead; Coll had his. That their paths had crossed like this was sheer ill chance. No matter what Johnny said, Coll had no intention of getting dragged back into a fight that was no longer his.

Without speaking, he set the flitter in motion. They were almost to the spot where Coll had first encountered Dayra when Johnny spoke again.

"Ye'll eventually get back in the game, ye know. Ye can't help it."

"Have you taken up clairvoyance in your old age, along with the grand dreams?" Coll snapped, irritated by his old friend's presumption.

Johnny nodded. "All ye need is something to believe in."

"Don't count on it. I had a lot of grand beliefs

81

in the past, and look where they got me."

"Maybe ye just didn't believe in the right things."

Coll couldn't stop the explosive laugh that burst from him. "You can't tell me you don't believe in the same things I did, old man."

"All those fancy words," Johnny said thoughtfully. "Yes, I believe in them. But they're not the most important things I believe in. Not by a long ways."

"Not . . . We were fighting for freedom! What's more important than that?"

Johnny started to speak, then stopped himself. An intensely thoughtful look stole across his features. He frowned at Coll; then his expression lightened as an almost imperceptible smile tugged at his mouth. His eyes glittered suddenly, alive with a thought that appeared to give him a great deal of amusement.

"Ye already know the answer t' that, lad," he said, settling back in his seat with satisfaction. "If ye're lucky, ye may just find that out one day. Maybe one day soon."

Dayra's ladder still hung where Coll had left it, but by now the tide, in its inexorable march up the cliff, had covered a good two-thirds of its length.

Johnny leaned out over the edge of the cliff, studying both the ladder and what was still visible of the rock face, his expression grim. "You found her climbing up this cliff?" he demanded, aghast.

"That's right. She'd slung the ladder over her

shoulders so it hung down her back. According to her, her fishing net and catch bag are tied to the other end."

"But how could she—she's fished here for years. She knows how to anchor that ladder!"

"I'm sure she does," Coll agreed. "I think someone deliberately unhooked the ladder and threw if off the cliff. Someone who frightened her very much and who threatened her brother and sister."

As succinctly as he could, Coll told Johnny what he'd found and what he suspected. Once he was gone, Johnny would be the only protection Dayra would have.

Using a longer, stronger rope they'd brought from the holding, Coll climbed down to where the Dayra's ladder was hooked on the protruding rock and quickly lashed it to a second rope so Johnny could pull it up.

By the time Coll climbed back up the cliff, Johnny was untying the net and catch bag, and morosely studying the new tears in the bag's sturdy fabric.

"Dragging over the rocks, I suppose," he muttered, not bothering to glance up as Coll crossed to stand beside him.

"Or other fish hoping for an easy meal." Coll eyed the lumpy bag, whose contents were unmistakable. Dayra hadn't lied about the fishing, after all.

"Whatever. Either way, it's not going to make Dayra very happy."

"It's only a catch bag," Coll said, picking up the

tangled net. "She can buy a new one. Easier than trying to repair that thing."

"Sure, if you've got the credits to be able to afford a new bag." Johnny rose creakily to his feet, then stooped to pick up the bag. He grunted at its weight and tried to get a better grip.

Coll took it out of his hands, easily swinging it over his shoulder with the net. "Come on, Johnny," he said, "how much can a bag like this cost?"

"More than Dayra can easily afford," Johnny snapped, obviously irritated by Coll's lack of concern. "With the Combine's taxes and trade restrictions, none of the settlers have any money."

His eyes rose to Coll's, a speculative gleam in their depths. "She'd be able to afford a new bag—and a lot more—if she were free of the Combine's control."

Coll shifted the dripping bag of fish, irritated by the appeal, and stomped over to the flitter. Trust Johnny to spot when he was softening, even by a little.

Johnny didn't try to push his point. While Coll piled the ropes, ladder, net, and heavily loaded catch bag in the back, he climbed into the flitter on the passenger's side, to all appearances completely uninterested in continuing the discussion.

He maintained his silence while Coll recovered his own bag, still lying in the grass where he'd abandoned it earlier, then headed the flitter back toward the holding. Only when they once more topped the rise overlooking Dayra Smith's holding did Johnny speak.

"Stop here," he commanded peremptorily.

Coll glanced at him, surprised, but the old man's gaze was fixed on the sprawling complex of stone buildings and higher stone walls below them.

"Not much to look at, is it?" Johnny asked, flicking one hand toward the holding. "A lot of rocks piled together enclosing a whole lot of not much of anything." His gaze lifted to scan the vast sweep of grassland that stretched on all sides. "Not much of anything anywhere except grass and rocks and more grass."

Coll kept silent, but he couldn't help following the direction of Johnny's gaze as the old man said thoughtfully, "There's a young woman down on that holdin' who's risked everything she has to build a future for herself and her brother and sister. She works from the minute she gets up in the morning until she goes to sleep late at night. She's too thin and she's always tired and she's almost broke. But in the year I've been here, I've never heard her complain. Not once. Not even when taxes to the Combine took over a third of the credits she'd earned last year."

Johnny shifted in his seat to stare at Coll. "You asked me why I'm here. I'm here for the same reason that Dayra Smith and every other settler on this planet is here, because I see a raw, new world where people can build a future for themselves, where they have a chance to avoid some of the mistakes we've made on most other worlds.

"The settlers on this planet represent every one of the seven species in the Combine. If they can break free of the Combine, if they can keep the profits they've worked for instead of paying them out in taxes that go to benefit other worlds than theirs, then they have a chance of building a society that could represent everything you and I have fought for all these years."

He paused, as if waiting for Coll to speak, then continued more softly. "They won't have that chance if the Combine ever gets too strong a hold here. Their best chance is now. Not next year or the year after. *Now*. That's why I'm back in the game, Coll Larren, to see if all those fancy words really can mean what we've always dreamed they could."

Johnny's persuasive voice washed over Coll like the tide, tugging at him, pulling him deeper. It would be so easy to give in to that insistent pull, so easy to let his hopes get ahead of his common sense.

"It can happen," Johnny insisted, as if sensing Coll's thoughts, "but not if the settlers don't get help. You could help them, Coll. Think what it could mean to them to know they had the help and guidance of the Sandman himself."

"I told you, the Sandman's dead," Coll said, biting his words off hard and sharp.

"Not to the people who keep on fighting for the dreams you gave up, Coll Larren. If you'd only think about it—"

"I don't have to think about it," Coll grated. "I know what it would mean, Johnny McGregor, and I want no part of it. The Sandman is dead and he's going to stay dead. Forever."

This time Johnny didn't push the issue. He simply sighed and said, "Ah, well, ye canna blame me for tryin'." Then he added, "We'd best be gettin' back. There's the fish to clean and supper to fix and Dayra will be needin' help with all of that."

Without comment, Coll set the flitter in motion along the path that led directly to the main gate of the holding.

Chapter Five

Johnny didn't waste any time. The minute he'd closed the holding gate and directed Coll where to leave the flitter and the fish, he'd bustled into the house to confront Dayra.

"Ye need help, lass," he was saying now, "and Coll Larren's the man to give it. I *know* him. All ye have to do is convince him to stay."

Dayra straightened resentfully, angry that her hired hand should repeat the same thought she was trying so hard to ignore. "I do *not* need help, Johnny McGregor, and I'll thank you to keep your nose in your own business, not mine."

"Ah, but ye do, lass. I helped Coll retrieve yere net and whatnot. Don't tell *me* that ladder just happened to slip off those hooks or that ye were climbing that cliff for fun."

"I—" Dayra snapped her mouth shut. She had

no reasonable way of refuting Johnny's arguments and he knew it. "Just how do you propose that I pay another laborer's wages?" she demanded instead. "If you're so anxious to have some help on the holding, maybe you'd consider a cut in pay of—shall we say half?"

Before Johnny had a chance to respond, Dayra said, "No, I thought not. So don't start telling me what to do."

The implication that Johnny was only driven by the credits he earned was absurd, of course. She paid him a pittance. It was all she could afford, but he'd never complained. If he went into Trevag or visited the surrounding holdings more often than she would have liked, it would have been unjust of her to deny him that small recompense. Working out here was lonely—she knew that better than anyone—and a gregarious fellow like Johnny McGregor must often find the silence burdensome.

Dayra's fingers tightened around the hairbrush she'd picked up from the table beside her when Johnny had started nagging her. Loneliness was not a subject she wanted to consider, especially not right now.

All she said was, "Would you mind helping Jason and Jeanella with the meal, Johnny? Please?"

"Oh, aye," the old man said gruffly. His eyes were not unkind as he studied her for an instant. "Just think on it, will ye, lass?"

Dayra nodded, too tired to continue the argument, no matter how politely it was conducted.

"I'll think about it, Johnny."

As Johnny disappeared down the hall leading to the kitchen, Dayra dropped her gaze to the brush she held. It had been her mother's.

For an instant Dayra wished that gentle, impractical woman were there with her. She would have liked to let herself be enfolded in her mother's whispering cloud of silk and scent. She would have liked to lay her head on her mother's shoulder and let her problems go away, even if only for a little while.

The thought of pillowing shoulders made Dayra's fingers tighten around the brush's polished wood handle. She remembered, all too clearly, laying her head against Coll Larren's shoulder. She wished she didn't.

With great care, she placed the brush on the table and picked up a hair fastener Jeanella had left after she'd brushed out Dayra's freshly washed hair. Her hair was still too damp to put up, but left loose it would be a nuisance.

Unfortunately, her abused fingers were stiff and awkward and the fastener refused to close, in spite of Dayra's efforts to force it. The fastener sprang out of her hand and fell on the floor, clattering and rolling across the stone toward the open door and freedom.

It didn't get far. Coll Larren, already half in the open door, bent and scooped it up before Dayra was out of her chair.

Dayra froze, then dipped her head, unable to meet his eyes.

Before she could come to her feet, Coll said,

"No, don't get up. I just wanted to talk to you . . . alone."

To Dayra, it sounded as if he suddenly wasn't certain the alone part was such a good idea, but that might have been her own discomfort and overactive imagination working. As she slowly settled back on her chair, he went down on one knee in front of her, his forearms propped on his thighs and the hair fastener dangling from his fingers.

"I told you I'm headed for Trevag," he said without preamble, looking up at her.

Dayra nodded, unable to speak. He was starting to twirl the fastener between his fingers, around and around and around in a mesmerizing circle that she couldn't stop watching, even though it made her all too uncomfortably aware of his hands and his voice . . . aware of *him*.

"If you don't mind, I'd like to stay here tonight," he said, his voice hypnotically deep. "It's late now. I'd planned to get there today—but I told you that, didn't I?"

Again Dayra nodded. She forcibly tore her gaze from his hands only to find herself looking into the forest dark of his eyes.

"Do you mind?" he said, this time with a touch of impatience.

"Mind?" Dayra dragged her thoughts back from wherever it was they'd gone, groping for the calm that had fled the moment he entered the room. "Oh! That you stay here tonight?" She shook her head so the heavy strands rippled with the motion. "No, I don't mind."

"I also thought that you—that maybe Johnny could take me on to Trevag."

He was leaving. Dayra frowned at the sudden realization that they'd been talking about his leaving all along, that he *wanted* to go. She plucked at a fold in her skirt, uncertain why that bothered her. "Of course. Johnny would be happy to take you. I certainly owe you that much, at least."

"Good." His twiddling stopped and he glanced down at the fastener, clearly surprised to find he was still holding it. "Here," he said, rising to his feet.

"Thank you." Dayra hastily snatched the fastener from his fingers. Glad of the distraction, she clumsily gathered up the heavy mass of her hair and tried to tie it back out of her face. Once again she fumbled, then dropped the fastener.

Coll grabbed it as it hit the floor. "Here, let me." Before she could protest, he had moved behind her and gathered her hair in his own hands.

Dayra tensed. To her suddenly supercharged senses, it felt as if his hands had ignited sparks along her neck and shoulders and back.

His fingertips brushed against her skin, just where the soft new hairs were growing at the nape of her neck. She jumped, as startled as if an electric current had surged through her, powered by his touch.

Perhaps it was the size of his hands or his lack of experience with such feminine articles as the fastener, but Coll wasn't any better at tying back her hair than she'd been. He would almost get the fastener closed when a heavy lock of hair would escape him. He'd retrieve the errant lock only to fumble with the fastener.

By the time he finally succeeded and stepped back, Dayra could scarcely breathe. An electric awareness had claimed her body, swamping her in a surge of sensation as disorienting as it was exciting.

She struggled for breath, wondering if she'd even breathed at all so long as he was touching her. Behind her, she could hear Coll breathing in quick, shallow pants, like a sprinter who'd just dashed across the finish line and wasn't certain if he'd won or lost.

For one tantalizing moment, Dayra savored the fantasy that he might have been as intensely aware of her as she'd been of him. Then rationality returned. She'd never had the capacity to stir a man's senses and never would. Coll Larren, like any man faced with a simple feminine task that was more difficult than he'd thought, had been frustrated by his clumsiness and the recalcitrance of the fastener, nothing more.

"Thank you," she said, tentatively poking at the heavy tail he'd made at the back of her neck. The tail was a little skewed with several long hairs tangled in the fastener, but it was good enough. Even if he'd left a hopelessly snarled mess she would have called it good enough so long as it allowed her to escape.

"Where can I wash up?" Coll asked before she could say more.

Was it only her imagination, or did his voice carry a subtle note of strain?

"You can take one of the guesthouses, if you like." Dayra pointed through the open door toward a row of three small, square buildings that stood alone on the far side of the yard. "We dine in the kitchen. I imagine we'll be eating soon."

Her own voice didn't sound normal, either.

"Thanks. I'll just grab my bag. . . ." Without finishing that thought, he sidled around Dayra and hurried out the door without glancing back.

Dayra didn't mind. She wasn't prepared to meet that disturbing gaze just yet. She rose from her chair, irritated by the sudden shakiness in her sore muscles.

Dinner and a good night's rest, that was what she needed. Tomorrow this stranger who had dropped into her life so unexpectedly would be gone and she could get back to her work and her worries about Talman Bardath. It would be a relief to deal with such relatively simple concerns.

There was, after all, a limit to how much danger she could endure in her life, and Coll Larren definitely exceeded the limit.

Dinner, Coll discovered, was an intimidating affair, at least to a man who'd never had much to do with children. It might have been easier if he could forget that brief exchange with Dayra, forget her hair sliding through his fingers like red-gold sun. He couldn't.

Every time he looked at her he remembered, and since Johnny had officiously seated him directly across the small table from her, he looked at her often, whether he wanted to or not.

From the subtle tension visible in the way she held her head and her careful, if unsuccessful, attempts never to glance at him, Coll suspected she was trying to forget, as well.

At least no one else had any inkling of his thoughts. Johnny blatantly kept his attention fixed on the bowl of fish and vegetable stew before him and the two children were too involved in their own discussion to notice.

When he'd entered the kitchen, Coll had found Dayra deep in lecturing Jason and Jeanella on why they were not to open the holding gates to anyone, not even Capt. Truva, unless either she or Johnny were present. She'd made no mention of the troublemaker Coll was convinced was responsible for her being forced to climb that cliff, but she did finish up with a standard, firmly adult warning against any undesirables who might seek entry.

The notion of general, all-around bad guys attacking the holding had appealed to Jason immensely. He was still plotting ways of dealing with them should they ever be so bold as to challenge his defenses.

Jeanella, Coll suspected, would have found the talk upsetting had it not come from her younger brother. Anything from that six-year-old oracle was greeted with the superior skepticism appropriate to an older and far more worldly-wise sister.

"They'd be tryin' to rob us," Jason stated in a tone of voice that allowed no room for doubt. "Take all our money an'—"

"We don't *have* any money. At least, not enough to matter," Jeanella objected. "There are lots and lots of richer people living in Trevag."

"Yeah, but somebody'ud see 'em there," Jason replied reasonably. "That's why they'd come here. But it'ud be all right, 'cause I got lotsa rocks piled on the top o' the wall that I could throw at 'em. That'ud scare 'em away for sure!" Evidently just the thought of his future defensive efforts made him thirsty, for he wrapped both his hands around his water glass and took several long swallows.

"You're dribbling, Jason," Dayra reproved him. "Please mind your manners. We have a guest, remember?" She didn't even glance at Coll as she spoke.

Jason thunked the glass on the table. "Are you gonna stay?" he asked Coll, running the back of his wrist over his wet mouth and chin, much to Jeanella's disgust.

"You're cleaning up the table on your side, Jason, 'cause *I'm* not going to," she said, pointing to the large ring of water spreading around the base of the glass.

"I set the table so you gotta clear," he shot back, not in the least abashed. He turned back to Coll. "Are you gonna stay? You could help me fight off any bad guys. I got lotsa rocks."

Coll had a mental vision of himself on top of the wall, pelting unwanted visitors with rocks that Jason had carefully stockpiled for his use. He didn't think it would be nearly as effective as simply sending the boy out to talk them to death or Jeanella to scold them into acceptable behavior. Sending the two together would have to be reserved for major encounters. You didn't waste that kind of intimidating firepower on just any random skirmish.

What Coll couldn't understand was the boy's ready acceptance of him. He'd never had much to do with children. His size alone was usually enough to scare them off, and the last baby he'd held had burst into tears the minute he'd touched her. Yet Jason not only was *not* intimidated, he seemed to regard Coll as a trusted friend after only a few minutes of conversation.

"Well?" Jason demanded, impatient. "Are you gonna stay?"

Coll hesitated, but he couldn't avoid the boy's questioning gaze forever. "No, I'm not staying. I'm headed to Trevag and your sister has said Johnny can take me there tomorrow." His voice seemed to rumble around the small kitchen and echo off the stone floors and walls.

Johnny looked up at that. His gaze darted from Coll to Dayra and back again. Whatever he saw in their faces evidently convinced him there was no mistake. He scowled at Coll, then glared at Dayra.

"You aren't really gonna go, are you?" Jason asked, staring at Coll. His mouth was open and his eyes were wide with disbelief.

"Coll was just passing through, Jason," Dayra said. "He—"

"Really?" Jason wasn't ready to give up yet.

Coll nodded. It was a simple gesture, but he found it curiously hard to make. He'd faced armed and angry men who were less unnerving than this one small, disappointed boy. At the same time, resentment bit at him that, even here, there should be demands he could not grant, expectations he could not meet.

"Can I go, too?" Jeanella demanded eagerly, breaking the tension. "Can I?"

Johnny broke in before Dayra could answer. "If ye haven't thought of yerself or the holdin', Dayra Smith, have ye thought of what our good Cap'n Truva might think if she finds your brand-new hired hand roaming the streets of Trevag tomorrow? It'll make her wonder about what a man like Coll was doin' on a holdin' like this. It'll make her wonder what *we're* doin', and well ye know it."

Coll's fingers tightened around the handle of his spoon. Johnny was right, on all counts. He *hadn't* thought of Truva's reaction, and he should have. He glanced up to find Dayra staring at him, a stricken expression on her face. Clearly she hadn't thought of it, either.

"Just as I thought. Ye dinna think of anythin' but yere own selves." He propped an elbow on the table and waggled his spoon accusingly at Coll. "Whether ye like it or not, Coll Larren, ye'll have to stay here, at least for a week or two. It won't hurt ye to do a little honest work for a change, and ye've nothin' else waitin' for ye in Trevag, in any case, now, have ye?"

Johnny was right. He should stay, for his own sake as well as Dayra's. He had no desire to become entangled in the captain's suspicions, especially now, when he was innocent of anything except a lack of purpose in his life. He had no place to go, nowhere he belonged, no work he needed to do elsewhere.

Remaining on the holding would solve a number of his more pressing problems. There was honest work for him here. He'd have a roof over his head and food in his belly. There were the children to think of, after all, and Dayra could use his help.

Coll tensed, angered by his sudden weakness. He didn't belong here. He was a fool even to consider staying, and yet. . . .

Across the table, Dayra was watching him with an expression of sudden concern, as if she'd somehow sensed the doubts and unadmitted longings within him, as if she'd heard all the things he hadn't said and never would.

Damn her sensitivity. She didn't want him to stay any more than he wanted to stay.

Damn him for having lingered even this long.

Coll pushed his chair back so abruptly its legs screeched in protest on the stone floor. Dayra flinched, but still her eyes held his. He stood, then grabbed for his own half-full glass of water and drained it in three long swallows, tilting his head back until the water ran out the corner of his mouth and down his chin and throat.

He thunked his glass down on the table, just as Jason had, and ran the back of his hand across his mouth. "If you'll excuse me?" he said. He didn't wait for a reply.

Once free of the house, Coll angrily paced the length of the holding wall until he ran into an intersecting inner wall. Without thinking, he turned and followed the second wall, and then a third and a fourth, too wrapped in his struggle to repress the yearnings and the loneliness inside him to notice that his path merely led him back to the house he'd so recently fled.

It was a sudden burst of childish laughter that brought him to an abrupt halt. He stopped in the grass near the house, listening to the sounds of the two children cleaning up after the meal.

The sun was setting, its light softening the gray stone of the house and reflecting off the windows in brilliant flares of pink and lavender. The wind had dropped until it was little more than a breath, carrying with it just a hint of moisture after the dry heat of the day.

Across the main yard, a light shone in the work shed where Coll had left the fish. Johnny, no doubt, concentrating on the messy job of cleaning fish.

He was tired, Coll realized. His leg ached. That climb up the cliff, coming on top of the long walk from the spaceport, had worn him out more than he wanted to admit. Not surprising, really, if he was honest. With the life he'd led for the last 15 years, he was entitled to feel old. A lot of the friends he'd fought beside had never reached 25.

Coll took a deep breath, then let it out slowly through his nose until there was nothing but a hollow echo in his lungs and he had to open his mouth to get the air back in. He envied his dead friends sometimes. There was something to be said for dying before your dreams did.

Inside the house, Jason laughed. Coll turned his head, listening to the murmur of human voices.

He could hear what sounded like an irritated protest from Jeanella, then Dayra's soft voice saying something that quieted them both.

Simple, ordinary family sounds, he supposed. It had been a long time since he'd been around any simple, ordinary family.

He waited, wondering what would follow. When nothing came but the rattle of dishes, he shrugged, ignoring the quick stab of disappointment that Dayra's voice didn't carry clearly all the way out here. He liked her voice. There was a sense-drugging richness to it that reminded him of ancient Andorian brandy—smooth, potent, and dangerous, yet undeniably irresistible.

Just thinking of it roused memories that made his legs a little unsteady. Probably just tired, he told himself, walking over to a small plot of mowed grass and plopping down. It had been a hard day. He was entitled to a little rest.

Laughter came from the house, but this time three voices shared in it. Even from this distance, Coll could identify each voice.

He'd been too long without a woman. That was the problem. After a while, deprivation could make a man's imagination work overtime. He'd seen it happen before. There was nothing especially appealing about Dayra Smith, certainly nothing that should start such warmth curling around in his middle. She was thin, overworked, and plain.

Coll thought of her eyes. All right, plain except for her eyes.

And her hair.

Unbound, Dayra Smith's hair was a glory that

would tempt a saint. And he was no saint, nor ever had been.

Coll jumped to his feet, irritated. He wasn't staying. He didn't belong here; he didn't belong anywhere, but he most especially did not belong here.

There were ways to deal with the risk that Capt. Truva represented. They could manufacture a story to explain why he'd left the holding. He could play the drunken lout, or Johnny could accuse him of petty thievery, or Dayra could say she'd fired him because he'd tried to make love to her.

Fire flared in his groin at the thought. Coll drew in a sharp breath, fighting against the unexpected heat.

That story might be the best way out, after all. To support the tale, he could go whoring in Trevag. That would have the double advantage of easing this sudden hunger and convincing Truva that the story was true. A pity he'd never been tempted by any of the women on the *Bendrake*. Most of them would have welcomed his advances, but not once in all the long, hellish weeks of his service on that ship had he thought of them as anything other than his crew mates.

What he needed, Coll decided, was something to occupy him for the next hour or so until full darkness, when he could legitimately plead exhaustion and go to bed. Cleaning fish wasn't the most desirable diversion he'd ever heard of, but it was the only one available right now.

What did it matter, anyway? By this time tomorrow he'd be safely in Trevag—even if he had to walk there—and Dayra Smith and her beautiful sister and precocious brother would be part of his past, just like everything else.

Coll woke while the dark still held sway over the world outside, uncertain what had brought him so suddenly awake.

He lay still for a few minutes, listening to the silence.

Nothing. Not even a hint of breeze rustling through the grass beyond the holding wall broke the stillness.

Go back to sleep, he chided himself, but it was too late. He'd spent too many years depending on his senses, even when asleep, to so easily ignore their warnings now.

Moving as quietly as possible, he donned pants and a pair of soft-soled shoes that were the only footwear he possessed besides his spacer's boots. For weapons he had his hands and the knife he usually carried inside his boot. It wasn't much, but the combination had served him adequately before and it ought to be sufficient now.

Fortunately, years of living as a hunted rebel had left him averse to closed-in spaces. He'd left both the door and the two small windows open when he'd gone to sleep, which meant there would be no noise from creaking hinges to alert whoever was out there in the dark.

Coll silently eased out the door. The largest of Far Star's moons was down, but the smaller moon cast enough light to expose any intruders who failed to keep in the shadows, the only way he'd catch them was if they were careless enough to make a noise . . . or he ran into them.

Once away from the thick stone walls of the small guesthouse, Coll paused. A whisper of air, too light to be called a breeze, brushed against his skin. Nothing else moved.

He waited in the shadows, willing his body to relax, willing his heart to slow and the beat of his pulse to ease so that he could catch any noise, however slight.

Still nothing.

He was about to give up and return to bed when he caught the faint chink of metal against stone. Coll shifted position, straining to identify the origin of the sound. It came again, then again, a little louder this time.

Someone was scaling the holding wall near the main house.

Despite her physical exhaustion, Dayra found it impossible to sleep. In the dark, all the fears and uncertainties she'd been able to push aside as long as she was active suddenly pressed in on her, biting at her like vicious, sharp-toothed monsters who had clawed their way into her mind.

Two weeks ago her past had caught up with her and now she didn't know what to do.

Five years had passed since Dayra had fled Talman Bardath. She'd just begun to think she'd escaped him forever when a man she hadn't recognized had accosted her on the streets of

Trevag, demanding she repay Bardath the money she'd stolen from him.

She'd ignored the man in Trevag. She couldn't ignore the attack on her or the threat against Jason and Jeanella.

If it had just been a matter of Bardath trying to hurt her sales in the markets in Trevag or wrest control of the holding from her, it wouldn't have been so bad. She could have dealt with that. There were people in Trevag who would be willing to help her and Far Star was a long way from Bardath's home on Edole. Besides, Bardath would find little of value in either the holding or her business. If he damaged those, he destroyed any hope of regaining even a small part of what she'd taken when she'd fled Edole.

That wasn't what he was after.

Dayra knew it; she just hadn't wanted to face the truth. By Bardath's standards, the money was trivial. He'd thrown that much away on a night's entertainment when it had suited him. No, what he wanted was revenge for the humiliation of having been cheated by the daughter of his mistress.

His whore, he would have said, if Triana wasn't around. Dayra had heard him say it, then laugh, pleased with himself for possessing a beautiful woman whom others desired, pleased with being able to sneer at her behind her back and denigrate everything she might have been to him, if he'd had the decency to let her.

Talman Bardath craved power. He despised those who didn't want it and trampled those who didn't possess it. As head of the Combine

Security Police, he'd become wealthy, but wealth, in itself, had no meaning for him. Its value lay in the power it gave him over others.

By stealing his money, Dayra had mocked his power and that was something Talman Bardath would never forgive. He'd probably spent ten times more money in tracking her down than she'd taken in the first place. It would be worth the expense if he could crush her, if he could show the world just how much it had to fear from him.

Considered carefully, the attack on her at the inlet had probably been a mistake. From Bardath's twisted point of view, there was nothing to be gained by violence if the victims had no chance to see the power that was so mercilessly destroying them.

Bardath didn't want her dead. He wanted her broken and groveling at his feet. Most of all, he wanted her to acknowledge that he was the one who had ruined her.

On the other hand, the threat against Jason and Jeanella had been deliberate. Dayra was sure of it. What better way for Bardath to destroy her than to take her brother and cast her sister into a living hell? He was an intelligent man. He knew how much she'd hated the life her mother had led. Before Triana had died, he'd made a point, every now and then, of blatantly waving her mother's dependence in Dayra's face.

If Bardath could get his hands on Jeanella, he wouldn't hesitate to sell her to the highest bidder on any one of the dozens of worlds where slavery and the vicious subjugation of women were not only tolerated, but encouraged. Given Jeanella's youth and developing beauty, he could ask almost any price and be sure he'd get it.

But Jason. . . . Why did he want Jason? The thug who had attacked her had made it clear that Jason was his primary target. Had he known, Dayra wondered, that Jason was Talman Bardath's son? Bardath knew, but that explained nothing. Jason had never meant anything to him before. Why should he matter now?

Tormented by her thoughts and the pain of her battered body, Dayra finally rose from her bed and crept to the window, hoping the night air would soothe her.

She hadn't bothered with the gown draped at the foot of her bed. As she sank onto the wide stone shelf beneath the window, Dayra was grateful for the worn cushion that lay there because the frayed cloth was soft and comforting beneath her skin. Against the protest of sore muscles, she tucked her legs under her, careful of her scrapes and the crusting scabs on her knees. Then she leaned forward so her arms rested on the ledge of the open window. The stone was cool to the touch, almost cold, refreshing after her fevered tossing in bed.

Outside the window, the world seemed awash in silver. One of Far Star's moons had set, leaving its twin master of the night sky. Few stars were bright enough to compete against its radiance, but then, this far out on the galaxy's rim, there weren't that many stars even on the darkest night. Dayra didn't miss them much. She liked this silver silence, and she liked the dark that followed.

The night breeze teased her with its touch and its soft, moist smell of grass and earth and salt sea. It caressed her face and throat, and Dayra responded by raising her arms and running her hands under the heavy mass of her unbound hair, lifting it so the air could reach her shoulders and drift down her back. The movement exposed her breasts and belly and Dayra automatically arched into the breeze, savoring the sensual brush of coolness across her skin. She stretched farther, dragging her hands through her hair, careful to protect her palms at the same time she let the silken strands sift down over the backs of her hands. She could hear the soft shushing sound as her hair fell into place, tickling her neck and back as it settled.

Dayra held her stretch for a minute, relishing the tension in her sore muscles, then slowly relaxed and once more leaned forward to cross her arms on the ledge. As she dropped her chin on her arms, her hair swung forward like a heavy veil, half hiding her body. Her breasts pressed against the stone, her nipples prickling at the cold.

Strange how aware she was of such tiny details, the nuances of the night around her. Thinking of Talman Bardath and his threats had done that for her, reminding her of the value of simple things and how easy it would be to lose them.

She wouldn't think of Bardath. Not right now. She wanted only to stare out the window and let the night enfold her, cloaking her nakedness in its encompassing dark.

Out there, Dayra could see the walls of the holding gleaming silver white against the black of the grassland beyond. The work sheds and storage buildings and guesthouses stood apart from each other, silver islands afloat in a sea of black. She couldn't see the door of the guesthouse where Coll Larren was sleeping, but the one small window on this side stood open.

Was he awake, as she was? Dayra wondered. Was he staring out at the night?

She leaned farther forward, straining to peer through that window and into the dark on the other side. She couldn't see anything.

It was absurd, but somehow it comforted her to know he was there. Tomorrow, when the sun shone and she was once again in charge, Dayra knew she would be angry at herself for having had such a thought. She would be glad to see Coll Larren leave. Right now, she was simply grateful for his presence.

Tomorrow she would be brave again. For tonight, she could admit she was afraid.

Chapter Six

Taking care to keep silent, Coll crossed the open space in front of the house and slid into the deeper darkness between the house and the massive holding wall itself. He wasted a second or two cursing whoever had built the house so close to the outer wall. If security was what they'd wanted, they'd made a serious mistake, but it was far too late to complain now.

From the sounds, which were clearer here, Coll guessed there were two visitors, one at the base of the wall, the second now climbing the outer wall. Once at the top, whoever it was would probably toss over another rope and climb down.

And then what? What was it they wanted so much they would come creeping in the night to steal it?

As answer, a head popped over the wall, followed by a torso and then a pair of legs, indistinct but unmistakable, even in the dark. A human, and probably male.

As the man turned to clamber down the inside, Coll darted to the base of the wall and pressed himself flat against the cold stones. A moment later, the unsuspecting visitor slid down the rope and right into Coll's waiting arms. A brief tussle, a muffled cry of alarm, abruptly cut short, and the intruder collapsed, unconscious, on the ground.

Coll didn't waste time tying the man up. His accomplice might have heard the faint sounds of struggle and either be coming after his friend or running away, and Coll wanted them both.

With practiced ease, Coll grabbed the intruder's rope and started climbing. Just before he reached the top, Coll paused, trying to determine by sound what the second man was up to. It wasn't hard. He was running away, tripping over rocks and getting his feet tangled in the long grass and cursing like a well-trained spacer.

As Coll slipped over the top of the wall and down the rope on the other side, the solar-charged lights on the inside of the compound came on. It seemed he wasn't the only light sleeper tonight.

Ducking his head to avoid looking at the light, Coll landed on the rough ground at the base of the wall and started after the second man. With the lights behind him, he spotted his prey immediately. Farther away, its metal shell dimly visible against the dark, Coll could see the flitter, whose motor had probably roused him in the first place.

Coll was gaining on the second man when the sound of a scream came from the holding behind him. With a regretful glance toward the flitter, Coll whirled about and raced for the holding as fast as the tall grass and uneven ground would permit him.

It took a minute or two to find the trailing rope he'd used to climb down. As Coll grabbed the rope, it shivered in his hand. He had only an instant to duck before the first intruder, the one he'd thought unconscious, clambered down the rope on top of him.

The struggle was fierce, but brief. Momentarily distracted by the sound of voices inside the holding, Coll turned his head a fraction of an inch and his opponent planted a solid hit on his chin. Coll's head snapped back with the force of the blow and he staggered back against the wall. The stones were hard, cold, and unforgiving.

Coll shook his head to clear it, then shoved off from the wall. There was no one left to fight. His assailant was already crashing though the grass in a desperate dash for the flitter, whose motor had just roared to life.

Still feeling slightly dazed, Coll grabbed the rope and climbed back up. He paused at the top to give his eyes time to adjust to the lights that now shone from half the buildings inside the compound.

Someone standing in the black shadows at the side of the house had no problem spotting him, however. "Just hold there, ye slime-rotted piece o' Woofrash gizzard, or I'll shoot ye where ye sit."

The corner of Coll's mouth twitched upward, in

spite of the ache in his jaw. There was no mistaking the accent. "Don't shoot, damn it, Johnny. It's me, Coll."

He shaded his eyes against the light, trying to spot his friend. "Come out of those shadows, you old dog."

"Coll? What do ye think ye're doin', rousin' decent people from their beds like this? And why, by all that's holy, are ye on top o' that wall?"

"Coll? Are you all right?" Like a being conjured from the union of dark and light, Dayra moved out of the shadows where Johnny lurked.

At the sight of her, Coll felt his heart skip a beat, then another. He couldn't see her face as she lifted it to him, but the light glowed through the long, loose gown she wore, outlining her slender form and gilding a bare shoulder and the glorious, tangled mass of her hair.

"Is he gone?"

For the first time, Coll heard the faint note of fear under the anger and indignation in her voice. "They're both gone . . . for now, anyway," he said, then grabbed the rope that still dangled over the wall and quickly climbed down.

She was waiting for him at the bottom of the rope, her hands clutching the fullness of her gown at her breast while the long skirt trailed on the ground behind her. As Coll dropped the rope and took a step toward her, she turned slightly, so the light hit her in profile. Only then could he see that her gown was torn and her shoulder, which only a moment before had appeared stained with gold, was marred by four parallel slashes that began at

113

the top of her right arm and ended at the inner curve of her breast.

"What?" Coll grabbed her arms and turned her to face the light. Fear—not for himself, but for her and what might have happened—made the muscles of his stomach clench and knot.

"Today seems to be my day for getting into trouble," Dayra said with a laugh—a very small, quavery, uncertain laugh. "I heard a noise and came out. I should have called Johnny, I guess, or you." She hesitated, then shrugged her injured shoulder, trying to force the torn edge of her sleeve back into place without releasing her hold on the front of her gown.

Coll gently tugged the torn cloth over her shoulder. His eyes fixed on the dark blood slowly welling in the gashes. Without thinking, he lightly traced the line of the cuts with the tip of his finger, down across her shoulder and over the soft swell of her breast to where it ended beside her breast bone. Her skin was warm beneath his fingers and he could feel as well as hear her sudden sharp intake of breath at his touch.

"How did this happen?" he demanded, forcing the question out between clenched teeth.

Dayra tightened her grip on the folds of her gown. "There was a man, lying on the ground. He was just starting to wake up and when I bent over him he . . . he grabbed me, tried to choke me. He ripped my gown and"—she hesitated, then forced herself to continue—"Johnny chased him off. We heard sounds of fighting."

She stared up at him, her eyes wide and dark

with concern as they searched his face for traces of the struggle. "Are you all right? He didn't hurt you, did he?" She reached up to touch his chin, as if to reassure herself that he was unhurt.

Coll flinched, then released her and ruefully rubbed his jaw. "I'll survive. What I want to know is, what were they after?"

At his harsh question, Dayra glanced over her shoulder at the house. When she spoke, the fear was back in her voice. "He was after Jason. And Jeanella, and maybe me. But mostly he was after Jason."

She might have said more but the sound of footsteps scrunching over gravel interrupted. Coll grabbed Dayra and pulled her into the darkest shadows between the house and the wall, sheltering her body with his.

An instant later, he straightened, embarrassed. He'd forgotten Johnny, who was checking the entire length of the wall, just in case.

Coll loosened his protective hold on Dayra and would have stepped back, but she let go of her gown and clung to him, instead. He glanced down, suddenly and intensely aware of how easily she fitted against him, of how warm her body was pressed against his bare chest.

"Don't go tomorrow," she said. "Please. I need your help. For Jason's and Jeanella's sake. I . . . I want you to stay . . . if you will."

"What do you mean he didn't get the boy?"

The simple question, spoken slowly and with icy calm, made the two uniformed aides blanche

115

and the man in front of the questioner lick his lips and gulp.

"He said a field unit from the local garrison was at the holding, and then that stranger caught them when they tried to get in later that night. The stranger has been there ever since and no one's left the holding in days," the man offered nervously.

"Then why didn't he retrieve the boy earlier, *before* the unit and this inconvenient stranger arrived?"

"He thought. . . . He said he thought the two children were with the sister in the flitter, that it would be easier to take them—"

"He *thought.*" The two words vibrated with scorn. "He doesn't appear to have the wherewithal to think." The questioner, a tall man dressed in an impeccably tailored uniform of the Combine Security Police, rose from his seat behind the broad desk.

The man in front of the desk flinched, but the tall man ignored him and instead crossed the room to stand before an impressive and constantly changing vid display of the galaxy. He didn't speak for several minutes, just stood staring at the display. Neither the aides nor the bearer of the unwelcome tidings ventured to break the silence. When he turned back to face them at last, the three automatically straightened to attention.

"Tell this fool you hired that he is to do nothing more. *Nothing.* Do you understand?" the tall man demanded.

"Yes, sir. Nothing."

"You," the tall man snapped, pointing to one of his aides. "Arrange for a fast ship to be standing by for me, ready to leave at a moment's notice."

"Yes, sir. Certainly."

"And you," he added, pointing to the second aide, "notify the garrison commander on Far Star to prepare for my arrival. Tell her. . . ."

The aide started to shuffle nervously under the tall man's quelling gaze, then immediately thought better of it and froze back into attention.

"Tell her Talman Bardath will be paying a personal visit," he said slowly. His smile made the three before him profoundly grateful that they were not the message's intended recipient. "Tell her I'm looking forward to a private discussion about, shall we say, dissident activity on her planet?"

The three hesitated, wondering if there were more instructions. The uncertainty dissolved the minute Bardath's right eyebrow raised in inquiry. "Well, gentlemen? Did you not understand my instructions?"

They were out of the room in the space of a heartbeat.

Coll found the parts he was looking for buried under a pile of junk in one of the work sheds. As he pulled the pieces out of the heap, he was conscious of an urgent desire to bury them again and pretend he'd never found them, that he couldn't yet finish the protective alarm system he'd been installing around the holding for the past ten days.

He turned the small bits of metal and silicon over

and over in his hands, studying them. They weren't very impressive, but they meant his freedom, a freedom he was increasingly loath to reclaim.

Ever since he'd given in to Dayra's fervent plea that he remain on the holding and help protect her family, he'd been torn by doubts and the strange, new longings that were tugging at his emotions, tempting him with impossible images of a life that was, he knew, forever beyond his reach. Even the children unconsciously conspired against him, insisting on drawing him into their lives as if he belonged there.

Jeanella often followed him about as he worked, watching him with those beautiful eyes of hers, content to be in his company without any need for conversation. There was nothing coquettish in her behavior, but Coll felt a hunger in her for companionship besides that of her family.

The child wasn't born for the hard life of a holding as isolated as this. Although she quarreled with her brother like any normal 11-year-old and did her assigned work without undue complaining, Jeanella silently longed to have people and beauty and soft things around her. Over the past days, Coll had come to think of her as a delicate bird, plucked from its garden and thrust into a harsh world that threatened to crush her if she couldn't learn to adapt.

Jason was another matter entirely. Curious and boundlessly energetic, the boy hadn't been intimidated in the least by Dayra's oft-repeated warnings to leave their visitor alone and let him work in peace. Instead, he popped up at all times, chattering incessantly and inundating Coll with his questions. To his surprise, Coll found he enjoyed the boy's company, even though the endless stream of questions sometimes wore on him. He'd even found himself laughing at Jason's silly jokes, and he wondered how long it had been since the last time he'd laughed like that.

And then there was Dayra. . . .

Coll squeezed his eyes shut, fighting back the images that came unbidden to his mind. Of Dayra sitting with her brother and sister after dinner, listening to them, sharing the small triumphs and discoveries and pains of their day. Of Dayra, alone, climbing to the top of the holding wall to watch the sun set while the wind tossed her hair in her eyes and pressed her shift against her breasts and belly and legs in ways that roused a painful heat within him. Of Dayra working among the vegetables and fruits that were planted in the fields enclosed within the holding's walls, her slender body moving gracefully between the close-packed rows.

The various crops she raised provided her livelihood, but as he'd watched her unobserved from the holding walls where he was installing the alarm system, Coll had sensed that the plants meant much more to her than mere profits. Dayra Smith drew her strength from the land and from the growing things that flourished under her care.

He hadn't meant to pry and he'd fought against the frequent temptation to set down his own work so he could watch her. Yet in spite of his good

intentions, Coll had more than once found himself following her with his eyes, wondering what
it would be like to see his dreams taking shape
beneath his hands as Dayra could see hers.

That thought, more than any other, reminded
him of how far apart they were, how different.
He'd had his dreams and had watched them
crack and chip, and then crumble altogether,
worn away by the cruel and constant abrasion
of reality. Dayra still had her dreams, and they
were blossoming under the warmth of the sun and
her hard work. Even her fears for herself and her
family were not enough to undermine her belief
in the future.

Coll glanced down at the small parts he held in
his hand, thinking of the tale she'd told him the
night she'd asked him to stay. She owed a man
money, she said, a lot of money, and the man
was demanding repayment before she was able
to pay him back. The man had threatened her
and her family, and for that reason, she wanted
Coll's help.

She'd sounded sincere, but Coll knew she'd told
him only a part of the truth, probably the least
important part. Not that it mattered. He didn't
want to know her secrets. He didn't want to feel
bound to her. He couldn't risk that.

That was why he had to finish the alarm system
and leave before he found he couldn't.

Setting down the parts he'd worked so hard to
find, Coll strode from the work shed. He'd tell
her he was going. Right now, before he had a
chance to reconsider. Johnny had said they would

be going to the market in Trevag in the next few days. He'd leave then, Coll decided. It would be easy that way.

She wasn't in any of the fields and he couldn't find her in the work sheds. Johnny was hard at work repairing one of the small, solar-charged cultivators Dayra occasionally used, but Coll decided not to interrupt him. He didn't want to answer any of Johnny's inevitable questions right now.

Frustrated, Coll headed for the house. Jason and Jeanella were supposed to be at their lessons at this time of the day, but they probably knew where their sister was. More important, they wouldn't be as curious about why he wanted her as Johnny would be.

The children worked at their lessons in the main room of the house, the room with the wall of windows overlooking the holding yard. Coll couldn't tell if they were there or not, because the angle of the afternoon sun had turned the glass into reflective panes of light, hiding everything inside. Without knocking, he turned the lever on the door and poked his head in.

It was all he could do to keep from gasping in shock.

The room was filled with greenery, like a lush garden or an exotic greenhouse bursting with exotic plants. Yet through the semitransparent greenery, Coll could still see the dim shapes of the room's furnishings. A table with two shabby chairs stood at one side of the room while a trunk and a long couch were pushed against the wall at the other side. Jason sat at the table, apparently engrossed in his studies.

Jeanella was sitting in front of what looked like a small computer placed on a table across from Coll. Her back was to him and she appeared unaware of his presence, too engrossed in whatever she was doing even to look up.

It took a minute before Coll recognized the equipment she was fussing over as a holographic projector, the kind used in classrooms to give children the opportunity to see and explore places and things that would otherwise be inaccessible.

As he watched, a shaft of color swept through the greenery, like the swift flow of light across the ground when a scudding cloud blocks the sun. In its wake, the light left the "forest" populated with a number of small, furry creatures and brightly colored birds from a dozen exotic planets, each as transparent, yet exquisitely detailed, as the trees they perched in. An instant more, and the birds and animals started to sing and squeak and chitter, adding their individual voices to the murmur of the breeze through the leaves.

Coll watched, amazed at the quality of the vivid holographic representation. It wasn't that holo-vid projectors were unusual—they were used in theaters and amusement parks across the Empire. He just hadn't expected to find anything like this here.

Apparently satisfied with the readings on her controls, Jeanella swung around in her chair. She didn't notice Coll, even though he was standing in the doorway with the sun shining behind him. Her attention was fixed on the holographic images around her. Her eyes glowed and her delicate features were alight with wistful pleasure as she watched a holographic bird with brilliant magenta-and-blue plumage hop from one imaginary branch to another. Then she saw Coll and the pleasure drained from her face to be replaced by wariness. She was, after all, supposed to be studying, not playing with a vid projector.

For a moment, neither spoke. When Coll realized she wasn't going to say anything, he said gently, "It's very beautiful. Where is it from?"

Jeanella hesitated, clearly debating whether or not to respond. "Some of them are birds we had in the aviary on Edole," she said at last. Her head came up as a scarlet bird with a large topknot seemed to sail over her. "I made some of them up, like that one. It's out of a picture book Mother used to read to us."

"You made it? The whole image?" He hadn't expected that. The projection was too . . . *real* to have been produced by a girl her age.

"Uh-huh." Jeanella watched him, waiting for him to protest her claim.

Instead, Coll simply stared at the miniature forest in front of him. Even though he could see the vague outlines of furniture through the image, it was hard not to get lost in the fantasy. Everything down to the smallest leaf had been crafted with a loving attention to detail he wouldn't have expected of any 11-year-old child. One glance at her face, stiff with defensive pride, was enough to convince him she spoke the truth.

"I'm very impressed."

Jeanella's chin came up a fraction. "I already did all my lessons. Dayra lets me work on my scenes if my lessons are done."

"Have you done many of these?"

"Umm . . . not many. On this system, anyway. I had more on the system we had on Edole, but it was bigger. It could handle a lot more." She gave the projection equipment a scornful glance. "This thing can't do very much. Not like the other one."

"At least *you* get to use it," Jason sneered from his corner. "Dayra never lets me play with it."

"That's because you make such horrible scenes of fights and stuff. Anyway, you're supposed to study your algebra," Jeanella said disapprovingly. "Dayra said so."

"I've *been* studying it," Jason responded indignantly. "It's none of *your* business, anyway. Besides—"

"Where's your sister?" Coll asked hastily, before the two declared war.

"Planting flowers in the garden," Jason responded.

"At the well," Jeanella answered at the same time.

"She's planting flowers," Jason objected, scowling at his sister.

"In the garden at the well," Jeanella amended with the superior air of a lady of 11 who knows precisely what value to place on information provided by a scrubby boy of six.

"Who made *you* the expert?" Jason demanded, totally unimpressed.

"She *told* me."

"Well she told *me*—"

"I'll find her!" Coll backed out of the door before he got caught in the crossfire. As he edged back out the door, Jason was making horrible faces at his sister. Jeanella, being the older and more dignified, opted for putting her thumbs in her ears and wiggling her fingers while she stuck out her tongue. If Coll remembered right, that made the honors about even.

Coll had heard Dayra mention her flower garden but he'd never been inside. There wasn't any need. The garden was located in the center of the holding, well away from any outside walls and not close enough to any buildings to be useful to anyone trying to sneak into the compound.

The garden, Coll discovered, was unlike anything he'd imagined.

It was constructed around an artesian well, whose crystal waters flowed out of the ground with a gentle burbling sound that echoed softly in the small, walled area constructed around it. Someone had carefully piled slabs of rock around the well and the channel the water followed as it flowed away, creating the image of a wild mountain setting. A glorious profusion of delicate flowers bloomed in the crannies of the rocks while dark green moss softened the shadowed recesses. A narrow stone path curved from the gate around the back of the spring, half hidden in the tall native grasses, where fragile wildflowers bloomed.

Flowering vines covered two of the stone walls enclosing the area, adding a sweet perfume to the cool, damp air. A young tree cast a lacy shadow across the water.

Coll gaped, surprised to find this small sanctuary in the middle of the holding. It took a moment for him to realize he was not alone. Dayra's head and shoulders poked above the rocks on the far side of the well. She was intent on some task that was hidden from Coll's view, unaware of his presence.

For a moment, Coll simply watched her, intrigued. Her profile was toward him, softened by the patterned shadows of the tree under which she knelt. Her hair, which had been so loosely piled on top of her head earlier in the morning, had worked itself free until nothing remained of her bun except an untidy loop at the nape of her neck. Even that was a temptation. Coll found his fingers twitching with a sudden desire to dig into that mass of shining hair, to set it free, then twist it about his hand in a thick, heavy coil, and carefully pin it up again.

Every once in a while, Dayra's shoulders would hunch and she would bob forward, once, twice in a quick, emphatic motion that set the loose locks of hair about her face rocking forward and back in response. Eventually, she sat back, as though studying her handiwork.

Apparently satisfied, she let her head fall back, crushing the knot of hair. Slowly, her eyes closed, and she circled her head from side to side, easing the cramped muscles in her shoulders and neck.

She let out a small groan of satisfaction, then opened her eyes and straightened, stretching to relieve the muscles of her back.

As he watched, Coll was aware of an uncomfortable tension in his body and a tightening in his groin. There was something so essentially feminine, so tormentingly sensual in her movements, that he couldn't help but respond. He didn't think he'd moved or made a sound, but Dayra looked up then, her eyes wide and startlingly blue in her thin face.

"I didn't hear you come in," she said.

Coll wasn't sure if he heard disapproval in her voice or not; he didn't want to go too far into the garden unless he was invited. When she didn't say anything more, he gestured at the garden around them. "It's very beautiful."

Her chin came up at that, as though she mistrusted his words or the purpose behind them. An instant later her expression softened. She glanced at the garden, then looked back up at him. "Thank you." She let her gaze drop, then pushed stiffly to her feet.

She wore a simple work shift and light work gloves, the fingers of which were encrusted with dark, damp soil that she carefully shook off before sliding the gloves off her hands. Both her hands and knees had already recovered from the battering they'd received, but she took care to protect them, nonetheless.

Although she hadn't invited him in, she hadn't kicked him out, either, so Coll ventured farther, careful to walk only on the stone path.

She'd been planting flowers on the mounded earth behind the rocks, he discovered. He could see the indentations in a circle at the base of each flower, where her gloved fingers had tamped down the dirt. That explained the rocking motion; she'd leaned forward to put extra weight on her hands so the earth would pack around the roots more firmly.

The individual plants looked very small and unimpressive against the dark brown soil, as though she'd simply stuck whatever was available into the ground, scattering everything in a haphazard pattern that crowded some plants together and left gaping bare spaces around others.

As though reading his mind, Dayra said, "It will take several years for some of these plants to reach maturity. They need space to grow. The rest like being close. You have to respect each plant's individual needs or it'll never thrive."

She bent and touched the leaves of a scraggly plant with gray-green leaves. "This is seshia, from the Bendax system. In five or six years it will be as tall as I am and covered with purple flowers year round." She brushed her fingertips across the delicate leaves of another plant, making them tremble. "This is pink zuulle. It grows wild on Edole, but I've had a hard time getting it to grow here. And this is misty moss, from Regulus. On its native world it's dormant half the year, but it seems to love the weather here on Far Star. It blooms year round and spreads like crazy. I'm using it as ground cover until the other plants get established; then I'll pull it up and move it somewhere else."

She spoke of the plants as she would of close friends, Coll thought, watching her. Each with its preferences and foibles; each treasured for its own sake at the same time it mixed with strangers from other worlds and climates.

She straightened and brushed back a stray lock of hair from her face with the back of her hand. It was a gesture that Coll was coming to think of as uniquely hers. He resisted the urge to reach out and push back the strands that remained.

"Is there something you needed?" she asked, flushing slightly under his scrutiny.

"Hmm?" Her skin would be warm, he thought. An almost imperceptible trace of sweat dampened her brow and temples. He longed to rub away the smudge of dirt at the edge of her jaw, then run the tip of his finger over—

"Did you find the parts you were looking for?" she persisted.

"Parts? Oh! Parts." Coll nodded, dragging his attention back to her question. "Yes, I found them."

"Oh." Her face fell. "So you've finished? The alarm system is done?"

"Yes. Well, almost. I'll be finished by tonight." Suddenly aware that he was staring at her, he dragged his gaze from her face. He didn't want to talk about it. Not yet. Instead, he gestured toward the garden. "Did you do this yourself?"

Dayra nodded, then frowned down at her hands, her attention caught by a smear of dirt on the side of her wrist. Turning from him, she picked her way across the soft ground to the far side of the well.

Coll stepped forward, automatically intent on following her, then stopped abruptly as his booted foot sank four inches. He looked down, startled, but instead of his own foot, his eye fixed on Dayra's. Coll felt an unexpected sexual warmth surge through him at the sight.

She was barefoot. From this angle, he had a perfect view of her slender ankles, the graceful curve of her heel, and the high arch on the inside of her foot. She stepped carefully, toe first like a dancer, which made her appear to float across the ground. She wasn't floating, however, for Coll could clearly see the imprint of her feet in the friable soil.

He stepped back onto the stone path, leaving a long, deep impression of his boot. The bottom of the impression was packed hard from his weight, in striking contrast to Dayra's prints, where the lumpy surface of the turned earth was still visible. Unlike him, she'd left the mark of her passing, but without forcing the land into her own shape. Yet her world blossomed under her care while his. . . .

A tiny puff of air caught in the middle of Coll's chest, forming a hard, little knot that made it difficult for him to breathe.

He glanced at the still-raw mound of dirt she'd been planting, then at the rest of the small area, where the wildflowers and blooming vines looked as if they'd always grown there. Suddenly the seemingly random pattern of her work took on new shape and meaning. She hadn't been sticking her flowers just anywhere, Coll realized. She'd been putting them where they belonged, where they could take root and flourish and become an integral part of the world she'd created, here inside the high stone walls of her holding.

Was she conscious of how she placed each stone, each new plant? Coll wondered. Or did she instinctively know where everything ought to go? Did she sense something in the ground she worked, some secret vibration to which she was attuned that no one else could feel?

As if from a distance, Coll heard a soft human voice, then realized Dayra was speaking to him.

" . . . and then I added the moss. You can't plant too soon, because the rocks and soil have to settle first. They have to find their own balance," she said.

She was sitting sideways on a large, flat rock, leaning forward as she rinsed her hands in the flowing water. Her attention was on her hands, not on him, and once again her hair had fallen forward to half hide her face.

Unwilling to leave his huge prints beside hers, Coll backtracked along the path until he could reach the rocks opposite Dayra. He cautiously settled on one rock, then propped one booted foot against another. He needed the extra support. Just looking at Dayra, being aware of her like this, was doing odd things to his sense of balance.

"The water's good," Dayra said, looking up at him.

The sunlight reflecting off the surface of the water cast a golden glow along her throat and the underside of her jaw. It made her face look softer, less sharp featured. Her eyes shone as brilliantly blue as the sky.

Coll felt his breath catch and his mouth go dry. He forced himself to swallow and tried to concentrate on what she was saying.

"There are actually four of these natural springs inside the walls of the holding," she added. "One of them flows into cisterns for use in the buildings. This one goes to the gardens. The rest I let run off since we don't need it. Not yet, anyway."

Coll watched as she bent forward and scooped up some water in her cupped hands, then brought it to her mouth and took a long drink. Tiny streams of water seeped over the edge of her hands and out between her fingers in a cascade of droplets that sparkled in the sun. He had to dig his fingers into his leg to keep from reaching out and catching the falling drops so he could taste them.

"It's very good," she said at last, opening her hands and letting the remaining water fall back. "Cold and sweet. Try it."

Coll heard her, but all his attention was fixed on her mouth. Water glistened on the surface of her lips and chin. A strand of wet hair was plastered from the edge of her mouth across her cheek. Unable to ignore the tormenting urge to touch her any longer, he reached across the narrow stream dividing them and carefully brushed the strand aside.

It was a fleeting caress, no more than the tip of his finger against her cheek, yet it sent a shock of electric awareness through him that shook him with its force.

For one second his eyes locked with hers. In them he read the same intense, almost frightening awareness he felt. He also saw the same tormented longing for something they both knew had no part in either of their lives.

He dropped his gaze to the swiftly flowing water that divided them. The sun flashed on the water's rippling surface, blinding him. Coll plunged his hands into the stream, scooped up the icy water, and bent his head to drink.

She was right. The water was cold and sweet. He scooped up more, but this time he splashed it on his face, then ran his wet hands through his hair, grateful for the coolness against his hot skin, hoping she wouldn't notice the slight trembling of his hands.

"It's very good," he said at last, when he was sure he could keep his voice steady. He pushed to his feet, then stepped back on the stone path, all without looking at her.

"I came to say. . . . Now that the alarm system's almost done—" He stopped, struggling for control and irritated by his sudden awkwardness. "There's nothing more I can do here. At least, nothing really useful. I heard Johnny say you had some deliveries to make in Trevag in the next few days. I'd like to go with you."

"So you're leaving?" Her eyes were wide with shock. She was still seated on the stone, her legs curved around behind her while her body turned toward him in a graceful arch that made her small breasts thrust against the fabric of her shift, but there was a tension in her body that hadn't been there a moment before.

"Yes," Coll said, thinking of that first night when the intruder had clawed her breast and shoulder. Even now he could remember how warm and silken soft her skin had felt when he'd traced the line of the gashes with the tip of his finger. His hand curled into a fist involuntarily, his fingertips tingling with that remembered warmth, that remembered softness.

"Yes, of course, you are." Her eyes dropped as she trailed a finger in the water, apparently fascinated by the tiny waves the motion generated.

"Well," he said, anxious to be gone—and very loath to leave. He ran his palms down the sides of his pants, drying them against the coarse fabric. "Best get back. There's still a little work to be done on the alarms."

He turned abruptly and walked out of the garden. His legs were shaky and he forgot about closing the gate until he was halfway across the compound. The gate could remain open, he decided. He didn't have the courage to go back.

For a long, long while, Dayra remained where she was, her gaze fixed on the gate through which Coll Larren had disappeared. The small garden seemed so much more . . . peaceful, so much safer now he was gone. His presence had disrupted the very harmony she had come to find, charging the

134

air around her with a masculine energy that was partly sexual and wholly unnerving.

So he was definitely leaving. She should be relieved. She'd spent the last few days regretting her hasty plea for him to stay, torn between anger that she should have let her fear overcome her and relief at the sense of security his presence brought.

So why did she feel so . . . so. . . .

She didn't know how she felt, but she knew her body ached, her face was flushed, and her breathing was only now beginning to return to normal.

Dayra brought her legs up, then pivoted around on her bottom so she could plunge her feet into the little stream. The shock of the icy water against her skin made her gasp. Propping her hands on the rock, she leaned forward, arms straight, shoulders hunched, and watched the swiftly flowing water surge around her ankles. She waggled her feet back and forth, studying the swirl of brown as the dirt on her skin washed away, then bent down and splashed water over her arms and up her legs to her knees. She scooped up a handful of water and dashed it against her face and throat, then straightened, tugged open the neckline of her shift, and dribbled water down her front, grateful for its coolness against her hot skin.

She should have been working in one of the other gardens. There was a lot to do and she *had* been planning a trip to Trevag. She had customers she'd neglected and the fruits and vegetables that were ripening had to be gathered soon or they'd spoil in the field.

Instead, she dragged her feet out of the water, tugged them in close to her hips, and wrapped her arms around her legs. Dropping her chin on top of one knee, Dayra stared down at the moving pattern of light and dark the sun made on the water's surface.

How could one man, a stranger, so easily disrupt her life in so short a time? In little more than a week, Coll Larren had managed to break through the defenses she'd spent a lifetime building. Defenses against men, against dependence, against her own emotions and longings. And he'd done it without trying.

Until a few moments ago, she'd thought she was the only one who suffered from the potent . . . *awareness* that had tormented and intrigued and upset her ever since he'd risked his life to save hers. Then she'd taken a sip of water and looked up to find his eyes fixed on her, looked up and seen all the lonely longing, all the hunger in him that she hadn't wanted to recognize within herself.

It wasn't right. For either of them. In a few days, Coll Larren would be gone. She knew without his telling her that he was a man with no roots, a man who feared involvement as much as she feared dependence. She didn't know how she could be so sure of that, but she was.

It wasn't her beauty that attracted him. She had none. She didn't know what he saw in her except a woman alone who shared his loneliness, but she was suddenly convinced that he was drawn to her by something more than mere lust or pity.

At the same time, it wasn't his appealing looks that attracted her. She'd never met a bigger, more intimidating male than Coll Larren. His features were too hard, his hair was too long and badly cut, his clothes too plain and worn for his appearance to be anything but unsettling. Yet despite his daunting roughness on the outside, on the inside he was a gentle and compassionate man whom any woman would value.

Not only value, but learn to love. Dayra wasn't ready to risk that.

Yet more important than her own desires was her urgent need for help in her stand against Talman Bardath. If she were alone, she wouldn't have been so afraid, but she wasn't alone. Jason and Jeanella made her vulnerable. She couldn't risk their safety, no matter how much it might gall her to admit she could not protect them by herself. Nor could she count on Coll to stand with her against Bardath and his minions. Not for long, anyway.

Once he discovered she'd lied to him—or at least that she hadn't told the whole truth—he was bound to be angry. Whatever he felt for her, it wouldn't be enough to make him stay. She was a fool to depend on him for protection, even for a short while, because when he left she'd be just that much less capable of defending her family by herself.

Whichever way she turned, Dayra found questions without answers, doubts without assurances, fears that had no end.

Dayra squeezed her eyes shut and wrapped her arms even tighter around her legs, drawing herself up into a huddled ball on top of the wide, flat rock. Despite the warmth of the sun against her skin, she shivered.

Chapter Seven

Coll finished cleaning and sharpening the mattock he'd used that afternoon, then put the tool in its place on the work shed rack. He ran his fingers thoughtfully along the newly sharpened edge. It was a crude and ancient tool to shape a raw, new world, but it served its purpose well.

It had to. When it came to technology, Dayra and the other settlers didn't have many options. The Combine's long-standing economic restrictions on the import of modern equipment to colony planets like Far Star had helped the government keep the local populations under control. Settlers who lacked modern communications systems and were forced to rely on hand tools and antiquated machines had little chance of successfully rebelling against their government. In spite of the difficulties, however, the dreams of owning their own land and shaping their own future, free of the smothering controls of the powerful businesses that dominated most of the developed planets, ensured a steady flow of hopeful colonists to settle the new worlds.

To his surprise, Coll had found an odd satisfaction in working with tools that kept him close to the ground he tilled. On the highly developed worlds, roboticized tenders and harvesters would have worked the fields, cutting the laborers' responsibilities to that of machine caretakers. He wouldn't have cared for that, but here, the heavy work provided unexpected rewards.

He'd spent the last three days, ever since he'd finished installing the alarm system, in preparing new beds for planting. The work was physically exhausting, yet he'd found a soul-satisfying pleasure in seeing the ever expanding square of turned earth. He was even conscious of a tinge of regret that he wouldn't be here to see the green plants begin to push up through the soil he'd prepared with such effort.

Something of his thoughts must have shown on his face, for Johnny, who'd been putting away his own tools, said, "Havin' second thoughts about goin' on to Trevag, are ye, lad?"

Coll straightened, then turned away from the tool rack. "No, of course not. I'm no farmer. You know that."

Johnny nodded. "Aye, I know that. I also know when a man's lyin' to himself, Coll Larren." The old man's expression softened. "Ye're not made t'be a drifter, lad. One day ye'll have to stop and put down roots. This'ud be a good place to start."

There was a wistful note of yearning in the old man's voice that Coll had never heard before. His eyes narrowed as he looked at his friend more closely, but Johnny didn't notice. He was staring out at the far side of the compound, where Dayra was playing a lively game of ball with Jason and Jeanella. The late afternoon sun, dipping to the horizon, lit their happy faces and gave a soft golden glow to the scene.

"You've grown fond of them, haven't you?" Coll asked gently.

"Aye, lad, I have." Johnny sighed, then dragged his gaze back to Coll. "I came here as a scout for the Alliance, as ye well know, but I've grown attached to the place, to the lass and the little ones. I never had a family, but if I had. . . ."

The corner of his lip twitched upward as his wry good humor resurfaced. "I suspect ye know what I'm talkin' about, lad. Now, ye canna tell me ye've not thought o' stayin'," he added as Coll started to protest. "I've seen the way the little ones trail after ye, and I've seen ye watchin' Dayra—more than once! Ye might just ask yereself if leavin' is what ye *really* want."

There was no reply possible. None, at least, that Coll was prepared to deal with. Instead, he said, "There are still a few things I wanted to tend to in that far field tonight. Would you mind finishing up in here for me?"

"If ye like." The expression on Johnny's face said he wasn't ready to end the discussion, but that he'd bide his time for now.

Coll sighed as he slipped out of the work shed, head down so he wouldn't be tempted to stop and watch Dayra and the children. There was no sense in tormenting himself with thoughts of what could never be.

Those thoughts had become far more difficult to resist since his conversation with Dayra in the flower garden. Nothing, not cold showers, hard work, or deliberately avoiding her could rid him of the tormenting memories of how she'd looked, what she'd said, how warm her cheek had been when he'd let himself brush the strand of hair away from her lips. It had been such a simple gesture, yet he'd replayed it in his mind over and over, remembering the feel of her, wishing he'd had the courage to claim the kiss he'd wanted so badly.

He had to remind himself he wasn't staying for long. He didn't belong and his continued presence on the holding could only put Dayra and the children at greater risk than they were now.

With the Combine Armed Forces' attention on the holding, there was always the chance that someone would recognize him as the Sandman. Coll didn't know if there was still a price on his head—it had been over two years, after all, since he'd last had any connection with the Rebel Alliance—but there was no sense in endangering Dayra just to find out.

Ever since Cyrus IV he'd drifted, kept to back streets and the back-street jobs where the soldiers and the police never came and no one ever looked too closely in your face or cared very much about your past. He'd moved from planet to planet by taking the same kind of berth that had landed him here on Far Star. He'd never lingered long in any one place. If you didn't stay, you were quickly forgotten, and that was just fine with him.

He'd never intended to end up on Far Star. Men like him were too conspicuous on sparsely settled planets like this. He'd certainly never intended to land in any situation where he would attract the attention of the military forces posted to the planet, yet he'd already been noticed.

Capt. Truva wouldn't forget him. In those cool gray eyes he'd seen intelligence and a stern dedication to duty that would preclude her forgetting a stranger like him.

He couldn't stay, but leaving was going to be one of the hardest things Coll had ever done.

Coll was halfway across the yard when he caught the faint sound of a flitter motor coming toward the holding. He stopped breathing, straining to guess the driver's intentions by the sound of the motor. An impossible task. The only way to find out who it was and what they wanted was to see for himself.

Dayra and the children caught the sound a minute later, but by that time Coll was racing past them. Pausing only long enough to give them a sharp command to stay put, he headed toward the stairs that would lead to the top of the holding wall near the main gate. From there he'd have the best view of the road leading to the gate and of the approaching flitter.

The flitter was a worn, battered work vehicle

just like Dayra's. Its occupants—two men, a girl, and a boy—appeared surprised to find the gate closed.

Coll was about to hail them when the clatter of feet on the stone steps made him whirl about. Jason threw himself down beside Coll and peered over the edge, clearly hoping for the chance to throw some of the rocks he'd stockpiled with such care. The four people in the flitter were definitely not who he wanted to see.

"Aw, that's just Settler Megat an' Alara an' Felix. We haven't seen 'em in weeks. Wonder who the other guy is?"

Before Coll could stop him, Jason jumped to his feet and shouted, "Hey, Felix! Didja hear we had soldiers visit us? An' I bit one!"

An instant later he was dashing back down the steps as fast as his legs could carry him. Coll followed after, shaking his head at the impetuous energy of six-year-old boys.

By the time Coll reached the bottom, Jason had turned off the alarms and was swinging the gate open to admit the visitors. Dayra had crossed to join them. Jeanella remained near the porch, watching the proceedings nervously. At sight of the children, however, her face lit up and she raced across the yard to greet the flitter.

"Alara!" she shouted excitedly as the girl, who was about Jeanella's age, climbed out of the flitter. "You have to see the new holo-vid I've been working on!"

Without stopping for introductions, the ecstatic Jason and Jeanella dragged their friends away, leaving to Dayra the task of greeting the two adults.

"Settler Megat! It's good to see you," she said as a burly, amiable-faced man dressed in the rough clothes of a settler unfolded from the passenger's side. The man gave an embarrassed grin in response, clearly uncomfortable, but just as clearly glad to see her.

"Hope you don't mind, Settler Smith," Megat said. "The kids have been pesterin' me to pay a visit for some time now, so when Settler Neur here suggested we come. . . ." His words trailed off as he indicated the second man, who was coming around the end of the flitter.

At sight of the tall, black-bearded man, Coll stiffened. The man looked like a farmer; he even moved like a farmer who had already put in a hard day's work and saw only more work ahead of him. But he wasn't a farmer. Or, rather, he wasn't just a farmer.

After years of living and working with people intent on rebellion, Coll knew instinctively when he was looking at a rebel leader, and he was very, very sure that he was looking at one now. Megat would be a follower, one of the rank and file, but the black-bearded man would be the one doing the planning and giving the orders.

At that moment, Johnny joined them. One look at the old man's expression was enough to tell Coll both that his assessment was correct and that Johnny was decidedly unhappy with the men's presence on the holding.

Neur glanced at Coll, his dark eyes frankly

assessing. Then he nodded at Johnny and politely turned to Dayra. "Settler Smith. Haven't seen you in the market for a couple of weeks so I thought, as long as I was visiting Settler Megat, I'd pay you a visit, as well."

"I always have work to do at home, Settler Neur," she said, just as politely. Her spine was suddenly straight, her chin up, her manner decidedly cooler than when she'd greeted Megat.

So she knows, too, Coll thought, casually crossing his arms over his chest. Or at least she suspects.

"I trust your crops are doing well," Neur said, surveying the holding. Apparently satisfied there was no one else around, he turned his attention back to Dayra. "I've heard Capt. Truva and her people paid you a little visit a couple of weeks ago."

"That's right," Dayra admitted reluctantly. "She said they'd heard rumors there were arms stored here. An absurd rumor, of course."

"Of course," Neur agreed. His gaze once more slid to Coll.

"How are your crops doing, Settler Neur?" Dayra asked calmly. "Well, I hope. It's so important to keep your energies focused on your fields, you know. If you let yourself get distracted by too many other things, your crops die."

Good for her, Coll thought, admiring the adroit way she laid out her position. It was a serious offense even to discuss rebellion, and Dayra clearly had no intention of running any risks, even with people she knew.

Neur frowned. "So I've heard. On the other hand, some things we all have to fight together." He paused for a fraction of a second, then added, "Like blight, for example."

No one took Neur up on his verbal offering. Coll could feel the silence stretch, then tighten, drawing them closer against their will.

"Ever seen a little insect called an ant, Settler Neur?" Dayra asked politely. "If I'm not mistaken, you've got something like them on your home world. I think you call them fire biters."

"I've seen them," Neur admitted cautiously.

"They're not very pleasant insects to have around, but they're not usually dangerous." Dayra frowned down at her hands, as if she'd just discovered they were in need of washing. "Not until you stir up their nest, that is. Then they turn vicious. They've been known to kill people on occasion."

"That a fact? Maybe the secret is to kill them first."

"Maybe the secret is to leave them alone and just walk around them."

"That's what a lot o' folks say," Neur agreed, pursing his lips thoughtfully. "The trouble is, sometimes your path leads right to their nest, whether you want it to or not."

Neur glanced at Megat, who was watching him nervously; then he abruptly turned his stare at Coll. "Of course, you can always bring in experts to help you deal with ants and blight and such things. It's often a lot more effective that way, wouldn't you say, stranger?"

147

Coll could feel his heart take a sudden, erratic jump. He forced his breathing to slow, his hands to remain still. He met Neur's challenging stare with a cold, flat stare of his own. "I wouldn't know. I'm not a farmer."

"Didn't think you were," Neur replied calmly. He turned from Coll to study the crude stone buildings around them. "Don't know about you, but I'm always intrigued by the folks who settle on a place like this. Most of 'em doing something different from what they did in the past. Take you, for example, Settler Smith," he said, waving his hand at her. "You don't look much like a fisherman *or* a farmer—no offense intended, you understand—but you've done well here, nonetheless."

"Maybe that's because I spend my energies tending to my own business, Settler Neur," Dayra replied tartly.

"Maybe. Me, I used to be a hotheaded fellow. Had a wife and kids and a little business on Kraleck II."

Coll tensed at the mention of one of the worlds whose rebel leaders he'd successfully helped some years before. If Neur noticed the reaction, he didn't comment.

"I was pretty happy with life, but I could see that I wasn't going to get much of anywhere, what with all the taxes and restrictions the Combine was forcing on us. So I joined up with the rebels who were trying to kick the Combine out." Again his eyes fastened on Coll, but this time he didn't blink. "We were lucky. We got the Sandman for an adviser. With him on our side, we won pretty handily and without losing too many lives."

Coll could hear Dayra's sharp intake of breath at Neur's mention of the Sandman, but all his attention was focused on the black-bearded farmer. "So what brings *you* here now, Settler Neur?" he asked with feigned casualness. "The Sandman's dead, so they say, but if your side won on Kraleck II, you could have kept going with your business."

The question brought a snort of real amusement from Neur. "Well, truth to tell, my wife liked the business better than she liked me. She filed to cancel our marriage contract and claimed the business as compensation." The amusement died. "I came here, hoping to start over, and now I find the Combine's working hard to get its teeth sunk as deep in our necks as they had on Kraleck II."

Neur abruptly straightened from his relaxed slouch. His gaze moved from Dayra, to Coll, to Johnny, and back to Dayra.

"There's a number of us planning a meeting in three days, after the market closes. It's at the Wild Comet and you're all welcome." He paused, then added, "We thought we'd talk about some crop problems, like blight and fire biters." He turned to stare first at Johnny, then Coll. "Experts are always welcome."

No one spoke for a long while after Megat had gathered his children and left with Neur. Dayra stood as still and stiff as a stone carving, but her eyes were alive with shock and a growing anger that Coll could tell was about to boil over and scald both Johnny and him.

Coll shifted uncomfortably. She was bright. And

quick. He'd known skilled Alliance operatives who couldn't have handled the conversation with Neur half as well and she'd put the bits of the puzzle together before most people would have known they had a puzzle at all.

Oblivious to the possibility that the children, who were playing nearby, might hear her, Dayra burst out, "How could you, Johnny McGregor? How *could* you? You're free to do whatever you please, but you have no right, no right *whatsoever*, to put me and my family at risk like this."

Johnny waved his hands vaguely, obviously distressed by her anger. "I meant ye no harm, lass. I—"

Her voice dropped, but her words were sharp enough to wound. "That's why Capt. Truva paid a personal visit to the holding, isn't it, Johnny? I've tried to figure out what made her come. Now I know."

Her jaw worked as she fought for control. "I'll pay you through market day, Johnny," Dayra continued, enunciating every word as carefully and quietly as if she were talking to a stranger who didn't speak her language, "but that's an end of it. You'll have to find work elsewhere. Do I make myself clear?"

"Now, Dayra," Johnny protested, shaken by her vehemence. "No harm will come to ye or the children, I promise. I wouldn't let that happen, no matter what."

Dayra ignored him. She swung around on Coll, her fury unabated and not one whit louder. "And you! I can't believe that *you* could . . . could—"

"I'm not, and I didn't," Coll said quickly, taking advantage of her stuttering. He wasn't sure why he felt so urgent a need to defend himself, but he knew he couldn't bear to leave her with such a low opinion of him. "I'm not involved with any rebel movement, Dayra. You have to believe me."

"Have you been?"

What was he supposed to say to that?

When he didn't respond, she turned from him to stare through the still-open gate to the grassy hillside beyond, which was just beginning to disappear in the gloom of twilight. "You were going to leave, anyway," she said, very low, her voice quivering with the intensity of her emotion. "I'm grateful for that, at least."

She took a deep breath, fighting to get her voice under control, then turned back to confront them. "I expect you both to keep on with your regular work until market day. I also expect you not to tell Jason or Jeanella about any of this. Once you've unloaded the produce in the market, your work will be done. After that, I don't ever want to see either of you again. Do you understand?"

Stunned, Coll tried to interrupt, to explain. "Dayra—"

She turned to confront him, eyes blazing. "I won't let you use me or my family, Coll Larren. I won't let *any* man use me. Not *ever.*"

With scarcely repressed fury evident in her slightest motion, Dayra spun around on her heel and stalked across the yard and into the house.

151

*　　*　　*

How could they do this to her? How could Coll
and Johnny betray her like this? Dayra had asked
herself the same questions several times in the
last ten minutes, and she still didn't have any
answers.

At least she'd had the good sense to tell them
they'd have to leave, Dayra assured herself as she
restlessly paced from one side of her room to the
other, then back again. She didn't need anyone's
help. She certainly didn't need help from men
who were willing to put two innocent children
at risk for the sake of their own ambitions.

Frustrated, Dayra kicked the edge of her bed,
wishing it could have been someone's posterior.
Johnny had been with her for over a year, for
stars' sake! She'd thought he was a friend, as well
as an employee. She'd thought she could trust
him, yet now she discovered he was working with
people who wanted to start a rebellion right here
on Far Star!

And Coll!

She didn't want to think about Coll. Yet even as
she silently vowed to thrust him from her mind forever, she found herself anxiously glancing toward
the window, wondering where he'd gone, what he
was thinking and feeling right now.

Was he really the Sandman? She'd heard of the
Sandman even on Edole, where being part of the
household of a senior Combine official meant the
rebels were discussed only in whispers and behind
closed doors.

The Sandman was a strange name for a man

who'd become a folk hero. One of the family maids, who was obviously half in love with him, had told Dayra he was called the Sandman because he was like the sand, always changing, always moving, shifting tactics with a speed and an ingenuity that drove the Combine leaders fighting him into frustrated rages.

It was hard to reconcile that image of the Sandman with the intense, lonely man whose very presence on the holding had disrupted her sleep for the past two weeks and made her waking hours an uncomfortable battle between rational good sense and the unaccustomed urgings of her heart.

If Coll Larren wasn't the Sandman, then she had accused him unjustly. If he was, and he had used her and her holding to hide his link with the rebels, then she was glad he would soon be gone. Glad!

Dayra slumped on the edge of the bed. That was a lie. She wasn't glad at all. She didn't want Coll to leave, not ever, not for any reason. And yet she had no choice. She couldn't put her family at risk. Not for anyone or any reason. She *couldn't*.

The next two days were some of the longest of Coll's life. He should have been grateful that Dayra was deliberately ignoring him—after all, he'd spent the previous two weeks trying to avoid her—but her carefully maintained emotional distance hurt in ways Coll couldn't even begin to describe.

Johnny was taking his banishment just as hard.

Over the past year, the old man had found a home with Dayra and the children and it would be difficult for him to leave. It didn't matter that it would be far easier for him to work with Neur and whoever else was plotting rebellion. Johnny didn't want to go, and Coll found he sympathized with the old man.

Tomorrow was market day in Trevag. The flitter was already loaded with all but the most delicate fruits and vegetables. With the exception of the few items he'd need in the morning, Coll had packed his things. The small house he'd used over the past couple of weeks was cleaned, his work in the fields finished.

There was nothing left to do but take Dayra on one last tour of the alarm system he'd installed. At the far side of the compound, Coll could see the main house, where Dayra was putting Jason and Jeanella to bed. The golden light pouring from its open windows and doors lit the darkness with a warm and welcoming glow.

Reluctantly, Coll descended the steps of his quarters and crossed the yard. Before he was halfway to the house, the lights went out, which meant Dayra ought to emerge soon. Just as well. He'd like to get this over with as quickly as possible.

Dayra, however, wasn't waiting for him when he reached the broad steps leading to the house. As the minutes passed and she still didn't appear, Coll decided he could wait sitting as well as standing. He'd put in enough hard labor during the past few days to last him for a lifetime and he realized suddenly that he was tired, both physically and mentally.

He dropped down on the top step, propped his forearms on his knees, clasped his hands, and stared out at the holding yard. Now that the house lights were off, Far Star's twin moons provided the only illumination.

Without birds or insects to give it a voice, the night was quiet. Only the wind was alive, soughing through the tall grass beyond the walls, whispering around the corners of the buildings in the compound. It was a soft wind, carrying just a touch of moisture from the nearby sea, and it felt cool against his skin. Coll savored it, relaxing under its soothing touch, relishing the silver darkness around him. A man could get used to enjoying a night like this, he thought. He regretted he'd never have the chance.

"I'm sorry. I didn't mean to make you wait."

Coll turned, startled. He hadn't heard Dayra's approach, which meant he was far more tired than he'd thought.

She stood just inside the darkened doorway, a vague black form dimly silhouetted against the deeper black of the room beyond. All he could see of her were her slender legs and her bare feet, captured in the moonlight that managed to creep through the open door.

"That's all right." He spoke softly, unwilling to break the stillness of the night.

She shifted position slightly. The moonlight, like the rising sea, flowed up her thighs and slender hips to wrap around her waist. He could see her hands hanging by her sides, the fingers curved in toward her body, relaxed. The rest of her remained wrapped in shadow. When she spoke, her voice seemed part of the passing breeze, unconnected with her corporeal body.

"Shall we?" she asked, her voice carefully neutral. "I imagine you're tired. I know I am."

She held out her hand and Coll felt the muscles of his belly and across his lower ribs tighten. It was as if she had gathered moonbeams in her hand to offer him, dipping deep until they spilled out of her palm and over her fingers.

Coll made no move to touch her and he hesitated a moment before rising to his feet. As he followed her down the steps, his brain told him she was simply intent on the task before them, but his imagination conjured visions of a magic far too potent for a mortal man like him.

The thought made him shake his head in disgust. He was a practical man, not given to absurd flights of fancy. Dayra was a plain and practical woman who still hadn't forgiven him for what she considered his betrayal. It was his weariness and the drab prospect of trying to find work in Trevag that had suddenly made him prone to extravagant thought.

He followed her across the bare ground of the compound. The grating of his boots on the hard-packed dirt was the only sound they made. She was barefoot and wary of sharp stones. Somehow that, too, seemed part of the magic.

Far Star's moons were high and bright. Because of the moons' different angles to the ground, the double shadows they cast crisscrossed on the ground. Coll watched his and Dayra's shadows as they walked, four silver-black masses that seemed to dance, to flow together, then break apart only to recombine with every new step they took. For each of them there was one longer shadow overlaid by a short, heavier shadow from the moon most directly above them.

To Coll's tired mind, the double shadows seemed like two visions of his soul. But which was real? Deep inside him, was there just one Coll Larren, or were there two? Or more? Was he the heavy shadow, the blackest one that moved so ponderously, as if chained to his body? Or was he the darkly silvered image that stretched so far ahead of him, as if trying to reach out to something still hidden in the night beyond?

He shook his head, trying to shake off such fanciful nonsense. He must be tired, indeed, if he could let his mind indulge in such absurd fantasies. But still he couldn't help watching as his second shadow blended with Dayra's when she mounted the steps at the far side of the compound that led to the top of the holding wall.

Fascinating how their darkest shadows never seemed to meet, Coll thought. If he stepped closer to her, if he took her in his arms. . . .

If he could do that, then black would merge with black and the silver shadows would stop their dancing. But only then.

"This is the main sensor for this side, right?" Dayra said, stooping to indicate a small black box half hidden in the stones at the edge of the wall.

"That's right." Did his voice sound as tight and strained to her as it suddenly did to him? Coll wondered.

"And this alarm can only be turned off from inside the house," she added, leading him farther along the wall to a second, somewhat larger black box.

Coll merely nodded, unwilling to trust his voice. She must have seen the motion, even in the dark, for she continued to lead the way along the wall, pointing out the various parts of the protective system he'd installed for her, seeking his confirmation that she understood how to operate it.

As they circled the holding, their shadows circled with them, stretching in front of them, then slipping to one side or the other, then falling behind before swinging round again to lead the way. It was, Coll mused, as if their shadow spirits were as uncertain as they were, reaching out to connect with the other only to slide away, afraid.

Dayra moved soundlessly over the stone pathway they followed, always just ahead of him, just out of reach. With her white shift and her unbound hair turned liquid silver in the moonlight, she seemed as one with the night around them, part of this world, yet floating above it, somehow apart.

By the time they completed the circuit, Coll was dizzy with the fevered imaginings of his mind and the even more tormented longings of his body. As Dayra started back down the steps, Coll muttered an excuse and knelt over the nearest black box, fighting to regain control before he rejoined her.

Whatever magic was abroad in the night

betrayed him, for instead of continuing on down the steps, Dayra came back to stand beside him.

"Coll?" she said hesitantly, looking down at him.

Coll groaned, but he could not refuse to acknowledge her. Her voice alone was enough to compel a response.

She was so *close*.

Tugged by the night wind, the hem of her shift brushed against his sleeve and as she bent over him a strand of her hair blew across his cheek.

She swayed, as if she, too, were captive to the wind's vagaries. Coll put out his hand to brace her. His palm pressed against the point of her hip as his fingers shaped themselves to the softer curve at her side.

He heard a soft groan, but wasn't sure if it was from his lips or hers.

She moved closer. He had to tilt his head back to look up into her face. What he saw there made him wonder if he were mad or dreaming. He didn't have a chance to decide, for at that moment Dayra placed her hands on his shoulders, leaned down, and kissed him.

It was a hesitant, very gentle kiss. Even as Dayra retreated, it brought him to his feet with a groan that Coll knew was his, for he could feel it being ripped from somewhere deep inside him. As he stood, he dragged Dayra into his arms, enfolding her in an embrace so powerful that she gasped.

As though reclaiming the breath he'd taken from her, Dayra slid her hands from his shoulders to tangle them in his hair and pull him down to her, seizing his mouth in a kiss that burned hot and hungry and wild.

Kiss followed demanding kiss as they clung to each other, wrapped in the exultation of a moment torn free of the world that bound them, unfettered by doubts or fears.

How long they remained suspended in the moonlight, caught between land and sky, Coll didn't know. The only thing he was sure of was that letting her go was the hardest thing he had ever done.

She slid from his arms without speaking, and when he reached to reclaim her, she wrapped her hand around his, restraining him. Her fingers trembled, ever so slightly, then stilled as she pressed them tighter against him.

He could move closer. Just an inch or two and it would be easy to draw her back into his arms. Coll could feel the heat of her body, even from here.

Instead, he pulled his hand from hers and stepped back.

Only once she was safely on the steps again did she speak. "I haven't thanked you for all you've done, Coll Larren," she said, her voice soft, but quivering with tension. "In spite of . . . of—"

"It doesn't matter."

For a minute she didn't reply; then she said, even more softly, "No, I suppose it doesn't."

She stepped down, into the dark at the base of the wall and back out into full moonlight, then turned to face him. Coll could see her upturned face, but her features were blurred in the moonlight.

She took a step backward, then another. The silence hung between them, an almost tangible thing of night and silvered shadows.

"Thank you, Coll Larren," she said.

With that she turned and slowly walked away, back to the house on the other side of the compound.

Coll watched Dayra go, her double shadows flowing across the ground behind her as if reluctant to leave. He waited until he heard her close and lock the door behind her; then he waited a little longer, listening to the dying night breeze, before he, too, descended the steps and retreated into his quarters.

Just before he drifted off to sleep, Coll turned to face the open door and the moon-drenched compound beyond. What had their shadows looked like, he wondered vaguely, when he had held her in his arms? What had they looked like as she'd slipped away from him?

Chapter Eight

Coll rose early the next morning. Rather than face Dayra over breakfast, he plucked several ripe poma fruits from the garden and ate them while he puttered at unimportant tasks he'd left undone. Since the flitter was already loaded, there was little left to occupy his remaining time. When the bustle from the main house indicated that Dayra was almost ready to go, he collected his bag, haphazardly stowing the few items he hadn't packed the night before, and crossed the yard to the flitter.

At the sight of Johnny casually leaning against the flitter, Coll stopped short. Johnny glanced up at him, clearly uncomfortable, but just as clearly determined not to move until he'd had his say.

"I wanted to tell ye I'm sorry, lad," he said quietly. "I know somethin' of how ye feel about

Dayra, and if it hadn't been for Megat an' Neur an' me, mebbe—"

Coll shook his head. "Don't worry about it, Johnny. I couldn't have stayed here, even if she'd wanted me to. You know that as well as I do." He pushed down the memory of the night before. It had been Dayra who had walked away, after all.

"Yes, well. . . ." Johnny bobbed his head in unhappy acceptance of the inevitable. After a moment's consideration, he plunged his hand into a pocket and, after a little rummaging, pulled out a handful of coins. "Take this, then, just to tide ye over until ye find work. I know ye refused to take Dayra's money an'—"

Coll shook his head, touched by the gesture. Johnny had rejected Dayra's offer of pay just as he had. The old man had never had much beyond what was needed for the Alliance's purposes. He wouldn't take his friend's credits, no matter how empty his own pockets were. "I've enough."

A barely perceptible smile tugged at the corners of Johnny's lips. "I'm tempted to call ye a liar, lad. I've never known ye to have much, and what ye did have, ye were as likely to give to others as keep for yereself and yere own needs."

His smile faded and he studied Coll gravely. "Whatever else may have changed in the past couple o' years, lad, I know that part of ye won't have altered. I dinna for a minute think it ever will."

"I told you, I've credits—"

"Not many, I'm willin' to bet."

Coll hitched one shoulder in a surge of combined irritation and embarrassment at his old friend's

163

unblinking gaze. "I've enough. Don't worry about me." He smiled wryly. "You're far more likely to get in trouble than I am, old man. You take care Capt. Truva doesn't catch wind of what you're up to."

Johnny shrugged. "The good captain knows somethin's up, but she has no proof. By the time she has it, we'll be close to winnin', anyway."

"Perhaps." Coll hesitated, shifting his bag from one hand to the other and back again. "Can you find someone to take your place, someone who'll watch out for Dayra and the children?" he said at last.

Johnny nodded, his old eyes fixed on Coll's with understanding. "Aye, I already have someone in mind. Dinna worry. They'll be fine."

Coll wanted to say more, but he couldn't, for at that moment Jason rushed into the shed with an excited whoop, closely followed by Jeanella and Dayra. Grateful for the interruption, Coll hastily stowed his bag in the carrier compartment along with the heavy bags of produce.

Without glancing at him, Dayra walked around to the front passenger's side. "You can sit with Jason and Jeanella in the back. There's more room, so you'll be more comfortable. Johnny can steer."

Dayra was grateful when Coll climbed into the back of the passenger section without comment and took his seat in the middle, by Jeanella. Dayra had managed to avoid him all morning. It was going to be difficult enough just to ride in the same flitter with him. Even though she'd never intended to kiss Coll, all her doubts and resentment over his deception had burned away in the heat of last night's kiss. If she'd had to sit beside him, where she could see his face, his eyes, his mouth—most especially his mouth—the trip would have been unbearable. It was hard enough just dealing with the memories.

The potentially more serious question, Dayra realized a moment later, was whether or not Coll could survive an hour of being squeezed in between an opinionated 11-year-old girl and a talkative six-year-old boy.

Jason had no such doubts. Since the top of the flitter was down, he didn't waste energy by using the door. He simply belly flopped over the edge and pitched himself, headfirst, into his seat.

"Jason!" Dayra's protest carried a world of exasperated adult expectations, all of which Jason ignored.

He squirmed upright in his seat and beamed at Coll. "This is great! I've been wantin' to talk to you all mornin', but Dayra said I wasn't suppose to pester you. You don't mind, do you? I got a lotta questions I haven't got to ask you yet." He gave Coll a fraction of a second to answer, then rushed on. "Did you ever travel on a fighter ship? You know, one of those really fast ships the Combine's usin' against the rebels. Where're you going next? Are you sure you can't stay? Really? There's lotsa—"

"Jason!"

There was no mistaking the warning. That didn't mean Jason wasn't willing to try to argue his way around it.

"Coll doesn't mind, do you?" Jason asked brightly, sure of the response he wanted. Before Coll could open his mouth, the boy draped himself over the back of Dayra's seat and said confidently, "Coll doesn't mind. Honest, Dayra. 'Sides, I wasn't goin' to pester him. I just—"

Dayra took a very deep breath. "At least keep quiet until we get on the main road. Can you do that?"

"Aw, Dayra—"

"Can you?"

Jason glanced back at Coll, then back at her. Evidently the expression on her face was convincing. He drooped, weighted down by the accumulated injustices of the adult world, and slid back into his seat. "I s'pose so," he said reluctantly. His small body slumped in dejection and the corners of his mouth fell.

Coll should have known enough to keep a straight face, Dayra thought a moment later. Evidently he didn't. The corner of his mouth twitched. It was just a little twitch, but Jason spotted it right off.

With a child's finely honed instinct for detecting weaknesses in his elders' defenses, the boy zeroed in on that twitch. "I got *lotsa* questions," he informed Coll, beaming once more. "But I'll wait!" he added hastily as Dayra started to open her mouth.

"Jus' till the main road," he added under his breath, clearly thinking she wouldn't be able to hear.

* * *

Talman Bardath sat alone in his private quarters. His ship was in orbit about the planet Far Star; he was waiting for the commander of the local garrison, a Capt. Truva, to answer his peremptory call, and he was restless.

The captain, it seemed, was not available at the moment. She was out with a patrol, her aide had explained nervously. Accessible only by the limited voice communicators available on the planet. He would have the captain respond to Domine Bardath's summons as soon as she returned. If, in the meantime, there was anything the aide could do to assist so distinguished a visitor. . . .

Bardath had growled his denial and cut the communications link, frustrated at being thwarted even in so insignificant a thing as this. He had spent his life working to control everything and everyone he could, but lately it seemed the fates conspired against him.

Now he glanced at the printout of the specially coded transmission he had received from Edole an hour earlier, just as the ship was dropping into orbit around Far Star. He knew the contents of the message by heart, for he had read it over more times than he cared to count. It lay on his desk, an insignificant slip of paper among so many other, more impressive documents.

The printout carried his death sentence.

There would be no more tests, no more chances, no hope. The last possible test had confirmed the specialists' opinion. He had, they said, perhaps three or four years left while he would still be

167

able to function, to think and plan and act. After that, the disease that was already spreading inside him would take over. Eventually he would turn into a slavering idiot incapable of controlling his own body, and then he would die.

It had begun almost two years ago. Slight memory lapses that were never more than irritating. A faint trembling in his hands that was annoying, but scarcely worthy of concern. When the doctors had first suspected that his symptoms might be the sign of something far more serious than the overwork he claimed, he'd laughed at them.

The idea that he would die was absurd. Death was an intellectual concept, something that applied to others, but not to him, not yet.

The doctors had insisted. He'd undergone more tests and more examinations. As head of the Combine Security Police, he'd had the best care available.

In the end, the specialists had been polite, but adamant. He had contracted Virisian fever, a viral infection that attacked the brain, slowly and implacably destroying the nervous system of its victim. There was no treatment and no cure.

That was when Bardath had begun to think about his own mortality. Even as he'd continued to fight against the judgment, insisting on more tests and more experts, he'd started thinking about a future when he would no longer exist.

And that was when he'd remembered his son.

Bardath thought of his son now. Jason was somewhere on the planet below. The boy had turned six two months ago, he knew, though he'd had to have one of his aides look up the boy's birth date.

There was so little he knew about the boy, and most of that had been gathered by his agents since they'd found him a month ago. He couldn't remember anything about the babe who'd lived in his house for over a year. All Bardath could recall was his anger when Triana had announced her pregnancy and the annoyance she'd caused him by being ill and unavailable when he'd needed a hostess or a companion for official functions. What value was there is possessing a woman as beautiful and desirable as Triana if she was fat and unable to leave her room? He hadn't been present for the birth and he'd given orders that the child was to be kept from his sight at all times. He'd actually been relieved when Jason and the little girl—what was her name?—had been taken away by that thieving older sister of theirs.

At the thought of the sister, Bardath growled, deep in his throat.

He'd never liked Dayra. She was too proud, too independent, too plain. She'd made her dislike of him abundantly clear and had defied him more than once. Not openly. The witch never did anything so blatantly unacceptable as fight or scream or insult him. It would have been easier to deal with her if she had. No, she had simply ignored him and done as she'd pleased, regardless of his wishes or dictates.

When she disappeared after Triana's death, he'd been torn between fury at her theft and relief that

169

she'd saved him the effort of getting rid of them. The fury had won out, but his early efforts to trace her had drawn a blank and he'd been diverted by other, more important concerns. Yet even as he'd temporarily suspended the search for her, he'd taken great satisfaction from knowing that he would find her one day. Revenge was always sweeter when his quarry thought he was safe and became complacent.

It had been ridiculously easy to find her this time. Now that she was an upright, tax-paying citizen, she'd been in the Combine's tax records. As simple as that.

Retrieving the boy had been more difficult, but Bardath had every confidence that Capt. Truva would provide the help he needed. As head of the Combine Security Police, he'd found that few refused his requests, and never for long.

When the communications link on his desk chimed to indicate an incoming call, Bardath smiled. With the captain's help, things should go more smoothly now. And once he had the boy. . . .

Trevag was as unprepossessing as Coll had expected, its buildings constructed of the same kind of native stone that had been used on Dayra's holding. Everything seemed made of stone or glass or the pressed grass used for just about everything else. The only exceptions were an odd door or two formed from wood or plasteel—symbols, no doubt, of the relative wealth of the buildings' owners. Even the broad streets were paved with crushed and compacted stone. Every so often Coll caught a brief flash of white light as the sun struck a bit of embedded crystal or mica, but there was little else except the grass in vacant lots to break the universal gray of Trevag.

Jason and Jeanella, to their obvious disappointment, were left in the safekeeping of a plump shopkeeper whose three children of varying sizes happily welcomed the addition of two playmates. As Coll watched the two of them follow their hosts, he was conscious of a numbing feeling of loss. He'd miss them. He'd even miss their incessant chatter.

There had been far too many good-byes in his life, he thought, resolutely turning away so he couldn't see Jason and Jeanella's mournful faces staring out at him from a first floor window.

A boy of perhaps 17 was delegated to carry in the sacks of produce that Johnny had set on top, specifically for this first delivery. The proprietress herself, whom Dayra addressed as Dame Mikella, didn't try to hide her curiosity over Coll's presence, but she asked no questions even after Dayra shared the story they had all agreed on that would most closely match the tales told Capt. Truva and still explain his presence in Trevag.

At the end of the recital, Mikella crossed her hands over her rounded stomach and studied Coll. "I don't blame you for wanting a little more lively place than a holding, but there's precious little work to be had here, and that's a fact."

Coll couldn't place her accent, with its long vowels and odd cadence, but a colony world

171

like Far Star attracted people from throughout the Combine. Among a thousand or so inhabited planets, it was easy to lose an accent or two.

"You might try old Sp'chula Brovas," Mikella added. "He's Andorian and as cautious with his credits as they come, but he's fair and his place is clean and well kept, for all he services the mines."

Coll murmured his thanks and said he would start looking after he'd helped Dayra unload the flitter and set up her stall in the market.

At the mention of the market, Dame Mikella glanced quickly at the passersby, then stepped closer and lowered her voice. "Watch yourselves in the market," she warned, looking directly at Johnny. "Capt. Truva's troops have been patrolling it pretty carefully lately. Rumor has it she suspects some of the settlers, and especially some of the miners, of talking treason. They haven't taken anyone for questioning yet, but you never know when they might start."

To all appearances, Johnny couldn't have had less interest in the warning. He was intent on digging out some nonexistent trace of dirt from under his nails and managing to look bored and anxious to get going, all at the same time.

Dayra, however, scowled. "Fools," she said, in a voice as carefully controlled as the shopkeeper's. "They'll stir up trouble to no good purpose and make it harder for us to make a living than ever."

"Indeed," the good Dame agreed. The arch of her eyebrow carried a far different message, one that was aimed directly at Johnny.

As though Dame Mikella's warning had triggered another concern, Dayra added anxiously, "Please keep a close eye on the children, Mikella. I don't trust Jason not to get into trouble and who knows what might happen if the soldiers are about."

"No need to worry. They won't go anywhere. Not that there's much trouble they can get into, in any case," Mikella added with satisfaction. "One of the advantages of being so poor and so far out is that Far Star doesn't attract much of the riffraff."

Her pale gray eyes fixed unblinkingly on Coll at that, as though warning him not to step out of line or threaten the peace of the settlement.

They made two more quick stops to do business with other, less talkative shopkeepers. Then Johnny cautiously steered the clumsy flitter through the increasingly crowded streets that led to the central square and main market.

From the vantage of a flitter seat that was now his and his alone, Coll studied the scene around them, grateful for the distraction. He'd spent far too much time since they'd left the holding staring at the back of Dayra's head, watching her every move and trying to guess the expression on her face, which she kept carefully turned away from him.

He spotted a Graun loaded with a heavy, cloth-wrapped burden slogging through the crowd. The pedestrians and flitter drivers around him readily gave way—Graun were known for their size, immense strength, and short temper.

They weren't so considerate of a gaggle of Yyeera who were disrupting traffic by flitting from one side of the street to the other, then back again for no discernible reason. No one had ever figured out why the creatures always moved in groups, or why they were so prone to sudden stops and starts and changes of direction. The Yyeera themselves couldn't explain it and didn't think it was important, anyway. If the rest of the galaxy's inhabitants chose to act as individuals instead of a group, that was fine with the Yyeera. They just didn't see any reason to lower themselves to that level for so trivial a concern as the convenience of others.

Coll spotted Andorians, Sessians, Morlites—even a Targ. So far as Coll could tell, every sentient species in the Combine was represented in the streets of Trevag. Judging by their clothes and the burdens they carried, they engaged in all the common trades and crafts. The only thing he couldn't spot was any hint of real wealth.

He also spotted a good number of armed Combine soldiers patrolling the streets, alert yet unobtrusive, their drab gray-green uniforms easily blending into the gray around them.

The market was built to one side of the open square that served as the city center. From the looks of the stalls they passed, the merchandise for sale was either food or locally manufactured goods, such as ropes or crude furniture like Dayra's, which was made from the ubiquitous pressed grass. What little came from off-world consisted of simple items useful to poor settlers who lacked the resources needed to produce such tools themselves.

Johnny stopped behind a vacant stall that bore a small sign indicating the space was reserved in Dayra's name for the day. With Coll helping, they quickly had the flitter unloaded and the bags of fruit and vegetables stacked in an orderly array around the cramped stall. The more delicate items had been packed in boxes woven from some sort of coarse grass or reed, and these were placed to one side, where they could be easily inspected without being trampled.

Coll was arranging the last of the items when he turned around to find an armed soldier in a Combine uniform standing over him, a look of suspicious disapproval on his face.

With carefully studied nonchalance, Coll straightened up. He was getting old, he thought. Old and slow and maybe stupid and deaf, as well. He should have heard the soldier's approach, despite the din of the market. He straightened slowly, his hands relaxed at his sides. Behind him, he could sense Dayra's and Johnny's cautious appraisal of this unexpected visitor.

"I haven't seen you here before," the soldier said, his eyes narrowing as he studied Coll.

"I've never been here before."

"That so?"

Coll hooked a thumb at Dayra. "I've been working for Settler Smith out on her holding."

The soldier glanced at Dayra. "Settler," he said, nodding politely. He turned his attention back to Coll. "You don't look like a farmer to me."

175

"I'm not. That's why I'm here now." He returned the soldier's stare, casual, not too challenging, but enough to let the soldier know he couldn't be intimidated. The man was middle-aged, with the hardened edges of a veteran who had seen a great deal more than he'd ever bargained for. He wouldn't be easily intimidated, either.

"I find I don't much care for the life—or the work," Coll added. "You wouldn't happen to know of anyone who's hiring in Trevag, would you?"

The soldier's unblinking gaze moved from Coll to Dayra to Johnny and back again. "No," he said at last, "I don't know of anyone hiring."

He paused and stared at Coll's powerful frame. His expression clearly said that Coll's appearance alone was enough to make him suspicious. "Exactly what kind of work are you looking for?"

Coll shrugged. "Anything that pays decent. Except the mines, that is. I'm not fond of mining."

"What's your name, stranger?"

"Listen, soldier," Dayra interrupted, shoving Coll out of the way so she could confront their unwelcome visitor. "Coll may be looking for employment later, but right now he still works for me and you're keeping him from it. You want to pay his wages? If not, I'd appreciate it if you'd go bother some other honest farmer and let us get on with our work. Right now you're in the middle of my stall, so I can't get out and my customers can't get in, and that's not good for business."

Dayra's challenge struck the perfect balance

between aggression and the indignation appropriate to an honest citizen prevented from earning an honest credit. Lacking any good reason for remaining, the soldier backed out of the stall, but his parting glance at Coll conveyed an unmistakable warning—Coll would be watched until further notice.

As the soldier disappeared in the crowd, Dayra muttered an imprecation under her breath. Her emotion wasn't all anger at the soldier's unwelcome visit, however. Her hands tingled from her brief contact with Coll's broad back as she'd pushed him out of her way. After spending the entire morning trying not to glance at him or brush against him as they worked, she'd upset all her good intentions with one thoughtless gesture. The uncomfortable heat threading through her body warned her she'd suffer for that mistake.

Before she could move, the Andorian running the adjacent stall casually strolled over. "It has been some weeks since we had the honor of seeing you here, Settler Smith," he said, bowing courteously to Dayra.

"Hello, Sp'char," Dayra said, distracted. She brushed back a loose strand of hair as she warily scanned the market around them. How many other soldiers were out there watching?

Although she avoided glancing at Coll, she could sense his own wariness. How much of that wariness, she wondered with a brief surge of hope, was owed to his reaction to her touch? Or had he even noticed?

"You'd best be careful what you say . . . and to

whom," the Andorian said, following her gaze. "The soldiers are everywhere these days, it seems, and they have ears where you don't expect them."

His heavy-lidded eyes half closed as he, too, studied Dayra, then Coll. "They are especially watchful of settlers whose holdings are remote . . . and of men who look as if they've spent their lives fighting." His gaze shifted to Johnny as he added, "On the other hand, they are not such fools that they limit themselves only to the obvious."

Johnny, who had remained silent throughout, met the Andorian's direct look with one of his own. "I don't suppose they do."

"Has there been much of this kind of harassment lately, Sp'char?" Dayra asked, forcing herself to concentrate on the issue at hand. The soldier's questioning of Coll might be just chance, but since it came on top of Truva's and Neur's visits to the holding and the discovery that both Coll and Johnny were connected with the rebels in some way, it was just cause for worry. The last thing she needed now that Talman Bardath had found her was to deal with additional problems generated by the local authorities.

"Let us say the soldiers are not as prone to remain in the background as they once were," Sp'char replied with the typical discretion of his race. "And several people have been invited in for a . . . conversation with Capt. Truva. But you have a customer, I see, and I must tend to my own affairs. Take care, Settler Smith."

With that, the Andorian returned to his stall,

leaving Dayra to try to forget both soldiers and the disturbing presence of one Coll Larren so she could concentrate on the business at hand.

"You're going to get in trouble." Jeanella stretched out the middle of the word trouble while frowning at her brother in elder-sister irritation.

"No, we're not," Jason assured her, unfazed by her disapproval. He once more poked his head out the window to study his planned escape route. "We're at the back of the house. Nobody will see us. All we hafta do is climb along this roof here, jump down to the roof next door, then slide down that pipe. See?" he added, twisting around to glance at the wide-eyed boy who hovered behind him with the nervous air of an untried warrior about to enter his first battle. "Easy."

"I don't know, Jason," the boy said.

"Come on, Arl. You're not scared, are you?"

The boy shook his head doubtfully. "Mama's not gonna like it. And what'll your sister say?"

Jason glanced at Jeanella scornfully. "Her? Who cares?"

"No. Dayra."

The reply generated a tiny flicker of anxiety that Jason quickly repressed. "She won't find out, either."

"I'll go, Jason! I wanna go!" A tousle-haired girl perhaps a year younger than the two boys was jumping up and down in her eagerness to be included.

"You can come, Mikky, but only if you do as you're told," Jason warned her in his best big-boy tones.

"Shara!" Jeanella burst out. "Are you just going to sit there and not do anything to stop them?"

Shara, a tall, plump girl who already looked very much like her mother, was clearly bored by the whole thing. "What can I do? Complain to Mama? They're not going to get into trouble. Mama lets us go into the market whenever we want."

"I'll bet you don't climb out the window first."

Shara grinned. "I don't know. That part of it might be fun."

Jeanella would have argued further, but Jason had already disappeared through the window. His voice floated back into the room, vibrant with excitement. "Come on! It's easy. All you gotta do is watch where you're going!"

Mikky was out the window after him in a flash, followed, a little more hesitantly, by Arl. Jeanella thrust her head outside, torn between telling on Jason and her own eagerness to explore the market and streets of Trevag.

A quick glance at the route Jason had proposed eased her doubts about the climb. Since the buildings of Trevag were all flat roofed and made of stone, there were plenty of hand-holds and foot-holds and more than enough good places to land if they fell.

She pulled her head back in and turned to Shara, still uncertain.

"Oh, go on," the older girl said, giving her a

push. "We might as well have some fun, too."

Thus encouraged, Jeanella clambered out the window and set off after the three younger children, who were already on the ground and headed toward the market.

Chapter Nine

She didn't need anyone's help, Dayra assured herself for the hundredth time since Coll and Johnny had left, glaring at the five bags and three small piles of produce remaining in her stall. These past couple of hours since they'd finished unloading the flitter had been some of the longest hours of her life.

She'd had a constant stream of customers, which hadn't given her any chance to mope, and yet she'd been painfully conscious of the fact that there was no one in the stall to help her, no one to share the satisfaction of the good sales she'd made. She'd grown accustomed to Johnny's wry humor and his offhand way of convincing customers to buy items they'd originally had no intention of buying, Dayra realized. She would have liked to have grown accustomed to Coll's quirks, as well.

Frustrated, she shoved a sack of mellian root lying on the ground to the side out of her way. The worn bag split at the seam, spilling the raw, dirt-encrusted roots around her feet.

She just might have burst into some heavy-duty swearing at that, but her incipient tirade was cut short before it could begin by the arrival of a squat, officious Morlite dressed in the uniform of a Combine customs officer. His porcine eyes peered out from under his bony brow ridges with an expression of smug superiority, but his clumsy fumbling with the two hand comps and the sheaf of official documents he carried was more irritating than intimidating.

"Settler Smith?" he demanded, glancing at the document on top of his pile. Before Dayra could respond, he thumped his stubby forefinger on the paper and snapped, "Yes, of course you are. Says so right here."

He shuffled through the documents until he found the one he wanted, then pulled it out and handed it to Dayra, his eyes still fixed on his paperwork. "You have to fill this out before you leave. List all produce sold and the price at which it was sold. Estimate an average price per unit if you sold at different prices. Calculate total sales; then check the table for the appropriate tax. I'll be by later to collect both the form and the taxes."

He started to walk away, but stopped abruptly and added with a dyspeptic frown, "Just make sure it's all correct, will you? I've got too much work to do to check the math of every back-country farmer who passes through this market."

He really would have left then if Dayra hadn't broken out of her astonishment sufficiently to wave the paper he'd given her under his nonexistent nose. "Just what is this? I've never seen this form before and I've already paid my taxes. And who are you, anyway?"

The Morlite tucked his chin in so tight the leathery folds of skin around his neck spilled over his collar. "What do you mean, who am I? I am the official representative of the Combine Tax and Custom Office for Trevag, Far Star, in the Mergaine quadrant. *That*," he added with a sniff, "is the tax and production report form now required of all merchants, farmers, and other vendors of edible produce. You are required to document your sales for both tax and economic tracking purposes. If you have any questions, read the instructions on the back."

His lipless mouth pursed unpleasantly. "That's assuming, of course, that you can read."

Before an astounded Dayra could reply, he waddled away, already deeply immersed in deciphering the next document in his stack.

"I *am* sorry," the Andorian, Sp'char, said, emerging from his stall. He'd been following the interchange while industriously, and very discreetly, engaged in tidying his now-empty stall. "I deeply regret not having informed you of this additional . . . necessity. It was implemented when he arrived in Trevag about a week ago. Those of us who are here at the market every day have, lamentably, grown accustomed to it."

Dayra scarcely heard him because she was

184

angrily following the Morlite's progress through the crowded market, torn between the desire to confront the creature and the equally strong temptation to shred his report and return the tattered pieces to him, with her compliments. The sight of Jason, Jeanella, and Mikella's three children dodging around a trio of Graun ended the silent debate instantly.

Jeanella quickly discovered that being free to roam in the market with friends who knew the area well wasn't anything like visiting it when Dayra was there to keep a close eye on them. Mikella's children were familiar with a number of dingy shops and back alleys that were a far cry from anything she'd ever seen before—and far more fascinating.

It also didn't take Jeanella long to realize Dayra wouldn't approve of her exploring such places, but that only added to the thrill of discovery. She didn't even mind Shara's slight smile of superiority whenever she asked a question that revealed her ignorance or gawked at something the older girl took for granted.

Well, not very much, anyway.

Jason never even noticed Shara's reactions, and he probably wouldn't have cared if he had. He certainly wasn't wasting any energy worrying about the possibility that Dayra would disapprove of his unauthorized adventure because he followed eagerly wherever his friends led.

Jeanella was trying hard to emulate her brother's casual attitude when she came around the corner of a market booth and spotted their sister. Every trace of her hard-won nonchalance disappeared in a flash.

"Oh, no! There's Dayra!" she wailed. "We've got to get out of here before she sees us. Where's Jason? And Mikky and Arl?"

The three youngest, oblivious to both the possibility of discovery by Dayra and the curses of the merchants and customers they were disrupting, were engaged in a wild game of tag. Squealing and laughing, they dodged in and out of stalls lining a narrow side street that opened onto the central square, heedless of the confusion they left in their wake.

"Nyah, nyah, can't catch me!"

"Can, too!"

"Gotcha! Now *you're* it!"

So engrossed was he in the game, Jason didn't see the tall, thin man blocking the way.

Jeanella did. Abandoning her intentions of remaining unnoticed, she shouted at Jason to watch where he was going.

Too late. With a wild whoop, he charged right into the hands of the thin man.

Appalled, Jeanella watched, waiting for the inevitable disaster. It took a moment for the truth to register. Instead of being bowled over by her brother's unexpected assault, the thin man grabbed Jason with an ease that suggested he was ready for the boy, then swept him under his arm, kicking and wriggling, and set off running down the street, away from the market and any possible pursuers.

It was only when Jason began screaming for help that Jeanella panicked.

A moment after Dayra spotted the children, the three youngest headed down a narrow side street, engrossed in their game of tag. For a minute, Dayra wavered between irritation that they'd disobeyed and amusement that Jason, as always, was the leader in this small mutiny.

Then she saw the thin man and her heart stopped.

It couldn't be he. Not here. Not now, when his target was within such easy reach, oblivious to the threat he represented.

An instant later Dayra saw the thin man sweep Jason up in his arms and heard Jeanella's scream. She was running before she realized what she was doing, madly vaulting over whatever lay in her path or dodging the startled market goers who crowded the open areas between the stalls.

Dayra was almost across the market when she suddenly heard the fast, rhythmic slam of booted feet striking the pavement behind her. The thin man's accomplice, she thought, her heart lurching as she remembered that two men had tried to invade the holding two weeks earlier, not just one. Desperate, she pushed herself to run even faster.

It was no use. He caught her just at the entrance to the side street where Jason had disappeared.

Dayra cried out in fear and fury, blindly flailing at him as she tried to turn so she could claw his eyes out. It was several moments before his deep, insistent voice pierced the mists of her panic.

"Dayra. Dayra! Stop struggling! It's me, Coll."

Dayra gasped in relief. "Jason—" She twisted in his grip, just enough so she could see her anger and fear mirrored in his face.

"I know. I'll get Jason. You get the other children and make sure they're safe." He gave her a small shake. "Do you understand?"

Dayra nodded. "Hurry! He's only a little boy!"

He released her so abruptly she staggered. Even as she turned to look for Jeanella in the gathering crowd, she could see Coll racing down the street after Jason and the thin man, zigzagging his way through the startled pedestrians and gaping merchants, ruthlessly shoving them aside if he couldn't get through any other way. Then a sobbing Jeanella was in her arms, closely followed by three other frightened children, and Dayra had all she could do just to keep them from breaking into hysterics.

At the sight of her, several of the passersby and merchants from nearby stalls surrounded her with offers of help, while others gathered in excited clusters to discuss the shocking event. Distracted, frightened, and unsure whom she could trust, Dayra refused the various well-meant offers of assistance as best she could, pleading instead for someone to fetch soldiers to help Coll.

Although several helpful souls immediately set off to do her bidding, the soldiers who had been so visible throughout the morning seemed suddenly to have vanished. By the time they arrived, Coll was already forcing his way back through the crowd, a subdued, wide-eyed Jason perched on his shoulders.

The instant Coll had worked his way through the press of people surrounding her, he swung Jason off his shoulders and set him on his feet.

"Jason!" Caught between joyous laughter and tears of relief, Dayra scooped up her little brother and hugged him to her fiercely. "Are you all right?"

Jason nodded, then abruptly buried his face in Dayra's shoulder and burst into tears.

As fear gave way to relief, Dayra had to fight down the urge to scold. There would be time enough for lectures and warnings. Right now, Jason needed comforting, and all five children needed to be taken back to Mikella's. But there was the matter of Jason's kidnapper to be attended to first.

Still holding Jason, Dayra turned on the two soldiers who had been so dilatory in responding. "Well?" she demanded. "What are you doing just standing there? Why aren't you trying to find the man who did this?"

"We were waiting for you—" one began.

"Can you describe him to us?" the second one said, frowning. "We'll get him. We won't allow this sort of thing to happen here."

"He was tall—almost as tall as I am—and very thin," Coll said. "Dark brown hair, cut short. A hook nose. He's missing a front tooth."

With each additional bit of information, the look on the soldiers' faces changed from stern resolve, to uncertainty, to what Dayra could only describe as fear. Which was absurd. Strained by worry, her imagination must have gone into overdrive. What could armed soldiers who were official representatives of the Combine have to fear from a common criminal?

"Are you sure about that, Settler?" the second soldier asked Coll, covering his unease with a determined air of authority.

"He's got it right. That's what the man looked like!" shouted one of the merchants who had been most solicitous of Dayra.

"His name's Pulanc. Adthor Pulanc. I seen him around before," another merchant added. "He's always causin' problems. You had oughta done somethin' about him afore now, an' that's a fact!"

The sentiment brought an angry murmur of agreement that only made the soldiers more nervous.

"If you managed to get the boy," the second soldier asked Coll, "why didn't you grab this Pulanc fellow at the same time?"

"What kind of question is that?" Dayra indignantly demanded, ignoring Coll's restraining hand on her arm. "Why aren't *you* out trying to find him?"

"I didn't grab him because I thought it was more important to get the boy back to his sister first," Coll responded. "I expected you people to capture him later."

Dayra glanced up at Coll. To someone who didn't know him, he sounded calm, but there was a subtle note of restrained anger in his voice that would have warned a more knowing observer to be wary.

"You are going to catch him, aren't you?" Coll added. Even the bystanders caught the note of warning this time.

"Of course," snapped the soldier who seemed to have appointed himself the leader of the two. He hesitated, then added, "That is, assuming he really did try to take the boy."

"Assuming!" Dayra choked. "Of course he did. Ask anyone here!" She tightened her one-armed hold on Jason at the same time she drew Jeanella closer to her. The other three children clung to her skirts, too shaken by the angry dissension among the adults to say a word.

"Well, there's always the possibility you could have arranged the thing yourself."

"You think I *staged* my brother's kidnapping?" Dayra demanded, furious. She squeezed Jason so tightly he gave a little whimper of protest. "Why would I do that?"

"I don't know. We've never had a report of people trying to kidnap children before," the soldier insisted.

"You never—"

"Would someone please tell me the meaning of this commotion?" an angry voice from the far side of the crowd demanded. An instant later, two armed soldiers pushed through the mass of onlookers, closely followed by an irate Capt. Truva. At the sight of Jason and Dayra, she stopped short.

Her gaze flicked to the first two soldiers, who immediately stiffened to attention, then to Coll, then to Jason. "Don't tell me. The boy bit someone."

Dayra stiffened in outrage. Before she could say anything she'd later regret, she clamped her mouth shut and ground her teeth together.

Coll had himself under better control. "Perhaps you should ask your men here," he said, gesturing to the two soldiers who were still at attention. "We've just finished explaining the situation to them."

"Well?" Truva said, turning to the two. Her arched eyebrow was even more intimidating than her curt query.

Reluctantly, the two recited the facts, putting, Dayra noted, great emphasis on Pulanc's description.

"Indeed?" Truva studied the two for a moment, much to their discomfort. "Discuss the matter with the sergeant. She'll tell you what to do next," she said, indicating one of the two soldiers who had accompanied her into the crowd. "Then see what you can do about tracing this criminal. After all, we can't allow children to be kidnapped in the market, now, can we?"

The two gratefully retreated with the sergeant, leaving Truva with one escort who moved closer, his hand on his weapon as a warning to anyone in the crowd who might consider jostling the captain—or worse.

Truva ignored her guard. Her attention was fixed on Jason, but Dayra could read nothing of the woman's thoughts in either her expression or her stance.

"What's his name?" Truva demanded without taking her glittering black eyes off Jason.

Dayra told her.

"Jason. Jason, look at me."

Jason responded by wrapping his arms tighter around Dayra's neck and glowering at the captain.

"Did the man who tried to take you hurt you in any way, Jason?" Truva asked, studying the boy's features.

Jason considered the question carefully. "He grabbed me, so I kicked 'im."

The corner of the captain's mouth twitched.

"An' I bit 'im, too."

"I'm sure he deserved it." Truva's dark eyes stayed fixed on Jason, as though she were searching for something. After a moment she nodded. "There is a resemblance," she murmured.

Dayra frowned, uncertain of the captain's meaning. She didn't resemble Jason that much and—

Horrified, Dayra suddenly understood whom Truva meant. Jason resembled his father. The resemblance would be obvious to anyone who'd met Bardath and had somehow connected the two.

Yet why would Truva make the connection unless Bardath had told her? And he wouldn't do that unless he'd somehow managed to get—or coerce—Truva's cooperation in stealing Jason. Which would explain the soldiers' sudden unwillingness to pursue the thin man once they had his description.

Dayra clung to Jason as the world swayed around her. If Truva had joined the ranks of Bardath's minions, how could Dayra possibly protect Jason and Jeanella? Or herself, for that matter?

Truva's dry voice interrupted her whirling thoughts, bringing her back to more immediate, practical concerns.

"I imagine you're anxious to get these children out of the market," the captain said. "Although these are all not members of your family, surely?" She barely gave Dayra a chance to shake her head before she added, "If you feel you need assistance, an escort, perhaps?"

"No! No escort." Dayra abandoned her hold on Jeanella to wrap both arms around Jason.

"In that case, good day, Settler Smith, Settler Larren." With a polite nod of her head and a sharp glance at Coll, the captain turned and disappeared into the crowd, closely followed by her anxious guard.

The rest of the crowd, seeing there would be no more entertainment, slowly drifted back to their own affairs, leaving Dayra and Coll and the children standing alone at one side of the narrow street.

Dayra glanced at Coll, wondering if it was just her imagination, or if she really had heard an unspoken threat in the way Truva had pronounced his name.

If he had, it hadn't fazed him. His eyes were fixed on her, warm and dark with concern. A surge of gratitude threatened to swamp Dayra. Just seeing him standing there, so big and strong and sure of himself, was enough to comfort her. She didn't want to think about what might have happened to Jason if Coll hadn't been there to rescue him.

"I can't thank you enough. If you hadn't been here—"

"We'll worry about that later." He gently brushed the back of his hand across her cheek and the hard line of his mouth softened. Then his eyes dropped to the four children still clutching her skirt. "Right now, I think we need to get some children back to their home."

Squatting on his heels so he was at eye level with the two littlest ones, he said, "I'm impressed at how brave you've all been. What would you say if I gave you both a ride to Settler Smith's flitter and then we took you home?"

Arl merely chewed on the knuckles of one hand and nodded, but little Mikky immediately launched herself into Coll's arms and wrapped her arms around his neck, clearly grateful for someone who would hold her. With one child in either arm, Coll rose to his feet.

Dayra shifted Jason to a more comfortable position—she couldn't bear to let go of him just yet—and set off toward the flitter with Jeanella and Shara on either side of her and Coll right behind.

A frantic Mikella greeted them at her front door. When she saw that the children were shaken but unharmed, she shepherded everyone up the steps and into the big, comfortable kitchen at the back of the house.

Herb tea, sweets, and a great deal of motherly clucking soon soothed the children into relative calm. By the time Jason got to the point of deliberately tormenting Jeanella and she retaliated with a sharp put-down, Coll knew they'd be all right.

It was Dayra he was worried about. Her eyes were, if anything, even wider with shock than the children's had been, their ice-blue color so washed out they were almost translucent.

Not that he needed so clear a window into her soul to know what she was thinking—he could feel the jumble of painful emotions emanating from her in an almost visible wave. Fear, relief, doubt, self-recrimination, and worry. Most of all, worry.

He ached with the need to comfort and reassure her, but there was nothing he could say, no promises he could make that would relieve her mind, and he wouldn't patronize her with cheering words that she would easily recognize as lies.

Whatever it was that threatened her and her family would not be vanquished by words, but by actions. The trouble was, he didn't know enough to act, and the chances were good that he wouldn't be able to stay long enough to help her solve her problems, anyway.

After two years of anonymity, of trying to pass through life like a shadow on dark streets, invisible and forgotten, he was coming close to being exposed. Truva had given him warning, both at the holding and by her look in the market today, that she would be watching him. And now that Neur had identified him as the Sandman. . . .

One would drag him back into a fight he had already given up; the other would turn him over to enemies who had never forgiven him the victories that had come at their expense.

Coll's fingers tightened around the mug he held. He had no real choice but to keep on running from his past, but Dayra. . . .

She had moved to the far side of the room to discuss something with Mikella. The two women had their heads together and were arguing about something; he couldn't guess what.

What was she going to do now? he wondered, watching her. She couldn't stay here, not for long, anyway. Her crops would die without care. She couldn't go back to the holding alone. Dayra had been justified in throwing Johnny and him out, Coll knew, but it couldn't have come at a more dangerous time for her.

At that moment, Dayra and Mikella broke up their discussion in the corner. From the firm set of Dayra's chin, Coll suspected she had decided her next step. Whatever it was, Mikella clearly wasn't happy with it. With a loud sniff of disapproval, the good dame gathered the five children and bustled them out the door, saying she had to get back to the shop and *this* time she wasn't going to let the five of them out of her sight.

As soon as they were gone, Dayra crossed the room to Coll.

"I know I have no right to ask for your help," she said, head high, "but I will."

Coll leaned back in his chair with studied casualness. He'd almost agreed to her request automatically, but she was up to something—he was sure of it—and he suspected it was something he wasn't going to approve of.

"Will you stay here at Mikella's for a little while, just a few hours at most? I'm going out and I'd like to be sure they're safe."

Coll studied her, trying to glean a hint of what she intended. "That depends."

"On what?"

"On where you're going and what you're going to do."

Dayra went rigid. "That's none of your concern."

Coll leaned farther back and stretched his legs out in front of him. "Then neither is Jason's and Jeanella's safety."

Dayra opened her mouth to protest, then shut it just as quickly. After a moment's frustrated consideration, she tried again. "I'm going to the rebel meeting at the Wild Comet."

"You're what?" Coll brought his chair back to its proper position with a crash.

"I'm not joining them. I just want to hear what they have to say."

Coll felt a tiny jab of panic, right under his breast bone. He leaned forward and stretched his hand out to her. "Listen to me, Dayra. You do *not* want to get involved with the rebels."

"And you should know?" Her challenge was direct and unflinching.

Reluctantly, Coll nodded. "I know." He dropped his gaze to where her hands had knotted into fists at her side. "The risk is too great, Dayra," he added, even more reluctantly. "The rebels, whoever they are, don't have the resources to mount an effective rebellion on Far Star. By the time they do, the Combine will have a stranglehold on all of you."

"So they should wait until there's no chance at all?"

Coll's head snapped up. "Better that than dead!"

Slowly Dayra sank into the chair across from him. She clasped her hands on the table in front of her, her gaze fixed on them as if she might find the answers she sought pressed between her palms.

With a groan, Coll dropped back in his chair. She didn't want to join the rebels. He knew that. She didn't want to be part of the Combine, either. She just wanted to protect her family from the dangers that threatened them, and she was prepared to fight for their safety without asking for help from others because she didn't know any other way to do it.

"Are you really the Sandman?" she asked at last, very quietly.

"I was." He sighed. "I'm not anymore. I left the Rebel Alliance two years ago."

When she remained silent, he said softly, "I wasn't using you as a cover for rebel activity, Dayra." He hesitated, then added, "I don't think Johnny meant to hurt you, either. He—you and the children mean a lot to him, you know."

Dayra nodded, then brought her gaze up to meet his. Determination had set a glint in her eye and compressed her lips into a thin, hard line.

"I may not have a choice about joining the

rebels," she said at last, her voice flat and uninflected.

Coll frowned, uncertain of her meaning.

"I told you that the attack against me two weeks ago was because of money I owed someone, money I couldn't pay back." She waited until Coll nodded, then continued. "That wasn't quite the truth. I didn't borrow the money, I stole it, and the man I stole it from is Jason's father."

That made Coll sit up.

Dayra continued as if she hadn't noticed his surprise. "He's an important official in the Combine. I've never known what his role is, exactly, and never really cared, but his influence must be greater than I thought, because he's got Captain Truva and the local garrison working for him, too."

He must have made some small noise of disbelief, because Dayra's eyes flashed cold fire.

"It's true!" she insisted. "Today in the market, when those soldiers were trying to accuse me of staging Jason's kidnapping? They were going to help until they realized who they were supposed to be chasing. Then it suddenly became my little plot, rather than an attack on Jason. And when Capt. Truva studied Jason like that, then said she saw the resemblance, I knew she wasn't talking about Jason's resemblance to me."

"That's absurd! The Combine Armed Forces don't like other people telling them what to do and there are darn few people who could make them do it, anyway. And Truva doesn't strike me as the type to pay much attention even then. Who is this man who has so much influence? What's his name?"

"Talman Bardath. He—"

"Bardath!" Coll wondered for a minute if the room was wheeling around him or if his head was just spinning with shock. He suppressed a wild urge to break into mad laughter. And he'd been thinking Dayra might be overstating things!

"Do you know him?"

"I know *of* him. He's the head of Combine Security. If anyone can tell Truva what to do, it's Talman Bardath."

Dayra frowned. "What is Combine Security? I've never heard of it."

"Most people haven't. It's a small, secret group that was set up to protect the Combine against spies and revolutionaries. Its members, especially its leaders, do whatever they please, wherever and whenever they please, regardless of law or questions of right or wrong. All they have to do is claim it's in the interests of Combine security and no one can question their actions."

Coll jumped to his feet and began pacing, shaken by Dayra's shattering information. Talman Bardath was Jason's father! He stopped abruptly and dragged his hand through his hair, trying to make sense of it all. At last he swung back and dropped into the chair facing Dayra.

"You're sure Bardath is Jason's father?"

"Of course, I'm sure! I wouldn't say so if it weren't true. Besides, I lived in his house for over four years. My mother—and Jason's—was his official companion."

"So you're not even Jason's full sister? You're only a half sister?"

"That's right, but what has that got to do—"

"Dayra, if Talman Bardath really is Jason's father, why is he trying to steal Jason back? Why doesn't he just take the boy openly? There isn't a planet in the Combine where he wouldn't be granted custody."

Dayra bit her lip, then took a deep, steadying breath. "I've thought about that. Almost as much as I've thought about why he would want Jason in the first place, because he never cared about him. Talman was furious with my mother for getting pregnant. He wasn't there when Jason was born and he never filed for legal recognition of paternity. I don't know if he ever even *saw* Jason."

"Then why—"

"Maybe he doesn't want anyone to know he has a son. Or maybe he doesn't want any publicity about what he's doing. I think it's to get revenge on me. He never liked me—he hated me, in fact. It must have made him furious when I stole his money." Her eyes widened suddenly. "I'm not a thief, you know! Not really! I took that money because I needed it to get away and start a new life for us."

She drooped suddenly and Coll had to force himself to remain in his seat. He wanted so badly to take her in his arms, to comfort her and tell her that everything would be all right, but he couldn't. Dayra didn't need lies right now, no matter how comforting they might be.

"I thought we'd be safe. I didn't think he'd ever

202

find us here." Dayra's eyes as they looked into Coll's were bleak and shadowed by the fear that must have been her daily companion ever since she'd fled with her brother and sister and her stolen money.

"Dayra, have you—" Coll stopped. He didn't want to ask his question, but he had to. "Have you ever thought about just letting Bardath have Jason? If he's the boy's father—"

Dayra jerked upright in her chair and her eyes suddenly flashed fire. "Never! I wouldn't let that man have a flea-ridden Borag pig, let alone Jason!"

"But why?"

"Why? You tell me he's the head of a ruthless organization that has no respect for right or wrong, and then you can ask me why?"

This time it was Dayra who jumped to her feet and began pacing.

"He's cruel—that's why," she said. "He likes to control people. When he can't control them, he destroys them. That's why he always hated me. He couldn't control me and he couldn't break me, no matter how hard he tried. The man's incapable of love or kindness or gentleness. How could I turn any child over to a man who can't be kind? I *won't* give him Jason!"

Coll said nothing. For a long while he just sat staring at Dayra, at her hair, which had once more worked free of its restraints, at her breasts as they rose and fell with each agitated breath, at the proud tilt of her head and the defiant tension in her slender body.

Here was a woman who worked a field with

hand tools because she could not afford either hired help or better equipment. A woman who regularly climbed up and down steep cliffs, despite her fear of heights, so she could fish for her family. Her beautifully shaped hands were scraped and callused from constant manual labor. She was dressed in a simple shift made of cheap fabric and she wore crude sandals instead of shoes, even though she must once have been accustomed to much finer things.

Despite all that, she had dared pit her wits and courage against a ruthless man with the vast resources of the Combine at his disposal. Not for wealth or principle or the desire for power, but for the sake of a little boy and a young girl who loved her.

When considered rationally, her struggle against Talman Bardath was doomed from the start. Yet when compared to all the years he'd spent fighting for abstract concepts like freedom and justice, Dayra's willingness to risk everything for the people she loved seemed eminently rational.

What had Johnny said to him that first day? That he would come back into the fight when he found something he could believe in? Coll knew he hadn't found that something yet, but Dayra had, and for now, perhaps that was enough. It would feel good to once more fight for something that mattered, even if it mattered to someone else.

Slowly, Coll rose to his feet. "Tell Mikella to be sure the doors are locked," he said. "I'm going to the meeting with you."

Chapter Ten

They reached the now-deserted market area before Dayra could finally get up the courage to question his sudden change.

"Why are you doing this?" she demanded, pulling Coll to a halt in front of a row of empty stalls. "Why are you coming with me?"

Beside her, a faded scrap of pink cloth caught on a stall divider fluttered in the wind, the only trace of life among the bare racks and mounded debris that were all that remained of the morning's frenetic bustle. The grimness of the scene reinforced the starkness of her thoughts, but Dayra refused to give in to the despair that had threatened to overwhelm her ever since Coll had revealed the extent of Talman Bardath's powers.

For the first time since leaving Mikella's, Coll met her questioning gaze directly, but Dayra found it was impossible to interpret the emotions hidden behind his dark eyes.

"I want to show you that joining the rebels won't help. Once you see that, then we'll think of some other plan, some way to divert Bardath and protect Jason."

Dayra's first thought was a protest that Coll should automatically assume he knew what was best for her. But then the significance of the single word "we" hit her and she gasped, stunned by the possibility that she might not have to wage her war against Bardath by herself.

She stared at Coll, unsure she had heard him right.

His attention had turned from her as he scanned the abandoned market around them. Although he appeared relaxed, almost bored, Dayra could sense an underlying current of tension vibrating through his big body as he searched for any hidden danger that might threaten them.

The setting sun had caught him in profile, outlining his hard features, highlighting the line of his jaw and the powerful arch of his throat.

Without bidding, the memory of Coll in the moonlight the night before rushed through her, threatening to drown her in a flood of sensation. She had fought against those sensations there on the wall and she'd lost, giving in to a temptation she'd never known before when she'd bent to kiss him as he knelt at her feet. Even now her mind could conjure the image of him, so powerful, yet so silent and dark in the silver light.

He'd looked up at her as she'd moved closer and

she'd seen the way the moonlight traced his features, just as the sunlight did now. Her nearness had forced him to tilt his head back even farther, until the brightest moon reflected in the black of his eyes like a light shining through the darkness she sensed within him.

She remembered the heat of him against her belly and thighs, the sudden fire that ignited deep inside her when he'd pressed his hand on her hip—for balance, she knew, and yet that simple touch had thrown her whole world off kilter. In an instant all her strength, all her good sense and self-control had evaporated in the heat flaring between them and she had bent and placed her hands on his shoulders and she had kissed him.

She'd never kissed a man before. That first tentative brush of her lips against his had set her heart racing and her blood pounding, but it hadn't prepared her for the aching hunger, the overwhelming need that had exploded inside her when he drew her into his arms and kissed her in return.

But last night had been a moment torn out of time, a moment that would not come again. Dayra knew that. The man beside her, who had so easily roused something in her that she'd never known existed, had his own demons to fight, his own future to find. Yet for now, he had said he would stand with her, help her in her struggle against Bardath, and with that, she would be content. With Coll beside her, she would not be alone.

Suddenly the market around her didn't look so empty and the fluttering pink rag seemed oddly festive instead of bedraggled. Even the trash left behind from the morning offered a promise of the human activity that would transform the area come tomorrow.

"Dayra?"

Coll's puzzled query broke into Dayra's thoughts, reminding her of the present and the challenges that lay ahead.

"Let's collect your flitter and whatever's left in the stall," he said, taking her arm. "I've got a plan."

"Damn!"

Dayra jumped at Coll's sudden expletive.

He was staring out the flitter's windscreen at one of the side streets of Trevag, a street filled with miners on leave, farmers, laborers, and no few members of the city's less desirable social elements. It was three blocks from the Wild Comet, the tavern where Neur had said the rebels were to meet.

Coll had brought them here by a convoluted route that had included stops at half-a-dozen stores, where Dayra sold her few remaining bags of produce and tried to drum up business for her next trip.

The process of going from store to store was not only profitable, but, according to Coll, a good way of hiding their intentions from the watchful eyes of the Combine soldiers patrolling the streets. From the frustration visible in the set of his mouth, Dayra guessed that the ploy had not been as successful as he'd hoped.

"This is the third time I've spotted that soldier," he said, indicating, with a slight nod of his head, an Andorian in the familiar uniform of the Combine farther up the street.

"Maybe this is where he's supposed to be. And surely we've spent enough time on legitimate business so that no one will wonder if we stop in the Comet for a meal," Dayra protested, tired of the delays. Even the mention of food had started her stomach growling.

"It's statements like that which prove you don't have any business working with rebels," Coll said without glancing at her. "For one thing, regular patrols don't follow the erratic course we have. There's no way we should have run into him this often, so we have to assume he's been detailed to keep an eye on us. For another, after Truva's visit to your holding, the Combine will wonder about anything you do, let alone if you do it anyplace where suspected rebels might meet."

"I didn't say I was going to work with the rebels," Dayra snapped, irritated. "But if I did, I'm sure I could learn to take care of myself, thank you."

"Not fast enough." Coll shifted in his seat until he was facing her. "For instance, you've been to Trevag before, I haven't, so I presume you know the city better than I do."

Dayra nodded, unsure where he was headed.

"We've just spent the last hour or so cruising the streets that surround the Wild Comet. If that soldier"—he indicated the Andorian with a tilt of his head—"tried to arrest us right now, do you know which of these buildings have back

209

entrances on alleyways that we might be able to escape through? Do you know where those alleys lead? And can you tell me which streets were most heavily patrolled and which weren't?"

Dayra's mouth dropped. "How would I know those sorts of things?"

"You'd know because you'd have been looking for the answers all the time we've been driving around from shop to shop. You'd know them because it might be a matter of life or death if you didn't."

When Dayra didn't respond, Coll said softly, "Don't worry about it, Dayra. I hope you never have to learn to think of things like that. Right now, though, trust me when I say we don't want to stop in the Comet for a meal. We'll get there," he added as she started to protest once more, "but we're not just going to stroll in while that Andorian is watching us."

At the moment, the Andorian in question was slouched against a building and staring at not much of anything, so far as Dayra could tell, but she was no longer inclined to argue. "So what *are* we going to do?"

Coll leaned closer. For a wild moment Dayra thought he might be about to kiss her, but his attention was on the soldier, not on her. "Do you still have those credits you were going to pay me?"

"The credits? Sure. Why?"

"I want them." Coll held out a hand, but this time his attention was completely focused on her.

Dayra couldn't help blinking. He was so *close.* Forcing down the thought, she dug into the small pouch sewn to the inside of her belt and pulled out several bills of credit. "What are you going to use them for?"

"I'm going to rent us a room for a few hours in that inn that's halfway down the next block. I'd pay for it myself, but I don't have enough credits even for that," he admitted a little sheepishly.

He took the credits and stashed them in his pocket, then sat back in his seat, but Dayra wasn't about to let him off that easily.

"Who rents rooms for a few hours?" she demanded. "And how is that going to get us in to the Comet?"

This time it was Coll's turn to blink. "You haven't heard of . . . ."

Her blank look must have convinced him she hadn't, because he said uncomfortably, "Uh, people rent rooms by the hour for . . . um . . . entertainment purposes, shall we say? If you and I check in to that inn, looking as if all we're interested in is a little entertainment, our friend over there is going to lose interest in us. At least, I hope he will, and I hope he won't be poking around the alley in back when we crawl out the window—"

"And head to the Wild Comet!" Dayra finished in triumph. An instant later, she flushed as the implications of Coll's plan finally filtered into her brain.

"It won't be hard," Coll assured her as he prepared to climb out of the flitter. "Just follow my lead . . . and keep your eyes open."

Dayra joined him on the street and immediately stiffened as Coll casually wrapped his arm around her and drew her close. He'd tucked her against his side so her breast pressed against his ribs and her thighs against the hard length of his. He smelled of sun and the dirt from the bags of produce he'd carried and, beneath that, of clean sweat and some totally masculine essence that made her dizzy. The heat of his body against hers was enough to addle her senses. It compounded her discomfort by tempting her to think of the fire a simple kiss had ignited between them the night before.

Crazy thoughts, and totally inappropriate for the moment, but Dayra found she couldn't think rationally when she was this close to him.

"Relax," Coll whispered in her ear, bending down so his lips brushed against her hair. "Pretend you're enjoying this or I'll make sure you never get to that rebel meeting."

Relax. Easy for him to say, perhaps, but Dayra sensed a tension within him that almost matched her own in intensity. The difference, she supposed, was that his tension came from the excitement of the hunt, hers from his tormenting nearness.

Nonetheless, she fell into step as he led her across the street and along the line of drab, single-story buildings that housed a variety of small shops. They moved slowly, like two people savoring each other's presence, oblivious to anyone else on the street.

In her case, at least, that was almost true, Dayra thought, struggling against the emotions and sensations tumbling through her. Almost true, but not quite. In the back of her mind, like a dark cloud threatening a storm, a presentiment of danger cast its shadow across her thoughts, chilling her in spite of the sexual heat Coll's proximity roused in her.

Three buildings short of the one they sought, Coll stopped abruptly and swung Dayra around into his arms.

"What—" Before Dayra could complete her question, he bent his head to lightly brush a kiss across her lips.

"Across the street at the corner," he whispered against her mouth, so low she scarcely caught his words. "The Andorian I showed you. Do you see him?"

He dipped to claim another kiss, but even as he did, he turned so that Dayra caught a glimpse of the soldier casually standing on the corner watching them. Her gasp of surprise and shock was swallowed in the warmth of Coll's open mouth as he ran his tongue across her lower lip.

"You see?" His breath flowed across her dampened lips, hot and tantalizing, yet even that wasn't enough to deflect the icy stab of doubt that struck her.

"Don't worry," he added, planting a kiss on her cheek just before he pulled away.

Dazed with the combination of sexual arousal and uncertainty Coll had stirred within her, Dayra followed meekly when he led her into the shabby inn that was their goal. As Coll arranged for a room at the back—away from the street noise, he told the clerk, but with some fresh air—she kept her face half hidden against his chest, glad for the support of his arm, which he kept tightly wrapped around her shoulders.

His embrace served a second purpose—in spite of her embarrassment, she might otherwise have been tempted to look out the door to see if the Andorian had followed them. Even without any experience in skulking, Dayra knew she couldn't risk it. It was bad enough to know that Coll had been right when he'd said they were being watched, without compounding the problem by letting the Andorian know they'd spotted him.

The inn's central hallway was poorly lit and lined with doors on either side. Dayra tried not to think about what might be going on behind those doors, but with Coll holding her hand so tightly in his own, it was impossible not to.

"Here," Coll said at last, sliding the key card into the lock and pushing the door open. With practiced ease he once more drew Dayra into his arms for a mock kiss, then swept her into the room after him.

"No one in the hall?" Dayra asked breathlessly, gratefully pulling free of his grip on her. Was it her imagination, or did his fingers trail regretfully against the back of her hand as she stepped back?

Absurd notion. Coll was already scanning the small room, intent on his next move. Without answering, he locked the door behind them, then crossed the small space to part the shabby curtains covering a dusty window and peer out. Through the gap he made in the curtain, Dayra could see the grim stone wall of the building opposite, nothing more.

"Looks good," Coll said, tossing a reassuring grin at her. He unlocked the window and carefully eased it open, then once more checked for any sign they were being observed. Waving to her to join him, he cautiously eased his big body out through the open window and dropped to the street below.

Nervous, yet conscious of a prick of excitement, Dayra poked her head out the window to find Coll just below her.

"Pull the window shut before you jump," he said in a low enough voice that someone in a nearby room wouldn't hear them.

Awkwardly, Dayra edged out on the stone sill, then tugged the window shut and jumped. Coll caught her, his hands tight against her ribs just under her breasts. Instead of immediately putting her on her feet, however, he slowly eased her to the ground as though reluctant to release her.

Dayra had no doubts about her feelings on the subject. The instant her toes touched the rough stone pavement, she pulled out of his grip, shaken by the contact and by the indecipherable look in his eyes. "Now what?" she demanded, angered by the slight quaver in her voice.

"*Now* we go to the Wild Comet." If he'd heard the quaver, he gave no sign of it.

They hurried down the dark, narrow alley, moving side by side but without touching until they approached the cross street at the end, when Coll once more slowed their pace and drew her against him. After a quick visual check to make sure neither the Andorian nor anyone else was following them, they crossed the street into the alleyway beyond, which led them to the front door of the tavern they were seeking.

Dayra had never visited any tavern, let alone one as rough as the Wild Comet, so she was unprepared for the heavy reek of ale and close-packed bodies that assaulted them the moment they walked in. Unwilling to admit her inexperience, she struggled to keep her breathing as shallow as possible, so as not to choke on the dank air, but her strategy didn't work. Three meters in the door her eyes started watering and she burst out coughing.

A dozen of the tavern's customers turned to look at her, obviously startled by so odd a reaction to their environment. It was, Dayra thought grimly, probably the only thing that would startle them. She had never seen so rough a bunch of individuals in her life. There were representatives of just about every species in the Combine present, male, female, and the sexless *yuwaa* of the gaggle of Yyeera in the corner. Not one of them bore any resemblance to the stalwart landholders and merchants she knew.

At least, that was her first impression. A moment later she was startled to have one of the roughest looking of the tavern's customers approach her, then bow slightly and say, "Settler Smith? We hadn't expected you to come. Has Johnny McGregor come with you?"

It required a moment's careful study for Dayra to recognize the man. "Settler Megat?" she said, amazed.

Megat smiled slightly. "Neur thought we should make it a little more difficult for the Combine patrols to identify us later." His smile disappeared as quickly as it had come. "Will Johnny be following you soon?"

Dayra shrugged. "I don't know. I haven't seen him for several hours."

Behind her, Coll said, "When did you expect him, Settler Megat?"

"An hour ago. A half hour at the very least." Megat shook his head. "Nothing we can do about it, I suppose, but he should be here." His voice dropped lower. "This is our first big meeting, you know. To plan, talk about what to do. . . ." His voice drifted off as he turned to study the assembled customers.

"*This* is your meeting place? The common room, where anyone can walk in?" Coll demanded, too low for anyone but Dayra and Megat to hear him.

"No, of course not," Megat replied, turning his attention back to them. "Our meeting's in the cellar. You get there through that hallway and down the stairs. There's a guard at the bottom of the stairs to keep strangers out."

As they headed down the stuffy hall, Dayra heard Megat begin a bantering conversation with another of the Comet's customers that included more vulgarities than she'd heard the man use in the past five years.

Without speaking, Coll pushed past her at the end of the hallway. After a quick glance at the tavern's common room behind them, he started

217

down the stairs ahead of her.

Dayra eyed the dark, narrow passage with misgivings. She couldn't see beyond a few feet, for the stairs took an abrupt right turn and disappeared in the shadows beyond. Swallowing nervously, she squared her shoulders and started down, suddenly anxious not to be left too far behind.

The guard Megat had warned them about was blocking a door that was half hidden in the darkness at the bottom of the stairs. It took a minute for Dayra to recognize him in the dim light. Another neighbor, only marginally less disreputable-looking than Megat. At sight of Dayra, he stepped back, a worried frown on his face.

"We hadn't expected to see you here," the man said. He ignored Coll—which was difficult, considering Coll took up most of the small space. In the darkness, with only the dim light from the stairwell behind him, he must have appeared even more intimidating than usual.

"Neur told us about the meeting," Dayra replied.

The guard opened the door beside him and directed them down a second dark hallway to a door at the end. As they groped their way through the dark, Dayra could hear Coll cursing softly under his breath. Clearly he didn't approve of the arrangements the plotters had devised for their meeting.

The second door opened into a large, dimly lit room filled with an even more bewildering mix of individuals than occupied the common room upstairs. Dayra followed Coll as he pushed his way to a spot against the wall that gave them a clear view of the proceedings, yet left them in the shadows.

At the moment, a heavyset Morlite dressed in the coarse, protective jumper of a miner was engaged in a strident argument with Neur, who seemed to be presiding over the meeting.

At sight of the Morlite, Dayra was abruptly reminded of the tax form she'd thrown away when she'd spotted Jason and Jeanella. Since the form was probably mixed with the rest of the market garbage by now, all she could do was hope its absence wouldn't cause her more problems the next time she came into Trevag.

It took a few minutes before Dayra could sort out the disagreement, which had something to do with an attack against the Combine soldiers posted to guard the mines. The discussion rapidly degenerated into an argument over who was going to direct the activities of the miners, the miners themselves or some central authority.

"We won't follow you, Thelat Neur," the Morlite snarled. "There're two of us already disappeared on one of your little expeditions and nothing to show for any of it. You don't know the mines and you don't know the soldiers that guard 'em."

"You miners can't just act on your own!" Neur responded hotly. "There has to be some central authority, some leader, or we'll never succeed. How many months have we wasted already, arguing about what to do and who's going to do it, rather than just pushing these Combine soldiers off our world?"

"Maybe somebody else should take over!" someone from the crowd shouted. Dayra couldn't tell who.

"That's right! We need someone who knows what he's doing!" another added.

As the cries of dissatisfaction and demands for new leaders swelled, Neur became more and more angry, hotly rebutting the protests from the crowd. Finally, frustrated, he burst out, "Who do you want then? Koravia, maybe? Or Forak?" he cried, naming two of the more famous names among the Alliance leaders.

"Thas a good 'un, Neur!"

"Sure! Why not?" another demanded. "Better yet, why don't we ask the Alliance to send the Sandman?"

That suggestion met with enthusiastic approval. Suddenly a dozen speakers added to the clamor, all of them wanting the Sandman or somebody like him to lead their cause.

Dayra could feel Coll tense at the unexpected uproar, but no one looking at him would have guessed that he was the object of their interest. His features were frozen in stern lines that gave no hint of his thoughts.

"They've already sent a representative," Neur protested.

"An' Johnny's done a good job, but he isn't a leader and never said he was!" someone objected.

Neur made no effort to identify Coll as the Sandman. Dayra couldn't tell if that was because he didn't want to expose Coll, or because he didn't realize Coll was in the room. Whichever explanation was the right one, she was grateful. She didn't want Coll openly dragged into the rebellion. For her family's sake, as much as for his.

The next 20 minutes were spent arguing about who was to lead the rebellion. The discussion might have gone on forever if Neur hadn't abruptly given in to their demands and agreed to contact the Rebel Alliance to ask for more help.

With that out of the way, the assemblage settled to a discussion of tactics that quickly revealed a common goal but widely divergent views as to how to reach that goal. Several settlers and miners mentioned conflicts with the Combine troops that worried Dayra with their hints of violence and growing discord. Most, it seemed, merely wanted to be free of the oppressive restraints the Combine forced on their operations, including the taxes that seemed to be increasing with every new mandate from the central government.

One thing was clear, however—everyone there had come to Far Star with the dream of building a future for himself and his family, and every one of them saw those dreams being eroded by a government half a galaxy away whose leaders understood none of the problems or challenges facing settlers every day.

As Dayra followed the main discussions and listened to the scraps of subdued conversation near her, she began to see that she was not alone in her dreams or her frustrations. The only real difference between her and everyone else in the room was that she had chosen to stand alone, to fight her own battles and to deal with her losses as best she could. The others had opted to work together for their common good, despite their differences and their lack of experience in what it took to start a rebellion or build a stable government afterward.

They understood what they risked, she thought, studying the intent faces around her, and yet they chose to act, anyway, regardless of the danger. Some of the people gathered here she knew. They had families, just like her: They had businesses or shops or small holdings that they could lose, just like her. Yet they were here, not as passive observers, but as participants committed to a shared dream of gaining the freedom to shape their own futures in a way that suited them, not some government bureaucrats a thousand worlds away.

Eventually, when the discussion showed no signs of slacking, Coll nudged her elbow and pointed to the door through which they'd entered, indicating by his look that it was time to leave. Dayra wasn't prepared to argue with him. She was tired, hungry, and confused, and she had a headache. But she was curiously energized, as well, as if something of the plotters' determination had rubbed off on her, despite her silence.

As she slipped out the door, Dayra caught the beginnings of a new argument regarding communications between the rebels in Trevag and those in Far Star's only other city, the spaceport. She nodded to the neighbor who still sat guarding the door at the foot of the stairs, but evaded his questioning look by keeping her eyes on the narrow steps as she climbed.

Deep in thought, she would have marched out of the inn without thinking if Coll hadn't stopped her before they reached the common room.

"You can't leave looking like that," he said, pulling her close, then gently brushing an errant strand of hair away from her cheek.

"Like what?" Dayra frowned, caught halfway between her unaccustomed thoughts and the sudden warmth that rose in her at his touch.

"Like a settler who's just gone to her first rebel meeting," Coll whispered in her ear.

It was her imagination, of course, but for a moment Dayra could have sworn he'd meant to kiss her. She blinked, embarrassed and afraid her confusion showed on her face.

"That's better," he said, once more placing his arm around her shoulders and drawing her closer still. "We need to get back. And I'd just as soon not leave the children alone with Mikella for any longer than we have to."

At the reminder of her brother and sister, Dayra pushed the troubled thoughts the meeting had stirred out of her mind. There would be time enough to think about what she'd seen and heard. For now, she had other problems to face, other responsibilities.

But Coll had been right about one thing. Joining the rebels was not going to help her protect Jason. She was as sure of that as she was uncertain of just about everything else.

The sun had set and the streets around them were dark except for the lights from windows in the taverns and inns that dotted the area. Fortunately, there were still more than enough people on the streets so she and Coll didn't stand out. No one bothered them or seemed to note their passing as they slipped through the alleyways and back to the room Coll had rented.

As he lifted her up to open the window, Dayra was grateful for the dark. It hid the sudden flush that his touch and the thought of the room beyond brought to her cheeks. The minute she was through the window, she retreated to the other side of the tiny room so he would have space to move. Unfortunately, her actions brought her up against the narrow bed pushed against the far wall.

The contact made her flush deepen, but it also reminded her that they were supposed to have been here for the past two hours, indulging in a little entertainment, as Coll had put it.

Grateful for something useful to do that would distract her thoughts, she bent to explore the bed, fumbling at the cover and the coarse sheets until she found the head of the bed and the two sorry lumps of fiber that passed for pillows. With one yank, she pulled back the cover and top sheet, then tugged at the edge of the second sheet until it worked free.

It didn't take much effort. By the time Coll was in and had pulled the window shut behind him, the bed was as close to the tumbled mess they would have produced as she could make it.

No, that wouldn't be quite right. The sheets

needed to be wrinkled, not just disordered. Dayra bunched the cloth, trying to compress it with her hands, but it was too heavy. Without stopping to think, she turned and plopped down on top of the heap, then wiggled, just enough to twist everything into a snarl.

It was the wiggle that did it, so far as Coll was concerned.

He'd kept himself well in hand throughout the long afternoon, despite the growing turmoil in his pulses. And even if there were a half-dozen other methods he could have used to shake off that Andorian, it hadn't meant he'd let things get out of control when he'd chosen this disreputable inn for their escape route. Hadn't he managed to restrain himself when he'd claimed all those kisses under the pretext of studying the area around them?

He'd suffered through that interminable meeting for Dayra's sake. A part of him had been intent on following the meeting and her reaction to it. Another part of him, a far more basic, instinctual part of him, had been aware of nothing but the curve of her mouth and the arch of her throat and the tantalizing, soft lines of her body beneath the shift she wore.

He'd even managed to restrain himself when they were alone in the alleyway and her slender body was pressed close against his. Granted, *he* was the one who'd insisted it was safer to keep up the image of self-engrossed lovers, but the excuse was legitimate, and no one had ever said you couldn't enjoy your job when the opportunity presented itself.

Admittedly, wrapping his hands around Dayra's waist so he could lift her up, then having her fanny go right past his nose as she climbed in through the window, had tested the limits of his endurance. But her wiggling in the middle of those tumbled white sheets was just too much.

"*What* are you doing?" Coll demanded, his hands firmly planted on his hips so he wouldn't be so tempted to put them on her.

Dayra glanced up, startled. She'd been so engrossed in her efforts she'd almost forgotten Coll. He was standing in front of the bed, but all she could see of him was a dark shape that was far too close for comfort.

"I'm . . . I'm trying to make it look as if we were really here."

For a moment there was nothing but silence strung taut with the unspoken recognition of a possibility neither of them wanted to consider. Then Coll groaned.

It was a very quiet groan, but Dayra bridled at the implied insult. She jumped to her feet, grateful for the dark so she couldn't see his face—and he couldn't see hers.

"What's the matter?" she demanded, suddenly realizing that he was a great deal closer than she'd thought. She could feel him, feel the heat from his body in the cool night air, and that awareness was an uncomfortable reminder of the night before.

"Your efforts aren't really worth much, you know," he said. His voice sounded oddly strained.

"Why not?" Dayra snapped, trying to edge past him without bumping in to him. Too risky, she decided after she took a tentative half step forward and felt her arm brush against his sleeve. She stepped back, determined not to move until he did.

"It doesn't matter," Coll said, fighting against the heat roused by her inadvertent contact. What insanity had induced him to respond to her question? There was no way in space he could answer without making things worse.

"No, tell me. I want to know," she insisted.

"It's . . . um. Look, we can discuss this some other time—"

"Not some other time. *Now.*"

"It's the dampness," he finally admitted, goaded. "If we'd really been here, the sheets would have been damp with . . . with sweat and . . . there'd be the . . . the scent . . . of our lovemaking."

Coll gasped out the last like a man under torture. Just the thought of Dayra, her skin hot and slick. . . . He groaned again, and hastily retreated toward the door.

Dayra scarcely heeded his reaction. She was too busy trying to control her own. She'd always wondered. . . .

No, she most definitely was not going to let her mind wander off in *that* direction!

Coll was fumbling with the lock. Dayra couldn't see him clearly in the dark, but she could hear his uneven, rapid breathing—which wasn't so surprising. Her own breathing was just as unsteady.

The clerk didn't even look up when Coll dropped the key card in front of him. He simply verified their room number and their time, then went back to his perusal of whatever was showing on the miniature vid viewer in front of him.

Dayra didn't have a chance to feel grateful, for Coll immediately wrapped his arm around her shoulders and led her out into the night.

"Put your arm around my waist," he hissed into her ear. "Remember our friend from the Combine."

She'd forgotten the Andorian. As Dayra slid her arm around Coll's broad back—a move that brought her even more uncomfortably close to his body—she tried to discreetly look around for the soldier who had followed them two hours before.

Coll forestalled her move by grasping her chin and tilting her face up to his. Before she could protest, he covered her mouth with his in a kiss fueled by fire.

Senses reeling under the unexpected onslaught, Dayra willingly yielded to the demands of his mouth on hers, matching his hunger with her own surging need.

The kiss was no attempt to mislead an observer, no teasing distraction. It was brutal and raw and honest, an admission of the hungry longings they could neither deny nor allow to rule them for long.

When they finally broke apart, Dayra's head was spinning and her body aching with the desire coursing through her, yet she was the first to pull free.

As she slid from his arms, Coll straightened, then tilted his head back, eyes closed, fighting for breath and the self-control that had deserted him. Then his eyes opened and he straightened up, forcing back his shoulders as if throwing off a burden that had weighed him down.

His voice still ragged with his uneven breathing, he said, "I think we'd better go before we're arrested for indecent behavior in public places."

Dayra was already three steps ahead of him.

Chapter Eleven

As it turned out, the Andorian who had followed them was no longer on duty, but Coll quickly spotted the slender human female who had taken his place. Unlike her colleague, she trailed after them without any attempt to disguise her interest. As Coll started the flitter, she stood across the street and watched them, silent and unmoving.

Not that the Combine's soldiers were his greatest concern right now, Coll thought in frustration. For the moment, he had all he could do to keep from revealing just how much one kiss had affected him.

What madness had possessed him to once more volunteer his help? Admiration for Dayra's courage and determination didn't explain it. Neither did raw lust. And it wasn't a simple desire to assuage his loneliness that drew him to her, either.

He'd endured loneliness for years without doing anything foolish.

So why had he suddenly promised to help her find a way to protect her family when common sense told him the task was impossible, anyway? The closer he came to an answer, the less certain Coll was that he wanted to know it.

It was the sight of Johnny, sprawled on the steps to Mikella's house, that finally roused Coll from his uncomfortable musings. Dayra was out and running before he'd brought the flitter to a full stop. He was only a couple of seconds behind.

Dayra's worry immediately turned to disgust when she rolled Johnny over and caught the strong smell of cheap ale emanating from his clothes. Johnny was oblivious to both her touch and his uncomfortable position on the stone steps. His limbs flopped, his head rocked back, and his mouth fell open. After a couple of seconds, he gave a loud snort, then a choking gasp, and commenced snoring.

Coll knelt and quickly checked the old man's pulse, then bent to sniff at his lips.

"I forgot about him," Dayra admitted, clearly torn between anxiety and anger. "Even when Megat said they'd expected him to arrive earlier, I didn't really worry. I never dreamed he'd be so upset that he'd drink himself into a stupor."

"He didn't," Coll said grimly as he gently shifted Johnny's head until it was in a less awkward position and the old man stopped snoring.

"What do you mean?"

"Johnny doesn't drink. Never has. He was

drugged, then doused in ale to make you think he was drinking."

"Who—"

"Truva," Coll said, keeping his voice low so it wouldn't carry to any possible listeners. "She's the only one who has the power to authorize this sort of thing. Or your friend Bardath, if he's on Far Star. But I can't see how interrogating Johnny will help Bardath grab Jason—or you."

"Interrogation? You mean, about his involvement with the rebels?"

"That's right." Coll rocked back on his heels and looked up at her, crouched three steps above him. Even in the dim light he could see her eyes had grown round with shock.

"They won't get anything from Johnny," he said. "As an Alliance adviser, he's been—inoculated, I guess you could say—against most of the known truth drugs. He won't reveal any information except under torture. Not that it matters. The fact that they can't get any information out of him is all the proof Truva and her people will need that he's linked to the Alliance."

Coll stood abruptly. "In any case, we're wasting time standing here talking. I didn't spot any observers, but—"

At his mention of observers, Dayra anxiously checked the street for any sign of their presence, then jumped to her feet and dashed up the remaining steps to pound on the front door. By the time a startled Mikella opened it, Coll was already carrying Johnny around to the cargo area of the flitter.

"What in stars' name?" Mikella exclaimed, pushing past Dayra and clattering down the steps toward him.

"Just a little over-enthusiastic celebration," Coll lied. He gently laid Johnny down on the pile of clean, worn produce bags that Dayra had purchased that morning. "I guess he made it back to your house, but couldn't quite get up the stairs. He'll be all right tomorrow."

"I've never known Johnny to drink!" Mikella thrust her head and shoulders into the flitter, then just as quickly pulled them out again. "Phew! Well, that's plain enough! But still—"

"Well, the sooner we get him to bed, the better," Coll said firmly. "And that goes for Jason and Jeanella, too. Are they ready to go?"

Instead of accompanying her friend into the house, Dayra remained by the flitter while Coll made Johnny as comfortable as he could. Not that his friend would notice much in his present state, but he couldn't just dump him as if he were another sack of produce.

"Shouldn't we try to sneak the children out?" Dayra asked anxiously, watching him. "If someone sees them—"

Coll shook his head. "You don't want to get Mikella and her family involved. Besides, if we're being watched, whoever it is that's watching will guess what we we're up to pretty quickly, anyway."

He slid out of the cargo area and closed the hatch. "I'm more worried about all that open country between Trevag and your holding than

I am about anyone spying on us right now."

Dayra bit her lip. "Should we stay here instead of going back, then?"

Coll casually scanned the street. Less than an hour after sunset and everything was shuttered and dark. Only a few people were still out.

"Whether it's Capt. Truva's people or Bardath's who are after you, they can get you here in Trevag as well as elsewhere. At least at the holding you have strong walls and an alarm system. It won't be much, but it's better than nothing."

Small comfort, but it was the best he could offer.

Dayra didn't have time to think up anything more to worry about because Jason and Jeanella both came racing down the steps right then, glad to be free of Mikella's strict supervision and anxious to be on their way home.

Talman Bardath was not happy about being kept waiting, especially when the woman wasting his time was a mere garrison commander. His displeasure only exacerbated his scarcely controlled anger that this Capt. Truva had made no effort to take the boy into custody as he'd demanded.

Now Bardath paced the spartan room that served as Truva's office and headquarters, his thoughts churning. Time was growing short. He couldn't afford to be away from Edole and Combine operations for long—there were far too many who would take advantage of his absence to undermine his position and his influence.

It would have been easier and far more efficient

if he could have sent his regular operatives to grab the boy and destroy the sister, but that was out of the question. He couldn't risk adding to his vulnerability by letting his enemies know he had a son, and they would inevitably find out if he used his own people. It was bad enough that he should be reduced to asking this arrogant captain for help, but at least out here she was too far from anyone of influence to be able to hurt him.

Blame it on the Virisian fever, but he hadn't been prepared for the sudden changes that had swept several of his strongest supporters from the Combine several months ago. They'd been replaced by softheaded fools who argued in favor of reconciliation with the Rebel Alliance and a loosening of central government controls over all member planets.

Bardath had no doubt that while he was gone they were actively, if discreetly, campaigning against him among the other members of the Combine. He wouldn't put it past a couple of them to have the devious kind of mind required to undermine him within the Combine Security Police, as well.

He would, Bardath knew, eventually have to step down from control of the Police. But not yet. Not until he had ensured his safety and his son's future. He had to be sure no one could destroy what he had built before Jason was old enough and experienced enough to be able to protect it himself.

Right now, few knew of his illness and those few, including the doctors who had treated him, would not reveal that information to anyone. They'd be too afraid. He'd made very sure they had good reason to be afraid.

By the time he could no longer hide the truth, he planned to be safely beyond the reach of those who would destroy him, if they could. And Jason would be with him.

The sound of the door opening brought Bardath to an abrupt halt at the far side of the room. He turned to face the door, drawing his features into an expression of displeasure that usually served to send his underlings scurrying.

It had absolutely no effect on the woman who came through the door, then turned to carefully shut it behind her.

Truva acknowledged him with a polite nod as she crossed the room to her desk. "Domine Bardath. I trust you have not been waiting long?"

"I am not accustomed to waiting at all, Captain," Bardath said, his words dripping cold disapproval.

"No doubt. But that is on Edole. You are on Far Star now." She calmly took her seat behind the desk and gestured to one of the two straight-backed chairs in front. "Please sit down. Would you like something to drink, perhaps?"

"No, I would not!" Bardath snapped. He ignored the chairs. "What I want is an explanation of why your people failed to take the settler and the two children into custody as I ordered. My sources tell me they were here in Trevag today. Surely your people are capable of handling an unarmed woman and two small children."

"They are. They are also capable of following orders—*my* orders, Domine—and those orders were to keep the three under observation, nothing more."

Bardath couldn't stop a harsh curse. "What do you mean, ignoring my specific instructions to—"

"You forget yourself, Domine!" Truva snapped, eyes flashing. "On Far Star, *I* am in command, not you! Until you provide me just cause for arresting them, those three will enjoy the same rights as any other citizen of the Combine. I wouldn't even have ordered them watched if I hadn't been curious about why they were such a threat that the head of the Security Police himself should come this far to oversee their capture."

"I do not have to explain my orders to anyone, Captain, least of all you!" Bardath snarled. "The security of the Combine requires—"

"That's a convenient phrase that you and your kind have used far too often, Domine!" Truva eased back in her chair, her eyes unflinchingly fixed on Bardath's. "I can't help wonder why, if security is your main concern, you should choose to use the services of petty thieves and thugs. Such creatures do not contribute to the Combine's internal security and never have."

"What do you mean?" Bardath demanded, suddenly wary. He wasn't accustomed to such cold defiance, especially not from a woman with no more rank than this one possessed.

"I am referring to Adthor Pulanc, a common

criminal and a blight on society who tried to steal the boy from the market today. It makes me curious. Especially since the boy's sister is far too poor to make kidnapping him a lucrative proposition." Truva paused, then added, "Unless, that is, someone else paid Pulanc to do it."

Damn Pulanc! And damn the fool of an aide who had hired him in the first place.

"I don't know anything about this Pulanc," Bardath said, leaning threateningly over Truva's desk. "What I do know, Captain, is that you have failed to obey my orders. No one, especially not a lowly garrison commander like you, has the right to ignore an issue of Combine security. Your superiors will not be pleased, Captain. Not pleased at all."

He straightened, then stepped back from the desk, his features cast in an icy glare that never failed to intimidate.

At least, it had never failed in the past. Truva sat staring up at him, unmoved.

"And what will *your* superiors think," she asked in a cool voice, "when they learn you're here, Domine? Do you think they'll consider Settler Smith and her brother and sister much of a security threat? Do they even *know* that those three insignificant people exist?"

Bardath barely managed to force down the rage that threatened to choke him. Losing his temper now would simply give the captain more of an edge against him. But the minute he had what he wanted. . . .

Without another word, Bardath spun around

on his heel and stalked to the door. Just as he opened it, Truva spoke, her voice heavy with exaggerated politeness.

"I regret my people have not been able to install a separate communications link in your quarters, Domine. The Combine does not provide outposts like this with much in the way of equipment, you know." She smiled pleasantly. "But please feel free to use our existing communications center any time you like. Or you can always return to your ship."

Bardath didn't slam her office door behind him. He didn't bother to shut it, either.

The trip back to the holding had never seemed longer to Dayra. Her imagination insisted on conjuring monsters out of the dark, and only Coll's presence managed to keep those monsters safely on the other side of the cone of yellow light cast by the flitter's headlights.

Coll sat without speaking, intent on steering the flitter over the unfamiliar trail. The pale illumination from the flitter's instruments cast an eerie blue-green light over his face, giving him the appearance of a spirit from the ancient tales her mother had told her when Dayra was young.

But there was nothing insubstantial or mystical about the man. At first glance, he seemed immobile, yet Dayra was achingly conscious of his slightest movement and every tiny shift of his weight.

By mutual consent, they didn't discuss any of the day's events, even after Jason and Jeanella fell asleep. Their few faltering attempts at trivial conversation quickly dried up, leaving them nothing to talk about.

She knew so little about him, about his past, about his dreams and fears and failures. He'd told her almost nothing about himself beyond his name and his search for a way off Far Star. He hadn't even really admitted to being the legendary Sandman. "I was," he'd said. "I'm not anymore."

So what was he? *Who* was he?

And what was she going to do now that she'd fallen in love with him?

Without the weight of the produce to slow them down, they made good time back to the holding. They'd seen no one after leaving Trevag, but once they were safely inside the holding walls, Dayra couldn't help murmuring a small prayer of gratitude to whatever fates were guarding them.

Jeanella roused enough to walk to bed on her own, but Dayra had to carry Jason into the house while Coll took charge of Johnny.

"Sleep well," Coll said softly, holding the door open for Dayra. "And don't worry. I'll check the holding and the alarm system before I go to bed."

But even after she'd tucked Jason and Jeanella in, tended to the small tasks left from the morning, then drained the solar-heated water tanks of every drop so she could indulge in a soothing bath, Dayra couldn't sleep.

Pulling a short robe over her nakedness, she drifted to an open window to stand in the flood of moonlight pouring into her room, wondering if the cool light might soothe her where warm water had not.

The silver light had more power than she'd thought, for it inexorably drew her to kneel on the stone shelf beneath the open window, then lean out until she could see the holding spread out before her.

It wasn't the holding Dayra saw, or not the whole of it, anyway. Her gaze fixed on the small stone house where Coll slept, just as it had fixed on the house the night before, and the night before that, and every night since he'd come.

That first night, battered and exhausted as she was, it had been comforting to know he was there. But with each succeeding night, the comfort she took in his presence had lessened, to be replaced by a growing unease for which she could find no explanation.

Tonight, in the flitter, her heart had given her the explanation her mind would not.

She loved him. As simple as that.

Except it wasn't simple at all.

Last night she'd claimed a kiss without thinking. It had taken hours before the fire he'd stirred within her died down enough so she could sleep, but she'd felt safe because she knew he would be gone today.

Today. . . .

The events of the day were a jumble in her mind, overlaid with so many emotions that Dayra found it impossible to sort them out. Beneath it all was the confusing welter of emotions that centered on one quiet, dark-eyed man who had come into her life uninvited and who seemed destined to linger whether she wanted him to or not.

And that was the core of the problem. Did she want Coll to stay, or didn't she?

Quite aside from her own feelings, Dayra knew she needed his help right now—for Jason's sake, if for no other. The attempted kidnapping in the market had shown her that.

Some part of her resented her dependence and longed for Coll to be gone.

Another, deeper part of her longed for him to stay, and that frightened her far more even than the threat against Jason.

Dayra drew her head back in the window and sank down to sit on the shelf, back against the wall and knees drawn up tight against her chest. Her gaze fixed on the moonlight streaming in the window, tracing the patterns it wove over the rough stone floor of her chamber.

It was easy to discern the outlines of the individual stones tonight because the moonlight was concentrated and directed by the window opening. It had been more difficult last night when she and Coll had walked along the top of the holding wall, for then the conflicting shadows cast by the two moons had hidden sharp edges and treacherous hollows.

If only the moonlight could show her the emotional outlines within herself as clearly as it did the stones of the floor beneath her!

Frustrated, Dayra tore her gaze from the moonlit floor only to snag it on her bed. It was a big bed, one of the many pieces of crude furniture that had come with her purchase of the holding. In her first weeks here, she'd found it difficult to fall asleep because she'd felt lost and adrift in a bed that was so much larger than the narrow beds she'd always known. Gradually, however, she'd come to appreciate its size, for it came to seem a secure and comforting refuge while she slept.

Now, the sight of the bed only served to confuse her more, for it stirred up vivid memories of another bed in another room when Coll had been only inches from her and the dark had enclosed them like a womb.

A regrettable comparison, Dayra realized an instant later as a now familiar but no less disturbing heat began to coil through her body.

She jumped to her feet, fighting for control, but as her glance slid from the bed to the open window, Dayra knew she had to get out of the room, at least for a little while, until she could get her thoughts and her body's reactions under better control.

She'd catch up on her record keeping, she decided, cautiously feeling her way down the stairs in the dark. She hated record keeping, and always put it off until she could put it off no longer, so there would be more than enough to keep her occupied.

Yet once she stepped into the moon-drenched main room, Dayra knew she wouldn't be tormenting herself with any mundane responsibilities. Not tonight.

With its shabbiness hidden in the dark, the room before her was transformed, reminding Dayra of a garden room in Jea'nel Shanti's mansion that had been one of her favorite hideaways when she was a young girl. That room, too, had had a wall of windows that let the light stream in, just as this one did. Outside the room, a small garden had offered escape into the world of imagination for the lonely child she'd been. When she'd asked, Jea'nel, Jeanella's father, had given her the small garden to tend under the supervision of the estate's master gardener. Dayra had grown to love that garden, the one place in all the universe that was her own and where even her childish hands could create beauty.

Tugged by the strings of memory, Dayra crossed the room and opened the door. As gently as the light streaming in the windows, the cool night breeze slipped past her and into the room.

Last night she'd stepped through a door and found Coll waiting for her. Tonight, the main yard was empty.

Across the yard, on the far side of the holding, Dayra could see the faint outline of the steps they had climbed last night and the dark line of the wall itself, black against the softer blue black of the night sky. The sight alone was enough to make her breath catch in her throat and set her heart pounding.

Hugging her arms tight against her, Dayra closed her eyes and leaned back against the doorframe, fighting against the unwanted flare of physical sensation. Oblivious, the night flowed around her, tormenting her with its possibilities.

Why had she opened the door? she wondered.

What had she thought to find on the other side? The long-ago garden . . . or Coll?

Her eyes opened, but this time Dayra stared at the opposite side of the doorframe rather than let her gaze wander. She pressed against the frame behind her, grateful for its solid support, and hugged her arms even tighter about her.

The memories would be far safer than the man, she knew, yet her body betrayed her, claiming that which her mind refused to acknowledge.

If only life were as simple as it had seemed when she was a young girl tending her garden! If only she had the power to entrance that her mother had possessed! If only—

Life was full of "if onlys," Dayra thought, pushing away from the door and reluctantly stepping back into the room. Before she could turn to shut the door behind her, her glance fell on a small chest pushed against the wall.

Dayra had taken very few possessions with her when she'd fled Edole five years earlier, but most of what she'd kept was stored in the chest, tucked away in safekeeping for Jason and Jeanella when they grew older. Somewhere in the chest was the only thing she had kept for herself, a gown that she'd worn to a formal ball Triana had given in celebration of Jeanella's birth.

The ball had been Dayra's first. She'd been 15 and nervous, yet thrilled at being allowed to attend. With his usual generosity and understanding, Jea'nel Shanti had ordered a special gown for her, one appropriate to her age, yet so exquisitely made that Dayra had felt, for the first time in her life, as beautiful as all the beautiful ladies whirling around her as they danced.

The gown was near the bottom of the chest, carefully folded inside a protective cloth. Beside it, tucked into a corner of the chest, Dayra found the small jewel case that contained the only two pieces of her mother's jewelry she hadn't sold. She carefully lifted out the jewel case and the dress, still hidden in its protective wrapper, then closed the chest and laid them on top.

Ignoring the pendant for the moment, Dayra pulled the gown free of its wrapper, careful not to snag the delicate fabric with her work-roughened fingers. The gown was light gold—to match her hair, Jea'nel had told her—and cut so that one shoulder was left bare. The skirt barely reached midthigh, a length considered appropriate for a girl of 15 at her first ball. An embroidered band that looped beneath one breast and around her back completed the simple outfit.

Fingers trembling, Dayra stood and slipped off the light robe she was wearing, then pulled the golden dress over her head. It settled about her as lightly as a feather drifting on air. Since she'd reached her full growth at the age of 12, Dayra had expected the dress to fit, but it was looser than before. She hadn't realized how much weight she'd lost because of the work on the holding.

It didn't matter. The gown was designed to be loose and the band took in whatever extra there was. And who was going to see her, anyway? The only thing left of the ball besides the gown she now wore was a holographic image Jeanella had created using recordings from the ball that Triana kept.

At the thought of her sister's carefully crafted images, Dayra crossed to the holographic projector, then turned the projector on and rapidly scrolled through the list of available programs until she found the one she wanted.

For a moment, she thought she'd miscued the projector; then she realized that the program, instead of projecting a compact image in the center of the room as it did for most of Jeanella's programs, was slowly creating an elegant ball room with dimensions equal to the room around her. Another moment, and ghostly couples began filling the open space in front of her, whirling to music that was as magical as they were.

For a moment Dayra simply watched, too caught in the fantasy to move. Then she cued the projector to keep repeating the recorded images rather than shutting off abruptly, and she slowly walked back to the chest, where she'd left Triana's jewel case. As she moved, the projector compensated for her presence by making the ghostly dancers appear to dance out of her way, as though she might somehow shatter the illusion by her passing through it.

As Dayra bent to pick up the jewel case, the silk of her skirt fluttered about her legs as if stirred by an eddying breeze. The brush of fabric against her bare skin was surprisingly sensual, but Dayra ignored the unsettling sensation and instead opened the lid of the case.

Inside the case, cushioned in its bed of silk, lay

a pendant made of precious, silver-colored *shabar* in the form of an eight-point star. A huge cabo-chon *porfhyr* was set in the center. In regular light, the stone would glow a deep, rich purple. In the moonlight, it shone a lustrous black against its metal setting.

Simple earrings, also of *porfhyr,* completed the set. The set had been her mother's favorite, and for that reason Dayra had kept it even though there had been other jewels of greater value in Triana's collection.

On impulse, Dayra fastened the earrings on her ears, then lifted the pendant from its case and clasped the heavy chain around her neck. With the combined weight of metal and stone, the pendant lay heavy against her breast bone. She touched it gently, letting her fingers explore the smooth dome of the stone and the sculpted lines of the setting, feeling the metal grow warm from its contact with her skin.

As her hand wrapped around this remnant of the past, tears welled in Dayra's eyes and a sharp pain lodged in her throat. She blinked, fighting back the tears, then swallowed.

There would be no tears. Not tonight.

Tonight imagination ruled, and in her imaginary world there were no past regrets, no future fears. There was only the dance and the moonlight and the moment—nothing more.

With that resolve, Dayra tugged off the fastener that held her hair and tossed it on the chest with the empty jewel case and wrapper. She ran her fingers through her hair so it tumbled free down her back and over her shoulders, then spun in a circle, pivoting on the ball of one foot. The silken fabric of the gown and the even silkier strands of her hair brushed against her bare skin with tantalizing delicacy, teasing her senses.

Eyes closed and arms out, Dayra whirled into the throng of holographic dancers, swaying slightly to match the rhythm of the music. Enthralled by the intoxicating power of memory and imagination, Dayra was oblivious to everything except the music and the movements of her body until a turn of the dance whirled her into Coll Larren's outstretched arms.

Chapter Twelve

Before Dayra had a chance to overcome the shock of dancing from imagination into reality, Coll had swept her back into the dance.

Through the moonlight they went as he led her in the simple steps of a *gavanne*, around and around and around until Dayra's head spun with the dance and the dizzying sensual heat he roused within her. Somewhere at the very edge of her awareness Dayra sensed the ghostly couples still swirling around them, but their pale presence only served as counterpoint to the dark, vivid reality of the man who held her.

Coll was bare chested. The moonlight sculpted the hard lines of his arms and torso in exquisite detail as he turned, outlining each perfect curve of muscle in a shifting pattern of cool silver and intriguing shadow. His face remained shadowed, for his head was bent toward her, his eyes gleaming as they fixed on her face with an intensity that made Dayra's breath catch deep in her chest, where it pushed hard against her breastbone.

He held her loosely, but Dayra was achingly aware of the slightest shift of the powerful muscles of his thighs, the faint twist of his hips as he brought her around with him in the circling rhythm of the *gavanne.* His right hand cupped hers, his fingers curling until the tips brushed against the back of her hand. His left hand pressed against the small of her back as he guided her steps. Dayra could feel the curve of his palm and the strong lines of each of his fingers through the delicate fabric of her gown. Somewhere deep within her brain a part of her wondered that the heat of his touch had not yet set the cloth afire.

She would scarcely have noticed if it had, for her body burned with the fierce hunger flaring inside her. Dazed with the heat and his touch, Dayra swayed closer.

He drew a deep, unsteady breath as the tips of her breasts brushed his ribs and her thigh pressed against his. Then his grip on her tightened and Coll pulled her closer still, until their two bodies melded in a swaying, heated rhythm that threatened to deluge her already overloaded senses.

"Dayra," Coll whispered, bending down until his lips brushed against her hair. His arms tightened even more about her and he whirled her around the floor as if desperately fleeing the flames consuming them.

It did no good. The motion only brought them closer. With each step her leg rubbed against the inside of his leg and her belly pressed against his hip. Dayra could feel the hardness of his arousal even under the constraining tightness of his clothing.

With a groan, Coll brought them to an abrupt halt, then dipped his head in a kiss that was as ruthless as the plundering of a barbarian warrior. Willingly, Dayra yielded. Her mouth opened beneath his onslaught, welcoming his tongue, his heat, his hunger.

He withdrew, but only for an instant, when Dayra could see his dark eyes glittering above her. Then he bent and lifted her off her feet, his arms around her, crushing her body against his. Once again he claimed her mouth with his, only to abandon it a moment later to lavish a hundred kisses along her jaw and down her throat.

However mad surrender might be, Dayra surrendered. She arched her head back as he trailed more kisses along her throat, then wrapped her legs around his waist in wanton abandon, just as she'd once wrapped them around his waist when he'd carried her away from danger. Now he swept her into it and Dayra scarcely heeded.

Beneath her gown she was naked. The rough cloth of his trousers rubbed her woman's flesh, punishing against her tenderness yet unbelievably arousing. She could feel his own response straining against the barrier that divided them. Without thinking, without wondering whence came her understanding, Dayra squeezed the muscles of her buttocks and thighs, pulling her lower body even more tightly against his.

Coll gasped. Impossibly, his arms tightened around her even more, until they crushed the air from Dayra's lungs. His fingers dug into the muscles of her back as he desperately tried to hold on, to make them one.

Then he groaned again and roughly dragged her legs from around his waist and set her on his feet.

Dayra clung to him, fighting his withdrawal. "No!" she cried, tangling her fingers in his hair and dragging his head down to hers. "No!"

"This is madness!"

"I don't care." The words caught her by surprise, yet even as she uttered them, Dayra knew she spoke the truth. She *didn't* care. Hadn't she resolved, just moments before Coll found her, to take the moment and the magic, and leave the past and future to take care of themselves?

Even though she had to stand on her tiptoes to reach him, Dayra claimed Coll's mouth in a kiss that was as wild and demanding as those he'd showered on her a moment earlier. Around them, the holographic dancers continued their endless whirl, oblivious to the humans in their midst. Dayra scarcely noticed, too caught up in the hungry need driving her to care whether there were imaginary observers to her actions or not. All that mattered was the feel of Coll's lips on hers and the way her body responded to the nearness of his.

An eternity later Coll pulled back. His breathing

was ragged, and even in the silver light Dayra could see the mad pounding of the pulse in his throat.

Hesitantly he brought his hand up to brush back a disordered lock of her hair, then gently ran the tip of his finger across her swollen lips and down her throat. He lingered briefly in the small hollow at the base of her throat, tracing small, tormenting circles on her skin before tracking the line of her shoulder across to her gown, then following the edge of her gown as it slanted down across her breastbone and the curve of her breast to the soft flesh at her side.

Dayra froze, her eyes fixed on his, her every sense attuned to his slow, tormenting movement.

Coll slipped the tip of his finger beneath the silken fabric just under her arm, lifting it away from her skin by the tiniest fraction of an inch. "I think it must be your finery that drives you mad," he said shakily.

"Do you like it?" Dayra could feel the way the uneven rise and fall of her chest alternately tautened and loosened the fabric stretched across his fingertip, trapping him against her, then freeing him, ever so slightly. Even so slight a pressure was torment, yet exquisite pleasure, all at the same time.

"I think. . . ." Coll took an unsteady breath, then another, struggling for the control he was so near losing.

His gaze dropped from hers to fix on the small mound his fingertip made beneath the edge of her gown. Slowly, with infinite care, he dragged his finger back up the length of the bodice, but this time he tugged the fabric down as he went, gradually pulling it free of her breast.

As the bodice slid down across the top of her breast, Dayra stiffened, then gasped as the edge caught briefly on the hard peak of her nipple. His finger slid closer, dragging the fabric down so it scraped across that small, aching point of flesh, then rolled over the yielding softness beneath.

When the back of his finger brushed against the lower swell of her breast, Dayra had to fight against crying out, and even then a whimper escaped her as he traced the soft curve, his finger trapped between her warm flesh and the edge of fabric.

Heat flared in the wake of his tormenting touch. Dayra could sense the almost invisible sheen of sweat forming on the skin of her throat and breast and belly. The muscles in her lower abdomen contracted involuntarily, almost painfully, but not so tormentingly as the muscles deep inside her that squeezed tight, then tighter still, searching for a fulfillment that was not yet hers.

Coll stopped, his gaze fixed on the point of her breast. He released her gown, but only enough so that he could cup her breast in the palm of his hand before he bent his head and lightly flicked her nipple with the tip of her tongue.

Dayra could not stop the cry that burst from her, yet if some part of her pleaded for release, the rest exulted in the fiery thrill that swept through her at his caress.

Heedless, she arched her back, offering her

breast to him at the same time she laced her fingers through his hair, trapping him against her.

Coll took what she offered, then claimed more.

His hands clamped on the curve at each side of her waist, holding her as he bent her even farther back so that her hips pressed into him and her thigh was hard against his erection.

Even as he suckled and kissed and bit at her breast, his arm slid around her back, supporting her and freeing his other hand to roam over the curve of her hip, down the length of her thigh to the hem of her skirt, then up once more along the soft, warm flesh of her inner thigh.

He came close, so tantalizingly close to the center of her that ached for his touch. But just as Dayra thought he would surely claim her, he paused, then slowly trailed his hand back down the length of her thigh until he was free of the clinging folds of her skirt. She could feel the tremor in his fingers, the quivering of his taut body against hers as he struggled for control.

Without thinking, Dayra pressed herself even tighter against his groin, twisting so that she could feel the hard length of him move as her body rocked against his.

This time it was Coll's turn to cry out. With a swift exhalation of air that was half groan, half gasp, he straightened and abruptly pushed her from him. Yet he couldn't release her, not entirely. His hands were pressed tight against her ribs, just below her breasts. Dayra could feel them curve over the hard edge of his hands, shaping themselves to his touch even now.

She started to protest his desertion, but the words died before they could be spoken.

He wasn't abandoning her. She could see the hunger in him, raw and dark. But where another might have claimed what she freely offered, roughly and without apology, Coll would not.

Instead, he fought for breath. When he could speak at last, he bent so his lips were close to her ear and whispered, "You asked if I liked your gown."

Dayra could only nod, torn between the mesmerizing glitter of his dark eyes and the aching heat within her. His hands had slipped up over her breasts, enclosing them in the warm hollows of his palms and fingers. Even though one breast was bare and one was not, she could scarcely distinguish the difference for his touch seared her skin equally.

"It is a very beautiful gown," Coll whispered, "but I would prefer—" His words caught deep in his throat as, still pressing gently, he slowly slid his hands up over her breasts to her shoulders. The friction of his skin against hers tugged her breasts upward with his motion, making her nipples ache.

The fingers of his hand closed around the golden clasp that held the band of Dayra's gown at her shoulder. She knew it would only take a moment for Coll to open the clasp, releasing the band and leaving nothing except the delicate fabric of the gown as a barrier between them. He didn't move.

"I would prefer," he said again, very slowly and

in a voice rough with desire, "to dress you in moonlight."

Dayra scarcely felt Coll open the clasp, but when the band uncoiled from around her body, a choked, joyous laugh burst from her throat and she reached to remove her gown.

Coll was before her. With one swift, fluid motion, he tugged her loose gown over her head and tossed it toward the nearest chair. She didn't even bother to check if it had landed on the chair or on the floor.

Her gaze was fixed on his face, trying to find some hint of his thoughts. It was impossible, for she stood facing the windows, open to the moonlight while his back was to the light, hiding his face in shadows.

For an instant, Dayra regretted her ready acquiescence, but only for an instant. Coll's sudden, sharp intake of breath and the tense stillness of his body as he studied her told her all she needed to know.

He found her beautiful, and that was enough.

The moonlight had cast her in silver, Coll thought, caught between the wonder of the moment and the aching, hungry heat that had consumed him since he'd stepped through the open door and found Dayra circling in the dance, alone in the lambent light.

His eyes devoured her, tracing every delicate line, each soft curve of her slender body. Even that was not enough to ease the aching—nothing would, he knew, until he could bury himself in her sweet flesh—but it soothed, at least for now, some hunger within him that lay far deeper than mere physical need.

She was so beautiful! He could scarcely remember his first disparaging dismissal of her. Too thin, he'd thought; her features were too sharp. But that had been a lifetime ago.

Now he saw her in his dreams like this: her slender body clad in nothing more than silver and shadow and the silken, unbound mass of her hair.

Was he dreaming even now? Coll wondered. Was this all an illusion designed to torment him? Or did Dayra really stand before him, her body strung tight and tense with the same tormenting sensations as his?

Suddenly hesitant, wondering if he could trust his own senses, Coll reached out to touch the tip of her breast.

Dayra tensed, then breathed deep. Coll could see the muscles of her belly tighten involuntarily.

It was enough to shatter the last vestige of the self-control he'd fought for so long to maintain. Coll swept Dayra into his arms and, heedless of the imaginary throng around them, crossed the room to the dark stairs leading upward.

Even the few seconds needed to climb to Dayra's second-floor room were torment, but Coll laid her down on the bed gently, then slipped free of her arms just long enough to shed the few items of clothing he wore before stretching out beside her in the wide, soft bed.

Here the moonlight creeping through the narrow windows was a dim and fragile thing, scarcely touching the dark corners of the room. It didn't matter. Coll needed no light, for the minute he knelt on the edge of the bed, Dayra slipped her hands behind his neck and drew him down to her.

That she was innocent, Coll knew, though he wasn't sure *how* he knew. But that didn't matter, either, for Dayra's own hunger, coupled with some woman's instinct made her open eagerly to his touch. As his hand sought and found the hot, wet flesh between her legs, she arched into him with a cry of joy.

That small cry shattered Coll's restraint. If he'd wanted to, he could not have prolonged the wait.

He didn't want to, and neither did Dayra. With a groan, Coll plunged into her, claiming her with one swift thrust.

Her body welcomed his with only slight resistance. A tiny gasp, as though of pain, then Dayra was moving with him, learning the rhythm of his motion and slowly finding her own as they rocked together in an age-old dance that melded them into one joyous whole.

The night slipped away, but Dayra scarcely heeded its passing, for each succeeding moment offered too many riches for her to grasp the whole. Even falling asleep in Coll's arms at last had been a wonder to be savored.

Coll left her just before dawn, concerned that Jason and Jeanella might wake unexpectedly and find them tangled in each other's arms.

Alone in the tumbled sheets, Dayra curled into herself, already missing his warmth and the solid strength of his body. When sleep refused to return, she piled the pillows behind her back, waiting for morning to dawn.

The pillow beneath her head and the sheets tucked around her still carried Coll's scent, fainter now in the cool morning air. Her body ached in unexpected ways and places, yet at the same time she felt satiated and strangely . . . complete. Content, Dayra rubbed her cheek against the pillow, savoring the lingering male essence, then burrowed deeper into her small nest.

The morning light came slowly, tentatively creeping through the open window on the far side of the room. The first rays struck the wall directly opposite, gilding it. As the sun rose higher, the light grew stronger, brighter. It slid down the wall and across the floor toward her bed, slowly filling the room as it came.

The dawn must feel as she did, Dayra thought, uncertain about what lay ahead, yet too tempted by the wondrous possibilities not to venture farther into the day.

When at last the golden beams found her in her bed, Dayra abandoned both her fanciful thoughts and any attempt to fall back asleep. Instead, she rose to straighten the room and gather clean clothes before she took her shower. It was as she bent to fling back the bedcovers that Dayra spotted her mother's pendant and earrings lying on the small stand beside her bed.

At sight of them, she paused, caught by the sudden memory of Coll gently removing each piece in the night, his touch sure and exquisitely gentle.

She could not remember exactly when he had done so, only that it had followed a wild and deeply satisfying bout of lovemaking that had left them both panting and flushed with satisfied desire.

Dayra picked the pendant up, dangling it on its chain so it slowly spun first right, then left, then back again. The cabochon *porfhyr* caught the light as it turned, its color varying from a deep lavender to a brilliant, regal purple.

As she studied the shifting colors of the heavy stone, Dayra couldn't help smiling. All her life she'd longed for the kind of beauty that could wear a jewel like this. Yet Coll had preferred her dressed in moonlight.

It was, she thought, exactly the way she liked him best, as well.

The sudden, intense heat that flared inside her at the thought of Coll, naked, drove Dayra out of her room and down the stairs. As tempting as it might be indulge in such lascivious thoughts, the night was past and the day ahead brought too many worries with it for her to linger so.

Besides, she admitted, her steps growing slower the farther down the stairs she got, if she thought too long about what had passed between her and Coll last night, a hundred doubts and fears would creep in to join with the ones she already possessed. Last night she had accepted each moment as it came; somehow she would have to be strong enough to do the same today.

Fortunately, only her robe and gown, both neatly folded on a chair in the main room, suggested that anything unusual had occurred the night before.

Coll had obviously picked up her clothes, shut off the holographic projector, and closed the door behind him when he'd left.

Dayra returned the gown to its protective wrapper, but when she picked up the jewel case, she found she could not let go of the pendant so easily. It had been her mother's, and her mother had been beautiful. Somehow, for the first time in her life, Dayra felt she'd earned the right to wear a thing of such rare beauty, too.

Without stopping to question the wisdom of her decision, Dayra fastened the chain around her neck, tucking the pendant under the top of her shift so it lay hidden, warm and heavy against her skin. Then she buried the gown at the bottom of the chest and headed down the hall toward the house's one bath.

If she'd still been tempted to think about last night instead of the day ahead, the shower solved her problem. Since the sun hadn't been up long enough for the solar heaters to replace the hot water she'd used up the night before, Dayra stepped into a shower so ice-cold that the shock of the water against her skin drove the air out of her lungs.

By the time she finally stopped shivering enough to dress, Dayra could hear the sounds of Jason and Jeanella stirring groggily in their small rooms at the far side of the house. She would, she decided, check on Johnny first, then fix breakfast, then. . . .

She sighed. There were so many things that had to be done today, pressing work on the holding that had to be attended to, yet none of it would matter if she and Coll couldn't devise a plan to keep them safe and outwit Bardath.

Preoccupied with her worries, Dayra was half-way across the compound before she finally heard the dull thumping coming from the main gate. She hesitated, her muscles tensing as her mind generated a dozen horrible explanations for the presence of unexpected visitors at this time of the morning.

Imagination, however, wouldn't answer the question of who was out there demanding entry. Resolutely squaring her shoulders, Dayra headed toward the gate. Coll got there before her, just as whoever was on the other side of the gate started shouting and banging against the massive gate with enough force to shake it.

"Open up in there!" someone on the outside bellowed. "Official Combine business! Open up *now* or we'll break down your gate!"

Dayra started to protest when Coll unlocked the gate, then she clamped both her lips and her fists together as tightly as she could. Combine soldiers really were capable of breaking the gate down if she didn't open it. She had no choice but to confront the soldiers and deal with their demands, whatever those might be. Reluctantly, she nodded to Coll, indicating he should open the gate.

Outside, at least a dozen Combine soldiers stood waiting. The sergeant in charge, closely followed by five troopers, strode through the open gate. Four of the five immediately surrounded Coll.

The sergeant and the remaining trooper stopped in front of Dayra.

Dayra crossed her arms across her chest and didn't budge. Anger and worry churned inside her, but she made very sure only the anger showed in her expression as she demanded, "What is the meaning of this outrage? Since when does the Combine have the right to threaten us? And this early in the morning, too!"

"Settler," the sergeant said at last, grudgingly. With his hard, cold gaze fixed on her, he added, "We are under orders to bring in your hired hand, Coll Larren, for questioning. As a citizen of the Combine, you are prohibited from interfering with our assignment. Do I make myself clear?"

With every word the sergeant spoke, Dayra's anger and fear grew. Appalled, she glanced at Coll, but his expression was too closed and cold for her to guess what he was thinking.

"Do you have a warrant?" Dayra demanded. There was absolutely nothing she could do if the soldiers insisted on taking Coll, but she wouldn't give in easily.

"That would only be necessary if Settler Larren were under arrest. He's not. But he *is* required to accompany us."

"May I ask why?" Coll tried to shove past the soldiers guarding him, to no avail.

"You'll learn why soon enough," the sergeant growled. He made a short, swift chopping motion with his hand. An instant later, two soldiers seized Coll's arms and jerked his hands behind him so a third could bind his wrists.

"You can't—" Dayra's cry of protest was cut short by the soldier accompanying the sergeant, who stepped in front of her, brandishing his stunner.

Before she could decide how to deal with this new threat, she was startled by a furious, childish screech, followed by the sound of running feet.

A second later Jason, still dressed in his sleep shirt, raced past Dayra and launched himself at the soldier with the stunner. "Don't you hurt my sister! Don't you hurt Coll!"

Jason was six years old and scrawny. The soldier was tall, broad shouldered, and powerfully built. He was also armed. None of his advantages helped, for Jason had flung himself forward with all the head-down fury of a charging Boravian ram. Whether he intended it or not, his aim was perfect. The soldier dropped his stunner, then clutched at his groin as he fell, groaning, to his knees.

Before the equally startled sergeant could react to the assault on his trooper, Dayra grabbed Jason and pulled him tight against her side.

"He's just a boy!" she shouted, seeing the sergeant reaching for his weapon.

The sergeant frowned, but the frown slowly changed into an ironic, lopsided grin as he studied first Jason, then the still-groaning soldier. When he looked back at Dayra, however, the grin disappeared. "In the future, keep him under control," he snarled.

With a gesture to the remaining soldiers to follow him, the sergeant wheeled about and stalked toward the skimmers waiting outside the gate.

Two of the soldiers stopped to retrieve their fallen companion. Their expressions of concern were severely undermined by their snickers, but the recipient of their attention was still too shaken to notice.

The remaining two soldiers, stunners in hand, shoved Coll into motion. He shrugged them off, even though they were almost as big as he was, and took two steps toward Dayra.

"I'll be all right," he said, even as the soldiers grabbed him again. "Just stay here. Where I can find you after I'm released."

Numbly, Dayra nodded. Her hands tightened on Jason's shoulders so that he squirmed, but she didn't let him go until after the soldiers had shoved Coll into the back of one of the skimmers, then slammed the doors shut and set the vehicle into motion. By the time Jason was out the gate, the powerful skimmers were a good half mile away.

The skimmer wasn't uncomfortable, Coll soon decided, but he couldn't say the same for being forced to sit scrunched in a narrow seat with his hands tightly bound behind his back. By the time the skimmer pulled to a halt over an hour later, the muscles of his shoulders and back were agonizingly cramped and stiff. As he tried to step out of the vehicle, one of the soldiers shoved him and Coll almost cried out with the pain.

Almost. He managed to bite his tongue before he did, but his forehead and upper lip were covered in a cold sweat by the time he regained his balance. He glared at his tormentor. His anger must have shown clearly, for the man blanched, then ordered him to get a move on.

The skimmer was parked in front of a large stone building located near the center of the walled garrison. Coll tried to see as much as he could in case escape became necessary, but his guards hustled him into the building before he caught more than a glimpse of the compound. Without stopping for further directions, the soldiers led him down a long, dark hall, then unceremoniously shoved him through the door of an equally dark room and slammed the door shut behind him.

Friendly folk, Coll thought, staggering. He regained his feet, then slowly pivoted, studying his surroundings. The room was small, with nothing more than a narrow window and one inadequate, solar-powered light for illumination. Since the light wasn't on and the window appeared to be shuttered, what little light there was managed to get in by sneaking around the edges. A small table and two shabby chairs, all formed from pressed grass, completed the room's charming decor.

Coll didn't think he was in any danger—at least, not yet—but this summary detention didn't bode well. Although the soldiers had passed the trip in ribald conversation, nothing they'd said had given him any clue as to the reason for his presence here now.

Not that it mattered. It had to have something to do with his past as the Sandman. He wouldn't even consider the possibility that it was due to his having attended the rebel meeting last night, for that would mean Dayra was at risk, as well. At the thought, Coll clenched his fists involuntarily, then immediately regretted the action because it made his cramped muscles scream in pain.

He forced his muscles to relax, trying to ignore the pain.

No, he was here because of who he had been, not who he was. Strange that his past should have caught up with him on a world like this, when he'd done so little to merit any official attention. In all his years with the Rebel Alliance, he'd only been taken prisoner once, and that had been when he was a youth and long before he'd become the Sandman.

Coll shifted his shoulders, trying to ease the strain on his muscles. With cautious probing, he'd discovered the soldiers had used titanium manacles to bind his wrists. The manacles were an antiquated device that he could get out of if he had to. He hoped he wouldn't have to. If he was here for some other reason than his past connections with the Alliance, he'd be a fool to reveal his rebel training.

Which left him with nothing to do except try to relax and not worry about Dayra.

Trying to escape would have been easier and a lot less taxing on his nerves.

Perhaps a quarter of an hour had passed when the door to the room opened and Capt. Truva walked in, closely followed by two armed soldiers.

Coll sighed. The coolheaded, intelligent captain would be a great deal more dangerous to deal

269

with than any brutal sadist intent on pounding information out of him.

"Settler Larren," Truva said with a cold smile. "How nice of you to meet with me."

"Captain," he said, nodding slightly in greeting. "To what do I owe the honor of your invitation? Your soldiers were so anxious to invite me here, they didn't even give me time to have breakfast."

"You'll live," Truva said dryly. With a slight toss of her head, she indicated the soldiers were to leave. She waited until they closed the door and their footsteps faded down the hall before she crossed to the table and propped her hip on the edge.

"Sit down, Coll Larren," she said, then added casually, "or should I call you Sandman?"

Coll didn't even blink. He'd been prepared for the question. "I don't know why you should, since that's not my name."

"What is?"

"Coll Larren. I told you that the first time I had the privilege of meeting you, Captain."

"So you did. But you know how it is in my line of work. After a while, you develop a very suspicious mind.

"So it would seem, if you've gotten in the habit of kidnapping honest citizens before their breakfasts," Coll said, letting a hint of insolence creep into his voice.

Truva didn't move, yet Coll sensed a tension in her body that was only just barely under control.

"Be glad you can still eat breakfast, Coll Larren—or whatever your name is. There are

over six million people on Cyrus IV who will
never have another meal."

Coll stiffened at the mention of the world and
the rebellion that had shattered every remaining
illusion he'd had about the value of what he'd
fought for.

"Nothing to say?" Truva insisted, leaning toward
him, eyes glittering. "Not even when I tell you that
I am from Cyrus IV, and that my sister died in the
slaughter that followed the rebellion *you* led?"

Chapter Thirteen

Truva watched him as a hunter watches her prey.

Coll neither spoke nor moved. He couldn't.

"Tell me, Coll Larren. Was freedom worth the price of six million lives?"

Still Coll remained silent. He'd spent the last two years looking for an answer to Truva's question—without success. He wasn't going to find it here in this room.

"One of my soldiers saw you in the market yesterday morning," Truva said at last. "He was a prisoner of war on Cyrus IV and saw you once when you came through the prison camp."

How many prisoners had they had? Coll wondered. Hundreds? Thousands? Prisoners were a part of war, an inescapable part of war if you didn't believe in mass slaughter. It wasn't the prisoners he remembered from Cyrus IV.

"The soldier said the rebels treated them well," Truva added. "He said they shared what food they had and kept them in decent quarters. Better quarters than they usually had, I imagine. He said he remembered you particularly because the Sandman had a reputation among Combine soldiers for being dangerous, but fair."

Truva abruptly took a deep breath, as though her words had choked her. She stood without taking her eyes off Coll, then turned and crossed to open the shutters on the room's one window. The light flooded in, lighting the front of her while leaving most of the rest of the room in gloom.

"My sister was eleven years younger than I," Truva said, staring out the window as intently as she'd watched him a moment earlier. "We are . . . were—" Truva took another deep breath. "I am from the Shintal people of Cyrus IV. For centuries the Harnaks dominated us, but we always fought back, always believed that someday we'd regain our freedom. Then, less than a hundred years ago, the Combine conquered our planet."

Truva turned back to face Coll, but she didn't move away from the window. From that angle, half her face was in shadow, and half was lit by the sun coming in the window. She looked, Coll thought, like a representation of the troubled world that had given her birth, half light, half dark, both sides joined, yet always separate.

Slowly Truva crossed to Coll, then sank into the second chair so that she faced him. Her eyes locked with his, unflinching. "When my sister told me that she'd joined the rebel movement on Cyrus

IV, I didn't hesitate to offer my help. I thought that after a hundred years our two peoples must have learned to work together, that we could handle the freedom that the Combine, the same government I worked for, had taken from us so long ago. That's why I became one of the spies within the Combine Forces that kept you supplied with the information that helped you win."

Coll stiffened as memory flared. "You were the one we called the Twin! All we knew was that the Twin had a sister. . . ." His words died away as he suddenly remembered the sister, a slender, intense young woman who'd been fiercely dedicated to the rebel cause.

Truva nodded. "I had a sister. Her name was Aleena. She was the only family I had, and I loved her very much."

For an instant the mask of cold self-control that Truva always wore slipped so Coll could see the agony inside the woman, the regret for what her actions had led to.

"When Aleena died along with so many others," Truva said, the mask once more back in place, "I swore that I would give the rest of my life to keeping the peace. If the Combine were still in control on Cyrus IV, Aleena would be alive."

She leaned toward Coll, her jaw set hard, her eyes glittering in the dim light. "I will not let you bring the kind of agony to this planet that you brought to my home world."

"It won't happen here!" Coll said, straightening in his chair in spite of the pain that sliced through his shoulders and upper arms. "These people haven't learned to hate like your people did. The government you support taxes them unmercifully, then prohibits them from importing technology that could make their lives easier, help them become more productive. Your wonderful peace offers them nothing but hard work and suffering!"

Truva nodded, but didn't back down. "I don't like a lot of what the Combine does, either, but at least it offers stability. The people of Far Star won't turn on each other as the people of my world did, but they're not ready to govern an entire world, either."

"Who says? You? Some bureaucrat on Edole? Those fat slugs who *are* the Combine?" In some part of his mind, Coll watched himself, astounded at his vehemence. But the rest of him, the part that had always believed in the rebel cause and that had been shattered by the tragedy of Cyrus IV, kept going. "The people who have settled Far Star are the ones best qualified to govern themselves. If they make a mistakes—"

"If? *If?* You've led successful rebellions on how many worlds? Ten? Twenty? How many of those same rebel governments have been able to guarantee peace and prosperity after they took control?"

"There aren't any guarantees, Captain. Not ever. You know that as well as I do."

"But there *is* history, and it says the Combine has kept the peace on a thousand plus planets for far longer than you or I've been alive!"

"It's been a repressive peace that's trampled

the rights of individuals. Your vaunted history is repeating itself on Far Star, Captain, and the settlers who risked their lives to build a home here are going to pay the price for it! If you—"

Two armed guards bursting through the door cut Coll's impassioned rhetoric short. The two stopped just inside the door, wild-eyed and nervous.

"You all right, Captain?" the senior-ranking soldier asked, training his weapon on Coll.

Truva, who'd jumped to her feet at their entrance, snorted in disgust. "Yes, of course I'm all right. Why wouldn't I be?"

"We heard shouting and we thought. . . ." The soldier's explanation trailed away at the expression on their commanding officer's face.

"The prisoner is still bound, as you can see, and I am armed," Truva said. "Be sure to close the door when you leave, and tell everyone I don't want to be disturbed, for any reason. Is that clear?"

It was abundantly clear. The soldiers retreated as fast as they came, leaving Coll and Truva alone again.

The difference was, their interruption had dissipated the emotionally charged atmosphere. Coll felt limp, drained of the unexpected vehemence that had tossed him into an argument he'd never intended to have again, for any reason, with anyone. What had he been thinking, spouting all the old platitudes he'd relied on for so long?

Truva appeared as drained by the encounter as he was. She sighed, then said in a carefully neutral voice, "We've been watching the rebels here.

They're still too disorganized and far too poor to mount a successful rebellion. But if you get involved, some of them—perhaps a lot of them—are going to die. I can't let that happen. Not after what happened on Cyrus IV."

Coll frowned. "What are you suggesting? I'm your prisoner. All you have to do is have me killed or—"

"I'm not killing anybody! Not if I can help it, anyway," she added, a little more calmly. "No, I want you to convince them that their plans are futile, stop them before they get started. You can do that. You're the Sandman, after all."

Coll sagged. Despite his vehement defense of the rebel position, he still didn't want to get involved. Not ever again.

He shook his head. "I'm not the Sandman. I'm not even part of the Rebel Alliance anymore. I left after Cyrus IV and I've been drifting ever since. I'm only on Far Star because I got booted off a merchant ship that stopped here."

"And Settler Smith?"

"The first person I found who gave me a bed and a meal in exchange for work." Coll was tempted to expand on his explanation, but he didn't want to attract attention to Dayra by seeming too anxious to explain.

"What about the rebel plans?"

Coll shrugged.

"What do you know about a shipment of arms to the rebels?"

"Nothing."

She tossed another dozen hard questions at him,

but Coll's response was always the same. He didn't know anything; he hadn't done anything; he wasn't the Sandman anymore.

There must have been something in his face that convinced Truva he was telling the truth, for her shoulders suddenly slumped. She looked tired and older than her years.

"There are still outstanding warrants for your arrest, you know," she said. "There's even a price on your head."

Coll nodded. He hadn't expected that two years would be enough for the Combine to forget the Sandman . . . or to forgive him.

Abruptly, Truva pulled a key from her pocket and came around to unfasten his shackles.

Coll grunted as his muscles protested the sudden release of tension on his arms. He stretched gingerly. As soon as he was sure his arms were in reasonable working order again, he turned to confront Truva.

"Why are you releasing me?"

Truva shrugged, then tossed the manacles on the table. "Say it's in memory of a young woman who died fighting for something we all thought we believed in."

She gestured to the door. "You're free to go."

"What about transportation?"

Truva pressed her lips together in irritation. "Find your own transportation. You got to that holding in the first place without our help."

Coll was halfway out the door when she called his name. He turned to find her standing stiff and straight in front of the shabby little table, staring at him.

"I don't believe you really left the Alliance, Coll Larren. I don't think you can. But even if you did, remember my sister if you're ever tempted to get back in. Think of Aleena."

By noon, Dayra had dug up a huge section of new ground she'd wanted to add to her cultivated area. She'd worked like a woman driven by demons, and because Jason and Jeanella were as upset by Coll's arrest as she was, she'd put them to work, too. Physical exercise was the best cure she'd ever discovered for worries.

With each bite of the spade into the hard-packed ground, Dayra imagined a blow struck against the soldiers who had taken Coll, then another against whoever had drugged Johnny and tried to abduct Jason. Every time she turned over a clump of earth, she imagined burying her worries and her fears beneath the dark soil. Yet still the questions ran through her head, around and around until she thought she'd go mad.

Why had the soldiers taken Coll? Was he safe? Had someone besides Megat recognized him as the infamous Sandman? Or was his arrest somehow related to Talman Bardath's attack upon her and her family? But then why would Bardath waste time taking Coll when he could just as easily have ordered the soldiers to take her and the children? Had he chosen this approach because he'd known she would suffer even more with worrying? If so, what was he going to do next? And what could she do to stop him and help Coll?

A hundred questions and not one answer. Dayra wished there was someone with whom she could share her worries. Johnny was still unconscious, though Dayra thought he'd now passed into real sleep, as opposed to the drugged daze he'd been in since they'd found him the night before. All she could do was hope the old man would be able to suggest some reasonable course of action once he did wake, because if not. . . .

Dayra gritted her teeth at that. If not, *what?* She couldn't just sit here waiting, afraid to act.

With each enumeration of her fears, Dayra's anger grew. Anger that any government should claim the right to barge into her home and take a man without justification. Anger that the same government that taxed her so heavily couldn't protect her or the people she loved—that it might, in fact, be actively working *against* her.

For the first time she truly understood what could drive people into open rebellion, people like her who stood to lose everything if their rebellion failed.

Even now she could see Coll as he'd looked this morning, hands bound behind his back and surrounded by armed soldiers. He hadn't been afraid, at least, not for himself, but she'd felt his concern for her as he'd tried to reassure her he'd be all right, that he'd be back soon.

With a sigh, Dayra stopped digging and straightened slowly to give her muscles a chance to ease. She was used to hard work, but she'd been digging with such ferocity the past few hours that her muscles trembled with exhaustion. Wearily, she leaned on her spade and let her gaze roam over the luxurious rows of growing plants that were the result of her efforts over the past few years.

But instead of seeing the bright green leaves or flowering creepers, she found her gaze drawn inward, fixed on a vision of Coll, half naked, with the moonlight sliding over his shoulders, across his chest, and back around as he guided her in the dance.

He was so . . . beautiful: a powerful man capable of incredible gentleness, a man of darkness who had somehow managed to illuminate her life in a way no other had. And now he was a prisoner of the Combine.

Dayra's hands tightened around the handle of the spade so fiercely she would have throttled it if it had been alive.

If Coll Larren had never walked into her life, if he hadn't stayed to help her yesterday, he might still be free. But he wasn't free, and Dayra cringed at the thought of what he might be enduring on her behalf. She knew the guilt was irrational—she wasn't responsible either for his actions or the Combine's—but she couldn't help thinking that Coll would have been far better off if he'd never rescued her from that cliff or gotten involved with her problems.

He might have been better off, but she wouldn't have been.

She didn't have a chance to explore that

thought, for right then Jason and Jeanella came stumbling across the lumpy, newly turned ground toward her.

"I'm hungry," Jason complained.

"I'm tired, and my hands hurt," Jeanella added.

"When's Coll gonna be back?" Jason asked.

"And why isn't Johnny awake yet? Is he still sick?" Jeanella persisted.

Dayra had lost track of the times she'd heard those same questions that morning, but at least her brother's and sister's complaints were comfortingly normal and could be dealt with.

"Come on," she said, abandoning her spade where it stood in the ground. "Let's check on Johnny. Then we'll fix lunch."

Johnny was still asleep, but he showed signs of being ready to wake soon. The three of them were almost to the house when someone suddenly started thumping on the holding's main gate.

"Settler Smith? Are you there?" The voice was muffled by the thickness of the stone wall, but Dayra recognized it an instant before her visitor shouted, louder this time, "Settler Smith! It's me, Megat. Open up! We need to talk to you."

Dayra almost laughed in relief that it wasn't the soldiers she'd feared it might be. Shooing her brother and sister into the house with instructions to fix their own meal, she crossed to the gate and unlocked it, opening it just enough so one person could slip through.

Megat, Thelat Neur, and a woman whom Dayra recognized from the rebel meeting the day before stood outside. A third man still sat in the driver's seat of Megat's battered farm flitter.

At Dayra's look of surprise, Megat stepped forward, "I'm sorry about coming unexpectedly like this, but Thelat . . . that is, *we* have a problem and we need your help."

"What kind of problem?" Dayra asked, surprised at the tension she sensed in her visitors.

"Can we come in?" Neur asked. "If you're alone, that is."

By "alone," Dayra guessed Neur meant, "Are there any soldiers here?" Although she had a far better appreciation for their concern than she might have had the day before, Dayra's stomach knotted in sudden nervousness.

"I'm alone," she said, opening the gate wide enough so the flitter could pass through. "Please come in."

Neur, Megat, and the woman followed the flitter. Megat helped Dayra close and lock the gate behind them while the other two openly studied the holding around them.

"Can I offer you something to eat? A drink of water?" Dayra asked, uncertain what her role as host to Far Star's rebel leader required she do next.

Neur shook his head. "Is there someplace private we can talk? Someplace no one can overhear us?"

Dayra's stomach added another knot to the one already there. "My brother and sister are in the house, and Johnny . . . Johnny's not feeling well. He's still sleeping, I'm afraid. Other than that"—

she shrugged, gesturing toward the other buildings and the high walls surrounding them—"take
your pick. No one will hear us, wherever we go."

Neur settled for the center of the compound,
away from either walls or buildings.

"We're here," he said without preamble, "to ask
your help in landing an illegal shipment of arms.
Tonight."

Talman Bardath sat before the holographic projector he'd ordered installed in his quarters. His
palms were damp and his stomach unsettled. In
his right hand he held a small recording disk that
he'd received only a short while earlier and that
he was now nervously turning around and around
between his thumb and fingers.

His nervousness annoyed him. The disk was
just a disk, after all. The difference was, this disk
contained a holographic image of his son, which
was as close as Bardath had come to the boy so
far.

When he'd learned that a laborer on Dayra's
holding was to be brought in for questioning this
morning, Bardath had demanded that Truva take
Dayra and the children into custody at the same
time. To his fury, Truva had refused, just as she'd
refused all his previous requests for assistance.

As a result, Bardath had been forced to recruit
what help he could from among Truva's soldiers.
It enraged him that he'd had to settle for so much
less than he wanted, and that he'd had to use
bribery when a command or, at most, a threat,
ought to have sufficed.

That fool Pulanc had been a mistake from the start, but if Truva would only give him a military skimmer, one large enough to carry him and his men, Bardath knew he could have raided the holding himself.

Truva wouldn't give him a skimmer; there was nothing else that was large enough available on the planet; and his transport shuttle wasn't suited for planetary hops. That left him dependent on others, people over whom he had no real control. Bardath didn't like that. He didn't like that at all.

Once he had the boy, Bardath fully intended to claim revenge on Dayra and Truva.

It enraged him that both his recovery of the boy and his revenge would be delayed, at least for a week or two. Those idealistic fools now on the governing board of the Combine were causing serious problems on Edole, problems only he could handle. His shuttle was ready, waiting to take him back to his ship for the return to Edole.

But once he'd settled the immediate problems on Edole, he'd come back, and next time he'd make sure things went the way *he* wanted.

At least now his people thought they'd found someone who might be coerced into helping them, someone Dayra knew and, Bardath hoped, trusted. That would make matters easier.

So far, the only thing he had of his son was this one holographic image, which was all the soldier had been able to take.

Bardath was finding it unexpectedly difficult to replay the image.

What did his son look like? he wondered. What

had Jason inherited from him? His eyes? His mouth, perhaps? Or his hair?

Fortunately, Triana had been intelligent, even if she had been weak. Since his own intelligence was near the genius level, Bardath knew there was a good chance the boy would be extremely intelligent, as well. Jason would need that intelligence, along with a talent for ruthlessness, if he were to have any hope of hanging on to the wealth Bardath would leave him.

He'd gone over all these points a thousand times, Bardath thought, eyeing the small recording disk he held. All that mattered was that the boy—his *son*—be intelligent and healthy. He didn't care about anything else.

So why, the first time he had a chance actually to see what Jason looked like, did he find it so difficult?

With an oath, Bardath shoved the disk into the projector.

The image was crude and tended to jiggle with each movement of the soldier, who'd begun recording just as Dayra had grabbed the boy and pulled him to her. Bardath couldn't tell from the image what it was Jason had done, but it had to have been something outrageous, because Dayra was trying to fend off someone else at the same time she was fighting to control the squirming boy. Jason was clearly angry and struggling to get free of his sister's grip, without success. He was just starting to calm down when the image cut off.

Impatient, Bardath cued the projector to continuously repeat the display, then hunched forward to study the pale, half-size figures of Dayra and Jason as they struggled together in the middle of his room.

Bardath grinned. The boy took after him in determination, at any rate. He certainly couldn't have gotten that kind of fighting spirit from his mother.

The more he studied Jason's crudely captured image, the more Bardath thought he saw a resemblance between them in the eyes and the mouth. The shape of the jaw, too, though he couldn't be absolutely certain, and maybe, just maybe, the shape of the head.

Rather amazing, really, if he thought about it. He'd never wasted time thinking about it before, but now. . . .

Bardath shifted his position, trying to find another viewing angle that would give him a clearer perspective on this small, determined creature who was his son, the part of Talman Bardath that would live on long after he was gone.

The garrison was located outside Trevag, but it was still a good distance from the sorry excuse for a road that led to Dayra's holding and a number of other holdings in the area. Coll had expected to spend the rest of the day hiking, but was pleased to get a ride with a neighbor of Dayra's whom he hadn't yet met.

The man, who introduced himself as Querrel, proved uncommunicative. That suited Coll. After the events of the past two days, he had more than enough to occupy his thoughts.

It might have been easier if his mind and heart weren't both still turned inside out from the magic of the night before. However long he lived, Coll knew he would never forget the wonder or the aching, hopeless need that had seized him when he'd stepped through that open door into a moonlit fantasy where time had ceased to exist.

And then Dayra had swept into his arms and he'd willingly surrendered to the moment. He'd held her so that her breasts pressed against his chest and her hips against his; he'd let his hands explore the subtle miracle of her body while her warm breath caressed his skin and her scent enfolded him; he'd—

Coll tensed in the uncomfortable side seat of Querrel's flitter, fighting against the physical sensations that threatened to shatter his self-control, even now. Last night he'd given in to the fantasy, to an impossible dream that had somehow seemed temptingly possible. But that was last night. This morning the real world had come crashing in and there was no escaping the consequences.

What did he do next? If he ran, he left Dayra vulnerable to Talman Bardath's machinations. If he stayed, he couldn't be sure that he'd outwit Bardath, but he could guarantee that Dayra would become a target in Truva's campaign against the rebels. She could lose everything—her holding, her family, even her life itself—if she were found guilty of consorting with a known rebel.

On top of it all, his confrontation with Truva

had stirred emotions within him that he'd thought dead forever. The words and ideas that had driven him to support the rebel cause still had the power to stir him, in spite of everything. Did that mean there was still some truth to all those dreams he'd followed for so long, or that he was simply too much of a dreamer ever to see the real world clearly?

Coll didn't have any answers by the time Querrel dropped him off at the branch in the road that led to Dayra's holding. Even walking the remaining three or four miles didn't achieve anything but making his game leg ache.

The sight of Jason, perched on the wall near the main gate, cheered him up. Coll couldn't help wonder if the boy had been sent to watch for his return, because the minute Jason spotted him, he jumped up and started frantically waving just before he disappeared down the steps on the inside of the wall. Even from this distance, Coll could hear Jason's excited shouts. A couple of minutes later, the main gate swung open and Jason came racing out.

"Coll! Coll!" he shouted, his arms flung wide as his scrawny little legs pumped hard.

Without thinking, Coll broke into a run, too. His game leg protested, but he ignored it. As Jason threw himself into his arms, laughing with delight, Coll had the oddest sense that this was what a proper homecoming should be.

Well, almost. Some small voice in his brain wanted to know where Dayra was, but that was all right. Wherever Jason or Jeanella were, Dayra wouldn't be far away.

And she wasn't. An instant later, she slipped through the open gate and dashed toward him. Coll froze, watching her while he listened to Jason's excited chatter with half an ear.

Her hair, as it always did by this time of the afternoon, had worked free of its restraints and was tumbling about her shoulders. With each stride she took, her breasts bounced and the skirt of her work shift rode up her thighs, higher and higher until it exposed almost the entire length of her slender, shapely legs. The same legs that had wrapped around his waist with such intoxicating strength the night before, Coll thought, fighting against the sudden stirrings within him.

Although he'd been about to put Jason down so he could take Dayra in his arms, Coll decided that prudence might be the better idea. At least, so long as Jason was around. If Jason hadn't been there. . . .

Dayra had no such restraints. With a choking cry of, "You're safe! They let you go!" she launched herself at him, flinging her arms around both him and Jason. "We've been so worried!"

If Dayra could ignore her little brother, Coll decided, so could he. As he wrapped his free arm around her, clutching her to him, he bent his head and claimed the kiss Dayra was only too willing to give him.

It was Jason who brought the kiss to an end. "Hey!" he protested, trying to squirm out of Coll's grip. "You're squeezin' me, you know!"

With an embarrassed laugh, Dayra pulled free of Coll's embrace. "I'm sorry, Jason. I was just so glad to see Coll—"

"That's all right," Jason said, patting his big sister's hand consoling. "I missed 'im, too."

Coll had never before had cause to think of his dark tan, but he was grateful for it now because it hid most, if not all, of the flush that stole across his cheeks. He wasn't accustomed either to blushing or to being welcomed so openly by people he cared about.

As he bent to set Jason back on the ground, Coll caught a hint of motion at the holding gate. He tensed, but immediately relaxed as he identified Dayra's neighbor, Megat, coming toward them.

"What's he doing here?" he asked Dayra casually, straightening up, but taking care to leave a protective hand on Jason's shoulder.

"Megat?" Dayra hesitated, then plunged ahead as though anxious to get a particularly unpleasant task over with quickly. "He and Thelat Neur and a few others asked for my help in"—she stopped, then glanced down at Jason as though she'd just remembered his presence—"in fishing," she continued. "Tonight."

Chapter Fourteen

"Fishing." Coll said the word very slowly and distinctly, watching Dayra's expression change from irritation, to anger, to a nervous uncertainty that was painful to see.

So this was where the arms shipment Capt. Truva had asked him about was going to be delivered, he thought. How much did the captain already know about the rebels' plans?

More important, how much did she know of Dayra's involvement? And just when had Dayra gotten involved, anyway? This morning, he guessed, after he'd been taken prisoner. Megat and Neur had dragged Dayra into their scheme without thinking of the dangers to which they were exposing her.

Or maybe they'd thought about them and decided such concerns were less important than their own needs. For anyone caught up in the rebel cause, it was all too easy to focus on the struggle and forget the difficult moral questions that came with it.

He knew, because he'd done the same.

Coll was torn between the urge to shout and storm and prohibit Dayra from getting involved— something he had absolutely no right to do—and the equally powerful need to know why she'd agreed to so dangerous a course of action in the first place.

All he said was, "We have to talk." He didn't have a chance to say more, for Megat was too close.

"Glad to see you're safe, Larren," Megat said heartily. "Upset us all to hear you'd been taken."

"Not enough, it would seem, Megat," Coll said dryly. He slid his arm around Dayra. "You can tell me about it over a meal. I haven't eaten since yesterday and I'm starved."

"Can I have somethin' to eat, too?" Jason asked, craning his neck so he could look up at Coll. He hadn't moved from where Coll had put him down, as though he was afraid if he strayed too far Coll might be taken away again.

"Of course you can," Dayra said with greater heartiness than she felt. She was far more conscious of Coll's casual embrace than she liked, and that made her nervous. "We'll all get something to eat. It's been a long day, after all."

It seemed strange to have Coll's arm around her as she walked, stranger still to have Jason and Megat see them like this. Yet at the same time it

293

seemed so natural, so very right. They fit together as if shaped for each other. His arm was warm across her back, strong and comforting when she needed both strength and comfort. The hard mass of his body against hers seemed all the protection she needed against a world that was becoming increasingly impossible to understand or control.

She knew Coll disapproved of her decision to help Megat and Neur, and that only reinforced the doubts that had assailed her ever since she'd agreed to it. On the other hand, she'd only agreed to get involved because of him, because she was angry that he'd been arrested and afraid for what might happen to him. If she hadn't been so worried. . . .

Dayra pushed the doubts from her mind. The decision was made and it was too late to back out now. She shifted so she could wrap her arm around Coll's waist, and it was thus they walked through the gates and into the holding yard.

Neur and his two companions were waiting for them, nervously prowling at the base of the steps leading to the house. Johnny, who had finally dragged himself out of bed near noon much the worse for wear, slumped on the corner of the steps, his head cradled in his hands. Even the excitement of Neur's illegal arms shipment hadn't been enough to rouse him to any enthusiasm.

At the sight of Coll, Neur strode forward. "Glad to see you're free, Larren," he said, in a voice clearly intended to assert his authority from the start. It would have been more effective if he hadn't looked so tense. "We didn't expect them to release you. At least, not so soon."

"Neither did I."

Dayra was glad she wasn't the target of Coll's piercing look. Neur evidently wished he wasn't, because he swiftly withdrew the hand he'd half extended in greeting. No one but a fool would miss Coll's disapproval of Neur's plans—or her involvement in them—but something about Neur's manner toward Coll indicated there was more to his nervousness than fear of a stranger's disapproval.

Coll glanced at Jason. "We have to talk, Neur, but Jason and I are both hungry. Aren't we?" he added with a grin when Jason beamed, pleased to be included in the conversation.

Reluctantly, Dayra slipped out of Coll's embrace and led the way into the house. The others followed her, one by one. Judging by their expressions, Dayra suspected they were grateful for any excuse to delay the conversation that would follow. Even Johnny managed to stagger to his feet and follow them.

Much to Jason's obvious disgust, Dayra didn't allow him to join the adults around the table. Instead, she gave him a sack full of food and booted him out the door, sending him off with instructions for him and Jeanella to take their meal in the flower garden, then find something to keep them occupied until she told them they could come back in.

Eventually Coll pushed his plate away, crossed his forearms on the table, and leaned forward, his gaze fixed on Neur. "Dayra tells me you're planning a 'fishing' expedition for tonight."

Neur had picked up another piece of dried fish, but at Coll's question, he scowled at the fish and tossed it back on his plate.

"That's right. We have a small shipment of arms coming in, our first. Because there's only one communications and observation satellite around Far Star, the ship bringing the arms is staying in low orbit on the far side of the planet. A shuttle will transfer the arms from the ship to a small, manned boat that it will drop just outside the area the satellite can monitor. The people on the boat will bring the arms to the Settler Smith's inlet, where we'll pick them up. The operation's been planned for weeks."

"You're going to have to change your plans," Coll said. He spoke in a flat, unemotional tone that nonetheless managed to carry an unmistakable note of authority.

Neur jerked back in his chair as if he'd been hit. The others, including Megat, remained quiet, watching.

"We *can't* change our plans! It's too late!"

"You'll have to. Truva already knows about the shipment."

"That's impossible! We've been most careful—"

"She asked me point-blank if I knew about an illegal arms shipment," Coll insisted, his voice sharper now. "She's been watching you for some time, and now she thinks I'm working with you. She let me go, but that doesn't mean she won't still be watching me—or you."

"But she won't know the details, the timing—"

"Are you sure of that?"

Coll's question made Neur snap his mouth shut on whatever else he was going to say.

Coll didn't hesitate to press his advantage. "When is the boat due to get here?"

Neur blinked and looked at his companions for support. He didn't get any. "At high tide, an hour past midnight," he said at last, grudgingly.

"Are you the only ones picking up the shipment?"

"No. There're sixteen of us. Several will be here in an hour or so; the rest will arrive just before the boat does. We didn't want to attract attention by having too many people here during the day."

Coll grunted and his eyes narrowed in thought. Dayra watched him, wondering what he was thinking. No, more important, she wondered what he was feeling. Would he ever tell her? Would she ever know him well enough to understand what he was thinking and feeling without the need for words?

Would he ever forgive her for having been the means by which his past had reached out and dragged him back?

"Do any of you have maps of the coastline around here?" Coll asked abruptly. "I have a plan."

It was cold. At this time of night and this close to the sea, the dampness, driven by the wind, cut through all but the heaviest protective clothing. Dayra shivered and thrust her hands deeper in her jacket pockets.

She was huddled in the lee of one of the four flitters parked near the edge of the cliff where Coll had rescued her almost two weeks ago. This time, instead of bright sun, a number of portable lights provided the illumination by which 11 people were working.

She was the only one not assigned a task, and Dayra couldn't decide if she was more resentful of being excluded or grateful for not being dragged out of the slight shelter provided by the flitter.

Perhaps it wasn't just the cold, she admitted to herself as Neur, closely followed by two other men who had arrived a little while earlier, disappeared over the edge of the cliff. They were climbing down her tenslon ladder, which was once more securely anchored on its hooks. Dayra couldn't repress a shudder at the thought of them dangling so far above the black, churning waters of the sea, which were now at high tide and halfway up the cliffs.

She hadn't been back to the inlet since the thin man had abandoned her there, and for the first time she realized it wasn't just that she'd been too busy to return—she'd been afraid to go there.

Tomorrow she'd come back, she decided. She'd bring the ladder and her net and catch bag, and she'd climb down. . . .

Just the thought of going back down that cliff was enough to make her stomach churn. Perhaps she wouldn't come tomorrow, after all.

Dayra frowned, ashamed of her readiness to postpone the inevitable. She'd eventually have to face her fear—better that she do it sooner, rather than later, because she couldn't afford the luxury of being afraid. Not when they needed the fish for food and for income.

She wouldn't think about it tonight. Tonight there were more than enough other worries to occupy her energies. What if Truva and her soldiers somehow found the boat before it could reach the coast? What if Coll's plan didn't work?

Dayra knew the garrison's technological capabilities were relatively limited, but what they had was far more sophisticated than anything the rebels possessed. This was the first time Neur and his followers had ever tried anything so complex as smuggling illegal arms. There was so much that could go wrong and they'd had so little time to revise their plans. Even Coll's ingenuity and experience might not be enough.

Not for the first time Dayra wondered if she should have stayed at the holding with Jason and Jeanella instead of leaving them in the care of Johnny, who had almost recovered from the drugging, and two of the settler women who had come with the others tonight.

Coll hadn't wanted her to come, but Dayra knew he'd only let himself be dragged into Neur's schemes for her sake. She couldn't leave him alone tonight. Especially when she hadn't yet found the opportunity—or the courage—to tell him she'd only agreed to help in the first place because of her fear for him, and her anger against the government that had taken him.

A tall, broad-shouldered figure passed in front of one of the portable lights to stand at the cliff's edge, watching whatever was happening below. There was no mistaking Coll, Dayra thought, not even in the uncertain light and with so many people bustling around, intent on their assigned tasks. It wasn't just his intimidating size or the easy, confident way he moved among these people he didn't know. It was something in the way he dominated everything and everyone around him without ever seeming to belong, as if he stood apart from them, forever alone.

His head came up and he raised his arm in a gesture of command. The lights caught him in profile, tracing his shape against the dark beyond. He looked, Dayra thought, like one of the gods of ancient mythology she'd read about as a child, a creature of power destined to bestride the world, a primal force shaped of fire and stone and darkness.

Dayra blinked, startled by the fanciful notion, and roughly dragged her wind-tossed hair out of her eyes. As her fingers tangled in the heavy locks, Dayra tensed, then flushed at the sudden, sensual memory of Coll's fingers sifting through the silken strands the night before.

They'd been lying facing each other with the coarse sheets twisted about their legs and their bodies heavy with the lassitude that had followed a wild bout of lovemaking. She'd been on the point of drifting into sleep when Coll had picked up a lock of her hair that had tumbled across her breasts.

With exquisite delicacy, he'd slowly curled the lock around his finger, then just as slowly uncurled it and drawn it over her shoulder and along her arm, teasing her with the soft brush of it against her skin. He'd abandoned the captured lock of hair at the point where her elbow lay against her waist and begun to trace tiny, enticing circles on the sensitive skin on the inside of her elbow. Before she'd fully realized what he intended, Coll had dragged the tip of his finger farther down the inside of her arm, where it lay close against her belly.

Even now, huddled in the dark and the wind, Dayra tensed, remembering the doubly tormenting feel of his fingertip against her arm as the side of his finger had burned a matching line across the soft flesh of her abdomen. His fingers had brushed against the inside of her palm, the curve of her fingers, yet when she'd tried to stop his tormenting exploration, he'd eluded her and gone seeking an even more secret, sensitive part of her.

Dayra squeezed her eyes shut, fighting to douse the flames that just the memory of Coll's gentle touch had roused in her. It didn't help.

With a muttered curse, Dayra opened her jacket and let the cold night wind cool her.

Strange that she should be tempted to indulge in such memories at a time like this. If only she had some task, something to keep her mind and hands occupied!

It might not help even if she did have something to do. Coll had claimed her last night, and even through the worries of the day just past he'd been so much a part of her, so much a part of her thoughts, that she could no longer remember what it had been like to exist without him.

As if summoned, Coll left the cluster of people standing near the edge of the cliff and came toward her. The wind tossed his hair back from his face and plastered his clothes against his body, but he seemed not to notice. There was nothing threatening in his demeanor, and yet there clung to him an aura of danger and dangerous deeds that was strangely suited to the setting. His gaze was fixed on her. Even in the darkness Dayra could feel its intensity.

"It would be more comfortable for you if you'd stayed at the holding," he said. He gave her no chance to respond, for he immediately drew her into his arms and bent to claim a hungry kiss.

Dayra gladly wrapped her arms around him, opening her jacket so her chest and belly were pressed against his. The heat of him drove out all thought of the wind and the dark and the presence of anyone save themselves and the rising fire between them.

Coll pulled away from her when the kiss threatened to become far more than just a kiss, but Dayra simply clung tighter, unwilling to let him go.

"Is everything going all right?" she asked, arching so she could look up at him.

"Yes," he said, his voice husky and a little uncertain, as though he was finding it difficult to talk. Without letting go of her, he turned and peered out toward sea, shading his eyes against the glare of the portable lights mounted near the cliff's edge.

"There they are," he said, pointing to a small light now bobbing wildly on the dark water. "Do you see them?"

Dayra nodded eagerly. It looked as if the boat which carried the light was getting close to the mouth of the inlet, where the water would be rougher. "Yes, I see them." Her grip on Coll tightened. "Will they be all right?"

"They should be. Neur said he'd handled boats before, and so have both his men." He laughed and drew her closer against his side. "I'm not sure he's ever managed a boat made of pressed grass, but that little hull that was in your shed seems to handle all right."

"So what happens next?" Dayra demanded, grateful for his solid bulk beside her. She wouldn't have wanted to risk her life on a boat she'd never tried.

"We wait, and we try to keep warm," Coll said, once more bending his head toward her. "And I just happen to have a few ideas about how we can manage that."

It seemed an age before Neur's little boat returned to the inlet. Dayra had expected to be able to watch their progress throughout, but the waves were high enough that she'd caught only occasional glimpses of their light.

At sight of them now, her legs started to tremble slightly, not from cold, but the sudden release of a tension she'd hadn't realized had gripped her so strongly. They were almost back and there was still no sign of any soldiers.

Maybe they'd overreacted to Coll having been questioned about an arms shipment. Maybe Truva had only heard rumors, not specifics. Maybe they would finish their work here without interruption and have a good laugh over their worries tomorrow.

A lot of maybes. Dayra couldn't shake the uncomfortable feeling that they weren't safe yet.

She moved closer to the cliff's edge, careful to keep out of the way of the others, who were checking the crude supports and the block and tackle rigging that would be used to pull the boat and its cargo up the cliff.

Below, Neur and his two companions were moving closer to the cliff. The light mounted at the front of their bobbing vessel cast distorted shadows on them and on the dark, churning water around them, creating a dark, twisted image like something out of a nightmare. When the boat moved so close to the cliff that she couldn't see them anymore, Dayra stepped back, shivering.

Whether Truva appeared or not, it had taken courage for those three men to set out in a boat they'd never handled before, knowing there could be no hope of rescue if anything went wrong. Before they'd climbed down the cliff, Coll had reminded them of the risks they were taking, but they'd gone ahead, anyway.

No matter how much she disliked Neur, Dayra could only honor him for his courage in acting on his convictions. If he and the other rebels won, she and just about everyone else on Far Star would benefit. If they didn't, Neur would be the first to pay the price. That thought made her feel ashamed of her own ambivalence toward their cause.

At that moment, the first of the men in the boat clambered over the cliff's edge. As soon as he was safely away from the edge, his safety rope was unhooked, then thrown back down for the next man. Neur came up last. All three looked pale with the strain and the heavy work they'd done in the past hour, but as their companions crowded around them with eager questions, they grinned and started recounting the details of their exploit.

It was Coll who cut them off sharply. "We still have the boat and the cargo to bring up," he said, waving everyone back to their assigned tasks.

Grateful for the chance to do something constructive at last, Dayra joined the people who were pulling on the ropes connected to the boat's bow. A second team handled the ropes tied to hooks on the stern. Between them, with much effort and no little amount of swearing from some of the men, they pulled the little boat, heavier now with its cargo, up the cliff.

Dayra couldn't help joining in the ragged cheer that went up as the dark hull of the boat swung past her, dripping icy water, then dropped into the crude cradle they'd made for it that afternoon. They'd done it! Coll's plan had worked! This part of it, anyway!

An instant later the cheers changed to oaths as two dozen armed, black-garbed forms materialized out of the night. Like demons released from a box, the creatures swarmed over the area, clubbing down anyone who offered resistance and seizing everyone else.

Panicked, Dayra turned to flee, only to find herself staring at a goggle-eyed monster pointing a stunner set on maximum force right at her. She froze, then slowly held her hands, palms out, away from her body.

It took a second for her eyes to adjust to having the lights behind her, instead of in front. Under the black uniform, the monster facing her was a Graun and the stunner he held was clearly military issue. The horrible eyes were night-vision goggles with adjustable, telescopic lenses. The goggles explained why she hadn't heard anything earlier. They allowed the soldiers to see everything without getting close.

The Graun waved the stunner, indicating he wanted her to turn around and join the other settlers, who were being herded into a group at the side of the lighted circle farthest from the boat.

Dayra's blood was pounding in her veins so hard she could scarcely hear, but her eyes weren't affected. As she carefully picked her way across to the area the Graun indicated, she strained to catch a glimpse of Coll in the confusion. For a moment, she couldn't find him.

Just before she could break into full-blown panic a second time, she spotted him being held by three armed soldiers a good distance away from the other settlers, almost at the far edge of the light. There was a dark stain across his cheek, but from this distance Dayra couldn't tell if the stain was dirt . . . or blood.

Fear, not for herself, but for Coll, knotted in her stomach. She'd done this. In her blind, stupid anger at the Combine for having taken him, she'd agreed to help Neur and Megat. Coll had been dragged in against his will because he'd wanted to protect her.

Even as she'd listened to him explain his alternative plan, she'd known what he was doing. She should have said something then, refused to let either of them get involved in Neur's plans. She hadn't said a word. She'd been too proud to admit she'd acted rashly, too unsure about which course was the right one, and so she'd said nothing at all.

Now they were prisoners and Coll was injured, perhaps seriously—all because she'd gotten involved when she should have kept her nose in her own affairs. At least Coll had predicted the soldiers' arrival, even if no one else had believed him. Dayra could only hope that the rest of his plan would go as well as the first part had.

Impatient with her delay, the Graun shoved Dayra between the shoulders. Reluctantly, she tore her eyes off Coll and moved to join the huddled settlers, who were now surrounded by silent, black-clad soldiers.

As she did, she spotted a soldier by the stern of the boat that now lay in its cradle like a beached whale. After a quick glance at the tarp covering the cargo in the bottom of the boat, the soldier stepped away from the boat and peeled off both goggles and black hood.

Truva! Dayra stiffened. Coll had warned them the garrison commander would probably accompany any troops tonight, but Dayra hadn't expected the woman to come dressed for a fight, too.

"Do you have them all?" Truva snapped as another soldier came up to her.

"Yes, Captain. And the man you wanted is over there, away from the rest," the soldier said, pointing toward Coll.

"Good. And the leaders?" Truva turned to study the settlers. Her gaze settled immediately on Dayra.

"Settler Smith?" she said, in a politely ironic voice. "I hadn't expected to see you here tonight."

"And we hadn't expected to see you or your troops, Captain!" Dayra said, hoping she could play this the way Coll had instructed them and grateful for her rising anger. It would be easier to face whatever lay ahead if she was angry instead of downright afraid.

She shoved past the soldier guarding her. He reached to grab her arm, but she jerked it away and strode over to Truva. With every step she expected the soldier to grab her by the neck and throw her to the ground, but Truva must have given him some sign to let her past because she got all the way to the captain without being tackled.

"I'm getting tired of this harassment, Captain," Dayra raged. "You raid my holding looking for arms. You arrest my employee, then force him to walk back, which meant I lost the better part of a day's work from him. Now this! If you think—"

"Quiet!"

Dayra shut her mouth. Which was just as well. Despite her anger, she was so scared her mouth had gone dry. She didn't want to ruin things by choking when she was supposed to be shouting.

Truva studied her unblinkingly for a moment, then turned to the soldier still standing beside her. "Take two of your people and empty out the cargo in that boat," she said. "Now!"

Chapter Fifteen

"There's nothing wrong with the cargo!" Dayra cried.

"No? Then why are you upset that my people would inspect it?" Truva demanded coldly.

"You have no right—"

"Stop shouting!" Truva hadn't raised her voice, but it easily cut through Dayra's protest.

Dayra swallowed uncomfortably. "I'm not shouting," she said, as calmly as she could manage.

"That's better. Now, perhaps you'll explain to me, in a reasonable tone of voice, exactly what's going on here."

"We're fishing. If I'd had any idea that fishing was going to—"

"Fishing!"

"That's right."

Truva glanced at Coll, where he stood, silent and

watchful, among his captors. Then she glanced at the cluster of men and women at the other side of the circle. She turned back to Dayra. "This hardly looks like a fishing expedition."

"Have you suddenly become a fishing expert, Captain?" Coll demanded. He tried to push past the soldiers around him and immediately found four stunners pointed directly at him.

The smudge on his cheek was blood, Dayra realized suddenly. She could see a thin trickle oozing down the side of his face. In the dim light, it looked black, not red.

"Keep him quiet," Truva snapped, her attention still fixed on Dayra. "I repeat, Settler, this does not look like a fishing expedition. Don't risk irritating me by lying."

Dayra swallowed uncomfortably. Coll had predicted this, too. Not that she'd be the one singled out for questioning, necessarily, but that one of them would. She only hoped she could handle it the way Coll had told them to.

"We are fishing, Captain. Nothing more." It wasn't easy keeping her voice steady, but it helped to know Coll was watching her. "Perhaps if you had climbed up and down a rope ladder with a net and a bag full of fish, you might understand why we wanted to try another approach."

"I might almost believe you, Settler, if it weren't the middle of the night."

Dayra shrugged. "On other worlds, fish tend to be drawn to the lights, so they're easier to catch. We hoped that technique would work here, as well."

"And did it?" Truva demanded impatiently. She was clearly growing tired of the discussion.

"You'll have to ask the men who went out in the boat. Your people interrupted us before we could unload the catch to find out," Dayra said, putting as much of a resentful sneer in her voice as she dared. Her stomach was twisted so tight with combined fear and nervous tension that she worried she might humiliate herself by throwing up.

Truva nodded to the soldier beside her. "Carry out your orders, Sergeant. Check the boat and everything in it."

"No! You can't do that!" The angry cry from the crowd of settlers brought Truva's head around with a jerk. Neur pushed forward, his eyes wild. "You can't touch that boat!" he shouted. "You have no right! Keep away from our boat!"

"They're going to take our fish!" another person cried.

As if on command, the settlers surged forward angrily, shouting protests and threats of retaliation for the soldiers' attack.

The soldiers, startled by this unexpected mini-rebellion, might have lost control if two of them hadn't been sufficiently quick thinking and brutal to club Neur and another man who was at the front of the group. As the settlers behind tripped over the fallen men, the remaining soldiers closed in around them, stunners at the ready. Since there were at least two soldiers to every settler, it didn't take long to restore order.

Capt. Truva had watched everything without moving, but the instant the settlers were back under control, she gestured to the soldier beside her. "Empty out that cargo," she snapped. "Now!"

Despite the continued cries of protests from the settlers, the soldier did as he was ordered. He and two others clambered into the boat, making it tilt dangerously in its cradle, and began systematically tossing out everything they found.

A tarp.

The light.

Two ropes.

A coiled net.

A couple of crude grappling hooks.

Some fish.

Then some more fish, promptly followed by even more fish.

Lacking any tools, the soldiers were reduced to tossing out the fish one by one. They'd bend down to grope in the shadowed bottom of the boat, then straighten, a slick, wet, scaly fish clutched in their hands, and turn to pitch the fish overboard. Then they'd repeat the exercise.

Some of the fish were so large it took two men to pick them up and toss them out. Some were still alive and squirming, which made the soldiers' task all the more difficult. Alive or dead, the fish were hard to handle and frequently slid out of the soldiers' grasp, forcing the increasingly frustrated troopers to try again.

Though Dayra watched as closely as she dared, she didn't see Truva move or change expression once during the search. Even the settlers' constant verbal hammering didn't affect the woman, although she must have seen that, underneath

313

their anger, most of them were thoroughly enjoying her discomfiture.

For her part, Dayra was finding it increasingly hard to maintain her image of outraged, innocent settler. She was too worried about what Truva's silence might mean.

Was the captain furious at not finding what she'd expected? Did she feel humiliated? Mocked? Despite the proof that there were no illegal arms in the boat, did she still suspect them of hiding something from her? How far would she go to find the arms she sought? Arms or no, would she be tempted to arrest them all, just on general principle?

The one time Dayra glanced at Coll, he was standing, arms crossed over his chest, watching the display impassively. He looked, she thought, just like an angry man who was fighting hard to control his righteous rage. It occurred to her that his pose might be no pose at all, but an honest reflection of his emotions.

Dayra didn't look at Coll again. She couldn't stand seeing him a prisoner, however temporarily, knowing he was at risk because of her. It didn't matter that he was perfectly capable of taking care of himself. He was a prisoner and it was her fault and that was more than enough to add guilt to the fear and worry already twisting in her stomach.

As the pile of fish on the ground mounted higher, the settlers' shouts grew louder and more enraged.

"Them fish are gettin' smashed, you bastards!"

"You'll pay for this!"

"That's our food! You wanta eat a fish that's been beat up like that?"

The soldiers ignored the angry squawking and concentrated on their unwelcome task instead. By the time the last fish went overboard, their expressions were set in hard lines of stoic suffering. There was no mistaking their relief as they threw out a tangled mess of fishing net, then bent down for one last inspection of the boat.

"That's it, Captain," the soldier who'd been given the assignment said at last. He leaned on the gunwale, panting heavily. "Do you want us to break up the boat, just in case?"

Truva ignored the howls of protest that greeted the suggestion and merely ordered the three to return to their skimmers and see if they could find something to clean up with. As the soldiers gratefully crawled out of the now-empty boat, Truva crossed to the mound of fish heaped on the ground and stood studying it for several minutes, eyes narrowed, her brow creased in thought.

Finally, she prodded one fish that had fallen farther away than the rest with the toe of her boot, then kicked it back into the heap and turned to Dayra.

"Fishing, indeed, Settler Smith," she said. Her eyes glittered, reflecting the light like the eyes of a predator would reflect the glow of a protective campfire.

Dayra tugged her jacket closed, aware, suddenly, of the cold night wind that was slowly dying away. "I tried to tell you."

"So you did." Without another word, Truva turned and crossed the lighted circle toward Coll.

Without hesitation, Dayra followed.

"Settler Larren," Truva said, coming to a halt in front of Coll. "We meet again. How pleasant."

"It might be if your men hadn't ruined so much of our catch, Captain," Coll growled, ignoring the warning hiss of one of his guards. With his arms crossed over his broad chest and the cut on his cheek still bleeding, he presented an intimidating picture of masculine power.

Truva was unimpressed. "I can't help wonder what else you might have caught in your nets tonight, Settler."

Coll remained silent, impassive.

Dayra stood to the side, prevented by one of the soldiers guarding Coll from getting too close. Her gaze darted from Coll to the captain and back again. The electric tension between the two made Dayra curl her hands into such tight fists that her nails dug into the palms of her hands.

Whatever challenge or warning passed, unspoken, between Coll and Capt. Truva, Dayra missed it, for an instant later Truva wheeled about.

"Release him," she said, "and the settlers." She strode to the edge of the light, then turned back, her dark eyes fixed on Coll. "I will do whatever is necessary to maintain peace on this planet, Coll Larren. Whatever is necessary. Remember that."

A moment later she was gone, swallowed up by the night. Her soldiers followed her, many of them walking backward, arms at the ready, to ensure the settlers didn't try to jump them in retribution.

Neur's people started to break into a ragged cheer, but a sharp look from Coll quelled them immediately. "We still have work to do," he said, striding toward the boat. "Let's salvage what we can of the catch and store the gear back on the boat. Then we can celebrate."

Dayra pitched in with the rest, grateful for work, any kind of work, that would keep her mind off that last challenge from Truva. There was more in the captain's words than just their surface meaning. Dayra couldn't figure out what it might be, but Coll knew. She was convinced of that.

Some things made sense, however. For the first time since Coll had explained his plan to them this afternoon, Dayra understood his admonishment to keep up the pretense of being fishermen even after the soldiers were gone. With their night-vision goggles, the soldiers could still be watching them, waiting to see what they would do next.

"Act angry and resentful, but don't appear elated or excited. Don't act as if you've just gotten the best of them, because you haven't," Coll had instructed them. "Don't ever let them think that you're anything but exactly what you say you are, and don't assume they aren't watching you just because you can't see them."

It wasn't hard to act angry or resentful, for that was the way they all felt after the soldiers' crude but effective trashing of the boat's contents. Fishing might not have been the primary reason for their expedition, but they could have used the fish nonetheless, and now much of the catch was too damaged to salvage. The harder part was not talking about the real reason for their charade, but Coll had warned them against that, too.

Working together, they made fast work of the cleanup. With the salvaged fish loaded in one flitter, the settlers left the flitter's driver with his smelly cargo and piled into the remaining three flitters. Their excitement on the return trip contrasted sharply with the tension that had kept them mute and watchful on the way out.

Only Dayra remained silent. She still had Jason and Jeanella to worry about. The memory of her last fishing expedition, when she'd returned to find that Truva and her people had searched the holding in her absence, was still too sharp and clear in her mind. She wished Coll was beside her, but he was in another flitter with Neur. The minute her flitter was inside the holding gate, she jumped out and raced for the house, anxious to check on her brother and sister.

Johnny greeted her at the door. One look at her face was enough to tell him all he needed to know about the success of their deception. He grinned, then nodded toward the children's rooms.

"They're sleepin', lass," he said, the old insouciance back in his voice now that the last effects of the drugs he'd been given had worn off. "They were nervous and restless, so Settler Korath gave 'em an herb tea that put 'em to sleep right off. She says nothin' will wake 'em till mornin', not even a spaceship landin in the holdin' yard."

Dayra breathed deep, relieved that none of her

guilty fears for the children's safety had been necessary. At least, not tonight. She started to ask Johnny how he felt, when the sound of eager voices coming toward the house distracted her attention and drew her back to the open door.

Outside, Coll was trying to make his way toward the house, with a notable lack of success. Neur and his people had surrounded him and were pelting him with enthusiastic congratulations and a barrage of questions.

"Do you think the smugglers got your message changing the rendezvous point?"

"When will we know if the rest of our group picked up the arms?"

"Do you think Truva guessed we were just a decoy? Will she hunt down the others? Will you help them, too?"

"Can you get us more arms?"

Coll reached the steps leading to the house, but when he couldn't go any farther, he turned to confront the others. "I don't *know* the answers to your questions," he shouted over their babble, his hands up, palms out, as though he could ward off their importunities with a gesture. "You'll have to wait until they can safely get a message back to you. If you—any of you—try to contact them or follow them, you run the risk of Truva following *you*, and then we'll all be arrested."

From her position in the doorway, Dayra studied the scene before her. The solar-charged lights mounted on the roof of the house cast a harsh glare over the eager faces that were turned up to Coll's. In the stark light, all the fears and hopes that

319

had driven these people to rebellion lay exposed for anyone to see.

It was frightening. Coll had shown them how to outwit their adversaries once, and already they dreamed of doing it again. They'd learned how satisfying it could be to triumph over the government forces that had controlled their lives for so long and now they were hungry for more successes and clearly convinced that only Coll could provide them.

Even Neur, who Dayra had thought craved the power of leadership as much as he craved freedom, was part of the eager, clamoring crowd. As though her thoughts had drawn him into action, Neur shoved to the front.

"If it hadn't been for you, Larren, we would all have been arrested, perhaps executed for treason. We need you on our side, we need the Sandman on our side. Will you join us?"

At mention of the Sandman, the others fell silent, confused at first, then even more excited as the implications of Neur's words sunk in. The legendary Sandman! Here, on Far Star! And he was on their side!

Even though Dayra couldn't see the expression on Coll's face, she could see the way the muscles in his shoulders and back tensed, sense the anger and the powerful uncertainty within him.

This was what he feared, she realized with sudden insight. He wasn't afraid of the soldiers or the fighting or the risk of dying. He wasn't afraid for himself at all. He was afraid for the people like the ones who stood before him and demanded his help, people who might lose everything they had, including their lives, if they became entangled in the rebellion they so badly wanted him to lead.

She was responsible for this mess, Dayra knew. If she'd turned Neur away this morning, Coll wouldn't be facing this dilemma now. She had to do what she could to rectify the situation and protect Coll, no matter how futile her efforts might be.

Without stopping to think about the problems into which she might be plunging, Dayra stepped forward to Coll's side. "Be quiet or you'll wake my family," she said, loud enough for all to hear. The wind had long since died and her voice carried clearly. "I'm tired and I imagine all of you are, too."

She glanced back at Johnny, who had followed her when she'd come outside to see what the uproar was about. "Johnny will show you where to sleep, if you'll go with him. We can talk more tomorrow. Today, actually. But only after we've had a chance to sleep on it." She wasn't really sure where Johnny would find enough beds or bedding for 14—or was it 15?—people, but that would be his problem, not hers.

At some point in the uproar, Johnny's usual cheerfulness had disappeared, to be replaced by an expression Dayra found impossible to read. He stopped at the bottom of the steps, then turned back to look up at Coll. In the harsh lights his face looked as if it had been carved into deep lines of weariness and old age.

"I told ye, lad. Ye can't stay out o' this, no matter

how much ye want to." With that, he turned his attention to herding the others toward the laborers' quarters and empty work sheds, where they could find temporary beds for what remained of the night.

At first there was some grumbling, but Neur's people were tired, too, and they eventually gave in, leaving Coll and Dayra alone on the steps.

Dayra shut off the house and outside lights, then returned to stand near Coll, close enough so he could touch her if he wanted. He didn't touch her. Instead, he remained still and silent, staring into the dark where Neur and his followers had gone.

Dayra waited, every fiber of her body strung tight with tension, not knowing what to say, what to do. Even standing an arm's length away from Coll she could feel the warmth of his body, hear the slight sound of his steady breathing. They were so close, yet because Far Star's moons had set, all she could see of him was the dark, almost shapeless bulk of his head and shoulders against the pale, distant stars.

When the silence had stretched until Dayra could bear it no longer, she said, "They would all have been arrested, perhaps killed, if you hadn't helped them tonight." Her voice quavered with her effort to remain calm.

Coll took a deep breath, then let it out slowly. "Yes," he said, nodding slightly.

"But you don't owe them any more than that."

Coll shook his head. "No, I don't owe them anything more." He still hadn't looked at her, hadn't moved, but his softly spoken words were heavy with repressed emotion.

He didn't say anything else and the silence lengthened until Dayra thought she would scream with the pain and the doubts she could feel warring inside him, tearing him apart. She blinked, fighting back the hot tears that threatened to blind her, then stretched out her hand and gently touched his arm.

He turned to her then, awkwardly, as if rousing from an unpleasant dream, and bent his head so he could look into her upturned face. Dayra knew he could not distinguish her features any more clearly than she could distinguish his, but when he bent lower, he unerringly found her mouth and claimed the kiss she was only too willing to offer him.

Dayra yielded eagerly to the pressure of his lips against hers, the probing heat of his tongue. He raised his hands to cup her face and hold her as he plunged deeper still, his kiss an anguished protest against the forces that pursued them.

Dazed by the fire that flared so easily in response to his touch, Dayra swayed, then reached for him, only to have him roughly pull back.

"Go to bed, Dayra," he said, his voice harsh, cruel. "The morning will come soon enough."

With that he turned and descended the steps, then disappeared into the dark.

Stunned at his abrupt departure, Dayra remained where she was, listening to the hard, grating scrape of his boots on the gravel. The sound of his footsteps was the only sign she had that he hadn't vanished. A moment later, even that sound faded away, leaving her with nothing but the lingering warmth his touch had stirred within her.

An animal sound that was half sob, half cry of protest, ripped from her throat.

Go to bed, he had said. How she longed to obey his command, but not alone!

Instead of retreating, Dayra remained where she was, wanting desperately to follow him, afraid he did not want her to. Did he find solace in being alone? Was it a refuge against her intrusion? Or had he abandoned her simply because he hadn't realized he could have chosen to stay?

How long she might have remained standing there, torn with indecision, Dayra didn't know. The instant she saw Coll on the top of the holding wall across from her, a tormented shadow against the dark sky, her doubts fled.

Heedless of any obstacles that might lie in her path, she raced across the open area to the far wall. She found the steps he'd used by the simple process of tripping over the bottom one in the dark. Fumbling and stumbling, she climbed the steps to the top, then carefully made her way along the wall in the direction she'd seen Coll headed.

She caught up with him on the walls that surrounded her flower garden. Dayra could tell the location only because she could hear the burbling murmur of the water and smell the mingled scents of the flowers, heavy on the night air.

Coll turned at the sound of her footsteps on the stone. "You shouldn't have come out here," he said harshly. "These walls can be dangerous in the dark."

"A lot of things are dangerous in the dark. Like doubts and fears and—"

"Dayra!"

The warning was clear. Dayra ignored it. "You only got into this mess because of me. I know that. And I wouldn't have agreed to help Neur if I hadn't been so angry over your arrest."

Coll drew in a deep breath at that, but Dayra ignored his reaction and kept on going. "Whatever's troubling you, you don't have to deal with it alone, Coll Larren. Not now. Not ever again, if that's what you want."

Dayra wasn't sure if it was she, or Coll, who gasped at that. She'd spoken without thinking, driven by feelings his own troubled emotions had stirred within her, but the minute the words were out, she knew they were right and utterly true. She would give anything to spend the rest of her life with Coll if he would let her, if he would have her.

For an eternity the only sound was the purling water in the garden below them. At last he moved a step closer and took her hand in his. His fingers were cold and they trembled, ever so slightly. Dayra scarcely noticed because the thudding of her heart suddenly drowned out everything else.

"Don't promise me forever, Dayra," Coll said. "Not until you've heard what I have to tell you. But then . . . if you want. . . ."

325

He curled his hand around hers so tightly Dayra could not have escaped if she'd wanted to. She didn't want to. When he drew her down to sit beside him on the wall, she went with him willingly.

The stone beneath them was cold and hard, but Dayra settled into his arms as easily as if they'd been sitting on silken cushions. Then everything faded from her consciousness except the comforting strength of his body against hers and the mesmerizing sound of his voice as he told her of his past, of his dreams, and of a world called Cyrus IV.

How long Coll talked he didn't know, but the first gray hint of morning was creeping into the sky when he fell silent at last. Throughout, Dayra had scarcely spoken, but just holding her had been sufficient to ease the pain of his tale.

He felt light-headed and he was glad she was still in his arms, anchoring him to the solid stone beneath them.

Somehow during his recital the fears and doubts and self-recriminations that had been so much a part of him for so long had magically dissipated. They would return, he knew, but not just yet. For the present, they were powerless compared to his fear that Dayra would rescind her promise to stay with him forever, now she'd heard his story.

"You're a fool, Coll Larren," she said, pressing even closer against him.

"A what?"

"A fool. Or maybe you're an arrogant fool. Probably the latter," she said, peering up at him from where he cradled her against his chest.

She freed her hand, which was crushed between them, and lightly traced the line of his cheek and jaw. "With a jaw like that, *definitely* the latter," she said.

Coll felt something within him tilt and spin out of control, but he was too stunned by her unexpected response to sort it out.

Dayra frowned, suddenly serious again, then withdrew her hand. "You can't accept responsibility for the madness of an entire world, Coll Larren," she said. "You helped them gain their freedom. They threw it away, but that was *their* choice."

"They wouldn't have had that choice if I hadn't helped give it to them." The words were harsh and burning, ripped out of him by his anger and pain. "Six million people died who wouldn't have if the Combine still controlled Cyrus IV. *Six million*, Dayra."

Coll hugged her tight against him, but his gaze was fixed on the horizon, where a tiny stain of pale yellow was slowly spreading across the sky. "How many will die if I help the people on Far Star?"

"How many will die if you don't?"

He stiffened angrily, then sighed and shook his head. "Neur is dreaming if he thinks they have the resources to fight the Combine. I can't work miracles, but some will think the Sandman can, so they'll join the rebels and then more will die than might have, otherwise."

And Dayra might be one of them. The possibility was too horrible to contemplate. Yet if she insisted on joining the rebels and he was there, too, he might be able to protect her from traps like the one that had almost closed around them today.

The doubts circled in his brain, around and around without resolution. There were so many unanswerable "what ifs" in this game, and they all came so close to driving him mad with their dangerous uncertainties.

"Coll?"

Coll glanced down, startled, to find her staring up at him.

"Do you . . . do you still believe in all those things you fought for? You know, liberty and justice and . . . and all that."

He laughed, a sharp, bitter laugh that burned like acid in his mouth. "Sure, I still believe in all those fancy words. I just don't think they're worth dying for. Not anymore."

Unable to meet Dayra's unblinking gaze, Coll turned his head to stare down at the carefully tended garden below them. Although the pale colors of dawn were slowly spreading along the horizon, the garden was still sleeping, wrapped in darkness.

In his mind's eye, Coll could see Dayra's footprints in the soft earth, leading away from him; he could see his own foot crushing down where she'd just stepped, obliterating her print and compacting the newly turned soil until it possessed neither texture nor shape.

Was that how it would be if he stayed on Far Star and helped the rebels? Would his interference destroy what these people were trying so hard to build?

As though sensing his dark thoughts, Dayra pulled free of his arms. Coll reluctantly let her go.

She turned to look out at the silent grasslands that swept away from them, glowing with the light of the sun that was just beginning to peek over the edge of the world.

"I have a dream," she said at last, her gaze fixed on the distant horizon. "A dream of the future when all this land is filled with animals grazing, or turned into fields that are producing enough food to feed hundreds, maybe thousands of people. I have a dream of a future where Jason and Jeanella are happy and safe and free to do what they please, wherever and whenever they please."

She swung back to face Coll, her eyes glowing with the intensity of the emotions driving her. "It's that dream that gets me up in the morning, even when my body aches and my hands hurt so badly I want to cry. It's that dream that brought me here and that makes all the hardship and suffering worthwhile, because there's always the chance it will come true someday."

She leaned closer and laid her hand against Coll's chest. Coll could feel the muscles of his chest tighten, as though the air he breathed had suddenly become trapped in his lungs. His pulse pounded in his throat.

"That's my dream, Coll Larren," she said. "I never realized just how fragile that dream is . . . until now. I never realized how much it depends on the dreams of people like you, people with dreams big enough to fill a whole world, and the courage to make them come true."

She leaned closer still, so close Coll stopped breathing entirely. "Hold fast to your dreams, Coll Larren. *Fight* for them, because they're the only ones that make dreams like mine possible."

Chapter Sixteen

Coll plucked Dayra's hands from his chest, but instead of pushing her away as he'd intended, he found himself wrapping his hands around hers and tugging her even closer.

"Are you saying that you want me to join the rebels on Far Star?" he demanded, confused by the warring emotions her words had unleashed in him.

At his sudden harshness, her eyes grew round with shock. "No, I . . . I wasn't even thinking about—"

Coll cursed, softly, but with feeling.

"No, of course you weren't." He looked away, ashamed to see the hurt in her eyes. He shouldn't have doubted her. Dayra had never asked anything for herself; she wouldn't have started now.

She tried to pull free, but he convulsively tightened his hold on her, unwilling to let her go.

His gaze dropped to her hands, half hidden in his. They looked so small and fragile compared to his, so delicate. And yet she was like an anchor for a storm-tossed ship; his hold on her was all that saved him from dashing himself to pieces on the rocks of his uncertainties.

As though she sensed his thoughts, Dayra worked free of his grasp, just enough to curl her fingers over the side of his hand so that Coll was no longer sure if he was holding her hand, or she was holding his.

The gentle pressure of her fingers against the back of his hand, of her flesh against his, were oddly comforting.

His thoughts churning, Coll turned her hands over, exposing the palms. Then he slowly ran his thumbs over the sensitive center, along her fingers, and back again. Her hand opened at his touch, her fingers stretching, trembling slightly. Her skin was warm and rough with calluses from so much hard work.

He could feel her watching him, wondering what he was thinking, but he didn't dare look up, didn't dare release her.

If only he could find the courage to believe in the future as Dayra did! Did she possess some secret knowledge that was hidden from him? The key to a treasure he'd never found? Perhaps if he could understand the source of her faith, then he could rediscover his.

"Tell me," Coll said, fighting the tension within

him. "How do you keep your dreams alive?"

He neither took his gaze off her hands as he spoke nor stopped the slow, exploratory sweep of his thumbs across her skin. "After everything you've gone through, how can you still believe in the future?"

She curled her fingers into her palms, trapping his thumbs.

Coll stiffened at the contact, but he kept his gaze fixed on her hands, afraid to face the concern he might see in her eyes.

"I believe, because I can't live without believing," she said. Her voice was pitched low. It vibrated with the power of her conviction. "I take what I have, and I make of it all that I can. That's all. I can't do anything more than that, and neither can you."

It sounded so simple when she said it. Take what you have, because that's *all* you have. Make what you can, because you can't do anything else, no matter how much you might wish you could.

It sounded like such a narrow vision of life and its possibilities, and yet with that little, Dayra was fighting for a future of virtually limitless possibilities. Because of her dreams and her faith in them, she would transform what she had into what she wanted, regardless of the hardships or the obstacles in her path.

Take what you have. . . .

Coll slipped his thumbs free of her clasp and once more wrapped his hands around hers, but this time he bent his head and brushed a tentative kiss on the back of her wrists. He could feel the sudden tension of her muscles, the barely perceptible twitch of her fingers at the touch of his lips.

From somewhere deep inside himself, Coll sensed a growing certainty, as if something of Dayra's confidence and strength had seeped into him. He brought his head up and found her watching him, her forehead creased in a frown of concern.

Take what you have. . . .

The words came without his willing them, without his even knowing they lay within him. Yet as he spoke, Coll knew he had never spoken more honestly than he did now.

"I love you," he said and watched the morning dawn in Dayra's eyes.

The holding yard was quiet, the house quieter still as they slipped up the stairs to Dayra's room. Everyone was sleeping, worn out from the excitement of the night before.

Everyone but them.

Coll tugged at the fastenings of Dayra's shift, fighting to control the euphoria, the raw energy surging through him. He wanted her so badly that every fiber of his being trembled and burned. His breath came in short, shallow gasps, as though the air around him had suddenly become too rarefied to serve his needs.

And yet as he knelt to drag off the form-fitting shorts she wore under her shift, Coll paused, caught by the naked heat of her, the sheer *aliveness* of her.

She stood before him, just as she had that first night on the holding wall when he had kissed her and the world had tilted off course. The rising sun bathed her in gold, highlighting the soft glow of her delicate skin and the silken sheen of her hair, which now hung loose about her shoulders and down to her waist.

Had he ever really thought her too thin? What a fool he'd been! Here, open to his gaze, was every soft curve, every firm, feminine line a man could dream of.

He laid his hand against the smooth swell of her thigh, where it joined her hip, then slowly traced the curves of her hip and waist with his palm, relishing the feel of firm muscle and soft, warm flesh beneath his fingers. She watched, scarcely breathing, and somehow knowing she watched made touching her even more sensually seductive.

Slowly, infinitely slowly, he brought his hand back down over her belly. Coll could feel the quivering tightness of her muscles, the barely restrained eagerness within her. His own muscles trembled, aching with the tension that held him captive to his growing hunger.

He scarcely brushed the dark gold mass of curls below, but she sucked in her breath as though he had ignited a hundred fires inside her. He could see the way her stomach muscles contracted in response, the way her rib cage expanded and her nipples peaked.

Without warning, Dayra knelt to tangle her hands in his hair and pull his head close to hers.

"I love you, Coll Larren," she said fiercely. "If you believe in anything, believe in that. Everything else can come after."

Coll believed, and in that moment he knew she was right—everything else would come after that simple, wondrous fact. She loved him, and he loved her, and for the first time in a long, long while the future beckoned.

But the future would have to wait, for right now the present had priority. Dayra claimed a swift, hard kiss, then knotted her fists in the front of his shirt and drew him to his feet. Laughing, Coll followed as she led him to the bed, then pulled him down on top of her.

"I'm not going to run away," he said, trying to extricate his shirt from her grasp so he could pull it off.

"I'm not taking any chances," she said, laughing with him, but abandoning his shirt to fumble with his belt, instead.

"Take what you have," Coll whispered, levering his hips off her so she could accomplish her self-appointed task.

"And make of it all you can." Dayra's fingers stopped their tantalizing exploration as her eyes locked on his. Her hands slipped in under his shirt and around to the sides of his waist, pulling him closer, and this time it was Coll's stomach muscles that knotted in response.

"So much, Coll," she whispered, soft enough that he had to bend his head to catch her words. Her hands slid up his back, pulling him closer still. "There's so very, very much."

And then she proceeded to show him just how much there could really be.

The sun was well up before Coll heard any sound from the people who had spent the night in the holding. He frowned, wishing there were some way he could keep the world at bay for a little while longer, knowing that it would intrude whether he wanted it to or not.

He glanced toward the window, but all he could see was bright blue sky and faint wisps of white clouds, lazily drifting past. The view was pretty enough, but he much preferred the view toward the other side of the bed, where Dayra lay sleeping.

He'd spent most of the past hour watching her sleep. He would happily have spent the rest of the day watching if he could. She lay on her side with her hand curved beneath her cheek and her hair tumbled about the pillows. Her back was to him, her body curled into his.

She'd fallen asleep that way, too tired and too content to notice the day was fully dawned. Coll hadn't tried to sleep. He couldn't have if he'd wanted to.

I love you. Three simple words.

It had cost him every drop of whatever courage he possessed to say them, and they had set him free.

He felt as though a weight had been lifted from his soul, as if the past had lost its power to twist and distort his present, leaving him to face the future unafraid.

Three words, yet what potent words they were!

Ever since Dayra had fallen asleep in his arms, Coll had struggled to comprehend just what had happened. He hadn't yet come close to understanding, but for the first time in his life, explanations weren't really necessary. It was enough just to feel the breath going in and out of his body, enough to feel Dayra's warm body pressed tight against him and to watch the slight smile that crossed her lips as she chased her dreams through sleep.

Take what you have. . . .

For the first time, what he had was enough—more than enough—and he was content.

Coll knew the minute he rose from the bed and pulled on his clothes and went downstairs that the world would come back to pressure him with its demands and necessities. But the world could wait for a little while longer, for he had no intention of leaving Dayra's side until he had to.

Coll shoved up on one elbow and leaned over to brush a whisper-soft kiss on Dayra's cheek. Still sleeping, she smiled, ever so slightly, then burrowed deeper into the pillow. The movement pulled the light blanket off her, exposing her to the morning air.

Gently, Coll lifted a heavy lock of hair that had fallen forward across her shoulder and tucked it out of the way so he could feast on the sight of her breasts. Half hidden in the twisted sheet and pressed together by the curl of her body, they tempted him with their soft roundness, teasing his body into remembering how perfectly they fit in his hands and how quickly her nipples hardened in response to his slightest touch.

He almost felt jealous of the pendant she wore, for it lay against one breast, its purple stone glinting in the morning light.

Coll longed to tug the sheet away and place a kiss on her breast, just where the pendant lay. He longed to wake her so that he could make love to her again. He didn't touch her. Dayra needed whatever rest she could claim before the rest of the world shoved in and demanded her attention. If only he could shelter her from all the hardships of this life she'd chosen!

Even that fleeting thought made him smile, imagining what her reaction would be if he were ever sufficiently demented to try. He couldn't run her life for her, and he had no intention of trying.

Which didn't mean he wouldn't do everything within his power to protect Dayra from Talman Bardath's threats. Unfortunately, in a situation like this, a defensive position was always more difficult to maintain than an offensive one.

Coll frowned, considering the problem. Perhaps working with the rebels was the wisest choice, after all. With their support, he had a chance of bringing down Bardath. Without it, he was damn near helpless.

The thought of once more getting into the fight against the Combine was tempting. More than tempting, Coll admitted. It made his heart beat faster just thinking about it.

What had Dayra told him, there in the dawn?

Fight for your dreams, she'd said. *They're the only ones that make my dreams possible.*

But how? He'd been over the problem a thousand times. The rebels on Far Star possessed neither the weapons nor the training they needed to succeed in their rebellion. There was absolutely no chance they'd have them before the Combine managed to consolidate its hold on the planet, which meant a rebellion, if it came, would be a very bloody proposition indeed.

How had Dayra succeeded? She lacked the machinery, money, and laborers needed to make her holding work. In spite of those limitations, she was slowly building the future she dreamed of.

Take what you have. Make of it all you can.

What did she have? What did any of the settlers have? Nothing! These were people who used tools like mattocks and hoes and shovels instead of modern machinery, pressed grass instead of wood, and handmade ropes and fishnets. What were they supposed to do? Catch the Combine soldiers in a fishnet? The soldiers wouldn't even look twice at—

Coll sat up abruptly.

Take what you have.

That little philosophy could be applied to a lot more things than running a holding. It might just work if you were running a rebellion, too.

By the time Dayra woke, dressed, and got downstairs, the morning was half gone. She could hear the sound of people talking and bustling about in the holding yard, but the only people in the house were Johnny and Coll. They were seated at the kitchen table, hunkered over cups of hot tea and engaged in an intense, low-voiced discussion that came to an abrupt halt the minute she walked into the room.

"Good morning," she said lightly, hoping the sudden rise in her temperature at the sight of Coll wasn't perceptible to anyone but her.

He looked so . . . so temptingly real and strong and sure of himself as he sat there, his elbows on the table and his big hands wrapped around his cup of tea. He was still dressed in the rough work clothes he'd worn for their little "fishing" expedition. A full day's growth of beard stubbled his jaws and chin. From the disorder of his shaggy hair, she guessed he'd used his fingers in place of a comb this morning.

Dayra tried not to blush at the memory of how eagerly she'd run her own fingers through those thick locks. She failed utterly. The sudden, discomforting flow of heat across her face made her tense, embarrassed by her lack of sophistication.

An instant later his eyes met hers and Dayra felt her cheeks grow even hotter. This time, however, it was from the heat he so easily roused within her, not from some absurd notion of propriety.

Coll Larren was a man of hard angles and rough edges. He had said he loved her and Dayra believed him because she could not imagine *not* believing him. But if there was to be any public acknowledgment of their love, it was up to her to make it. She knew instinctively that he would not force himself on her, would not demand of her more than she was willing to give.

At the same time, the thought of telling the world—of just telling Johnny—about her love for Coll was frightening. Not because she mistrusted Coll, but because she mistrusted herself. It was one thing to admit she loved Coll when she was in his arms and the world was safely shut away, quite another to put her love out where life could take its try at trampling it. She'd stood alone for so long that she was afraid to let herself depend on anyone, even someone she loved as much as she loved this strong, gentle man who watched her with understanding lighting his eyes.

It was that understanding that gave her the courage to walk around the table to Coll's side, then bend down to offer a hesitant kiss.

The instant Coll's lips touched hers, Dayra's hesitation vanished. She bent lower to claim a hotter, hungrier kiss, then run her fingers through his hair just as she'd longed to do since the moment she'd stepped into the room.

When she at last pulled away, Dayra was dazed and shaken, trembling with the force of the emotions burning within her. She was also certain, absolutely certain, that she'd made the right choice, whatever the ultimate consequences might be.

"Good morning," she said again, very softly.

"A very, very good morning," Coll said, just as softly, reaching to touch her lips with the tip of one finger. He smiled, and in that smile glowed a promise that needed no words for it to say all that Dayra longed to hear.

Dayra might have stood that way forever, her eyes locked with Coll's, her body so close to his that she could feel his warmth, even though they weren't touching, if Johnny hadn't finally cleared his throat in a very loud and very awkward, "Ahem!"

Startled, she whirled around to find the old man watching her and Coll with a comical combination of embarrassment and satisfaction lighting his weather-beaten face. Before she could move away, Coll wrapped his arm around her waist and dragged her down to sit on his lap.

"Johnny and I were just discussing the possibility of a rebellion here on Far Star," he said, "but there are a number of things we need to discuss with you first."

Talman Bardath had long ago learned to maintain an expression of poised hauteur when he was in the public halls of the Combine's central headquarters on Edole, regardless of what he was really thinking and feeling. His enemies were too numerous and too willing to take advantage of any weakness, however slight, for him to let his guard down by indulging in so much as an irritated frown.

That was why his present inability to control his fury only enraged him more. He'd hadn't yet struck anyone, but his clenched fists trembled with his craving for a physical outlet to his inner violence.

At least he had the satisfaction of seeing everyone in his path scatter in fear as he approached.

343

The word of his rage preceded him, it seemed. There was some satisfaction in that. Not everyone was foolish enough to think they could challenge him without suffering the consequences.

Bardath slammed open the door to his suite of offices and stalked across the open reception area, roaring out orders as he went. He didn't stop to see if his orders were obeyed. His secretaries and aides knew better than to defy him. He'd made sure long ago that they knew how extraordinarily unpleasant the penalties for not obeying could be.

Once in his private office, he vented his rage by sweeping the stack of papers and recording disks on his desk to the floor, scattering them so it would be an hour's work just to put them back in order. When that proved insufficient relief, he tried hurling a valuable sculpture against the far wall. The sculpture shattered in a thousand tiny fragments, but Bardath scarcely heeded the destruction. He was already angrily pacing the length of the room, his mind churning.

Ble'nara Ro, the newly named chairman of the Combine Central Committee, had demanded he— he! Talman Bardath!—explain the actions of the Security Police in a dozen different instances. How dare that small-minded, moralistic little rat of a man challenge him in an open meeting as if he were nothing more than a minor functionary! And five of the Committee members had encouraged Ro's questions, including one member who owed her seat to his support!

That left only four members of the Committee who hadn't yet opposed him. Three of them would never dare confront him, Bardath knew. All he had to do was threaten to reveal the information he held against them and their careers would be destroyed forever. But ensuring they wouldn't speak against him didn't guarantee they would defend him in a Committee debate, either.

The fourth, whose influence on the Committee even Bardath didn't dare challenge, had generally supported his activities. But that didn't mean he would continue to support them, especially if the Committee swung toward Ro and against Bardath and the Security Police under his direction.

At the thought of Ro's increasingly effective campaign against him, Bardath snarled in rage. In the almost three weeks since his return from Far Star, he'd spent all his energies in trying to stop the man's depredations. Unfortunately, Ro had taken brilliant advantage of his absence. It wouldn't be easy to put a halt to his activities now that he'd been named Chairman.

Bardath kicked at a pile of papers that had fallen in his path, cursing fluently. If he hadn't been so distracted by this damnable disease that was slowly killing him, he would never have allowed Ro the opportunity to gain a seat on the Committee, let alone the Chairmanship. But in the first months of diagnosis and treatment, he'd let far too many things slide. Now his greatest enemy, a man who had consistently opposed him for years, was in a perfect position from which to destroy him.

At the thought of Ro as Chairman, Bardath ripped a small, exquisite tapestry from its mounting, shredding it in the process. Even the

345

destruction of the tapestry was not enough to allay his rage.

He should have had Ro killed long ago, but the balance of powers between them had always made it difficult to move against the man.

Until he found Triana's necklace and the recording disk he'd hidden in it, Bardath knew he'd have no chance of reining in Ro. The disk contained the only information he had that might give him leverage over Ro and his followers on the Committee. All he had to do was make sure that no one ever saw the full recording, which could be as dangerous to him as to his enemies.

But he had to get the disk first.

Damn that slut Dayra for having sold off her mother's jewels! His people had traced all the rest of the pieces, but no one had yet discovered who had purchased the *porfhyr* pendant.

He'd never liked the bitch, but now, with the loss of the disk added to her theft of both his money and his son, he had more than enough reason to claim his revenge. She'd pay, and pay heavily, for her treachery.

A firm knock at the door to his office stopped Bardath in midstride. At his snapped order to come in, the door opened to admit a cold-eyed senior officer in the uniform of the Security Police.

"You sent for me, Domine?"

"Assemble thirty of your best people. I want them heavily armed and ready to leave in two hours." Truva would learn to regret having refused to help him the first time around. Bardath was looking forward to teaching her.

"You're returning to Far Star?"

Bardath nodded. "We'll use the same ship I used two weeks ago. Make sure it's ready to leave as soon as your people are on board. I'll join you then."

"As you wish." The officer placed a recording disk on the desk in front of Bardath. "Dor just sent this from Far Star. The man you control inside the holding has taken some holographic shots of the boy, as you ordered." With that, the officer saluted, then executed a smart about-face and left.

Bardath stared at the disk.

His son.

He'd almost worn the earlier recording disk smooth playing it over and over, trying to trace the subtleties of the boy's resemblance to him.

For the first time, Bardath wondered if it was really worth the expenditure of time and energy required to bring Ble'nara Ro down. At best, he only had three or four good years left to him before the disease destroyed his mind. Since Jason could not hope to take over his position within the Combine, perhaps he would be wiser to give up his political powers now. That would leave him free to focus on preparing the boy to assume control of the personal empire he'd built over the years.

At the thought of conceding defeat to his enemy, Bardath involuntarily clenched his hands into fists. He'd never allowed anyone to get the best of him. He wasn't going to start now.

This time he would not linger on Far Star. Too

many people now knew of his purpose there for it to be worth the effort of disguising his motives. With 30 of his best people to support him, he would humble Truva, destroy Dayra, and reclaim his son. Then he would return to Edole and do whatever was necessary to bring Ro down, as well.

His son and his fortune were the only immortality he would ever know. He would let nothing endanger them. *Nothing.*

Chapter Seventeen

Of all the hard work she'd done over the past five years, Dayra decided that cutting the tall, coarse grass that grew in such profusion on the far side of the holding was the worst. The grass, which had been used to make the holding's doors, gates, and some of its crude furniture, oozed a sticky sap that made handling it a detestable chore. She'd harvested the grass in small quantities when she needed glue, but she'd never before had to cut so much of it at one time.

At least she finally understood why the people who regularly worked with this stuff charged such high prices for their products. There had to be some compensation for the misery of being coated with the goo on a daily basis.

The only consolation was that the others working with her weren't managing the job any better. All of them were covered with the sap. Their clothes would probably have to be washed two or three times before they could be worn again.

Fortunately, they shouldn't need more than this one batch of grass. If they did, Coll could just find someone else to help, Dayra decided. She had no intention of suffering through this a second time.

Every time she stopped long enough to consider the matter, she was amazed all over again at how much life had changed in the three short weeks since Coll had agreed to work with the rebels. The holding was filled with people now, every one of them busily engaged in producing the supplies they would need when they finally moved against the government. And that, according to Coll's plans, would be soon, before Truva and her people could figure out what they were up to. There were now too many people scattered across Far Star who had joined the rebels when word of the Sandman's presence leaked out for the secret to hold for long.

Dayra had to admit she'd enjoyed having so many people around. The rebels were pitching in to do their fair share, so they hadn't created as much extra work as she'd expected. As payment for the additional food they consumed, a number of them had helped her clear and prepare the remaining fields inside the holding, work that would have taken her another year or two to complete on her own.

The "fishing" expedition that Coll had organized to protect the arms shipment had provided a valuable lesson in cooperative efforts on which they'd been quick to capitalize. The boat was taken out almost daily now. Several of the settlers were proving to be first-class fishermen. The larger catches they brought in not only provided the food needed to feed so many people, it gave them extra they could sell in the market at Trevag.

Johnny and Megat, who had been chosen as the chief message carriers, used the excuse of selling the fresh fish to travel between the holding and Trevag regularly. They'd even worked in a couple of trips to the spaceport and the mines when information needed to be shared quickly.

So far, none of the government soldiers or market inspectors had expressed any suspicion over their frequent trips. According to Johnny, they were more than happy to receive a fresh fish or two in exchange for ignoring the fact that he and Megat didn't always file all the required reports on their sales.

Dayra glanced over at Megat, who had volunteered to help harvest the sticky grass. He didn't look as if he were relishing the experience, but then he'd been down-in-the-mouth for the past couple of weeks. Missing his kids, probably. When Dayra had asked him where Alara and Felix were, he'd snapped that they were with friends near Trevag, then stomped off. She hadn't dared ask him again, despite Jeanella's and Jason's frequent promptings.

Thinking about the past weeks wasn't getting the present work done, however. Dayra sighed and picked up her bundle of grass, then carried it over to the crude hoist they'd rigged at the top of the holding wall.

Although the hoist was strong enough to lift her up, as well, Dayra decided to take advantage of the chance for some time to herself by walking around to the main gate.

The past three weeks had brought far more changes than just the new people and the almost ceaseless activity around the holding. Finding herself in love and in the middle of a rebellion, all at the same time, was an exciting, frightening, and thoroughly unsettling experience, and she still hadn't quite adjusted.

For Jason and Jeanella's sake, she and Coll had filed as Companions with the registry office in Trevag. The relationship was neither as binding nor as complicated as a full marriage, but she still had trouble grasping the differences it had brought into her life.

For the first time since her mother's death, someone else had a say in the decisions she made and the life she chose to lead. It was one thing to have to consider the effect of any decision on her brother and sister, quite another to acknowledge the right of another person, even someone she loved as much as she loved Coll, to support or oppose her choices.

Not that Coll had tried to control her. If anything, he might pay a far heavier price for her meddling in his life than anything she would ever suffer. More than once over the past weeks, when he thought he was unobserved, she had seen in his eyes, in the tension in his body, the fears that hounded him constantly now.

His fears were not for himself, she knew, but for the safety of those he led. Every time she caught his worried frown, Dayra felt a stab of guilt that she was the one responsible for dragging him back into a struggle he'd already renounced.

Beneath her guilt lay her fear that she'd drawn Coll into the rebellion—a rebellion she'd never before considered joining—because she wanted his help in defending Jason and Jeanella against Talman Bardath. She didn't want to believe that she could be that despicably self-serving, but every time she saw the worries he hid from everyone else, she couldn't help doubting her own motivation.

And yet, when night came and they could be alone together at last, all the doubts and fears and frustrations that plagued her during the day disappeared as if they'd never been. Safe in Coll's arms, she was discovering a world of infinite pleasures and subtle delights she'd never before imagined. ·

Whatever the future held, Dayra thought she could face it so long as Coll was by her side to face it with her.

The minute she rounded the end of the holding wall, Dayra realized she might need Coll by her side very quickly. Three military skimmers were visible in the distance, and they were headed straight to her holding.

She didn't need to shout a warning. The lookout posted on the holding wall had already spotted them and was alerting the others to the unexpected visitors.

Well, not totally unexpected, Dayra admitted to herself as she hurried along the base of the wall. Coll had warned them to expect a visit by someone—sooner, rather than later, he'd said.

Truva's soldiers and spies were neither blind nor stupid, he'd reminded them. They would spot the unusual activity on holdings and small settlements around Far Star. They'd certainly notice the absence of so many people from their accustomed haunts. Even without the sophisticated communications and monitoring equipment available on more developed worlds, it wouldn't take them long to figure out where all those people had gone.

Once again, Coll was right. Thank the stars he'd also given them instructions on how to handle a visit such as this.

Dayra reached the main gate just before the first two skimmers veered off to approach the entrance at widely separated angles. It didn't take military training to see that their positions gave them a wider angle of attack and made them difficult targets for anyone in the holding who might be shooting at them.

The third and smaller skimmer came right up to the gate at a sedate pace that suggested peaceful intentions, but gave the other two skimmers time to get in place in case a fight developed.

Even knowing there was nothing in the holding that would rouse suspicions, Dayra couldn't help feeling nervous. Beneath the nervousness, however, lay a growing anger at the intrusion.

It was the anger, properly restrained, that she let show in her expression as she squared her shoulders and prepared to face the skimmer's emerging occupants.

Two Grauns, stunners at their sides, climbed out first. Immediately behind them came two human males, similarly armed. The four took up positions on both sides of the skimmer that would give them each a clear field of fire in case of need.

Even as she waited for whoever remained in the skimmer to emerge, Dayra couldn't help wondering at her sudden awareness of concepts like fields of fire and angles of attack. It was amazing how quickly one could develop that awareness if one was on the wrong side of the law.

As the skimmer's remaining passenger climbed out, Dayra stiffened in surprise.

"Capt. Truva," she said in as coldly polite a tone as she could manage. "We hadn't expected the honor of your company quite so soon after your last visit."

"No doubt," Truva responded dryly. She tilted her head back to study the top of the holding wall. "I rather expected a more impressive reception than this, Settler."

"If you'd let us know you were coming, we might have arranged something more to your liking, Captain. As it is, we're rather busy right now." Dayra smiled sweetly, knowing Truva would not mistake the meaning behind the expression. "Perhaps you'd like to come back later."

"Perhaps. However, as long as we're here—"

The little-boy voice that interrupted Truva was unmistakable. "I got my rocks, Dayra! You want me to throw 'em?"

Appalled, Dayra whirled around, her heart in her throat. "Jason! You get down from there this minute!" she shouted. "If you throw even one rock, you'll go to bed without supper! Do you hear me?"

At that moment, Johnny's head popped above the edge of the wall, right beside Jason.

"Come down from there, ye little pest," he said. No one could mistake his tone, not even a six-year-old boy bent on mischief. When Johnny wrapped his arm around Jason's waist and dragged him off the top of the wall, Jason didn't try to fight. He simply went limp, which would, Dayra knew from experience, make him even harder to carry.

"I'm sorry, Captain," she said shakily, turning back to face Truva. She wished her hands weren't gummed over from cutting the grass. Her hair was falling into her eyes and she very much would have liked to jerk it back, just to relieve the tension that Jason's little escapade had generated in her.

"You should keep a closer watch on your brother, Settler," Truva said, clearly irritated.

"He's six years old, Captain!" Dayra said sharply, goaded by Truva's haughty disapproval. "Or don't you remember what it was like at that age?"

Truva stiffened, but refrained from taking up the challenge. Instead, she said, "I am here because of rumors that illegal arms are being held here, and that this is a meeting place for potential rebels. Do you have any objection to my people searching your holding?"

Dayra sighed, trying to regain her composure

and still maintain the pose of indignant landholder that Coll had advised would be most appropriate. "I don't suppose it would make much difference if I *did* object, would it, Captain?"

"Only in the amount of effort I would have to put into getting through that gate, Settler," Truva admitted. "It would be much easier for both of us if you simply let my people pass."

Resigned, and grateful that so blatant a display of power was bringing her anger back with a vengeance, Dayra stepped aside. "The gate's open, Captain."

"Thank you." There was nothing in Truva's voice to indicate any real gratitude. She gestured to two of her soldiers, who hurried past her and, weapons in hand, cautiously pushed the massive gate partway open.

At the sight of the busy crowd of people inside the holding, the soldiers hesitated, then even more cautiously swung the gate all the way to the side so the captain's skimmer could enter.

The holding's occupants dropped whatever they were doing the minute the skimmer appeared. Some chose to stay right where they were; others, either more bold or more curious than their friends, strolled toward the gate with every appearance of people who weren't sure whether to be irritated or pleased by having their work disturbed.

Everything looked perfectly normal, Dayra decided. Normal, that is, if she'd regularly had almost 40 people living and working on the holding.

Although Truva had clearly expected to find

more than the usual number of people in the holding, she just as clearly hadn't expected to find so many. That everyone had been employed at tasks that didn't look at all like rebel plotting was even more obviously a surprise to her.

"What are all these people doing here, Settler?" she demanded, with extra emphasis on the "what."

"They're working, Captain."

"That's absur—*What* are they working on?"

Dayra shrugged. "A variety of things. Do you want a guided tour? Or would you rather your people just snoop around until they're bored to death?"

"I warn you, you're trying my patience, Settler."

"And you're trying mine, Captain!" Dayra snapped. The anger was an excellent front for her growing nervousness. She'd thought Coll would be here to help her by now, but she couldn't see him anywhere. Surely he wasn't going to leave her to handle Truva all alone? "I'm growing tired of your suspicions. There are no arms here, Captain, any more than there were the last two times you barged in."

Truva evidently decided not to escalate hostilities any further, because she clamped her mouth shut, then turned to wave a second skimmer through the gate.

Among the skimmer's occupants were the two Mmmrxs who'd used their olfactory talents to search the holding the first time. At least, Dayra assumed they were the same ones. She'd never been able to tell the creatures apart.

Once Truva had her temper back under control, she said more calmly, "I would appreciate it, Settler, if you would tell me why so many people are working here. That's assuming, of course, that you haven't suddenly come into a fortune and hired them to work for you."

Dayra didn't bother to smile. "We're working together, Captain. We decided if one collaborative fishing expedition could be so successful, it was worth seeing what we could achieve in other areas."

It cost her an effort to refrain from any mention of Truva's disruption of that expedition, but she managed to keep her voice as politely calm as Truva's as she led the captain on a tour of the various work areas.

"We're making rope, here," she said, indicating an area heaped high with the long, thin grass that could easily be braided into a strong and flexible, if crude, rope.

"And over there, they're using the finer ropes to make fishing nets. I imagine your people have already told you about all the fresh fish we're getting into the market in Trevag, Captain," she added.

To her surprise, Dayra realized she was almost beginning to enjoy the deception. Perhaps she had more rebel blood in her veins than she'd thought. "We're getting an excellent price for the fish, far better than anything I ever made on the dried fish I sold."

As Dayra led Truva past the big vats where several people had already started to process the grass they'd gathered that morning into a sticky glue, she suddenly remembered how gummy her hands and arms and clothes were. In the nervous strain of dealing with the captain, she'd forgotten both her appearance and her own discomfort.

For one wild instant, Dayra considered brushing up against Truva and ruining her beautifully starched uniform, but decided to restrain herself. Deliberate provocation wouldn't get her anything but more trouble.

In the spirit of open communication, Dayra even tried to take Truva on a tour of the various fields inside the holding. The captain demanded to explore some of the buildings, instead.

To Dayra's relief, they found Coll in one of the work sheds. He was industriously mixing something with a mortar and pestle and didn't appear to be aware of their existence until Dayra spoke.

"I know you're acquainted with Coll Larren, Captain," she said. Even though she tried, she couldn't keep a note of anger from creeping into her voice. The memory of Coll's arrest was still too unpleasantly vivid.

"Yes, I am," Truva murmured. Her gaze was fixed on the small mound of leaves and seeds heaped beside Coll on the workbench. "May I ask what you are doing?"

"Me? I'm trying a new blend of herbs and spices from Dayra's garden," Coll said with a charming air of innocence. "Would you like to try it?" He shoved the mortar with its ground contents under Truva's nose.

The captain immediately sneezed, then sneezed

again, more violently. Her eyes were watering as she hastily backed away.

"What the devil is that?" she demanded, barely controlling another sneeze.

"Pepper. A sort of pepper, anyway," Coll replied. "Dayra's found that traditional pepper plants don't seem to grow well here on Far Star, which is why all the pepper's imported and damned expensive. We figured if we could develop something similar, we could sell it at a considerably lower price and still make good money."

"If the smell's anything to go by," Truva snapped, "you'll make a fortune." She wiped the tears from her eyes and moved farther away from the bench before adding, "I trust you haven't forgotten our little conversation, Larren?"

Coll didn't move, didn't even alter his expression by so much as the twitch of a muscle, yet Dayra was suddenly conscious of a cold and angry tension within him that hadn't been there a moment before.

"How could I forget, Captain?" he said with exquisite calm. "You made your points with great clarity."

Truva glanced at Dayra, as though debating the wisdom of saying more in front of her, then looked back at Coll. "I'm not waging war against you or anyone else, Larren. But I won't let people's lives be destroyed as they were on Cyrus IV. Change that comes through violence won't benefit anyone in the long run."

Dayra could see Coll's fingers tighten around the mortar he held, but his voice when he spoke was perfectly controlled. "And what about non-violent change, Captain? Where does that fit into your vision for the future?"

"I'd welcome it. I'd even help it along, if I could. But there's no way you and these hotheaded dreamers can overthrow the Combine here on Far Star. We're too well armed and too well trained. We have communications systems you lack. We have transportation you can't match. You can't win, and if you try, a lot of innocent people will die. I can't permit that. Don't force me into a confrontation that neither of us wants."

Once started, Truva clearly found it impossible to stop her impassioned plea. As though she could permit nothing to come between her and Coll, she grabbed the mortar out of his hands and slammed it down on the workbench, then leaned close enough so she could stare directly into his unblinking eyes.

"Listen to me, Larren. Things are changing in the Combine. Ble'nara Ro has just taken over the Chairmanship of the Central Committee. He's got good people backing him, people who are working toward the same goals you and I are. But they need time, time they won't have if they get hit by rebellion."

"How much time, Captain?" Coll was making no effort to control his emotions now. His eyes were blazing, his shoulders rigid with the anger that gripped him. "A year? Ten years? A hundred? How long do people have to wait before they get a fair chance at living their lives without a restrictive government breathing down their necks?"

Truva didn't answer. Like a runner just finishing an impossibly long race, she took a deep breath, then another, and straightened until her shoulders were as stiff and straight as Coll's.

Dayra watched the exchange, her heart racing, her lungs burning because she could scarcely breathe, she was so tense and confused. Had she really understood what she'd just heard? Did Truva really want change as much as they did? Was her rigid adherence to the letter of the law really motivated by a desire to avoid bloodshed, rather than a passion for power? Had they misjudged the situation so badly? And what did it mean for Coll and Neur and Megat and all the others who were risking so much on the hope of freedom? What did it mean for her?

She had questions, but no answers, and it didn't look as if she'd get any soon. Coll and Truva were too caught up in their own conflict even to remember her presence, let alone concern themselves with explanations.

Johnny's arrival in the work shed came as a welcome interruption. The old man strolled in as calmly as if he'd expected to find his friend and the commander of the Far Star garrison locked in a battle of wills and as if he considered having a dozen soldiers searching the holding an everyday occurrence.

"Ah, Cap'n!" he said cheerily, coming to a halt beside Dayra. He hooked his thumbs in his belt, thrust his shoulders back, and beamed on all and sundry. "Have to apologize about the boy, I'm afraid. He'd been sore disappointed we've not let him pelt any visitors with all those rocks he's gathered. Been readin' too many silly stories about robbers and brigands and what not, ye understand. We havena been able to convince him there are none o' their like here."

With a visible effort, Truva forced herself to relax before turning to face Johnny and uttering what Dayra was beginning to suspect was her favorite word.

"Indeed?" Truva said in a carefully controlled voice. "For the sake of my people and their safety, I trust you've confined the little monster."

"Oh, aye, that I have. He's locked in his room for now, but he's prepared to make his proper apologies if ye'd like to speak to him, Cap'n."

Truva's right eyebrow rose a quarter of an inch. "I'll forgo the pleasure, if you don't mind." She stared at Johnny for a long moment, then glanced at Dayra before once more fixing her steady, disconcerting gaze on Coll.

"I've warned you twice, now, Settler," she said, her voice carefully uninflected. "That's once more than I usually do. I don't intend to repeat myself a third time."

With that, she turned on her heel and stalked toward the work shed door. Just before she stepped out into the sunshine beyond, she hesitated, then turned back. Her eyes locked on Coll's. "Remember Aleena," she said, and then she was gone.

For a moment, Dayra could only stare after her, startled by the last, inexplicable reference. When she looked back at Coll, she was even more startled to find him carefully dumping the spicy contents of the mortar on the floor of the work shed.

"What—"

"I'll explain later," he said, taking her elbow and Johnny's and leading them out the door.

The soldiers seemed to have completed most of their search, without success. As two armed soldiers and one of the Mmmrxs headed toward them and the work shed, Coll politely pulled Dayra out of their way. Johnny stepped back, his attention firmly fixed on the trio, but Dayra wasn't interested in either the soldiers or the Mmmrx. She wanted to know what Truva planned on doing next.

She was about to start after the captain when a sharp, angry squeal of surprise from inside the work shed stopped her short. A moment later the two soldiers emerged dragging a coughing, wheezing, teary-eyed Mmmrx between them.

"Tsk," Johnny murmured beside her. He cocked a knowing eye at Coll. "Ye really should clean up yere messes, ye know. Poor creature can hardly stand, what with all them strong spices in its nose."

The only response Coll offered was a regretful, "Tsk, tsk," before he grabbed Dayra and dragged her off toward the two skimmers parked in front of the main gate.

It took a couple of minutes before Dayra realized he was making a careful mental note of the number of soldiers and their species.

"Remember," he whispered as they approached Truva's skimmer just as the captain headed toward them from the opposite side of the holding. "Act angry, but not too angry. You're the landholder and you want them out of the way so everyone can get back to work."

With that, he abandoned her to face Truva alone while he crossed the holding yard toward the front steps of the house, from which vantage point Jeanella was anxiously watching everything going on around her. Dayra cringed at the sight of her sister's forlorn figure. In the upset of the past half hour, she'd forgotten both her brother and sister. Thank the stars Johnny and Coll hadn't.

She didn't have a chance for too much self-blame because Truva, closely followed by three of her soldiers, came to a halt in front of her a second later.

Drawing a deep, steadying breath, Dayra tried to ignore the fact that one of the three soldiers was a huge, fanged Targ, and concentrated on dealing with Truva, instead.

"Well, Captain, did you find your illegal weapons?" she demanded.

"Not yet, Settler, but we will eventually, I assure you."

"You can't find what doesn't exist," Dayra snapped back.

She was having a hard time concentrating on Truva with the Targ so very, very close. It towered over her, its upper lip curled back to display its fangs to maximum advantage. Dayra could see every one of its 12 claw-tipped fingers twitching, as though it were just waiting for permission to tear her to shreds. She could only hope Truva's presence would keep the beast in line.

As though sensing her appalled fascination with the Targ, Truva glanced up at the huge, furred creature, then looked back at Dayra, a cold, barely perceptible smile on her lips. "The Targ are very effective soldiers and dangerous fighters," she said. "They're enormously powerful, impervious to stunners, and completely fearless. There are two of them assigned to the garrison in Trevag."

Dayra swallowed uncomfortably. "Since I don't know anyone who's thinking of fighting your soldiers, I don't imagine it matters how good the Targ are, Captain."

Truva's smile widened noticeably. "I just thought you might be interested."

With that, she gave an order for her soldiers to regroup before climbing back into her skimmer. The still-wheezing Mmmrx was shoved in after her. Three minutes later both skimmers were out the gate and headed back toward Trevag, closely followed by the third skimmer, which had remained outside the holding walls.

The settlers didn't even wait until Truva and her people were out of earshot before breaking into a raucous cheer.

Dayra didn't feel like joining in the celebration. She was still fighting down the sick feeling of dread that the Targ's presence had stirred deep inside her. They couldn't fight a creature like that. No one could. Coll and Johnny and Neur and all the rest of them were mad even to think of trying.

The sight of Coll with his arm around Jeanella's shoulders crossing the yard toward her was what finally roused Dayra from her horrified reverie. With difficulty, Dayra forced a smile onto her lips and a totally false note of good cheer into her voice as she said, "There you are, Jeanella! I'm so glad you had the good sense to keep out of the way of those soldiers."

"Guess what, Dayra?" Jeanella demanded, her eyes alight with eager excitement. "I'm going to help Coll! I'm going to be a rebel!"

Dayra had just gotten her stomach to settle into its proper place after her encounter with the Targ, but it twisted right up again at her sister's enthusiastic announcement. "You *what?*"

"That's only if I can get my hand on the equipment I need," Coll said soothingly. He gave Jeanella a conspiratorial grin and a hug, then turned back to Dayra. "Do you have anything like an ant around this place?"

"A . . . a *what?*"

"An ant. You know, those six-legged biting insects that dig in the ground. I thought I'd go in for a little bug collecting."

Chapter Eighteen

The holding seemed strangely silent after so many weeks of frenetic activity. Coll was making a last check of the flitter to be sure that everything he'd loaded the night before was in its proper place and he hadn't forgotten anything, but he stopped for a moment to take a last, lingering look around him.

Although dawn was still more than an hour away and Far Star's twin moons had set long ago, there were enough solar-charged lights on around the holding to show the outlines of the silent buildings and the massive stone wall beyond. Everything looked peaceful, yet oddly expectant, as if the holding were silently awaiting the future and all the generations that would be born inside its walls in the long years to come.

Strange, how much his perceptions had

changed. Once, he'd looked around him and seen failed hopes and the mockery that life could make of ambition. Now he saw the promise of a dream. All because one slender woman with a heart and a soul big enough to hold the future had taught him what it meant to believe.

He could only hope the confidence she'd given him hadn't launched him on a fool's quest.

The scrunch of footsteps on gravel drew his attention. He turned to find Johnny coming out of the shadows toward him. "Do you have anything more to load in the flitter?" he asked.

"Nary a thing. Nothin's been left behind. Do ye have everythin' ye need?"

"Yes." Coll cut the word off short, hoping his old friend wouldn't catch the worry behind it.

He *had* to have everything they needed, because there was no going back now. The settlers who had been working at the holding over the past few weeks had left late yesterday, scattering to their homes for one last visit before they converged on Trevag today. Later this morning, people in the spaceport and at the mines, as well as in Trevag, would launch simultaneous attacks against the Combine forces stationed on Far Star. If everything went well, the fighting would be over by nightfall. If it didn't. . . .

"It's too late to worry now, lad," Johnny said softly.

Coll grimaced. "I know that." He closed the cover of the flitter's cargo area. "But there's so much that can go wrong, and this is such a crazy, cockeyed scheme—"

"Aye, so it is, and that's exactly why it has such a good chance o' workin', lad. The soldiers won't worry about the kind o' cargo our people will be carryin' into market today, an' even Truva won't expect somethin' like this."

"Let's hope not." Coll frowned. "Today's only the start of our worries, anyway. Even if we succeed, there's still the Combine to deal with, a government to get started, a—"

"There's a hundred other worries come after, lad, an' we've gone over every one. Are ye forgettin'?"

Coll sighed, then shook his head, frustrated. "You're right, of course, but I can't help worrying . . . for Dayra's sake, as well as for everyone else's."

At least Megat had agreed to stay behind with Dayra at the holding. He hadn't wanted to, but Coll had pressured the man until he couldn't refuse. Just knowing there was someone on the holding to help Dayra if anything went wrong made Coll feel a little better.

Dayra was coming across the yard toward them now, a small bag of food that she'd prepared for them dangling from one hand. At sight of her proud bearing and determined stride, Coll straightened up. He scarcely noticed when Johnny climbed into the flitter and started the motor.

Dayra walked right up to him and wrapped her arms around him, laying her head against his chest and squeezing as hard as she could. Coll hugged her back, then gently tilted her chin up so he could steal a kiss. Her lips were warm and Coll

371

could taste the salty wetness of the tears that had escaped her.

"We'll be all right," he said and kissed away the tears that stained her cheeks.

"I know."

"You just have to look out for yourself and Jason and Jeanella."

"I will."

"Megat is still here."

"Yes."

Coll brushed his face across the top of her head, treasuring the silken caress of her hair against his skin. There wasn't anything to say they hadn't already said long ago.

"I love you," he said, very softly.

Dayra's response was a hearty sniff as she fought against the tears that threatened her. "And I love you, Coll Larren."

Once more Coll bent to claim a swift kiss. Then he eased out of her embrace and climbed into the flitter. "We'll be back as soon as we can."

Dayra merely nodded and stepped away. Johnny brought the flitter up on its cushion of air, then eased it toward the main gate that Megat was holding open for them.

Coll twisted around in his seat, straining for one last glimpse of the woman he loved, but Dayra was already lost in the shadows behind him.

From this high above Far Star, Bardath could clearly see the sun's first rays striking the buildings of Trevag and the Combine garrison on the city's outskirts.

He didn't have much of a chance to admire the sight, even if he'd wanted to, for the shuttle pilot was bringing them in on a steeply angled approach to the garrison's landing field that left little time for gawking. Behind him, 30 of his Security Police and ten crew members from the ship they'd left in orbit stirred restlessly, eager to be started on the mission.

Bardath didn't plan on wasting any time in Trevag. At this time of the morning, the landing area would have only minimal staff, as would the transport garages. It shouldn't take more than a few minutes to commandeer the three military skimmers they'd need. His men were heavily armed and had orders to use any and all force necessary to get the skimmers. He wasn't going to be thwarted by Truva this time around.

In any case, Capt. Truva wouldn't be a problem for long. The two people Bardath had left on Far Star had already documented a number of instances when the good captain had been too lax with suspected rebels or too willing to accommodate the settlers' demands, regardless of existing Combine regulations. That information alone ought to be enough to have her called before a military tribunal.

Bardath's lips twisted in a smile of grim satisfaction. Truva would regret having defied him. He was going to take great pleasure in destroying her military career. If he was lucky, he'd even be present when she was tried. He'd enjoy watching her expression as she realized who was destroying her and why.

But Truva would have to wait. Jason and his two sisters were far more important right now.

According to the informant his people now controlled, the three would be alone on the holding while everyone else was at the market in Trevag today. Bardath didn't care if they were alone or not. No one was going to stop him today. Absolutely no one.

As he'd expected, none of the people they encountered seriously opposed their landing or their requisition of the three skimmers. Not after a couple of high-powered stunners were clearly displayed, at any rate. Leaving the shuttle pilot with firm instructions to remain in the communications center inside Truva's headquarters so he could serve as the link between the skimmers and the main ship, Bardath ordered the rest of his people into the transports.

The two people who'd remained on Far Star over the past weeks served as guides as they pulled away from the garrison. Bardath growled when they told him it would take a little over an hour to reach the holding that was their destination, but there was nothing he could do about it except endure the trip with what small patience he could muster.

At least he could comfort himself with the knowledge that he would have his son in less than two hours. Bardath couldn't decide whether he most enjoyed contemplating that fact, or the equally pleasing thought that he would have Dayra Smith in his power, as well.

After all, he had so many interesting plans for both of them.

*   *   *

Coll and Johnny reached Trevag without incident shortly after dawn. An armed military patrol stopped them just inside the city and demanded to search the flitter. Coll couldn't tell if they really expected to find contraband arms, or if the soldiers were merely bored after a long night. They found nothing that interested them, in any case.

Taking care to maintain the appearance of hardworking settlers delivering their wares, he and Johnny stopped at several places to drop off some of the nets, ropes, pots of glue, and other items manufactured over the past weeks. The people they dealt with were ready for them, tense with the combination of eagerness and fear that was common before a battle. At each stop, the report was the same: everyone was in place; everything was calm.

With each stop, they drew closer to the Combine garrison. Because it was here they would face the strongest opposition, Coll had decided that he and Johnny would lead separate groups of rebels, striking from different angles and working their way toward the headquarters building as swiftly as they could. Fortunately, they had a large number of supporters already in place who were prepared to sabotage critical points, such as the garrison's headquarters, the weapons storage areas, and the landing field first. If the people inside failed to achieve their objectives as quickly as possible, the fight might turn deadly.

Coll could only hope it didn't.

As it always did once he was committed to a

fight, a sense of calm and strong, focused energy took hold of him. It was too late for doubts, too late to wonder if he'd considered all the dangers or made the right decisions. From now until the battle ahead was finally won or lost, he could not allow himself the privilege of thinking about anything but the struggle at hand.

He would have to leave the worrying to Dayra, Coll told himself grimly. She'd have plenty of time to indulge.

Dayra paced from field to field and back again, too restless and worried to concentrate on her work even though the sun had risen some time ago. Jason and Jeanella were engaged in a wild game of chase, dashing around the holding as heedless as wild beasts. Like her, they were finding relief from tension in ceaseless activity. Unlike her, they seemed to be managing to fight off the worst of their fears. She wished she could so easily escape her thoughts.

Megat was even more restless than she was. He'd disappeared immediately after closing the gate behind Coll and Johnny's departing flitter, but Dayra had spotted him several times since, pacing mindlessly from one place to another, his expression drawn and worried. She'd thought about seeking him out, just so she'd have someone with whom to share her worries, but had decided to leave the man alone. He undoubtedly resented having been assigned to guard her and the children. Forcing her presence on him now might well make things more difficult for both of them.

She felt so helpless. The fighting would have begun by now and there was nothing, absolutely nothing, she could do to help.

Dayra was halfway through her endless circle around the holding when she caught the sound of angry shouting, closely followed by a shrill screech from Jeanella. She was in a dead run three steps later.

As she burst through the open gate separating the field from the central holding yard, Dayra caught a flash of motion from the corner of her eye. A second later, someone tackled her from behind, sending her sprawling over the rough gravel.

Desperately, Dayra rolled away from her attacker and tried to scramble to her feet. He was faster. As she lunged upward he wrapped his arm around her waist and pulled her, kicking and flailing madly, against him.

Dayra twisted in his grip, fighting to get enough leverage either to break free or to claw his eyes out. It was hopeless. The man was huge and immensely strong. At the moment when she thought he might well crush her, someone else jerked her out of his arms.

It wasn't to rescue her, however. Before she realized what was happening, her hands were brutally pulled behind her back and her wrists shackled. In desperation, Dayra tried ramming her head and shoulders into her attacker's belly.

"Enough!" the first man snarled, grabbing her by the back of the neck. "We won't hurt you, but you'd best not push your luck. It isn't you he wants most, after all."

377

The second man, the one who'd bound her, snickered. "Not to worry, love," he leered in her face. "If he throws you out, we'll take you in. Providing you give good entertainment, that is."

"Shut your face, you fool," the first snarled. "He's sent others to the mines on Caldera for less than that."

At the threat of the infamous mines, the leering oaf backed off. Dayra felt a brief flash of relief as he moved away from her; then she caught sight of the two military skimmers and the cluster of armed men in the middle of the holding. Her stomach twisted viciously with the sudden return of fear.

No, it couldn't be. . . . Surely the soldiers couldn't have beaten Coll and all the others. Not so soon. . . .

Dayra squeezed her eyes shut, willing her panic to ease and her mind to work. When she was sure she had herself under control, she opened her eyes.

It took a minute for the truth to sink in. The men who held her and the men by the skimmers were dressed in the uniforms of the Combine Security Police, not the Armed Forces. Their invasion of her holding had nothing to do with the rebellion, and everything to do with Talman Bardath's threats against her.

The fear surged back, but this time Dayra was prepared for it. Whatever else she did, she couldn't let fear keep her from thinking clearly.

If only Coll were here! He'd know what to do, know how to handle—

Dayra cut the thought off, before it had a chance

to work its way even deeper in her consciousness. Perhaps if she hadn't allowed herself to depend on Coll so much, if she hadn't relegated so many of her responsibilities to him, this never would have happened.

She never should have let herself come to depend on anyone else, Dayra told herself fiercely. She never should have let down her guard, thinking that someone else would take the responsibility for protecting them. *Never.* If only—

Stop it! She didn't have time for regrets. Not now.

As the two men who'd caught her roughly dragged her toward the skimmers, Dayra tried to concentrate on what she was seeing, tried to guess what might come next. She didn't recognize anyone. Not until the crowd parted and a tall, elegant man stepped forward.

Dayra's stomach twisted again, even harder. Talman Bardath!

The man who'd first grabbed her shoved her forward, making her stumble. Bardath made no move to help her. Instead, he watched, his eyes glittering, as she struggled to regain her balance; then he said, very coldly, very quietly, "So we meet again, Dayra Smith."

Dayra swallowed, shaken by the naked threat in his voice.

Bardath came closer. Dayra flinched, but forced her chin up so she could meet his icy gaze directly.

"You have caused me a great deal of . . . shall

we call it annoyance? Yes, I think annoyance will do." His eyes narrowed and his lips thinned. "I don't like to be annoyed, Dayra Smith. You should know that. You should have known that five years ago."

"Don't tell me you were sorry to see us leave, Bardath," Dayra snapped, putting on as bold a front as she could.

"Not then, no. On the other hand, I didn't like losing either my money . . . or the jewels you sold."

"Those jewels were Triana's!"

"I gave them to her."

"No, you didn't! I—"

Bardath cut her protest short with a vicious backhand across her mouth.

Dayra's head snapped to the side from the force of the blow. She staggered, but managed to keep her feet. She ran her tongue around the edge of her mouth and tasted the sharp tang of blood. Her lips were already beginning to swell.

Her head spinning, Dayra turned back to confront Bardath. She'd gain nothing by not fighting back. Talman Bardath trampled those who were foolish enough to plead for mercy.

"Where are Jason and Jeanella?" she demanded.

"They're safe. I must say, your brother is extraordinarily quick with his teeth and feet."

"If you've hurt them—"

"There wouldn't be a thing you could do about it," Bardath interrupted. His upper lip curled back in a horrifying mockery of a smile. "As it happens, I haven't hurt them, and neither have my men. Jeanella's sale price would be considerably diminished if she were injured. She promises to be just as beautiful as her mother . . . if she lives that long. I'd hate to lose my chance to recover some of what you stole from me just because of any undue violence now."

Dayra's mind reeled. The thin man hadn't just been trying to frighten her. "Even you wouldn't be so despicable."

"I regard it as being practical, nothing more."

"And Jason? What are you planning to do with Jason?"

For a moment, she didn't think he was going to answer her. Then he turned and gave a sharp order for his men to move back towards the skimmer and away from them. Bardath waited until his men had retreated out of earshot before turning back to her.

"Jason is my son," he said.

"I'm surprised you admit it," Dayra said with as much of a sneer as she could manage. "You didn't seem to remember he existed after he was born."

Bardath appeared to consider his reply before saying, "Circumstances change. Jason is my only heir and it has occurred to me that it is time he learned to manage the kind of wealth he will someday inherit from me."

Dayra frowned. There was an odd note in Bardath's voice that hinted at something—she didn't know what—that she ought to understand. Something it was important she understand.

"But tell me, Dayra Smith," Bardath continued, not giving her a chance to pursue her thoughts, "why is it you haven't asked about what I intend to do with you? Don't you care? Or do two children mean so much to you that you'd put them before your own safety?" His voice was deliberately mocking, carefully calculated to unsettle her with its unspoken suggestion of the terrible fate that awaited her.

Dayra shrugged with as confident an air as she could manage. "You'll never get your money out of me if I'm dead. And I know you wouldn't be thinking of selling me into the kind of slavery that you have in mind for Jeanella."

Bardath laughed at that. "That goes without saying. Although. . . ." His voice trailed off as he studied her, as if he were seeing her clearly for the first time since she'd been shoved in front of him.

"There *is* something different about you," he muttered thoughtfully, staring at her as if he expected to see the explanation he was looking for written across her forehead.

An instant later he shrugged and said, "You're wasting my time. I want to know what you did with your mother's jewelry."

Dayra gaped at the unexpected turn in the conversation. "I sold it. You already know that."

"And my people have traced most of it. Most, but not all." For a moment Bardath stared at her, as if weighing what he would say next. "The one piece I can't find is a *porfhyr* pendant set in a star-shaped, *shabar* setting. You do remember the piece, don't you?"

The last wasn't a question, Dayra knew, but a threat.

She felt her lungs constrict, as though her rib cage had suddenly shrunk from the withering force of Talman Bardath's stare. What would he do if she told him she was wearing the pendant now, under her work shift?

She didn't care to find out. He must want it very badly if he had gone to the trouble of coming to Far Star after it. But *how* badly did he want it? Could she use it to trade for her freedom and the children's? If so, how?

"I remember the pendant," she said slowly, as though searching her memory. "I sold it with the rest. I don't remember who bought it. It wasn't important. I just wanted the money."

"You didn't want just the money," Bardath snarled suddenly, wrapping his fist in the front of her shift and dragging her closer to him. "You were mocking me, trying to show you could steal from me and get away with it. I don't tolerate anyone mocking me, Dayra Smith. Not anyone. Not ever."

He shook her until her head snapped back and forth uncontrollably. Dayra scarcely noticed the pain his violence caused her. All she could feel was his hand and the pendant that lay just an inch or so below where he'd grabbed her shift.

What if he accidentally bumped the pendant? What would happen to her, to Jason and Jeanella, if he found what he was looking for so easily?

"All right! All right!" she shouted at last. "I didn't sell it!"

Bardath hesitated, then gave her a last, vicious shake and shoved her away so hard she almost fell. "I know you didn't sell it. My people would have traced it by now if you had."

"No! You don't understand!" Dayra said, hoping she managed just the right note of desperation. "I didn't sell it on Edole! I brought it with me. The pendant and a set of earrings. I thought I might need money in the future, so I kept them, in case."

"Where are they, then?" Bardath was almost trembling with the eagerness of a hunter close to his prey.

"The . . . the earrings are in a chest in the house, in the main room. I sold the pendant."

Bardath reached for her in a sudden resurgence of fury. "You said—"

"I said I brought it with me!" Dayra barely avoided his grasp. "I sold it in Trevag last year. I needed to buy seed and—"

"Seed!" Bardath was controlling his anger with difficulty. "Who'd you sell it to? Give me a name. . . ."

"I don't know who bought it. I swear!" she added when it looked as if Bardath would strike her. "It was someone visiting Trevag, someone from off planet. I can show you where—"

Before she could expand on her lie, one of Bardath's people came running up. "Domine! Domine Bardath!"

Dayra couldn't help noticing he kept safely back out of Bardath's reach.

Bardath whirled around, clearly infuriated with the interruption. "What is it?"

"We just got word from the shuttle pilot. They're under attack, Domine! Rebels have struck the garrison, the landing field, the city—they're everywhere! The pilot's already cut off from the shuttle. He says the control center will probably be overrun in just a few minutes and wants to know what your orders are."

The man was panting and wide-eyed, clearly alarmed by the unexpected news. Even as she felt elation surge through her, Dayra knew he'd made a mistake by revealing his fear to Bardath.

She was right. Bardath turned the full force of his wrath on his hapless subordinate.

"What do we care about rebels, fool? Surely you aren't afraid of a few scruffy settlers playing soldier? Or are you?"

"No. No, of course not, Domine! It's just—"

"Shut up!" Bardath turned away abruptly, already concentrating too deeply to worry about one panic-stricken man. He took several steps to the side, then stopped, and immediately came back.

"Tell the pilot to contact the ship. Have them send down the escape shuttle. Have them send it here. They can land in this open area without too many problems."

"But, Domine! The escape shuttle only holds two people and—"

"Are you questioning my orders?" Bardath demanded in a low, deadly voice.

"No. No, of course not, Domine! It's just—"

"Then do as you're told. Now!"

"Yes, Domine! Of course!"

"And have Lt. Pliath bring me the informant. Immediately."

The man didn't bother to respond. He was scuttling backward even as he saluted. When he was a safe distance from his commander, he turned and fled without regard for dignity.

Bardath turned on Dayra. "What do you know of this rebellion?" he demanded.

Dayra hesitated, uncertain how to respond. What could she say without endangering Coll and the others? What would help her?

If only Coll were here to tell her what to do, to help her outwit Bardath! He'd get her out of this mess.

Even as the thought slipped into her mind, Dayra ruthlessly squelched it. She couldn't depend on Coll for help. She couldn't depend on anyone except herself, and she couldn't afford to waste time wishing things were different.

"Well? Tell me!" Bardath didn't have to raise his voice to sound menacing.

"I don't know much," Dayra admitted, grateful that that statement, at least, was true. There were numerous details of Coll's plans she knew nothing about. Coll had said it was safer that way. Once again he'd been proven right. "They're attacking in Trevag, the spaceport, the mines. I don't know their plans."

Something in her expression must have convinced Bardath she was telling the truth because he relaxed slightly—not much, but enough to let Dayra relax a little, too. At least the rebel attack had distracted him from his threats against her and the children. For now, anyway.

A moment later, her relief came to an end as she saw Megat, hands bound as hers were, being led across the holding yard toward them. For a moment Dayra was conscious of a sharp pang of guilt. She hadn't thought of Megat once since she'd heard Jeanella scream. If his battered face was any indication, Bardath's men had beaten him fairly severely when they'd barged into the holding.

Dayra's sympathy lasted only until Bardath began questioning Megat.

"Why didn't you tell us about the rebellion?" Bardath demanded.

The cold fury visible in his face was enough to make most men quail. Megat didn't even blink. "You only wanted to know about her," he said, jerking his head in Dayra's direction. "Her and the kids. So that's what I told you."

Dayra wondered suddenly if the ground had shifted beneath her feet. *Megat* had betrayed them? But why? She got her answer immediately.

"We still hold your children," Bardath said. There was a world of deadly intent in his words.

Megat didn't miss any of it. His jaw set stubbornly. "You said you'd set them free if I did as you wanted. You said—"

"You're in no position to talk about what I or my people might have told you," Bardath snapped, his rage once more escaping his usually rigid self-control. "I want to know about the rebel plans."

"They're hitting Trevag right now. And the spaceport. I don't know how many of them there are or anything like that. If I did, I'd be fighting with them instead of being here."

Bardath appeared to consider forcing the issue, but opted to abandon it, instead. "Get him out of here." He didn't even bother to look at Megat as he gave the order.

"What about my kids?" Megat shouted, infuriated. "What about Alara and Felix? If you've hurt them—"

His protests were cut off when the man on his right suddenly clubbed him into unconsciousness. Bardath's men grabbed Megat before he hit the ground. As they dragged him off toward the work shed where he'd been held earlier, the toes of Megat's boots left parallel grooves in the dirt.

At the sight of those tracks, Dayra swallowed hard. She'd known Bardath was dangerous, but somehow this careless violence had shaken her far more than his threats.

Her brief rage against Megat had died as quickly as it had come. She could understand the reasons for his betrayal. She'd do the same for Jason and Jeanella, if she had to.

Bardath turned back to her, his eyes flashing dangerously. "Now, as for you. . . ."

Chapter Nineteen

Coll ducked around the end of an administrative building near the center of the Combine garrison. Across the way, he could see five of the rebels assigned to him taking up their positions beside a second building. Behind him, two more rebels should have reached their cover behind a skimmer he'd already disabled.

An instant later, the decoy team of two rebels came racing through the open area between the buildings, hotly pursued by seven Combine soldiers, including one of the Targs.

The decoys, hampered by the heavy personal body shields they wore as protection against the soldiers' stunners, barely cleared the rebels' position before Coll gave a shout, signaling his people to move. They broke from hiding with wild whoops and bloodcurdling yells that startled their quarry, giving the rebels a momentary, but essential advantage.

With smooth efficiency, two of the rebels sent their fishing nets sailing out, tangling five of the soldiers in the rough mesh. The five went down in a confusing welter of arms, legs, heads, and weapons. Before any of them could recover sufficiently to fire a stunner through the nets, two more rebels moved in to disable the soldiers with hypo-sprays that would leave them unconscious for several hours. A third, wielding a container of glue manufactured from the grass Dayra and the others had gathered, poured the gummy substance over the firing mechanisms of every weapon the soldiers carried. It only took a few seconds to make sure no one would ever use the weapons again.

At the same time the fishing nets descended, Coll leaped for the massive soldier nearest him. With a quick flick of his wrist, he tossed a handful of spice in the soldier's face.

Within two steps the soldier dropped his weapon and fell to his knees, choking and gasping for air, tears streaming from his eyes. He was too convulsed even to notice when Coll bound him, hand and foot, in a rope coated with the grass glue. Once the soldier recovered from the spice, he'd find it impossible to break free because his struggles would only bind him tighter.

While Coll dealt with the human, the remaining two rebels brought the Targ down by means of heavy, three-stranded ropes they whirled about their heads, then released. The ropes, weighted at all three ends with rocks from Jason's collection, went spinning through the air until they hit the Targ. The momentum of the rocks immediately wrapped the ropes around and around the creature's arms and legs, bringing it to the ground with a crash.

Before the Targ could recover, one of the men unstoppered a jar slung from his belt, then tossed the jar's contents on the Targ. The tiny, antlike insects inside the jar began to burrow their way under the Targ's fur and away from the light. The instant they hit the Targ's skin, the huge creature began writhing and snorting, too distracted by the tormenting, ticklish feel of the insects' minuscule claws to care about its captors.

Coll had debated using the ants. Tickling, especially for a creature whose skin was as sensitive as the Targ's, could become a form of torture. Unfortunately, the Targ was impervious to stunners and hypo-sprays—and just about everything else available. The insects wouldn't hurt it, and the Targ's hour or so of suffering had to be balanced against the deaths and injuries it would cause if it were loose.

Coll grinned, thinking of the holographic images of a rampaging Targ that Jeanella had created. The hand-held projectors had been intended for classroom use, not battle, but they'd been good enough to confuse two separate field units of Combine soldiers. No one liked facing an angry Targ, including the soldiers from the garrison.

So far, there had been no deaths and only one injury, a Combine soldier who'd broken his arm when he'd become entangled in a fishing net and fallen. Coll could only hope that their record would hold and that the rebels at the mines and the spaceport had had similar luck.

After a quick check to be sure the seven soldiers couldn't work free of their bonds, Coll gave the sign for his people to move forward. Their objective now was to take over the garrison's headquarters and capture Capt. Truva and her senior staff. The captain should be in the building's control center because it was the best place for her to maintain contact with field units deployed throughout Trevag and across Far Star.

The hardest part of the actual fighting lay ahead, Coll knew. For the first time the rebels would be facing soldiers in fortified positions who were forewarned about their weapons and tactics and who would be prepared to deal with fishnets and glue and ropes weighted with rocks.

At least, Coll was hoping that was what the soldiers would be expecting. Surprise was still the most important ingredient in their strategy.

Coll and his team encountered no more opposition before they reached their preestablished positions near Truva's headquarters, but they heard the sounds of fighting coming from several different directions.

At least the rebel supporters who worked inside the garrison had provided good information, Coll thought, studying the area around them. Some of that information would be essential once they stormed the headquarters building. He hoped their people were already in place inside, but he couldn't tell. Not from this angle.

From here on out, the Combine's restrictive policies regarding colony worlds would be working against the soldiers as much as they had worked against the settlers earlier. The rebels had a chance of seizing the headquarters building only because the Combine Armed Forces hadn't been willing to pay for more modern security equipment and an adequately staffed garrison. If Truva hadn't been forced to rely on settlers to fill some of the essential jobs in her operations, the rebels wouldn't have had anyone inside her headquarters to act as spies or saboteurs.

Coll frowned and ran his hand over his beard-stubbled jaw. There was still so much that could go wrong. He could sense the excitement that gripped the men who followed him and it worried him. Overconfidence could be as dangerous—and as deadly—as a Combine soldier. He'd warned the rebels against it numerous times, but they were buoyed by their relatively easy successes so far and eager to tackle the soldiers' final stronghold.

Success now was really just the beginning, Coll knew. Even if they managed to overthrow the Combine forces on Far Star, they would still have to deal with the Combine Central Committee and all the other resources the Committee could draw on.

The rebellion wasn't over yet. It wasn't even close to being over.

Sternly, Coll quashed the doubts that were rising to plague him. He'd done everything he could to prepare for what lay ahead. He couldn't do anything else. Certainly not right now.

Out of the corner of his eye Coll caught a flash of movement, then another. The other rebel teams were moving in to take up their positions around the main building.

He shifted position, moving so he could have a clearer view of his own team. A moment later he spotted Johnny, then Neur. So far as Coll could tell, everyone was in place. They'd all made it this far.

Now for the next stage.

At a prearranged hand signal from Coll, everyone dug into the packs they carried and pulled out the weapons they'd kept hidden until now, the weapons that Neur had smuggled in only a few weeks before—long-range stun rifles and projectile launchers. If the rifles failed to put the soldiers out of commission, the exploding canisters filled with large quantities of the potent spice they'd been using ought to do the job. And while Coll and his people eliminated the soldiers posted outside the headquarters building, the rebel supporters inside would be busy disrupting operations there.

At a second signal from Coll, the rebels began firing. The stun rifles worked, but the canisters of spice were even more effective, especially the ones that broke through the building's windows. In the small, poorly ventilated rooms the spice would be overwhelming, and there would be no protective filters to screen out the spice because the rebel supporters had destroyed them days ago.

As doors and windows opened and choking, wheezing, watery-eyed soldiers began pouring out,

Coll waved his people forward.

With a roar of excitement only partially muffled by the protective masks they wore, the rebels darted out of their hiding places and raced toward the building. A few of the defenders tried to shoot back, but the tears produced by the spice blinded them, making it impossible for them to aim.

Coll was at the head of the group that stormed the main entrance. As he burst through the door, he felt a quick stab of satisfaction that he wasn't wearing shackles this time; then he was too busy fighting to think of anything else.

The rebels inside had cut off the power supply to the building, leaving only emergency lights to illuminate the scene. Spice hung heavy in the air, making the rebels' eyes water despite the masks protecting them against the smell.

As they forced their way down the stone-walled central corridor toward the main control and communications center in the heart of the building, the soldiers fought back, but with rapidly dwindling enthusiasm. The hand-to-hand combat was still brutal—and unavoidable since the dim light and close quarters meant both sides would be as likely to hit friend as foe if they used their weapons.

Coll led his team into the center of the fighting, desperately trying to force his way through to the control center as quickly as possible, before Truva and her people had a chance to destroy any essential communications equipment.

For the first few minutes neither side gained a clear advantage; then a second group of rebels burst through the windows of one of the rooms and a third charged through a side door. Their presence turned the tide. One by one, the demoralized soldiers backed away from the fighting and raised their hands in a sign of surrender.

Coll didn't waste time on them. Closely followed by three of his team, he charged on down the hall, then up the stairway that was supposed to lead to the control center. At the top of the stairs, the corridor turned sharply to the right. Coll turned right and ran directly into the gaping muzzles of five high-powered laser rifles, all of them pointed straight at him.

Fatherhood might not have been quite what he had envisioned, after all, Talman Bardath decided, glaring at the recalcitrant six-year-old boy who was his son.

Nothing would be gained by losing his temper right now, however. With great deliberation, he took a deep breath, then sat at the opposite end of the battered sofa from Jason.

"Now, Jason," he said in as reasonable tone as he could manage. "I think you'll find living with me quite exciting. You'll live in a comfortable home with servants. Anything you want, you can have. You won't have to work in the fields as you do now."

Jason scowled and crossed his arms over his chest in blatant defiance. "I like to work an' I don't want to leave Dayra and Jeanella. I don't want to leave Far Star."

"I'm sure once you see—"

"I'm not gonna go an' you can't make me!" The

scowl deepened. "I wanna see Dayra! *Now!*"

"Dayra's tied up right now," Bardath snapped, unable to restrain his exasperation.

That statement, at least, was the literal truth. After Dayra had tried to break out of the small workroom where she'd been confined, Bardath had ordered his men to gag her and bind her hand and foot to a chair. Despite his threats, she'd persisted in her absurd story of having sold the pendant to someone from off-planet, someone whose name and home world she'd conveniently forgotten.

If he'd had more time, Bardath knew he could have forced the information he wanted out of her. He didn't have more time. The rebellion on Far Star had created a number of difficulties, the most pressing of which right now was the loss of his shuttle. The problem was, he didn't know if the shuttle pilot had been able to relay his orders to the spaceship's captain to send down the escape shuttle, or if the captain would obey the secondhand orders even if he'd received them. Ship's captains were notoriously cautious about risking their shuttles on unauthorized landing areas.

On top of all this, to discover that his son was an obnoxious, independent-minded brat was almost too much. Jason would come around eventually—he wouldn't have a choice—but Bardath didn't appreciate this particular complication. Not now.

If—when—the escape shuttle landed, he'd have to bind Jason and his sisters. Loading the two-man shuttle with four people, even if two of those people were just children, would make the return trip dangerous enough without adding the possibility of mutiny. Bardath had seen enough of Jason and Dayra to know they were quite capable of causing serious problems. The other sister, Jeanella, wasn't really important, but she might provide useful leverage against Dayra, so he didn't want to leave her behind if he didn't have to.

"I want to see Dayra an' Jeanella!" Jason insisted, more loudly. He slid off the sofa.

For a moment, Bardath thought the boy was going to throw a temper tantrum. He was wrong. Without warning, Jason landed a hefty kick on his shins, then raced toward the open door and the spurious freedom beyond.

Bardath's angry shout instantly brought two of his men to the door. Jason ran right into their hands. The fight wasn't quite as uneven as might have been expected, however.

The men quickly discovered that holding on to a squirming, kicking, fist-swinging small boy without hurting him wasn't as easy as it looked. Since Bardath had given strict orders that Jason wasn't to be hurt, their options were limited. Eventually, one of them grabbed Jason's feet while the other wrapped his arms around Jason's arms. The result was awkward, but effective.

As soon as his men disappeared, fighting hard to keep in step without dropping their struggling, squealing burden, Bardath limped back to the sofa and sat down. Jason might be small, but he'd already mastered a vicious kick.

Despite his irritation, Bardath couldn't repress an unexpected feeling of pride in his spirited son. The boy had courage and quick wits. Those traits would serve him well in the years ahead.

Bardath sighed and closed his eyes, leaning his head back against the wall. He tired so easily these days. The disease hadn't seriously slowed him down yet, but it had made keeping up his usual active schedule far more difficult. He would have to slow down soon, however, if only to conserve his remaining strength.

At least now he had a good reason to go on, despite the difficulties that lay ahead and the ultimate horror of the disease itself. He'd spent a number of hours over the past few weeks reviewing the holographic images of Jason, tracing the points of resemblance between them. It wasn't quite as easy to spot the same characteristics when Jason was shouting or scowling—Bardath didn't think he'd ever set his jaw or stuck out his lower lip quite like his son had—but they were there. He'd seen them.

Bardath opened his eyes to stare, unseeing, at the far wall.

His son.

Strange how much meaning those two words had taken on.

His future. The part of him that would live long after he himself was gone.

Was it really worth the time and energy he'd need to destroy first Dayra, then Truva, then Ble'nara Ro and the other Committee members who opposed him? Wouldn't it be better to spend the days and years that remained to him training Jason to take his place?

Bardath tried to imagine living with the knowledge that he'd allowed his enemies to get the best of him. He couldn't do it. It would be difficult enough to face the daily evidence of his own mortality without his enemies being alive to mock his decline, as well.

He pushed to his feet, shaking off his suddenly morbid thoughts. What he needed was action. He'd wait another half hour for the escape shuttle, Bardath decided. If it hadn't arrived by then, they'd return to Trevag in the skimmers.

After all, the rebels might have attacked the garrison, but without more sophisticated weaponry than they could possibly possess, there was no way they could win. The Combine soldiers were better trained and better armed. They'd defeat the rebels in the end. They probably already had.

Coll straightened up slowly, hands out to show he was no threat. The five soldiers facing him didn't blink or drop their weapons by so much as a hairbreadth, not even when the rebels following him came to an abrupt halt on either side of him.

"I had expected your last visit to discourage you from coming again, Coll Larren," a woman's voice from behind the soldiers said. An instant later, Capt. Truva appeared beside them, her gaze firmly fixed on Coll.

"I won't say it was your hospitality that brought me back, Captain," Coll replied calmly, motioning to his people to remain where they were. "I'm here to accept your surrender on behalf of the people of Far Star."

Truva's lips twisted in a mocking grin. "Indeed? Strange. I could have sworn it was *my* guns that were pointed at your chest."

Coll didn't even glance at the soldiers, who had noticeably tensed at their commander's words. All his attention was on Truva. "Call off your people, Captain. There's no purpose to be served by any more fighting. We've won and you know it."

When Truva remained silent, he said, more softly, "Surrender, Captain. There's been no blood spilled so far. Do you want to be the one responsible for spilling it now, when it can't make a difference? Is that what you've been working for since Cyrus IV?"

Truva stiffened. Her head came up defiantly and her eyes flashed. But only for an instant. Then her face twisted with remembered pain and her shoulders slumped.

"Lower your weapons," she said wearily, not even bothering to glance at her people. "He's right. There's nothing to be gained by bloodshed now. I'm not sure," she added a moment later in an almost imperceptible whisper, "that there ever was."

The escape shuttle arrived just as Bardath was about to order his men into the skimmers. He ignored the pilot's anxious explanations and concentrated instead on getting his three protesting, squirming prisoners and himself into a vehicle designed to hold no more than two passengers.

"Take your men and head back for Trevag in the skimmers," he told his senior officer. "Truva should have the rebels under control shortly; then you can bring the shuttle up."

And if they couldn't get into Trevag and back to the ship within the next couple of hours, he'd leave without them, Bardath thought. He'd already wasted more time on this whole affair than he could afford. He wasn't wasting any more.

The escape shuttle was slow and clumsy to operate under the best of conditions. With two extra passengers, no matter how small, it became even slower and a positive beast to maneuver. Bardath cursed and sweated, forcing the awkward vehicle to respond against its will. In the future, he silently promised himself, he'd take a bigger, better-equipped spaceship, even if that meant adding a few days to his journey.

Dayra watched Bardath struggle with the controls, her mind racing, trying to guess what would happen after they reached the ship. A hundred different scenarios had already occurred to her, none of them pleasant.

Her mouth was painfully dry from a combination of fear and the cloth gag Bardath's people had used to silence her. She'd already given up trying to work free of the cords that bound her hands and feet, but at least her captors had retied her hands in front, rather than behind her. She had the use of her fingers, even if she didn't have much freedom of motion.

She was grateful she couldn't see Jason and

Jeanella, who were bound and gagged as she was and strapped to cleats on the shuttle's walls behind her. She'd seen their wide, frightened eyes when Bardath's men carried them on board, and the anger the sight had roused within her had made it impossible for her to think straight for several minutes. She couldn't afford distractions, not even the distraction of worrying about her brother and sister.

So far as Dayra could see, their only chance of escape would be with this same escape shuttle. If she could somehow work free of the safety straps holding her in the seat, she might have a chance to take over the shuttle just after they docked within the ship even if her hands and feet were still bound. Assuming Bardath got out first, or at least stood in the hatch so she could kick him out, she might be able to seal the outer door and take the shuttle back into space before anyone could stop her. Fortunately, the shuttle was primarily designed for emergencies, so there ought to be some control somewhere that would put it into automatic pilot and send it back to Far Star.

It wasn't much of a plan and it had almost no chance of working, but she had to try. Once she was on the ship, Bardath would have the crew to help control her. There was also a good possibility that she'd be separated from Jason and Jeanella, if for no other reason than to make any attempted escape more difficult. Any chance of escape that remained would disappear entirely the minute Bardath's people came back on board and they left Far Star for Edole.

Of one thing she was sure, Bardath wouldn't have bothered to bring her if he wasn't convinced he could force her to tell him what she'd done with the pendant. She'd already considered his possible reaction if he found out she was wearing it, and she had decided she'd prefer to think about something else.

What she preferred to think about was Coll and how much she wished he were here to help her, how much she wished she could talk to him, touch him, see him. Such thoughts were dangerous—and dangerously seductive.

Coll wasn't here and he couldn't help her. He probably didn't even know Bardath had returned to Far Star; by the time he did, it would be far too late.

There was no one who could help her now but herself, Dayra reminded herself for the hundredth time. Absolutely no one. She was on her own, and if she didn't do something soon, it would be far too late to do anything at all.

Taking care not to attract Bardath's attention, Dayra began working her bound hands around to the fastener on her seat's safety straps. By the time they were ready to dock, she was free of the straps and had worked out the exact moves needed to take control of the shuttle.

Now if only Bardath would cooperate. . . .

In order to prevent further violence, Truva began a systematic broadcast to other Combine bases and field units that hadn't already been captured by the rebels, ordering them to put down their arms and surrender. Most of her effort was unnecessary because the rebels had overrun the Combine control centers both at the spaceport and the mines. Only two field units were still fighting. Three more were on patrol away from any of the settlements and so hadn't yet heard of the rebellion, let alone the rebel victory.

So far, only one fatality had been reported, a miner who had tried to commandeer a Combine skimmer and crashed it, instead. There were a few injuries like the soldier with the broken arm, but far fewer than Coll had expected. Even the Targs had been picked up by rebel units and were presently being "de-bugged."

"I have to give you credit," she said to Coll. "I wouldn't have thought it possible. Certainly not with the kinds of 'weapons' you were using."

"Give the credit to a wise woman I know," Coll said. "She said the only way to succeed is to take what you have and build your dreams out of that. Obviously, she was right."

"Not so obviously, but it worked, anyway." Truva slumped into a chair near the central communications console. "So, what comes next, now that the easy part's over?"

Coll grinned wryly. "You know, you're one of the few who's recognized that." He chose a chair near Truva's and sat down, then propped his feet up on the console. The fighting *was* over and the reaction was beginning to set in for him, too. He felt as tired as Truva looked.

"Now we see if we can take advantage of those changes in the Combine that you mentioned." He dropped his gaze to the toe of his boot and added, "I thought you might be able to help us out there. We—"

Johnny interrupted by bursting into the control room, closely followed by two armed rebels who were escorting a third, obviously frightened man between them.

"We've got trouble, lad," the old man said.

Coll brought his feet down on the floor with a crash. Johnny never admitted there was trouble until it had turned into *serious* trouble.

"This fellow here," Johnny continued, indicating his prisoner with a jerk of his head, "is a shuttle pilot for the ship that Talman Bardath brought into orbit around Far Star early this mornin'."

"What?" Truva straightened indignantly in her chair. "Bardath returned to Edole."

"Accordin' to this fellow, he came back. He and thirty o' his men landed this mornin', just after dawn. They took three o' yere skimmers, Cap'n, and headed to Dayra Smith's holdin'." Johnny's eyes grew hard and dangerous looking. "Seems they had information she'd be alone today."

"Infor— Who told them? No, never mind that now." Coll was out of his chair and across the room before anyone could blink, let alone stop him.

"What were they planning?" he demanded, grabbing the front of the pilot's shirt and pulling the man up on his toes. "Where are they now? Have they taken the people from the holding? Where are they headed?"

"I . . . I don't know," the man sputtered, clearly

terrified. "They didn't tell me their plans. All I know is they were at that holding, wherever it is, when you folks attacked the garrison." As quickly as he could, the man explained his role as communications go-between and told them of Bardath's order to send the escape shuttle.

"Well, did they send the shuttle?" Coll was struggling to control his growing rage . . . and fear, but he wasn't ready to let the man go yet.

"I don't know! We got cut off. I don't *know* what's happening! You gotta believe me!"

Coll believed the man, and he reluctantly released him. He badly wanted to strangle somebody right now, and the man who had brought Bardath down to Far Star was as good a victim as any.

"We found 'im trying to sneak across to his shuttle," Johnny said darkly.

"We can stop the skimmers when they return," Truva said thoughtfully, "but there's not much we can do about Bardath if he's already used the escape shuttle to return to his ship."

Coll turned to stare at her, caught by something he heard in her voice. "You sound as if you already know what's going on," he said suspiciously.

Truva shook her head. "I don't know anything about this. I know Bardath was trying to get the boy—who I assume is his son—the last time he was here."

"How do you know that?"

"Bardath wanted me to arrest your Dayra Smith and the children when he was here last time. Or he

407

wanted me to help him arrest them. He didn't seem to care, so long as he got his hands on them."

"You *knew* of his plans and you did nothing?"

"What was I supposed to do?" Truva snapped back. "For all I knew, all three of them could have been guilty of some crime elsewhere."

She frowned, then said, "Talman Bardath is a murdering, thieving slime who represents all the worst of the Combine government. He may be losing his power, but he's not powerless yet. I infuriated him just by refusing to help him or to give him the skimmers and soldiers he wanted. If I'd openly opposed him, he would have had me removed from my position and replaced with one of his people, instead. Would you have wanted *that*?"

Coll shook his head, but didn't respond. Truva was right. There wasn't much she could have done. As it was, she'd risked a great deal for people she didn't even know.

And none of their arguing was accomplishing anything, anyway. But if she'd been willing to risk so much before, perhaps she would be willing to risk even more now.

The vague outlines of a plan began to take shape in Coll's mind, but there were so many different factors to consider, so much to lose if he was wrong.

"I have an idea, Captain," he said slowly, his gaze fixed on Truva. "But I'll need your help."

Chapter Twenty

The instant Bardath opened the hatch, Dayra jumped. She hit him with her shoulder, propelling him out of the shuttle and onto the spaceship's docking-bay floor in an ungainly sprawl. Only the gag in her mouth kept her from biting her tongue with the force of the blow.

She staggered, off balance because her hands and feet were still bound, but managed to grab hold of the edge of the hatch and pull herself back in. Another awkward leap brought her to the hatch controls.

Her hands shaking with fear and the adrenaline rush of the fight, Dayra punched the buttons that would close the hatch, desperately praying the automatic closing sequence was faster than the sequence for opening had been.

It wasn't.

Bardath was on his feet and through the hatch as it started to close. Enraged, he brutally shoved her aside, then slammed the control panel with his fist, shattering it and halting the closing sequence.

Dayra watched the hatch grind to a stop, still not quite halfway across the opening. A wild, agonizing scream of despair and denial reverberated inside her mind, echoing her brother's and sister's muffled cries of fright from behind her.

At the sound of their panic, Dayra felt a new and coldly murderous rage blossom within her. Her only chance of escape was gone, but there still was a way for her to protect Jason and Jeanella.

She could kill Bardath.

As Bardath swung around to strike her, Dayra ducked, then rammed him in the belly. He doubled over, gasping for breath and clutching his midriff. Before he could straighten up, Dayra shoved him against the hard metal edge of the hatch. Her bonds severely limited her range of movement, but she had the advantage of the strength she'd gained through hard, physical labor. Bardath gasped as he struck the hatch, then groaned. Dayra wasn't sure, but she thought she caught the sound of a bone breaking. She hoped it was something important.

She staggered back, fighting to regain her balance. Too late. One of the ship's crewmen dived through the half-open hatch, knocking her feet out from under her. She fell back, striking her head against the edge of the pilot's seat.

Bardath ordered her to get up. She couldn't move. Dazed and sick from the force of the blow,

Dayra sensed a wall of darkness reaching to engulf her. Yet an instant before she could give in to that welcoming void, she caught the muffled moans and cries of her brother and sister.

With a deliberate effort of will, Dayra fought against the darkness, pushing it back. She *couldn't* give in. Not while Jason and Jeanella were still in Bardath's clutches.

A moment later the crewman grabbed her by her heels and dragged her out of the shuttle, heedless of any hard, rough edges she might hit in the process. Something sharp ripped her sleeve and scraped her skin, drawing blood. Dayra welcomed the pain. It helped focus her energies on the goal of destroying her enemy before he could destroy her.

The crewman released her feet, letting them drop on the metal deck with a hard thump. Dayra rolled to her side, then painfully struggled to her knees.

Bardath was there in front of her, clutching his left arm to his side. He might have been a feral dog, his features were so distorted with rage and pain. He hit her with his right hand, then hit her again.

Dayra slumped to the deck. Bardath grabbed the front of her shift and dragged her back to her knees.

The pendant! Dayra's mind fought back against the pain. She'd been so caught up in the fight to escape that she'd forgotten the pendant and the slight hope of escape it offered.

Bardath released her and swung back his

remaining good hand to hit her yet again. From somewhere, a man in the uniform of a Combine spacer leapt to grab Bardath's arm.

"That's enough, Domine! I'll not have anyone beaten on my ship, not even by you!"

Bardath tried, and failed, to break free of the man's grip. "What do you care, Captain?" he snarled. "She's nothing but a thieving slut."

Still reeling from the force of Bardath's blows, Dayra scarcely heeded the argument. She couldn't even stay on her knees without Bardath's grip to hold her up. She barely managed to sit down rather than fall over. Her shoulders drooped. It was all she could do to keep her head up and her eyes fixed on Bardath.

"Capt. Leroth!" A strange man's voice came over the ship's intercom, piercing the hostility that held Bardath and the ship's captain. "There's an urgent communication for you from Capt. Truva, the commander of the Far Star garrison. Shall I put it on the speaker for you?"

The captain released Bardath's arm. "Go ahead, Lieutenant," he said, clearly relieved at the interruption.

"Capt. Leroth?" Truva's clear, unmistakable voice echoed in the almost empty docking bay. "As you know, we have had some trouble with insurgents here, but I am pleased to report that my people have managed to put down the rebellion and take the rebel leaders prisoner."

At Truva's words, Dayra's heart constricted. She was afraid even to consider the possibility that Truva's prisoners might be Coll and Johnny, but if Truva didn't have them, what had happened to them? What about everyone else who had risked so much?

As though he could hear her thoughts, Bardath stared at her, a gloating, vicious, satisfied smile on his face. He didn't bother to add his congratulations to Leroth's, but Truva's next words drove the smile off his face.

"As you know, Captain," she said, "Combine regulations require that traitors be sent to Edole by the swiftest means possible. To comply with that regulation, I will use your shuttle to bring up the two most important rebel leaders. I have reason to believe that both of them are members of the Rebel Alliance. I request that you take them back to Edole with you—under armed guard, of course."

Before Leroth could respond, Bardath interrupted angrily, "This is Domine Bardath, Captain. My mission is far too important to be delayed for anything so trivial as a couple of incompetent rebels. The shuttle pilot must be sent to pick up my people so we can get underway. I will request that Edole send a ship to pick up the rebels, but I can't offer any more help than that."

And he wouldn't offer that much if he didn't have to, Dayra thought, watching his expression. Her muscles screamed from the tension that gripped her. *Were the prisoners Coll and Johnny?*

"Your shuttle pilot was seriously wounded in the fighting, Domine, but he did inform us of your situation," Truva said. "I've already sent your people some help. Once I've delivered the prisoners into Capt. Leroth's keeping, I'll return to Trevag so your shuttle will be waiting by the time your people get back to the garrison." There was a long pause, then Truva added dryly, "I look forward to seeing you again, Domine."

There was a sharp click, as though the communications signal was broken, then another click as Truva's voice once more came over the intercom. "By the way, the prisoners' names are Coll Larren and John McGregor. Truva out."

Dayra collapsed in a heap, an anguished cry of pain and denial caught in her throat, her eyes burning with tears for all the dreams that now would never be.

"Are you sure you want to go through with this, Captain?" Coll asked, his gaze fixed on Truva's impassive face. "Right now, you're just a dishonored garrison commander who lost a battle. The minute you step onto that ship with us, the minute you actively help us rescue Dayra and the children, you're on our side. If you're taken prisoner, you'll be classed as a traitor and executed, just like us."

Without blinking, Truva glanced from him to Johnny to the ten rebels who were donning Combine military uniforms in the back of the shuttle.

"I'm quite sure," she said calmly. "I've never liked Talman Bardath or anything he stood for. I wouldn't mind spiking his guns, even once." The edge of her mouth quirked upward ever so slightly. "And who knows, anyone who can defeat an armed garrison using fishing nets and glue pots might just be able to build a working government, too." She shrugged. "It ought to be interesting to watch, at any rate."

"Then if you'll do the honors. . . ." Coll turned, offering his hands to be tied behind his back. He'd already slipped a stun gun under his belt within easy reach and the shackles had been fixed so they wouldn't lock.

As Truva fastened both his shackles and Johnny's, Coll bent to peer over the pilot's shoulder and out the forward port. Bardath's ship was already visible ahead. Coll gritted his teeth, trying to fight down the mingled rage and fear that rose in him every time he thought of Dayra and the children in that monster's grasp.

The original shuttle pilot had said there were five crewmen left on board, including the captain. With Bardath, that meant there were six trained fighters against him, Johnny, Truva, and the ten untrained rebels who had eagerly volunteered to help.

The numbers and the element of surprise were on his side, but Bardath had experience and a knowledge of the ship on his. He also held three hostages who might now be anywhere on the ship. If Dayra and the children were separated, it would be even harder to rescue them.

As Coll weighed the odds, considered the options and the possibilities, he was conscious of a cold, hard certainty taking root within him, a sureness of purpose that was stronger, even, than the anger and the fear.

For the first time in a long, long time, he did

not question what he was about to do, did not consider the dangers he was asking others to bear. The safety of Dayra, Jason, and Jeanella came first, regardless of the price.

The docking procedure and the opening of the shuttle door seemed interminable.

Johnny, his hands tied behind his back just as Coll's were, was grim and silent, as bent on vengeance as Coll was. Behind them, the rebels in soldiers' uniforms made small, nervous rustling noises as they checked their equipment, making sure they had everything right.

To all appearances, Truva was as cool and detached as she always was, but Coll sensed a restrained eagerness in her, as if she were glad of the chance to act after so many years of being caught between one side and the other.

The shuttle's hatch opened to reveal the ship's small docking bay. As Coll followed Truva out of the shuttle, he could see all five of the ship's crewmen in position around the bay, stun guns ready, awaiting delivery of the "prisoners."

Bardath, his left arm held tight against his body by a protective sling, was standing by Capt. Leroth. His anger at Truva's arrogant determination to have her own way showed clearly in his expression and his stance. Coll was scarcely out of the shuttle before Bardath advanced on Truva and began to berate her.

Coll paid no attention to Bardath's tirade. His attention was fixed on Dayra, who was watching him, eyes wide and filled with horror, from where she was huddled against the side of the bay.

He was so relieved to find her that it took him a minute to realize she'd been cruelly bound, hand and foot, then lashed to a stanchion. She was gagged, as well, but the gag could not hide the dark bruises that were beginning to form on her cheeks and around one eye. Her hair hung about her shoulders in a disorderly tangle and one sleeve of her work shift was torn. He could see the bright red stain of blood around the edges of the tear.

At that moment, Coll silently vowed to kill Talman Bardath.

Coll had killed before, but always in the heat of battle. This time was different. This time he would make sure that Bardath knew exactly why he was dying and who was killing him. This time Coll would allow no doubts or misplaced moral scruples to stop him.

Talman Bardath would pay for what he'd done, and Coll Larren would collect the payment.

Johnny came to a stop beside Coll, but he took care to leave them both room to maneuver once the fighting started. He'd already slipped out of his shackles and pulled the hidden gun out from under his belt, ready to move at an instant's notice. Coll followed suit.

The uniformed rebels spread out behind them, stun guns in hand. To the ship's crew, they would look as if they were ensuring the "prisoners" had no chance of escape, but their positions gave them a clear view of the bay and every one of their opponents. Taking over the ship should be a relatively simple operation.

Neither Jason nor Jeanella was anywhere in

sight, but Coll didn't worry about that. Unless there were more people on the ship than the shuttle pilot had told them, the children were safer out of the way. It shouldn't be hard to find them once Bardath and the crew were taken care of.

By now, Bardath had worked himself into a rage over Truva's refusal to obey his orders. The ship's captain and crew were watching him, too bemused by his emotional display to pay attention to much else.

At that moment, Truva gave the signal they'd agreed on. Johnny brought his gun around and fired on Capt. Leroth once, twice. The captain dropped to the floor, unconscious. Behind him, the startled crewmen were also dropping, felled by the rebels' heavy fire and greater numbers. It was an easy victory.

Or it should have been.

Since it would have been inappropriate for Truva to come on the ship with a gun in her hand, she'd been forced to carry her stun gun in its holder at her side. She reached for her weapon as she gave the order to fire, but Bardath was quicker. He pulled his gun from its hiding place inside his sling and shot her, then grabbed her as she fell.

Contrary to regulations, Bardath had chosen to carry a deadly laser gun instead of the more versatile stun gun. Heedless of the damage he might wreak on the sensitive systems inside the ship, he backed toward the exit, holding Truva's body as a shield in front of him and firing wildly at anything that moved.

Before anyone could move into a position from which to shoot him, Bardath reached the door leading to the rest of the ship. With a last wild volley of shots, he shoved Truva's body away and leapt through the open door. The door crashed shut an instant later when he hit the emergency controls on the other side.

Cursing, Coll shouted orders for Johnny to take some of the rebels and break through the door's emergency controls while the rest tended to Truva, who was unconscious and bleeding heavily. He darted to Dayra's side, suddenly terrified that one of Bardath's stray shots might have hit her.

She hadn't been hit, but the minute her gag was out she began to cry. The crying only made her angrier, and Coll had to snap at her to stay still so he could unfasten her bonds.

"That scum! That monster!" she raged. "He'll be sorry if he hurts Jason or Jeanella! Can't you get that off any faster? Thank the stars you're all right! When the message came through, when I thought you were taken prisoner, I. . . . Oh, Coll!"

The last was uttered in a wail as Coll untied the last cord and swept her, trembling, into his arms. Coll's own hand shook as he pressed her head against his chest. He buried his face in her tangled hair and held her even tighter, heedless of the tears that spilled, unchecked, down his cheeks.

"Dayra, Dayra," he murmured, over and over again, as if her name were an incantation capable of dispelling the horror of the past hours.

"I didn't think you'd come and I was so afraid," she whispered, her own tears thickening her voice.

"But now you're here and—" She straightened up abruptly and pulled free of his embrace. "Jason and Jeanella! We have to—"

"I'll find them, I promise," Coll said fiercely. "They'll be all right. But Johnny has to get the door open first."

Heedless, Dayra tried to get to her feet. The instant she put her weight on her feet, she gasped and collapsed against Coll. "I can't walk! My legs—"

"Your bonds were too tight. You'll be all right in a little while," Coll soothed, helping her sit back against the wall.

"But I—"

"Let me take care of Bardath," Coll said and hoped she couldn't hear the murderous intent in his voice. "Trust me."

For an instant, Dayra hesitated. Her gaze locked on his. She grabbed a handful of his sleeve as if she expected to hold him back with so tenuous a grip. In her eyes Coll saw an inner struggle that had nothing to do with him and everything to do with her own inability to let go and rely on someone else.

Somehow Coll knew, without really under-standing how he knew, that entrusting Jason's and Jeanella's safety to him now was the hardest thing Dayra had ever done. It was one thing to ask for his help in defending a stone-walled holding, quite another to put the lives of her brother and sister in his hands like this.

And yet somehow, out of her love for him, Dayra

found the courage to do just that. "Be careful," she said and let go of his sleeve.

He started to stand, but Dayra grabbed his sleeve again and pulled him back down beside her. "I don't know why, but Bardath is searching for this pendant," she said, fumbling to unfasten the necklace she wore hidden under her shift. "Perhaps you can use it to bargain with or . . . or whatever."

Her hand trembled slightly as she extended the pendant and chain to him. This time she made no move to stop him as he rose to his feet.

"I love you, Coll Larren," she said, looking up at him.

Coll felt the muscles in his chest and belly tighten, trapping the air in his lungs. Of all the responsibilities he had ever borne in his life, this was the greatest, and the one he accepted most gladly.

"And I love you, Dayra Smith," he said, very softly. Then he turned and crossed to where Truva lay.

"She's lucky she's still alive," said one of the rebels who was tending to her. He pointed to the gaping wound that Bardath's laser gun had made in Truva's shoulder. "Be careful! He's shooting to kill."

Johnny and four others were still struggling to open the door Bardath had locked. "Just about through," Johnny said, his face set in hard lines of determination. "One o' the crew roused enough to tell us where the little ones are. We'll get them first, then Bardath."

The instant the door was open, Coll and Johnny set off at a dead run, heading for the living quarters where the crewman had said the children were being held. The four rebels who had helped open the docking bay door were right behind them.

They didn't need to go far. Bardath was coming along the corridor towards them with the laser gun in his injured hand and Jason, still bound and gagged, slung like a sack of vegetables over his other shoulder.

At sight of them he hissed in anger, fired a couple of shots in their direction, then darted down another corridor that ran at an angle to the one they were in.

"He's headed to the escape pods!" Coll shouted, racing after him. Johnny was right behind him.

Even hampered by his injured arm and Jason's weight, Bardath was already out of sight by the time they reached the side corridor. Fortunately, the ship was a standard Combine military vessel. The only place Bardath could go was the emergency exit where the escape pods for this side of the ship were stored. Everything else was a dangerous dead end.

Just to be sure, Coll directed the men with him to search the side corridors. By the time he reached the assembly area located directly behind the exit, only Johnny was left.

Two open doorways led from the assembly area to the exit, one at each side. For safety reasons, the exit couldn't be sealed off. That still left a lot of cover for Bardath, who only needed a couple of minutes to activate one of escape pods, which would automatically take him back to the planet below. The pod couldn't be guided, but if Bardath destroyed its emergency beacon, it couldn't be easily found, either.

And Bardath had Jason.

Johnny, stun gun at the ready, was already moving around toward the door on his side of the comm center, but Coll motioned him to wait. There was still one chance to draw Bardath out.

"Listen, Bardath," he shouted. "I have the pendant you've been searching for. What would you say to a trade, the pendant for the boy?"

"You're lying!" Bardath shouted, panting heavily from the strain of running while carrying Jason.

Even this far away Coll could hear the note of pain in Bardath's voice. He smiled grimly. He'd never taken pleasure in another person's suffering—until now.

"Dayra was wearing it under her shift. Do you want me to describe it?"

There was a long pause. Coll thought he could hear Bardath cursing under his breath. He also thought he could hear Jason's muted sobs, but couldn't be sure. After all, the boy was gagged and might well be unconscious.

At the thought, Coll gritted his teeth, fighting to control the anger building inside him. Bardath would definitely pay for his sins, but not until Jason was safe.

"All I want is the boy," Coll shouted. "If you'll send him out, I'll give you the pendant. I'll give you the whole damn ship. We'll take the children and Dayra and the shuttle. You'll have the ship and the pendant. What do you say?"

"Take the girl and that bitch, the older sister," Bardath shouted back. "The boy stays with me."

"No deal." Coll's eyes locked with Johnny's. In his friend's angry gaze Coll read the same hunger for revenge that was churning in his own gut, the same implacable determination to destroy Talman Bardath.

Dayra and the children were the only family Black Johnny McGregor had ever had. They were the only family Coll had ever had, and he loved Dayra more than he loved life itself.

Suddenly, he realized that this wasn't about all the things he and Johnny had fought for as part of the Rebel Alliance. It wasn't about freedom or justice or right or any of the other grand things he'd thought were so important.

For Johnny, and for him, this fight was about protecting the people they loved. If Dayra and Jason and Jeanella weren't safe, then none of the other things he and Johnny had risked so much for meant anything at all.

Coll's grip tightened around the stun gun he held. Johnny would follow his lead, whatever he decided.

They could wait and hope that Bardath couldn't cram both himself and Jason into one of the pods, or that they could quickly trace the pod once it landed on Far Star. That course of action prolonged Jason's suffering and put him at greater risk as Bardath became more desperate.

Or they could storm Bardath now and take the chance that Jason wouldn't be caught in the cross fire. Johnny was older, slower, his reaction time considerably less than it had been when he was younger. If they attacked, the chances were very high that either he or Johnny would be shot, perhaps killed.

Attack now . . . or wait.

It was his decision.

A muscle in Coll's jaw jumped. If he could be sure that Bardath would aim at him first, instead of at Johnny. . . .

He frowned, then pulled Dayra's pendant out of his pocket. The stone flashed a deep purple in the overhead lights, reminding Coll of how brightly it glowed against Dayra's breast when the morning light caught it, of how it turned black in the light of the moon, a dark jewel on the pale silver white of her skin. He juggled the pendant in his palm, weighing it thoughtfully.

There were no guarantees, but it was the best he could do. It was his decision and he and Johnny would have to live with it . . . or die with it.

Coll met Johnny's steady, questioning gaze. With a jerk of his head, he indicated they should attack. Johnny nodded, then silently moved closer to the door on his side. Coll shifted his grip on his gun and glanced over at Johnny. They were ready.

A fraction of a second before he gave Johnny the sign to move, he tossed the pendant through the doorway, then dived through the door after it.

Coll was shooting as he hit the floor. He rolled, then came to his feet, still shooting.

He was too late. Johnny hadn't made it through

the door. He was already crumpling to the ground as a brilliant crimson stain blossomed on his chest.

Bardath, too, was sagging, but Coll hadn't knocked him out completely because he was struggling to bring his gun up, struggling to focus on Coll.

Coll shot him again, then again. Bardath fell like a rock. He'd be unconscious for hours with the combined hits from the stun gun.

A quick glance showed Jason safely curled against a command console, his eyes wide and red-rimmed from crying.

"Hang on," Coll said. His heart twisted. He could imagine how frightened the boy must be, but he didn't have time to help him now. Johnny needed his help far more urgently.

He was wrong about that. Johnny would soon be past anyone's help.

At Coll's hesitant touch, Johnny opened his eyes and smiled weakly.

"The lad's all right?" he asked, struggling for breath.

Coll nodded, fighting against the pain and grief that threatened to choke him. There was no time for that. Not now. "He's fine. Just scared, I think, and a little shaken up."

Johnny sighed, then coughed. Bright red foam appeared at the corner of his mouth. "That's all right, then."

He closed his eyes, his breathing harsh and labored. Coll could hear the bubbling of the foam in his throat and the thin hiss of air going in and out through the hole in his chest.

After a moment, Johnny opened his eyes again, but this time his gaze was vague, unfocused. "Ye remember what I said, lad."

"I remember," Coll said, leaning closer so he could catch Johnny's words. Hot tears stung his eyes and his throat hurt with his longing to cry. He couldn't cry now. There was so little time left.

"A good place . . . to put down . . . roots," Johnny said. "A good place. . . ." He gasped, fighting against the encroaching darkness with the last measure of his failing strength. "She's a good lass. Name yere first . . . lad . . . Johnny, eh? After me."

And then he was gone.

Coll didn't know how long he remained kneeling beside his friend as his tears streamed down his cheeks and fell to mingle with Johnny's blood.

He didn't know how long he might have gone on like that, but the four men who had followed him and Johnny so short a time before brought him back to an awareness of his surroundings. They stood in the doorway without moving, staring into the room, wide-eyed with shock.

Slowly, Coll rose to his feet, creaky and awkward like an old man. Just as slowly, he crossed to where Bardath lay.

Pain ripped through him. It was Bardath who should be dead, not Johnny.

Coll bent and picked up Bardath's laser gun. He glared at the weapon, turning it over and over in his hands. It would be so easy. Just shoot Bardath now and have done with it. So very easy. . . .

With a curse, Coll straightened up. He had sworn he would make Bardath pay for what he'd done to Dayra and the children, sworn he would kill him. But Johnny had died instead and now Coll found he couldn't pull the trigger. He wasn't a murderer and there were other things that were more important, things that demanded his attention.

"Get him out of here," he said harshly, not caring if the men saw his tears. "And destroy this," he added, holding out Bardath's laser gun.

A small, scuffling noise caught his attention. Coll turned to find Jason staring at him, too frightened to move.

Coll swore and immediately crossed to the boy and pulled out the gag, then untied him. For a moment, Jason just looked at him; then he threw his arms around Coll's neck and burst into tears.

As Coll hugged the boy to him, murmuring soft, meaningless words of comfort and assurance, he was aware of a strange easing of his own pain and grief. He had spent his life fighting for the future, Coll realized, and now the future was here in his arms, scared, tired, and in desperate need of love and comfort, but safe.

This was what he'd fought for, Coll thought, feeling Jason's tears warm on his neck, his little body heavy in his arms. This was what Johnny had died for.

He had made a hard decision, but so had Johnny, and Coll was suddenly sure—absolutely, positively sure—that it had been the right one, no matter how bitterly high the price.

And maybe that was the secret to it all, the answer he'd sought for so long but had never found until now. He'd wanted the future, but he'd never accepted that there was always a price to be paid, a sacrifice to be made. Always.

Coll slowly rose to his feet with Jason still in his arms, then turned to find Dayra standing in the doorway.

Her tears cut wet tracks across the bruises on her cheek. Her chin trembled and her lips were so tightly pressed together they'd almost disappeared. She glanced from Jason to Johnny and back again, and then, with a soft, gasping sob, she came stumbling across the room and into Coll's embrace.

For a long, long while, Coll wasn't sure exactly who was holding whom. Dayra hugged Jason and him, and Jason and Coll hugged her back. It was impossible to sort out the tangle of arms, and Coll didn't care, anyway.

That was another thing he was learning about the future. It wasn't easy to hold, and it wasn't always easy to know if it was holding you, instead.

But it was always there, if only you believed.

Dayra held both Jason and Jeanella in her lap, even though it had been a tight fit to get the three of them in the copilot's seat on the shuttle.

Her brother and sister were asleep, unharmed but worn out by their ordeal and their grief. Their heads were pillowed on her shoulders, their arms and legs tangled around each other. She held them both as tight as she could, afraid of waking them, but even more afraid of letting them slip out of her grasp, even for a moment.

Yet even as she clung to them, she watched Coll as he guided the shuttle back to Far Star. He'd insisted on taking the craft, leaving the pilot and ten rebels he'd brought up with him to take charge of the ship and watch over their prisoners.

In the back of the shuttle, two benches had been rigged out of the seats. One held Truva, who was in stable condition but still unconscious. The other held Johnny's body, which was wrapped in a dark blanket taken from the ship.

Although they'd had no time to talk, Dayra sensed that Johnny's death had a deeper meaning for Coll than could be explained by the loss of a friend and colleague. Despite the weariness that was evident in his face and in the way he moved, Dayra could feel a change in him, as though. . . .

She hesitated, groping for the words that could explain what she felt. It was as though Coll had found a secret he'd been searching for all his life, the answer to a question he'd been asking since forever.

She didn't understand it, any more than she understood the changes she could feel within herself.

"Trust me," Coll had said, and she had.

Not because she had no other choice, and not because she was depending on him to do what she could not.

430

No, she had trusted him because . . . because she trusted him.

Dayra smiled. It was an absurd explanation. She didn't care. The children were safe and Coll was beside her and that, for now, was enough.

There would be time to grieve for Johnny. They would all need that release, for he had been far more than just a friend.

Johnny would always be missed, but for now Dayra wanted to think of him as being here with her, just as Jason and Jeanella were here, asleep in her arms, just as Coll was sitting beside her, intent on his work.

Coll changed the shuttle's course slightly, bringing it down toward Trevag at an easy angle. Suddenly Dayra could see Far Star in the shuttle's view port, a dark jewel against the black sky. One of the twin moons was already out of sight, the second just slipping below the far horizon. At the other side of the planet, the side toward which they were descending, Dayra could see the first soft glow of the coming dawn.

As she watched, enthralled, the sun rose over the edge of the world and suddenly all was golden light and the night went scurrying away from them into oblivion.

Coll turned to her, then. In his face Dayra could read the pain and weariness of the past hours, but she could also see, deeper and stronger still, the infinite love that was for her and Jason and Jeanella and the family that they would someday make between them.

He stretched to lightly brush his fingers against

431

her hand, where she held Jason.

"We're going home," he said.

Dayra smiled and nodded, and didn't mind the tears that suddenly welled in her eyes.

"We're going home," she said.

Epilogue

It wasn't until Coll crested the hill near the holding that he could feel the breeze coming up off the sea ahead of him. It ruffled his loose work shirt, cooling the sweat on his skin and tossing his hair in his eyes.

It also reminded him that he'd promised to let Dayra trim his shaggy locks today. According to her, it wasn't fitting for the head of the newly installed government of the newly independent world of Far Star to be so unkempt. Coll hadn't heard anyone complaining, but he'd do anything to please his wife, even if it meant submitting to her surprisingly strict notions of official decorum.

Coll smiled. Dayra was a fine one to talk about decorum. Her hair still tumbled out of its practical bun at every opportunity and when she was working, she was as likely as not to have a smudge of dirt on her chin or a tear in the simple shifts she wore. It didn't matter. He loved her looking that way—almost as much as he loved the way she looked when they were alone and she was wearing nothing at all.

At least now, with the growing profits from their cooperative fishing venture, she didn't have to work as many long, hard hours as she had before. From this vantage point at the top of the hill, Coll could see the two cranes that raised and lowered the co-op's fishing boats into the bay where Dayra had once clambered up and down a rope ladder by herself. The small fleet, crewed by settlers from the nearby holdings, was kept busy harvesting the immense wealth of Far Star's sea.

The co-op had been Dayra's idea. Though it had been in operation less than a year, it was already making many of the local settlers wealthy enough to buy some of the luxuries that were starting to flow into Far Star's markets now that the Combine no longer controlled trade.

Coll turned to look back down the hill, tracing the path he'd made through the tall grass from the fields where he'd been working all morning. Dayra had used her profits to buy specially manufactured farm equipment capable of handling Far Star's extraordinarily rocky land. Her dreams of rich, productive fields stretching to the horizon were beginning to take shape in these first tilled hectares of land outside the protective walls of the holding. The wheat and quinoa and *flassa* they'd planted were just beginning to ripen, promising a rich harvest in the months ahead.

So many changes, Coll thought, yet none could compare to the changes within himself. He'd come to Far Star by chance, adrift and discouraged, yet it was here on this raw, new world that he'd found the inner peace and sureness of purpose he'd sought all his life.

More than that, he'd found a happiness he'd never dreamed possible—a happiness that hadn't come from his grand dreams, but from the love of a woman who had taught him what it meant to believe.

If Johnny had lived, he would have grinned and said, "I told ye so!" Coll often found himself wishing his friend were here to prod, and laugh, and challenge his decisions. He would have liked to have had the benefit of the old man's wisdom. One thing Coll was sure of, he would never forget the lesson Johnny had taught him with his dying— that everything worthwhile had its price, and that there could be no looking back.

They'd buried Johnny inside the holding. Dayra had planted a tree to shade his grave and flowers to cover it with bright blossoms year 'round. The beauty of the spot was a constant reminder of all they owed him, and of the friendship they'd lost with his death.

The sound of a flitter motor roused Coll from his reverie. He turned to see Jason, his head barely topping the steering bar, guiding Dayra's old farm flitter up the hill. The expression on the boy's face betrayed the struggle he was waging to keep the flitter down to a reasonable speed. Coll had no doubt that Dayra's presence in the passenger's seat was responsible for Jason's circumspect behavior, but he couldn't prevent a twinge of protective worry at her venturing out with her reckless little brother when she was over six months pregnant.

With difficulty, Coll restrained himself from trying to help her out when Jason brought the flitter to a jerky stop. Dayra had already warned him she wouldn't tolerate any help until she was so big she couldn't get out of a chair by herself. Until then, she'd said, laughing, he'd just have to get used to the idea of having a wife with a stomach that seemed to grow larger and rounder every day.

The minute Dayra was out of the flitter, Jason started down the hill toward the sea, and this time he was moving at a considerably higher speed than he had coming up. Dayra didn't bother to check. Instead, she turned and came through the tall grass toward Coll. Even though her frown spoke of unpleasant news, Coll was content to wait for her to come to him. He took too much pleasure in watching her to waste even this fleeting opportunity to savor the sight of her.

In spite of her growing belly, Dayra's movements were as graceful as they'd ever been. There was a slight sway in her walk now and her hand rested protectively on the curve of her stomach, but she gave no other sign her pregnancy had affected her. Heedless of the rocks that might lie hidden in the tall grass, Dayra fixed her gaze on him with a steady, ice-blue intensity that sent a jolt of pure longing through Coll.

As she came closer, he extended his hand to her

and drew her into his arms, then bent to claim a hungry kiss. His body easily accommodated the additional roundness of hers. When Dayra drew back at last, Coll tightened his hold on her and dropped his hand to caress the swelling arc of her belly. The wonder of her and of the child she carried was enough to keep him silent, not caring what unwelcome news she might be bringing.

"Truva just called," Dayra said, placing her hand over his to stop his gentle exploration of her stomach. "Bardath committed suicide two days ago."

It was Coll's turn to frown. "How?"

"He hanged himself in his cell. I guess he couldn't endure losing everything like that." Dayra hesitated, then added, "You know, sometimes I wonder if we did the right thing by turning over the recording disk we found in the pendant. Without that evidence against him, maybe—"

Coll gave her a gentle shake. "Talman Bardath deserved the punishment he got, and more. You don't think he would have hesitated to use the disk for his own purposes, do you?"

"No, but it's so hard to think of him locked up like that, knowing he was dying and that he'd lost everything—his position, his wealth . . . even his son!" Dayra shook her head in frustration. "I can't forgive him for the way he treated my mother or for his kidnapping Jason and Jeanella and killing Johnny, and yet . . ."

"And yet you can't help thinking about how you'd feel if you were Talman Bardath."

Dayra blinked, considering the idea, then snuggled closer into Coll's embrace. "I guess that's it."

"Don't waste your energy worrying about him, Dayra," Coll said, resting his chin on the top of her head as he cradled her body against his. "Bardath chose his own path in life. If the recording disk hadn't convicted him, something else would have. But then *we* wouldn't have had anything to give the Combine in exchange for a guarantee of Far Star's independence. That disk has helped make life better for a lot of people, Dayra."

"I know. It's just . . . I'm so happy now, I can't imagine the kind of despair that would lead someone to commit suicide."

Coll grinned. "Can't you, my love? Then what in the world makes you want to climb in a flitter when Jason's handling it?"

Dayra laughed, then gave him a playful slap on the arm. "Jason's doing very well. He didn't try to gun it even once! And *you're* the one who insisted on teaching him, remember?"

"For self-preservation, only!" Coll protested, putting his hands up in mock surrender. "Once Jeanella learned, you know very well we couldn't have kept him from taking that flitter. Better that he learned how to handle it properly!"

"If you're so worried about my safety, you can just take me back to the holding yourself. I sent Jason on to the fishing docks with some supplies they needed and he won't come back any sooner than he absolutely has to."

"Really?" Coll's grin widened. "Hmmm. With Jason gone," he said slowly and very thoughtfully, "and Jeanella in Trevag with Mikella's kids, you and I have the holding all to ourselves . . ." He gave Dayra a leering smirk. "That being the case, what would you say to a little debauchery in the middle of the day?"

Dayra grinned. "I'd say that sounds like a great idea, so long as it isn't just a *little* debauchery!"

This time it was Coll's turn to laugh. He wrapped his arm around her shoulders and dragged her back against him. "I think we could manage more than just a little—if we tried. But I'm afraid you're going to have to walk halfway. I left my flitter at the bottom of the hill."

"I can manage that. But we'll need to get a move on. Jason might come back on time, instead of three hours late!"

Side by side, they made their way down the hill with only an occasional pause for a kiss or two. When they reached the flitter, Coll helped Dayra into her seat. As he walked around to his side, his eye was caught by the trail he and Dayra had left behind them in the tall grass.

They'd been so close together, they'd left only one broad path instead of two narrower ones. Rather than coming straight down the hill, the path jigged around rocks and curved away from uneven ground and every once in awhile it even wobbled from side to side. The wobbly parts were where he and Dayra had been so absorbed in each other, they hadn't noticed where they were going. From here, Coll could see at least three of the places where they'd stopped to share a kiss and enjoy the view—the grass was flattened in a slightly wider circle in each of those spots.

In contrast, the tracks he'd left on his way up

the hill were much more direct and far narrower. There weren't any wide spots. Not one. Alone, there'd been no reason to stop, no distractions to get him off course.

The trails were rather like life, Coll thought, tugging his door open. There would be any number of distractions in the years ahead, and even more reasons to just stop and enjoy the moment. With Dayra beside him and the babe yet to come, he might not cut a straight path through life, but the journey would be far more exciting than any he had ever made alone.

As the flitter lifted on its cushion of air, Coll glanced over at Dayra. She was watching him, a gentle smile lighting her face.

"I love you, Coll Larren," she said, very softly.

Coll smiled, secure in the greatest gift he had ever been given; then he turned the flitter and headed toward the broad gates that stood open, awaiting their return.

Letter to the Readers

Dear Reader:

Coll Larren and Dayra Smith had their fair share of troubles. In my next book, *Hidden Heart,* Tarl Grisaan, heir to the Controllorship of the planet Diloran, is just beginning to find out what trouble really is.

Having to assume the role of a silly fop was unpleasant, but at least it's given Tarl a chance to figure out what's been going on under his uncle's despotic rule. It was sheer bad luck—or good luck, depending on how you look at it—that landed him in the bed of the breathtakingly beautiful and undeniably naked woman who helped him escape from the armed patrol he'd run into during one of his nightly forays into the city. But having to accept that same woman as his slave is something else entirely. After all, as daughter of the leader of the Zeyns, his family's traditional enemies, Marna of Jiandu isn't likely to be Tarl's most enthusiastic supporter. Quite the contrary, in fact. Without realizing that the man she gladly welcomes into her bed in the dark of night is also the fool to whom she's been given as a slave, Marna confesses to Tarl, her nighttime lover, that she's supposed to kill Tarl, her daytime owner, and make the assassination look as if it's the responsibility of another of the warring factions on Diloran.

If that all sounds confusing, just wait—it gets worse!

In the meantime, I enjoy hearing from readers who love futuristic romances as much as I do. My address is P.O. Box 62533, Colorado Springs, CO 80962-2533. A self-addressed, stamped envelope for reply is appreciated.

Sincerely,
Anne Avery